Dear Reader,

Bluebird was written in a summer without sunlight.

A pandemic had struck, changing living situations and work schedules. Taking away friends and lives, and all in a time of unrest, racial injustice, and unprecedented division in our country. And no matter what the views or political affiliations in that sunless summer, there seemed to be one common denominator to the chaos.

Fear.

And I was writing about a time dominated by fear. The aftermath of a world war. Fear of all the terror that had been. Fear of what the post-war world might look like. Project Bluebird was a real experiment born out of that very real fear, a CIA secret that left a permanent and little-known stain on our nation's history—because our fears of Communism, the Soviet Union, even our fears of "other" ethnicities, were not so different from Hitler's Nazis, and they led America, through Project Bluebird, to commit some of the same, terrible deeds.

The reality of our past and our present seemed impossible to escape and impossible to reconcile.

It can be hard sometimes, when you're living and writing in the depths of night, to remember that the light is real, too. That night only happens because the sun is still there, hidden on the other side of the world.

To remember that for every choice made in fear, someone chooses courage. That for every harm, someone will seek its justice. That for every Project Bluebird, there is a Powell House. A real place of refuge far ahead of its time. One, small shining example of what our nation can choose to be when love lights the path.

Even a global pandemic can mean slowing down, spending time with family. Finding time to finish a book.

Bluebird shone a light in a difficult time for me. It reminded me that light exists now, whether we can see it or not. Because that is the power of story, even when you're the one writing it.

In love,

Sharon Cameron

Title: Bluebird

Author: Sharon Cameron

On-Sale Date: October 5, 2021

Format: Jacketed Hardcover

ISBN: 978-1-338-35596-3 || Price: $18.99 US

Ages: 12 and up

Grades: 7 and up

LOC Number: Available

Length: 464 pages

Trim: 5-1/2 x 8-1/4 inches

Classification: Young Adult Fiction:
Historical / United States / 20th Century; Historical /
Europe; Romance / Historical

---------------- *Additional Formats Available* --------------

Ebook ISBN: 978-1-338-35598-7

Scholastic Press
An Imprint of Scholastic Inc.
557 Broadway, New York, NY 10012
For information, contact us at:
tradepublicity@scholastic.com

Acclaim for other books by Sharon Cameron

Praise for *The Light in Hidden Places*:

A Reese's Book Club YA Pick

"Beautifully written and meticulously researched. Sharon Cameron captures the extraordinary story of one of history's hidden heroes. Every devastating moment is both gripping and powerful."
—Ruta Sepetys, *New York Times* bestselling author of *Salt to the Sea*

"Harrowing, heartbreaking, and yet so full of hope."
—Jennifer Donnelly, *New York Times* bestselling author of *Stepsister*

"Haunting and lyrical. An incredible true story of bravery, survival, and defiance."
—Alan Gratz, *New York Times* bestselling author of *Refugee*

"Sharon Cameron's exciting novel weaves together the lightheartedness, sheer terror, and incredible inner strength of this young woman, my mom. This book exceeds all my expectations."
—Ed Burzminski, son of Stefania Podgórska

★ "Authentic writing and well-researched history combined with the gripping and terrifying subject matter make this a must-read for historical fiction fans . . . Cameron's remarkable, heartbreaking true story of one woman's bravery and selflessness in World War II Poland will intrigue both teens and adult readers."
—*School Library Journal*, starred review

★ "Cameron's wide-ranging research and deft storytelling abilities combine to create an astoundingly authentic first-person narration. Her exquisite prose conveys in riveting detail exactly what it was like for Stefania to live through the horrors she witnessed."

—*BookPage*, starred review

"A true story of faith, love, and heroism . . . An inspirational read."

—*Kirkus Reviews*

"Empowered by thorough research—an author's note details events after the war—Cameron successfully conveys horror and bravery in this powerful and captivating novel. A memorable read."   —*Booklist*

"Cameron's novel is heartbreakingly real in its attention to detail and its ability to pack emotional punches."

—*Bulletin of the Center for Children's Books*

Praise for *The Knowing*:

★ "Both a politically charged adventure and culture study, this thought-provoking dystopia stands firmly on its own."

—*Booklist*, starred review

"Diverse, well-drawn characters abound, but in the riveting power struggles that ensue, women are dominant players, ruthless ideologues willing to sacrifice all that interferes with the goal. The intricately woven narrative threads come together in a suspenseful denouement sure to leave readers hoping for another installment."

—*Kirkus Reviews*

"Cameron is a writer of prime caliber." —*School Library Journal*

Praise for *The Forgetting*:

A #1 *New York Times* bestseller
An Indie Next List selection
A *BookPage* Teen Top Pick

★ "A well-crafted fable for our time."
—*Kirkus Reviews*, starred review

★ "This fantasy is a marvelous achievement."
—*School Library Journal*, starred review

"[An] absorbing adventure."
—*Publishers Weekly*

"*The Forgetting* is Sharon Cameron's fourth young adult novel, and she's grown adept at blurring the lines between fantasy, dystopian and science-fiction genres. Cameron reminds us, through Nadia's documented memories, that we must learn to appreciate the truth as much as question it, exploring the morality tucked within the fallacy of memory."
—*BookPage*, Teen Top Pick

Praise for *Rook*:

A YALSA Best Fiction for Young Adults selection
An Indiebound Indie Next Top Ten selection
Winner of the Parents' Choice Gold Award

"The suspense kicks right off in this action-packed tale, quickly wrapping readers up in the drama."
—*Romantic Times*

"Full of derring-do and double crosses, this romantic adventure is thoroughly engrossing." —*Kirkus Reviews*

"Cameron crafts a brilliant homage to *The Scarlet Pimpernel* yet also manages to make her telling unique . . . [T]he many twists, turns, betrayals, and lucky breaks will keep readers breathless until the very end." —*Bulletin of the Center for Children's Books*

"*Rook* is sure to be a read all readers will remember." —*Portland Book Review*

Praise for *The Dark Unwinding*:

A YALSA Best Fiction for Young Adults selection
Winner of the SCBWI Crystal Kite Award

"Utterly original, romantic, and spellbindingly imaginative." —*USA Today*

"Haunting thrills unfurl." —*Entertainment Weekly*

"Gripping twists, rich language, and an evocative landscape." —*Publishers Weekly*

"[A] singularly polished piece." —*The Horn Book*

"A strikingly original, twisty gothic tale that holds surprises around every dark corner." —Judy Blundell, author of *What I Saw and How I Lied*

Bluebird

Also by Sharon Cameron

THE LIGHT IN HIDDEN PLACES

THE KNOWING

THE FORGETTING

ROOK

A SPARK UNSEEN

THE DARK UNWINDING

Bluebird

SHARON
CAMERON

Scholastic Press
New York

Library of Congress Cataloging-in-Publication Data available

ISBN 978-1-338-35596-3

10 9 8 7 6 5 4 3 2 1   21 22 23 24 25

Printed in the U.S.A.   128

First edition, October 2021

Book design by Abby Dening

For the seekers of justice
and those that help them find it

CHAPTER ONE

—— *August 1946* ——

IT IS A LAND WITHOUT RUBBLE.

Eva leans over the top rail of the ship, gazing across the leaden sea. And there are no piles of charred stone. No smoking pits or chunks of broken concrete. Just walls. A city of them. Whole and strong-looking, rising brick by solid brick. Beautiful, unbombed buildings floating in a bank of gray and sooty fog.

This is a new world now. That's what they'd told her. The old world is ash. Burnt like paper in the fire winds of Berlin.

Sometimes, Eva thinks, people tell you lies.

There's supposed to be a statue, but she can't find it in the mist.

Up onto the first rung of the rail and Eva leans out again, hands free, knees braced against the metal, hooked in place by her shoe heels. She can see the tops of heads and hats on the lower deck, water churning into foam far below them. And the city spreads, bigger, closer, anchored to the moving horizon.

She closes her eyes. Lets the wind snatch her hair. Slap her cheeks. It's like driving fast with the windows down. Like diving off a cliff.

It feels a little like flying.

When she opens her eyes again, the city is lost to the fog bank and an island has taken its place. She can see children down there, playing in the haze, jumping up and down on a sea wall built to keep them from falling into the harbor. The children are fascinating. These children don't know about unexploded grenades. Or teetering walls that collapse when climbed. And no one here is going to shoot them for their shoes.

She'd forgotten there could be children like that.

The barest brush of a moth wing, and Brigit is beside her. Eva steps down quickly to the deck and takes Brigit's hand. Brigit smiles at the children. A smile that lights the fog. And then the second mate hurries past and she cringes. Shrinks into herself. The mate touches his cap, like he has a hundred times, disappearing catlike down a ladder, and Eva puts her arm through Brigit's arm. Tightens her grip on Brigit's hand.

Brigit is not like the children. She will never be like the children again.

Sharp heels come clicking across the deck.

"Eva! Brigit!" says Miss Schaffer. "What are you doing up here? Where are your hats? Where are your bags?"

"Our suitcases are in the cabin, Miss Schaffer," Eva replies.

Her English is careful. Correct. But she doesn't understand Miss Schaffer's use of the word *bag*. The suitcases they were given do not even resemble a sack. It's hard to know what Brigit understands, because Brigit does not speak. But she must have learned a little English, because Eva sees her hand dart suddenly to her head, as if surprised not to find a hat there.

"Well, hurry, please," Miss Schaffer fusses. She has a clipboard clutched to her chest, a badge with an eight-pointed black-and-red starburst sewn onto her sleeve. "We couldn't have you greeting America with bare heads. It would be indecent."

Indecent, Eva thinks. The opposite of *decent*, which means "nice." Civilized. She'd known many indecent people in her life, and most of them had been wearing their hats.

Miss Schaffer disappears down the stairwell, and the second mate comes back up the ladder. And now that Miss Schaffer isn't near, he gives an extra smile to Eva. A sly one. Because she let him kiss her. And put his hands on her blouse. For aspirin. When Brigit was sick and the doctor said others were sicker.

"Fair is fair." That's what the second mate had said.

And then Brigit has a foot up on the rail, her body pitching forward, over and down to the lower decks. Eva grabs a handful of skirt and yanks her back again.

You have to be quick with Brigit.

"No," Eva whispers, taking her hand again, patting her arm. "Not that way."

She never should have let Brigit see her up on the rail.

The second mate shakes his head, disgusted. But Brigit was only trying to see the children. It's Eva who would have jumped. Or let herself fall.

The second mate doesn't know it was Eva who put the dead rat in his laundry bag.

Fair is fair.

"*Kommen Sie mit,*" Eva whispers. Her German is only for Brigit now. She leads her away from the rail, away from the mate, down two flights of stairs into the electric-yellow light of belowdecks. Around the corner, and Eva opens a small wooden door.

Their hats are side by side on a narrow bed in the narrow cabin they have shared across a wilderness of sea water. Eva hates the cabin. The walls are too close. But she can turn the lock whenever she wants, and this, she loves. The other passengers love it, too. The other passengers are afraid of Brigit.

They probably should be.

Eva turns the lock now and sits Brigit on the only chair.

She straightens Brigit's blouse—not as white as it had once been, but crisply ironed—pulling the buttonholes downward where they want to gap across her bust. Then she pins on Brigit's hat. It's an ugly hat, black-coffee brown and without shape, but Brigit makes it beautiful. She blinks two clear blue eyes, while Eva turns to the mirror. Eva's hair is wild and the color of Brigit's hat. She'd pinned it up the night before, like her mother used to make her do. To tame the curls.

Anything tame is gone now. Lost to the sea wind.

Her mother is gone now, too. Burned up with the past.

Eva squashes her own hat on her head and then smooths her skirt, feeling for the papers she has sewn inside the lining. Safe. She stands up Brigit and checks her skirt. The papers are safe there, too. She can feel them. Will anyone else be able to feel them? How thoroughly will they be searched? What if the plan doesn't work?

The man said it would work.

She knows the man tells lies.

Eva turns to the basin, playing with the water like she's washing her hands. Brigit cannot be allowed to see fear.

So she breathes. And breathes. And pretends to wash her hands.

Then Eva dries her hands and gives Brigit her suitcase, wrapping each of Brigit's fingers around the handle. She smiles when she doesn't want to.

"Time to go," she says. "Stay with me, yes?"

Brigit blinks.

Eva picks up her purse and her suitcase, and they step out of their small, safe cabin for the last time, up the metal stairs, and out into the smell of a harbor. Flags snap along the halyards, the anchor motor buzzing the boards beneath her feet. Brigit cringes. The lower deck is swarming now—refugees and war brides and bits and pieces of families—hanging over the rails, yelling and crying, waving their arms and their handkerchiefs. The docking point is in sight and it is also swarming, people cheering and crying and waving their arms and their handkerchiefs.

There is no one down there waving for her.

Eva turns Brigit quickly toward the bulkhead, getting her back to the noise and the crowd, pulling down her hat brim to make a little tent around her face. Brigit holds out her hand like she's been taught, and Eva gets two buttons from her purse and puts them in Brigit's palm. Brigit smiles, touching the buttons, distracted, and then Miss Schaffer comes, clicking on her heels.

"There you are! Eva Gerst and Brigit Heidelmann." She ticks two boxes on her list. "You have your papers?"

Eva holds up two sets of papers, the ones she will allow Miss Schaffer to see. The ones she will not allow her to see are rustling in their skirts. Miss Schaffer nods, and moves on down the line she is forming. There are thirty-eight in their group, from toddlers to grandparents, Polish, French, Ukrainian, Latvian, and Hungarian. Eva and Brigit are the only Germans. Because Germans are the enemy.

But they all have new suitcases. The lucky ones. Coming to America. Leaving hell like a dream behind them.

Or bringing it with them.

"Show the man at the desk your papers," Miss Shaffer shouts at her line. The noise of the cheering is deafening. "Nothing to be afraid of! Just answer the questions truthfully, and there won't be a thing to worry about . . ."

Only Eva will not be answering truthfully. And Brigit will not be answering at all.

The movement of the ship slows to nothing, the flags hang limp, and the deck boards go still beneath Eva's feet.

America.

They wait a long time. Brigit gets bored with her buttons. Eva adds a blue one, held back for this purpose. The gulls wheel and squawk. And at last their line moves down the gangway, people carrying trunks and cases, tagged bundles propped on their heads. Eva takes away the buttons and holds tight to Brigit's hand. One step. Two steps. The dock comes closer, closer, the crowd calling out names, the babble of so much English wild and strange in Eva's ears. The man in front of them is crying with happiness.

So much hope. But hope isn't what Eva came for.

She's come for justice.

Their feet land together on solid ground. American ground.

And suddenly, America is enormous.

A beam of sunlight finds a crack in the clouds, coloring the ship, the faces. Eva sees the statue now, on its own island across the water, arm held high to the sun. Brigit raises her chin. She has always loved the light. Her smile is beatific. Angelic.

"Welcome to America," says a man. A young man, pausing on his way to somewhere. Men always pause for Brigit. He has a short haircut, a duffel bag on his shoulder, and a uniform. Army.

So he has been to hell, too.

Brigit cringes and Eva steps a little in front of her. The young man in the uniform doesn't notice. He tosses something shiny into the air.

Eva drops her suitcase to catch it. A little candy, wrapped in gold foil, glittering like a gem. Brigit stops shivering, distracted. She knows something sweet when she sees it. She smiles until she dimples.

"Thank you," Eva says, and at the sound of her voice, the young man's face goes hard. Like gun metal.

"Kraut," he says. And spits on her shoe.

CHAPTER TWO

—— *February 1945* ——

IT'S A ROAD WITHOUT CARS.

Long, straight, stretching empty through the pastureland to the hazy horizon. Lying just beyond the crest of the hill. Just beyond the reach of her steering wheel.

This is what she came for.

Inge stomps the gas, the car surges, and the tires leave the earth.

It feels like flying. Like falling.

Then the car crashes down again, bouncing the girls into the roof. Annemarie squeals.

"Inge! You'll get us killed!" But she is laughing with the glory of it. The daring of it.

Inge is nothing if not daring. She hits the gas again, jerking the wheel a little too hard around an ice-rimmed puddle. The car skids, throwing them sideways, then rights itself. Mud splatters the windows.

"Your father will see all this dirt!" Annemarie protests.

"Papa is a pussycat," says Inge. "And anyway, he's away." He's always away.

"Then your mother will see!"

This threat is more serious. "I'll pay Kurt to clean it," Inge says, picking up enough speed to make Annemarie squeal again.

She'd confess to stealing Papa's car and driving it to Berlin before she'd let Mama find out Annemarie had been in the passenger seat. Mama says Annemarie is of the lower classes. Just because she lives on a farm that Mama's papa used to own. But the head of their club, Frau Koch, says there is no caste or class in the new Germany. That all German blood is valuable. That children should not listen to their parents, because their parents are old. Youth is the future. The youth will rule Germany.

And anyway, Mama is only jealous because Annemarie is tall, blond, and perfect, and Inge is not.

Inge pushes the hair from her eyes. Mama is ridiculous.

There could never be a better Nazi than Annemarie.

Inge takes a hard turn into a wooded lane, zipping down the narrow track. Then she puts both feet on the brake, skidding ruts into the mud, slamming Annemarie forward and then back into the seat cushion. They're hidden from the main road, beside the shaded path leading to Annemarie's farm.

"You're a terror," says Annemarie. But she's still laughing. Then she looks hard at Inge. "Are you sitting on a book?"

Inge pulls her skirt down over *An Examination of Racial Degeneracy,* the thickest, most comfortable-looking book she'd been able to pull from Papa's shelf. She's sixteen to Annemarie's almost eighteen, but Inge still can't see over the steering wheel. Not without help.

Annemarie rolls her eyes. "Why do I let you talk me into these things?"

"Because it's fun. And you know what else is fun? Getting kissed."

Annemarie leans forward, her face serious. "Inge! Who have you been kissing?"

"Kurt. Yesterday. In the toolshed."

"Kurt? You shouldn't have! What would Frau Koch say?"

"That he was of good German stock. But really, Annemarie, why would I tell Frau Koch?"

"But what about Rolf?"

Inge strengthens her grip on the steering wheel. "What about him?"

"It's just that . . ." Annemarie looks upset. "You're so lucky. Rolf has a perfect pedigree. Inge, you didn't . . ."

"Of course not! No babies. Not like you in a year or so."

Annemarie pushes Inge's arm, giggling, and Inge laughs, even though she isn't sure it's funny. Last week, after their club meeting, Annemarie had whispered that she'd decided to be like Frieda Hoffmann. When Frieda Hoffmann turned eighteen, she'd told her mother she was taking a course in Hamburg, when really she'd gone to a lovely mansion in Berlin to meet an SS officer to have a baby with.

A baby for Hitler, Frau Koch says, a good German baby, is the greatest gift a girl can give to her Führer.

Just not, maybe, with your mother's chauffeur in a toolshed.

"You haven't said anything, have you?" Annemarie asks. Annemarie might have to tell her mother she's taking a course, too.

Inge gives her protest some drama. "I would never!" But Annemarie still looks unhappy, so she adds, "And I won't let Kurt kiss me again, either. If that makes you feel better."

"You shouldn't. It's so unfair to Rolf. Rolf is a hero."

Inge examines her skirt hem. She's been hearing about heroes at least once a week since she was thirteen. The brave young soldiers winning glorious victories for Germany, defeating the Communist aggressors and all their allies. She's sewn shirts for them—with the other girls from their club, on their social nights—written cards, packed hundreds of boxes of candies and cigarettes to send to the front. Rolf is winning the war that will begin a thousand years of German rule. A pilot, from the perfect family. He's also ten years older, a friend of her father's, and has a gap between his front teeth.

Kurt will have to join the army soon, now that he's old enough.

Annemarie sighs. "Your father is the nicest man in the world and you're going to break his heart. Go home and be good and I'll see you at the meeting." She opens her car door. "And don't get into trouble!"

"Me? I never get . . ."

And then a rumble comes fast across the sky, shaking the air. A plane, so low their hair flies with the rush of its wind. The birds take flight, the evergreens creaking and thrashing overhead, but the branches are too thick to see more than the plane's passing shadow.

"Luftwaffe," says Annemarie. "Going to fight the Communists."

"To victory," Inge whispers automatically. She doesn't mention that the engine hadn't sounded German.

She will turn on the radio when she gets home, no matter what Mama says.

Annemarie waves and hurries away down the path, glancing furtively at the sky while Inge backs up the lane. The drive home isn't any fun now. It's just a drive.

Tall, formal hedges grow along one side of the road, trimmed around open iron gates. Inge turns smoothly between them, into a long, sloping driveway, leaves the car in gear, and cuts the engine. She knows exactly how far she can coast. The car glides past the stable, the tennis courts, the little copse of trees where the nuthatches live, swinging into its spot in the garage behind the house with barely a sound.

Kurt is there, waxing the hood of her mother's Mercedes. He

watches her park, sees the mud, and shakes his head, a shock of light brown hair showing beneath his cap. It's his fault, anyway, Inge thinks. He shouldn't have taught her how to drive.

But this means Mama is home.

Inge hops out and picks up the book she's been sitting on. It smells vaguely of Papa's pipe. "Back already?" she asks. As if it doesn't matter.

"I left her at the front," Kurt replies.

Then Mama won't have seen that the car was gone. Inge wants to wilt with relief. Annemarie might be the bigger secret, but what Mama would say if she knew Inge could drive is more than should be imagined.

"Did she have Erich and Adolf with her?"

"And Helga."

Helga is the nanny. The new one. She won't last long.

"And Herr Gundersen is here for violin," Kurt goes on. He leans into his work, buffing out the wax, sweating interestingly with the effort. He nods at her father's car.

"You'll have to pay me to wash that," he says. His tone is sly. A little wicked.

Inge holds the heavy book tight to her chest. Papa always says that no one does anything for nothing, and that this is fair. If someone does something for her, she has to do something for them. But "pay" might mean something different to Kurt. And she is not Annemarie.

Kurt straightens. "Honey cakes. Two of them. Out of the oven."

Inge grins over the book, suddenly happy again. Kurt winks, and she tucks her hair behind her ear.

One more visit to the toolshed couldn't really hurt anything.

Still smiling, Inge slips out of the garage, across the garden, through the back door, and into the kitchen. Frau Kruger waves a hand at her from behind a cloud of steam, and then Inge is on the staircase, the one meant for the servants. She pauses. The screech of a badly played violin is coming from the parlor, which would be Adolf; Erich is actually getting quite good. She'd been good. Very good. At the piano. But Mama had stopped her lessons. Her teacher, Mama said, focused far too much on foreign composers. That nonsensical romanticism is bad for a mind like Inge's. Now she has to practice "Clair de Lune" when Mama isn't home.

The violin starts up again. Inge hugs the book tight and runs up the steps, placing her feet exactly where the creaks are not, putting one eye to the crack of the door to check the upper corridor. When no one is there, she slides out, over the thick, silent carpet, and into her father's study.

Inge breathes in the stale tobacco, but the smell is nearly gone now. Wanting Papa home is selfish, because his work is important. Vital to Germany. Vital to the war. Even the Führer thinks so. But she wants him home, anyway.

There's a hole in the row of books on the shelf behind the desk, where *Racial Degeneracy* belongs. Inge gets on her tiptoes and pushes it back into place, between Rudin's *Heredity and Racial Hygiene in the National State* and *Permission to Destroy Life That Is Unworthy of Life.* Her fingers go still on the last one.

Papa says that emotion must never enter into judgment. Emotion makes correct choices difficult, and that is weakness. "And who will you be?" Papa would say, ruffling her hair. "One of the weak or one of the strong? Tell me what you think, my *Vögelchen.*"

Strong, she'd told him. She'd be one of the strong.

Inge's fingers touch the gold letters of the book spine. "I am Inge von Emmerich," she whispers. "I belong to Papa, Mama, Germany, and the Führer. They love me, and I love them." Like Papa taught her. Twenty times when she opens her eyes in the morning, and twenty times at night, just before she sleeps. Or whenever she is . . . uncertain.

Lately, she has been more uncertain. Lately, she's been thinking thoughts she shouldn't.

Then she remembers the airplane.

Inge turns to Papa's desk, pushes aside a stack of files, and reaches for the radio. The knob clicks and the dial wakes up, the yellow glow brightening like a slowly opening eye. The study is alive again, humming with soft, garbled words coming clearer as the radio warms. There's no need to tune it. There's only one broadcasting station allowed. And then she sees the edge of a folder, sticking out from the bottom of the stack.

It has her name on it.

Why would Papa have a file with her name on it?

"Inge."

Inge steps instantly away from the desk, hands going guilty behind her back. Mama is standing in the doorway.

"What are you doing?" Mama asks. Her blond hair has faded to silver gray, pulled back into a bun that is smooth, sleek as steel. Like her voice. Not a syllable out of place.

Mama crosses quickly to the desk, her heels soundless on the carpet, and turns the radio knob until it clicks. The warm glow fades and the room is cold and dead again. Mama looks down on her. Then she pulls back a hand and slaps Inge's face.

Inge's head snaps to one side. Her cheek is on fire, but she doesn't cry. German girls don't do that. Mama is waiting, watching, to see if she will.

She won't.

Inge closes her eyes.

Mama hits her again.

I am Inge von Emmerich. I belong to Papa, Mama, Germany, and the Führer. They love me, and I love them. I am Inge . . .

Only, this time she sings it in her head. To the tune of "Clair de Lune."

"Go to your room, please, Inge," says Mama. "And put a clip in your hair."

Inge slides around her mother and leaves the study. She can hear the violin downstairs. It's Erich now, playing Stravinsky, and it's beautiful. Even though Russian music is much worse than French. Or that's what Frau Koch says. Inge walks without hurrying down the corridor, head up.

I am Inge von Emmerich . . .

Cold light filters through the lace curtains at the window, making the blue satin spread on her bed look shiny and slick. Inge sits at her dressing table, knees perched beneath its ruffled cover, ignoring the barrette Mama told her to use. She picks up a brush, twining her short, dark hair around her fingers, trying to tame a curl. Mama had tried to lighten her hair when she was little, having the maid comb lemon juice through it and sending her to sit in the sun until her skin burned. It hadn't worked. Her hair had gotten darker, anyway.

She doesn't want to look in the mirror. She doesn't want to look at the red slap mark on her cheek.

Mama really is jealous of Annemarie. Because Annemarie's mother won the medal for bearing children and she did not. Because Inge is supposed to be better than Annemarie and she isn't. Because music is something that Inge is good at and Mama is not.

These are thoughts Inge is not supposed to have.

She feels a twinge of pain in her middle.

So she goes to the window and pulls back the lace curtain instead, where the nuthatches nest in the oak tree. Papa had given her a nuthatch once. Soft and sweet, summer-sky blue with blushes of orange. Because Papa loves her.

Rolf says he loves her. In his letters. That her eyes sparkle like the sky. But isn't it strange that his letters are lies. Her eyes don't sparkle. They aren't even blue. And to her knowledge, she's never actually smiled at him. Especially like a sunrise.

Maybe Papa told Rolf to say those things. Maybe Papa told him to write those letters. And what had happened to that little bird? She can't remember.

These are also thoughts Inge is not allowed to have. They hurt. They make her sick. She drops the curtain and thinks them, anyway.

About a jealous mother. French composers. Hair she shouldn't have. Violets in a field, bunched in her hands. A file hidden beneath the other folders. A file with her name on it. And Inge thinks of a word. One word before the click of the knob. One clear word before Mama took the voice of the radio away.

America.

CHAPTER THREE

── *August 1946* ──

EVA WATCHES THE young man with the duffel bag walk away, disappearing into the noisy crowd on the dock. And then she whispers, "Nothing to worry about, Brigit. Look, he's shined my shoe for me."

She picks up a piece of newspaper from the ground and cleans the spit off her shoe. The shoes had been a prize in the clothing box at the displaced persons camp—black pumps with an ankle strap— too small to fit anyone else. They make her taller. Eva lets the newspaper go blowing when she's done, curling and twisting off into the sea air, disappearing like the fog. She takes Brigit's arm and opens her candy for her.

"Eat it," she tells her. "It's good."

Brigit does, sucking on the chocolate and licking the wrapper. The other passengers from the boat are starting to pool up around them like a blocked stream.

"Move along," says Miss Schaffer, a crying toddler on her hip. "Stay together, please. Walk with me. Come away from the edge, Edgar!"

The group is slow and wayward, like sheep badly herded, while ship horns blare and seagulls cry and fleet children and fast English run together bewilderingly over the dock. And below the noise, somewhere around the level of her knees, in the lining of her skirt, Eva can hear paper rustling.

There's a building at the end of the dock. Like an enormous shed. There are no bullet holes in it. Through the open doorways, she can see desks, set up like checkpoints on a road, and at the far end is a white picket fence, holding back masses of people shouting to their families. A few of the passengers run past the desks, hugging and kissing over the fence, and men in red and navy uniforms let them for a few seconds before pulling them away again, guiding them back into line.

Eva feels her blood humming, buzzing through her veins. They will say no. They will tell her to go home, when there is no home. Question her. Beat her. Spit on her shoes. They will lock her in a cupboard. A tiny, dark cupboard, where there isn't enough air. They will take away Brigit and put her in a hospital. In a camp.

Miss Schaffer says they don't have concentration camps in America. But anything that anyone tells you at any time could be a lie.

She will not let Brigit be put in a concentration camp.

Brigit is picking at the hem of her skirt. She must have heard the rustling, too. Eva pulls her hand away, tucking it back into the crook of her arm. She gives her one button. Brigit cannot get upset. She can't allow Brigit to hurt anyone. Not here. Not now.

They get in line. Miss Schaffer fusses and clucks. Eva turns down the brim of Brigit's hat, so she can hide. They inch closer. And closer. Until they are inside the shed. Until they are standing in front of a desk, where a woman stamps their papers. And then another desk, where a different woman examines more papers and uses her stamp. And then they stand before the next desk. And this time, it's a man. In a uniform. Army. Like the boy who spit at them.

Eva moves her body slightly in front of Brigit. She has to be convincing. Her English confident. The man needs to think she is nice. Decent. That she has something to offer.

He needs to believe all her lies.

He needs to see the tiny mark that has been put on the bottom corner of their papers.

She's afraid he won't see it. She's afraid Brigit will know that she's afraid. Eva lifts her chin and smiles. The smile must look a little fierce, because the man glances up once, and then again, startled.

"Papers?" he says, holding out a hand.

Eva lays their papers on the desk. Brigit is picking at her skirt again. Eva pulls her hand away. The man reads, tilting his head to get a look at Brigit's face. He reads more and looks surprised. They had told Eva he would look surprised.

"How long did you live in Berlin?" he asks.

"Eight months," she answers. "The French Zone after."

"And before?"

"In Dresden," Eva says. It isn't true.

"Hmmm." The man looks up at Brigit. "And what about you?"

Brigit's attention has been caught by the whirl of an electric fan.

"I said, what about you, fräulein? Don't you answer?"

"No," Eva replies. "She does not."

The military man sighs, forehead wrinkled, and goes back to his list. He knows, Eva thinks. He's seen others who have had a bad war. That's what the doctors said. That Brigit had "a bad war." But this man, with his close-clipped hair and the burn scars on his left fingers, he understands that hell leaves its mark. He shuffles through the stack and finds their sponsorship papers. He reads one page and then another. His brows go up.

"And how old are you?" he asks.

Eva opens her mouth. And she can't speak. The man at the desk is waiting, expectant. But he doesn't have his own face. He has her father's face. The knit brows. Pressed lips. And she can hear her father's voice. Piercing. Like breaking glass.

How old are you? How old?

Eva blinks, and the man behind the desk is staring, his brows now all the way up his forehead. He is not her father. He looks nothing like her father. But she can almost smell the tobacco. Sweat trickles down Eva's spine.

"Eighteen," she whispers. "And Brigit is nineteen."

"Are you sure about that?"

"Yes," Eva hisses. She knows why he's asking. Because she took too long. Because she's too little. Because Brigit looks twenty-five and like she belongs in a magazine. He's not completely wrong, but it makes her mad. "That is the age on our papers. You can see the numbers, can't you?"

He looks down at the typing.

"Do you see everything on my papers?"

She's not supposed to do that. She's not supposed to point out the mark. They told her not to. The man's brows furrow. Eva's breath is coming fast.

"Do you say that I am lying?"

Brigit whimpers, and Miss Schaffer's clicking heels are hurrying across the concrete from somewhere behind them. The man at the desk glances up and shakes his head.

"Calm down, sweetheart. One look into your big eyes and I'd swear on a Bible you were forty-one. Or eighty-four."

He's not completely wrong about that, either.

He shakes his head again, and stamps Eva's papers with blurry red ink. He does the same to Brigit's. Eva hears Miss Schaffer exhale. He puts all the papers back together, taps them on the desk, handing them to Eva in a neat stack.

"Skip the medical exam and go straight through," the man sighs. "And take it easy on us, fräulein."

Eva tugs and Brigit shuffles, reluctant to leave the fan. Brigit may be taller, but Eva is stronger. Her heartbeat matches the rhythm of her shoes. Faster, faster. With a rustling in her skirt. Past the other desks, other lines, trickles in the long river of people waiting for the dam of America to break.

They sit on a bench, and when Miss Schaffer and the rest of the passengers have moved beyond the desks, they sit again, this time on a bench on a ferry.

And here comes New York. With its strong, whole walls unbroken by bullets or bombs. Glass glinting with reflected sun. Taller and taller. Closer and closer. A city set afloat in the sparkling bay.

They pick up their suitcases again. Eva hangs on tight to Brigit and her purse. Off the boat and into a hallway, where their shoe heels echo. Up a set of steps. Through a heavy door and straight out onto a busy sidewalk.

The walls surround them like brick mountainsides in a canyon. Trucks and cars chug and stop, chug and stop, up and down both sides of the street, horns honking, men shouting, shoulders bumping. A bicycle whizzes past. Eva can smell rubbish, bread, perfume, the sea, and the leavings of a dog.

America.

And no one has stopped them. No one came running after to tug on her sleeve and say no, never mind. Brigit cowers at all the unexpected movement. At the noise. The people. But Eva closes her eyes. Fills her lungs.

It worked. The plan worked. Just like the man in Berlin had said it would.

She'd made a rotten deal.

And now, in America, she will break it.

Fair is fair, though she doubts the man in Berlin is going to agree with her.

She says the names. Soft, fast, under her breath. Twenty-seven names.

Twenty-seven reasons for justice.

Twenty-seven reasons to find her father.

CHAPTER FOUR

—— *February 1945* ——

INGE SWAYS WITH the moving car, her eyes on the passing farmland, the hills a purpling smudge in the distance. The same color as her bruising cheek.

She doesn't resent her slaps. Fair is fair, after all. She knew Mama had forbidden the radio. She took a risk, and she'd lost. If you flout authority, Papa says, then you deserve your punishment. Like in the camp where he works, rehabilitating the enemies of Germany. Teaching them to obey. To be better. To be useful and productive. She had disobeyed, and so Mama had to hit her. To teach her to be better. That was fair.

Only today, Inge had seen something. A look when Mama drew back her hand. A tiny lift in the corner of her mother's mouth.

She hadn't known before. That Mama enjoyed hitting her.

But her mother only wants to make her better because she loves her. Doesn't she?

Inge sneaks a look at Mama, tall and silent beside the other window. Mama is angry because there was a dead bird in the Mercedes. One of the nuthatches. On her seat. Kurt swears he doesn't know how it got there. That it must have gotten trapped in the car.

She looks at Kurt's cap, at the short hairs on the back of his neck. If Kurt did know who did it, he'd never tell.

I am Inge von Emmerich. My name is Inge . . .

She says it again. And again. Like she was taught.

But she doesn't feel sure. She feels a little sick.

The car hits a pothole as they come into Wernigerode, not unusual for late winter, but Mama tells Kurt that his driving is the problem. That he's been sent by Communists to punch holes in her tires. That the enemies of Germany will be glad when he bends her axle. She tells him for a long time, while Inge wonders why Germany has so many enemies. The Führer says it's because some people are born bad.

She's never seen Hitler, but Mama has, and Papa has met him. When Papa is away, Mama plays records of the Führer's speeches, while Erich and Adolf run trucks and trains on the parlor rug. Jews, the Führer says, are not like Germans. They do not understand authority. They are natural criminals. Pickpockets and drug dealers and bank crooks. A virus infecting the people of Germany.

Ruth hadn't seemed like a virus. And she hadn't been much of a criminal. She'd only been twelve, with a yellow star sewn to her coat. Allowed to operate the cash register and fire the bread ovens at her family's bakery, both deeply impressive to eleven-year-old Inge. But Ruth did read books that weren't allowed. Interesting books. She'd let Inge borrow one once, sneaking it into her bag. *War of the Worlds*, about men from Mars attacking England. Inge had read it by flashlight, eyes wide beneath her ruffled satin blanket.

She'd been hurt when Ruth left without saying goodbye.

Inge thinks about that book of Ruth's, still hidden behind her wardrobe. She thinks about the radio. And Papa's stolen car. Maybe she's the natural criminal. The one who was born bad. Mama seems to think so. But Kurt got rid of all the mud, so Mama hasn't found out about the car. Or Annemarie. Or the toolshed. She doesn't even know about "Clair de Lune."

Inge smiles out the window.

She needs to get those cakes for Kurt.

The car slows through the narrow streets, the turrets and spires of the old castle watching over the little city from its clifftop. There haven't been any bombs in Wernigerode. Not like in other places, where the army had to drive back the enemy. Here, it's just as it's always been, except for the people who had to move away. So that Germans only live with Germans. Kurt drives past a boarded-up tailor's shop. Two more turns, and the bakery. With the new baker in it. Past the Balters's old house, empty because they wouldn't allow their sons to join the Hitler Youth. And then Mama sits forward in her seat, peering out the window.

There's a Block Warden on the sidewalk, his brown Nazi uniform a little tight across his middle. He has a clipboard. Writing the name of the farmer going into the doctor's office.

That farmer should be careful, Inge thinks, saying what he's going to the doctor for. The Block Warden can take your name straight to the Gestapo.

Mama turns, looking back down the street. There's another Block Warden taking a woman by the arm, just outside the locked-up church. And when Kurt slows to a stop in front of Inge's clubhouse, there's another. Gray-headed, shriveled, a veteran of the last war, the red of his swastika arm band bright beneath the banner that says LEAGUE OF GERMAN GIRLS. He's whispering to Frau Koch.

Inge hops out of the car. Mama leans over to say something, but Inge pretends not to hear and slams the door, waving to a group of girls coming down the sidewalk.

"Hello, Inge!"

They fold Inge into their chattering knot, and she walks with them, right past the Block Warden without sparing him a glance. She hasn't done anything.

Or not anything he could possibly know about.

Their clubroom is old, half-timbered with squeaking floors, bright with butter-yellow plaster and a red bunting of black swastikas hung crisscross along the ceiling, fluttering as more girls come through the door. Hitler looks down at her from his portrait on the wall. Inge smiles. Relaxes. Hangs her coat on a row of hooks. The room is loud with chitchat. She unclips the barrette from her hair and stuffs it in her uniform pocket, refusing to notice a sympathetic glance or two at her cheek. And then she listens.

There's an extra current in the room today, an urgency to the talk. Soft. Beneath the surface, like a radio tuned between the stations. A girl behind her is whispering, and Inge catches the words "shot by an airplane."

She turns, but the girl has already moved away.

That couldn't be true.

Annemarie comes hurrying in, her cheeks bright, long blond braid neat down her back. She waves, and then Frau Koch is tromping toward the front of the room. Inge finds a seat, adjusting her posture before Frau Koch gives them one, sharp clap of her hands. The talk stops instantly, the creak of the chairs fading into silence.

Frau Koch looks them over. She's a large woman, strong-looking, and Annemarie has smacked Inge's arm more than once, giggling when Inge tried to get her to admit whether or not she thought Frau Koch could single-handedly pull a plow. Inge catches Annemarie's eye on the other side of the room. Annemarie shakes her head no, biting back her smile.

"Belief and beauty," Frau Koch says into the quiet. "Where

does our belief come from? From where do we draw our faith?"

"From our Führer," they say as one. "The savior of Germany."

Inge looks at the portrait of Hitler. What must it feel like, to be a god?

"And from where do we draw our beauty?"

"From a pure heart and pure blood," reply the girls.

"And why are we here?"

"To send our blood to every corner of the earth and fill the world with Germany's nobility."

The girls stand, and Frau Koch sets a record on the player. The needle scratches, skips, and the music begins. They draw in one, collective breath.

Our flag flutters before us
into the future we march side by side
We are marching for Hitler . . .

The League of German Girls doesn't sing this song like the boys of the Hitler Youth, marching down the street with drums and flags. The girls' version, Inge thinks, is more musical. Though she wouldn't have minded the boxing and the jumping off buildings into nets, like Kurt says the boys do. She glances at the chart on the wall behind Frau Koch, with the various eye colors and skin tones for choosing a suitable husband. She should see where Kurt falls on that chart.

Or maybe she shouldn't.

Our flag is the new age
And the flag guides us to eternity
Yes, the flag is more to us than death.

Frau Koch waits for them to sit and settle, plants her feet, and puts her hands behind her back.

"I have something to say to you. There has been discussion amongst some of our girls. Talk that criticizes the defense of our Fatherland."

So that's what the Block Warden had been saying, Inge thinks. The rumor about someone being shot by an airplane. There had been another rumor, a few months ago, whispers that the girls in Berlin had stopped their regular meetings and were training to run the signals instead, alerting the guns to enemy aircraft. The Block Warden hadn't wanted them to talk about that, either. Mama said it wasn't true. Signals were a soldier's job. Hitler would never allow it. And no one could have been actually shot by the enemy in Wernigerode.

But they had been checking the doctor's office, Inge thinks.

"In the League of German Girls," Frau Koch says, "to criticize our war against aggression is to doubt our Führer. And to doubt our Führer is treason! Is there any girl here who doubts her Führer?"

Her gaze rakes through them like machine-gun fire.

There is not one breath or the scuff of a shoe.

"Good," says Frau Koch. "Then we will continue our preparations for the celebration of the Führer's birthday. Rise and stack your chairs against the wall. Annemarie Toberentz, please pass out the hoops."

Chairs scrape, and the girls move to do as Frau Koch says. Inge exchanges a look with Annemarie as she passes. Annemarie knows what's coming, and so does Inge. The floor is cleared, the hoops passed out, and the girls arrange themselves in rows. Inge makes sure she is in the back, out of Frau Koch's line of sight.

Another record goes onto the player and the music begins.

"Two, three, four, and up . . ." says Frau Koch.

They begin their routine. Hoops lift upward, and around, and around, and then the other way. The effect of all the hoops moving together is a little mesmerizing, and will be even more so at the celebration, in their costumes with the wreaths of ribbon and the short, white skirts that show their legs.

Frau Koch claps. "Stop!" she shouts. She lifts the needle from the record. "Some of you do not have the correct form. Annemarie, come forward!"

No one is surprised. They'd all been waiting for it. It's not even Annemarie's fault. But resentment crackles in the air, anyway, especially after their scolding. Annemarie walks forward slowly, head up.

"Show us the second position," Frau Koch says.

Annemarie lifts her hoop high to one side, her opposite leg back, toe pointed, long braid yellow down her back. Her body is straight, steady, her face serene.

"Look at her legs, girls." She lifts Annemarie's skirt to the thigh. "See how long and taut? Each muscle perfectly defined. This is the way a German girl should look. This is how we show our grace and good health. Our Führer deserves nothing less."

Only he won't even see it. He'll be at the big celebration. In Berlin. The collective thought ripples through the silence as if someone had said it. Frau Koch narrows her gaze.

"Perhaps our Führer might come to Wernigerode, instead, to inspect our performance more closely. Perhaps I will write and invite him."

The idea falls on the room like a bomb. Inge's eyes dart to the portrait. Would Hitler see her legs?

"Before our next meeting, each of you will do fifty leg lifts each night, until your thigh and calf muscles look exactly like Annemarie's."

This will require the supernatural. Frau Koch hears the unvoiced moan.

"You will please observe Annemarie's form for one minute," she says, looking down instantly to her watch.

The room seethes as they study Annemarie's legs. But Inge is looking at her face. She knows Frau Koch embarrasses Annemarie, holding her up as their ideal all the time. But why be embarrassed when you are exactly as you ought to be? What's cruel is to point out all of Annemarie's perfection while making her hold that hoop up in the air. It must hurt.

Annemarie doesn't quiver. She doesn't even change her expression. But she does cry. One tear, leaking from the corner of her eye. Inge shakes her head.

German girls do not cry.

Annemarie's tear trickles down to hide in her hair, but what is plain to see, Frau Koch doesn't notice. And then Inge realizes Frau Koch isn't looking at her watch. She's looking beyond them, at the back of the room. Inge turns her head.

Mama is standing in the doorway to the clubroom.

It's like an invasion. An attack. Mama shouldn't be here. It's not her place. With her plucked eyebrows and shiny purse and that fur on the collar of her coat. The smooth skin of Mama's cheek is tilted just a little, studying Annemarie. Then her gaze slides over the rows of uniforms and braids and finds Inge.

Inge feels the comparison. She feels it exactly. She snaps her head forward.

Something is wrong. Mama would never be here if something wasn't wrong.

She knows. About the car. About Kurt. She thinks of that corner of Mama's mouth and fear crawls down her neck. Creeping like a spider.

"Excuse me, Frau Koch, for interrupting your class." Mama's voice is cool. Calm. "But I need Inge, please. Immediately."

Or maybe it isn't that at all, Inge thinks. Maybe it has something to do with airplanes. Maybe it has something to do with what the radio said.

With America.

The enemy.

CHAPTER FIVE

——— August 1946 ———

EVA CLUTCHES HER purse and her suitcase on one side, Brigit on the other, a tide of people breaking past them in waves. The street beyond the ferry building is a bit like a dock, only with cars and trucks instead of tugboats and ships, plowing through a sea of pressed suits and workmen's caps, red lips, and clean gloves. A woman walks past them with a veil on her hat and a dog on a leash. Her eyes meet Eva's and dart away.

And Eva feels the comparison. She feels it exactly. They all look away. Even the old man sitting on a pile of newspapers on the corner. Gazes brushing past her face like the tip of a finger across a hot iron.

They know, Eva thinks. They know I am not decent.

And then she sees why they are in such a crowd. They're standing beneath a sign with a bus drawn on it. Eva backs up, holding tight to Brigit's arm. Brigit is looking straight down. Only at her feet. Carrying her suitcase. Like Eva taught her. Until they reach the strong bricks of the building. The people waiting for the bus are divided neatly in two. White faces to one side, brown to the other. As if there's a fence Eva can't see.

They'd told her America would be like that.

Miss Schaffer herds them a little closer to the rest of the group, yet another toddler on her hip, a small boy so tired his head lolls on her shoulder. He has a tag on his sweater, like a parcel to be picked up. All the little ones do, and that is exactly what begins to happen. Men and women, mostly women, arriving with yet more paperwork that is compared to the tags and then they take the confused children away.

Eva watches the people who take the children. She looks at their hems and their fingernails and their eyebrows and their shoes. You can learn a lot about a person from these things. This one has unworn heels three inches high, dark red nail polish, painted eyebrows, and a skirt that has never been let down. Rich. Plenty of time to think about herself. Another man has shiny shoes with a flattened heel, navy pants with a fraying cuff, and a frown line between his brows. Working, but tidy. He doesn't take a child. He leans against a streetlamp, smoking a cigarette.

Eva wonders who is coming for her, and what their fingernails will look like.

The bus comes and takes the two crowds away. Two more gather in their place. One white. One brown. One on each side of the invisible fence.

Hitler would have thought America should be like that.

Brigit tries to sink down and sit, but Eva won't let her. The street is filthy. Eva gives her the blue button, the best one, hat tented around her face, her back to the busy street. A cat comes to sniff at their ankles. A lean tabby with green eyes. Brigit smiles and reaches down, and the cat scratches her hand. A thin line of blood wells up. And so do two tears.

"No, Brigit," Eva whispers gently, dabbing at the wound with a handkerchief from Miss Schaffer. "We do not cry."

Brigit stops crying, but her mouth is turned down. Eva watches. Wary. Pain can make Brigit upset.

It can make her dangerous.

A car pulls away from the curb, belching black smoke, and another takes its place, dark blue, dusty and a little battered, making the traffic behind it honk at the inconvenience. The engine chokes, and a woman slides across the front seat, swinging black pumps to the pavement on the safer side. Everything about her is medium. Her height, her weight, the brown of her hair, the beige of her suit, the cream-colored blush of her cheek. But she has a badge on her sleeve, a pointed starburst like Miss Schaffer's.

"Miss Schaffer!" the woman says. "Lovely to see you and so sorry to make you wait. It was difficult to find a parking space. Are these our girls?"

Miss Schaffer doesn't have a moment to answer before the woman turns to Eva and Brigit, strips off a glove, and holds out a hand. Her fingernails are short. Rosy pink.

"I'm Elizabeth Whittlesby, from the American Friends Service Committee, but you can call me Bets. I hope you aren't too dreadfully tired. Are you sisters?"

Eva takes the woman's offered hand, which is difficult because Brigit is clinging so hard to her arm. She didn't catch every word Elizabeth Whittlesby said, but she did get the last question. Eva shakes her head.

"Oh, just good friends, then. Fine. It's nice to have a friend. Especially during such times. Are these your bags?"

Why do Americans call a suitcase a bag? But Eva only nods, leaning over to put Brigit's suitcase back into her free hand and pick up her own. Elizabeth watches, sharp eyes taking in Brigit's scratches, then she turns to Miss Schaffer.

"You have paperwork for me to sign?"

Miss Schaffer flips pages on her clipboard, and Eva sees the paperwork happen like everything else seems to happen with Elizabeth Whittlesby. Fast.

"All right, girls? Ready to go?"

Eva doesn't know if she's ready, because she doesn't know where they're going. She doesn't know what anything will cost. Miss Schaffer said everything would be explained when they arrived, but so far, nothing has been explained, and now, Elizabeth Whittlesby is watching Brigit in alarm. Brigit has been shrinking into herself, cringing, ever since the cat. Now she's beginning to shake.

Whatever Eva owes them later, Brigit needs to go now. Off the street. To somewhere quiet, where Eva can take care of her. Before she screams. Or attacks someone. Before the police come. Or soldiers. Or a doctor.

They'll take Brigit away.

Eva pulls Brigit toward the car, but Brigit resists, whimpering.

"I'll take the bags, shall I?" asks Elizabeth.

"Come, Brigit. *Kommen Sie mit . . .*" Eva whispers. But Brigit has gone rigid, and now Eva sees why.

There's a boy in the back seat of the car.

A young man. He lifts a hand, sliding across the seat to roll down the dirty window. Brigit's breath is coming in short, agitated puffs. Breaths that will soon have noise. A lot of noise. Eva steps in front of Brigit, takes her hands. The window glass creaks downward.

"Hi," he says.

"Look at me, Brigit," Eva whispers. "Look at me . . ."

"Say, do you like music? How about the harmonica?"

Eva looks back. There's a flash of silver in the young man's hand, and before she can register what it is, he holds it to his mouth and music blares out. Eva jumps. The tune is cheerful, jaunty, jangling, and strikes her as a little off-key.

She hates it.

But Brigit doesn't. Her eyes go wide and she smiles, fear slipping off her like a jacket. The old man sitting on the newspapers laughs and claps, and the man with the shiny shoes turns his head, watching while he smokes. Brigit relaxes, takes a little step beyond Eva's protective grip. Someone passing on the street yells for them to "pipe down already."

"Oh, go pipe down yourself!" Elizabeth Whittlesby says good-naturedly, shutting their suitcases in the trunk. She hurries to the passenger side, scooting back across the front seat to the steering wheel as the young man finishes his tune with a fanfare. He opens the car door, wipes the harmonica on his pants leg, and offers it to Brigit.

And Brigit gets in the car. Just like that. Beside a boy. When a word or even a glance from any sort of male has sent her into fits for a year. When it had taken Eva months to learn how to calm her, hour upon hour creating every little trick and stratagem. And this young man had just done it in seconds. Without even trying. He slides over to make room, and Brigit takes the harmonica, turning it over and over in her hands, her dimples denting her cheeks. He looks up at Eva and smiles.

His shoes are hidden beneath the front seat of the car. Short nails, hands and face and forehead bronzed by the sun. Brown jacket, dark hair, and dark brows that don't tell her much of anything, because sitting underneath them are two of the most extraordinarily beautiful hazel-green eyes.

And she is extraordinarily angry with him.

Eva drops into the back seat beside Brigit, cramming them all together, and shuts the car door. Hard. Her skirt rustles. Elizabeth twists around.

"Did everybody meet? Miss Gerst, Miss Heidelmann, this is Jake. Our resident chief in charge of getting rid of the blues."

He lifts a hand. Eva doesn't know what "getting rid of the blues" means, and she can't look at Jake, so she turns to the window instead. The man with the shiny shoes is still smoking, watching their little drama, and Miss Schaffer, who suddenly looks like security to Eva, is waving goodbye, her hand barely at the level of her waist. Eva waves back, just a little. Miss Schaffer looks tired. And relieved to see them go.

Maybe she knows about the second mate.

"Now then, girls," says Elizabeth. "Let's hit the road, shall we? We have to get you home."

CHAPTER SIX
—— February 1945 ——

KURT DRIVES HOME fast, skidding through the streets until they are back in the countryside, trees and pastureland zipping by. Mama is a statue, staring out the window, swaying only slightly with the bumps. Inge meets Kurt's glance in the rearview mirror. He doesn't know, either.

Then it's not about her. Or the car or the toolshed. Mama would have never interrupted a League of German Girls meeting for something less than a disaster, and there is the corner of an envelope sticking out of her purse. An envelope that wasn't there before. Inge wants to ask, when she knows she shouldn't ask. She ventures a whisper.

"Is it Papa?"

"No," Mama snaps.

"Rolf?" she guesses. But Mama doesn't answer.

When she was ten, Papa took her to a military parade. Just the two of them. He'd held her hand in his, and they had laughed and cheered while the band played and the tanks rolled by. Inge had thrown flowers for the soldiers to step on, marching their way to victory. It had been exciting. Special.

It's impossible to think that something could have gone wrong with the war. How many times has she been told that Hitler would not allow it?

But why, then, has Mama forbidden the radio?

Why was there an airplane that had not sounded German? And rumors that the Block Warden tried to stop?

Inge quietly clips back her hair.

Kurt pulls the car between the tall hedges and circles around the drive to the front door of their house. It's a stone house, with sculpted trim along the gables that has always reminded Inge of icing dripping down a cake.

"Come back with the car in twenty minutes," Mama tells Kurt.

Inge bites her lip. They step out into the graveled drive, and as soon as Kurt has pulled away, out of sight, Mama hurries.

"You are to pack a bag," she says on her way up the steps. "One bag. Take three changes of clothes and a coat."

"But where are we . . ."

"I have no time for your questions. Fifteen minutes and you will be standing at the front door. Go!"

Inge hurries into the entry hall. Mama must have already called ahead from Wernigerode because she can hear an argument between Helga and Adolf floating down from the boys' bedroom upstairs, while one of the maids is packing up the silver in the dining room. Grandmama's silver going into a box is the most frightening thing Inge has seen yet.

She doesn't like the front stairs. There's an empty space underneath them. But this time she runs up them anyway, across the balcony, throwing open her bedroom door and then the door of her wardrobe. She stands there, staring. What to choose when you don't know where you're going? But Mama did say to take a coat.

Inge tosses a sweater, two blouses, a skirt, the loose dungarees she uses for exercise, and her pink party frock onto the bed. One pair of sturdy lace-ups, her pink heels, three sets of underthings, and when all this is in the initialed suitcase Papa gave her for her birthday, she grabs a hairbrush, her pins, a necklace, and at the last second, a book on the Romantic composers, hidden underneath her bed behind the ice skates.

The lid snaps shut, and then Inge is out of her room and into the hall. She turns around again and comes back out with her tennis racket and her toothbrush now crammed inside the suitcase.

And there is Papa's study, the door still ajar.

There is a file in that room. On Papa's desk. A file with her name on it.

She takes a step toward the study, and then Erich and Adolf burst into the hallway, a harried Helga pushing them in front of her. Helga looks startled, wide-eyed, a little frantic. A mouse brushed by the wing of an owl.

Then again, she always looks like that.

Who wouldn't, trying to please both Mama and the boys? When pleasing them almost always means two completely opposite things?

"Inge!" Adolf complains. "Tell Heggie I want my trains!"

"Stop being such a baby," Erich replies. He's ten to Adolf's seven, taller than him by a head, hair darkening from the corn silk blond of childhood to a pale brown. "Mama said clothes only."

Inge thinks of her tennis racket.

"And you know what will happen when you whine," Erich goes on. "Do you want to get Heggie in trouble?"

It's a good question, because getting Helga in trouble could be exactly what Adolf wants. And Helga knows it. Her eyes skitter down the stairs, where Mama is barking instructions to someone in the dining room.

Papa says that you have to let people solve their own problems. That coddling the weak with kindness only encourages their weakness. That kindness is unfair to them, because it cannot make them strong. But what Adolf's doing is unfair, too.

"We won't be gone long," Inge says cheerfully. "And think how hard your trains would be for you to carry, Adolf. Your suitcase would be so heavy."

Mama said three changes of clothes. So three days. They would be back in three days.

"And . . ." Inge adds, "maybe there will even be trains where we're going. Real trains, instead of toy ones."

Adolf's face perks up and Helga throws Inge a grateful glance, bustling her charge toward the stairs. Erich frowns.

"Inge, what happened to your face?"

Inge bites her lip. If Erich doesn't know, then he wasn't the one who put the bird in the car. He's done things like that for her before. And Mama doesn't suspect. Inge smiles at him. Big and bright. Like there's a holiday. Or ice cream.

"Just bumped the door," she tells him. "It was stupid. Hurry, before Mama gets mad."

Erich frowns and picks up his suitcase, glancing back on his way down the stairs. Inge looks to the study door.

Why would Papa keep a file about her? Like one of his patients?

My name is Inge von Emmerich. I belong to Papa, Mama, Germany, and the Führer. They love me, and I love them . . .

"Inge!" Mama calls. "We leave you behind in one minute!"

Three days, and they would be back. Of course they would be back. Packing up the silver was probably just a precaution. Three days is not so long to be away. And it will be so easy to sneak into the study then. When Mama is out shopping. Or asleep.

My name is Inge von Emmerich.

Inge grips her suitcase and hurries down the stairs, leaving the study door open behind her.

CHAPTER SEVEN

August 1946

EVA RESTS AN elbow on the car door. Elizabeth Whittlesby is talking with a cigar-smoking man in front of a solid-looking apartment building dotted with holes that are open windows. The fog is gone, but the air is humid, stale, the breeze blocked by lines of hanging shirts, pants, and underthings strung crisscross between the buildings like mismatched bunting. But there are children playing, as unconcerned as the ones at the dock, and the woman selling bread from her front stoop can tell them all to kick their ball elsewhere by their first names.

There are no separate groups in this neighborhood. No invisible lines or fences. Because Eva can't see a face that is anything other than white.

This is where she's supposed to live now.

It doesn't look like anyone here would want to kill her. Or spit on her.

Then again, they don't know her yet.

It is so hot in the car.

Eva uses her free hand to pull the hat from her head and shake out her sweaty hair. Brigit is still holding the harmonica, her head lolling on Eva's shoulder. Eva arranges Brigit's rustling skirt away from Jake, making sure not to look at him. Making sure he can't get a good look at her, even when he's trying. He drums the seat with his fingers, and the rhythm is like music, but unexpected. Interesting.

She turns her face to the window. When they'd come to her with their plans—when she'd made her rotten deal—she thought they'd be sending her to a camp for displaced persons, like Düppel Center in Berlin, or Biberach. With dormitories and barracks and rows of iron-framed bunks, a bowl of porridge, a can of meat, and one glass of milk each day. Where she would be one face in a hundred. A thousand. Where she could slip away, come and go unnoticed, and do what she came to do.

But America is not a war zone. Here, you'd never know there had been a war. And New York is so much bigger than she'd thought. And Elizabeth Whittlesby hasn't taken them to a camp. She's taken them to an apartment building. Like normal people. With rent. And the three American bills she has hidden in her bra are not going to be enough.

She'll have to have a job. Immediately. When her only real skills involve pot scouring and lice combing and putting together a Quonset hut. And she won't be able to share the apartment. The men there might not have a harmonica. She and Brigit will have to have a room to themselves, with a lock—a good lock—where it's safe to leave Brigit while she works. When leaving Brigit alone is a disaster waiting to happen.

Maybe she could bring Brigit with her. America must be full of jobs where no one minds when the employees bring their crazy friends along.

Only, Brigit isn't crazy. Not really. Or if she is, it isn't her fault.

It's Eva's.

And while she's doing all that, how is she supposed to find her father?

She's going to fail those twenty-seven names before she's even begun.

The woman in the displaced persons camp had said she was lucky, because the American Friends Service Committee, the AFSC, would help them "adjust." "Adjust," Eva thinks, must mean "make them fit," like filing down cogs in a machine. They will be worked. Shaped. It will probably hurt.

What she's come here to do is going to hurt, too. But it will be worth it.

Because it will be justice.

But no one has said what Elizabeth Whittlesby and the AFSC are going to ask in return.

She has nothing left to give.

Eva adjusts Brigit's sleepy head, which is leaving a sweaty place on her shoulder, and leans her cheek on the window frame, trying to find a breeze. She closes her eyes.

And for one, brief flash the sun is snuffed and the window is a wall, a wall so tight, so close to her face that she can't get enough air.

There isn't enough air.

Her eyes fly open, and she's in a hot, sunny car with Brigit, fingers tapping music on the other end of the seat. She breathes. Breathes.

And then she looks hard at the street corner.

There's a man leaning against the iron trunk of a streetlight. A man with shiny shoes, pressed pants, and a frown line between his eyes. Smoking a cigarette. Just like he had been outside the ferry building.

Eva stares straight ahead, before he can see her looking. And something inside her shifts into gear. Ready.

"Uh-oh," says Jake, watching Elizabeth's conversation. The man in front of the apartment building is flinging cigar ash while he yells. Jake opens the car door. "Don't go anywhere, okay?"

He trots over to Elizabeth, but whatever Jake tries to add to the conversation, it doesn't work like it did with Brigit. More gestures, what looks like pleading, and in another minute, both he and Elizabeth are walking back to the car, shoulders drooping. Elizabeth plops down into the driver's seat, and to Eva's relief, Jake gets in the front beside her. The man on the street corner grinds his smoldering stub beneath the sole of a shiny shoe.

"Of all the nerve!" Elizabeth exclaims, and smacks the steering wheel with a gloved hand. Brigit starts, eyes half-open. Eva takes her arm, careful to speak with a voice that is soothing. Calm.

"What is happening, Miss Whittlesby?"

Jake looks back and raises a brow. "She speaks!"

"Call me Bets," says Bets. "And I'll tell you what's happening. Mr. Gabertelli has done a dastardly thing and given your room away. Just because somebody else paid him a higher rent for it. Can you believe that?"

Of course, she can believe it. Why would someone turn down a higher rent?

"What a lout," Bets goes on. "And he kept the deposit money, too! Just because the boat came two days late." She huffs, and then she sighs. And starts the car. "Oh, well. Maybe he needs the higher rent."

Jake chuckles. "So says every landlord in every city everywhere, Bets."

"I don't know," she says. "You never know what's really going on with somebody else. Maybe he has six kids or something . . ."

Bets steers around the playing children. The engine chugs and then roars. They pass the man with shiny shoes, just opening the door to a beige car dappled with rust.

"Maybe times are tough and he needs milk for the baby," Bets muses. "Maybe he doesn't have any choice, you know?"

If Bets had just arrived in Berlin, Eva thinks, she'd already have her purse stolen. And her car. And possibly her clothes.

"Maybe I should send one of the girls over to check on the Gabertellis. See if they need anything . . ."

Jake's beautiful eyes glance over his shoulder, and he shrugs once at Eva, like *What can you do about it?*

Isn't it odd, Eva thinks, how a look or a gesture can transcend a language. And how sometimes it can't. Why is he here?

Everybody wants something.

"So what are you thinking, Bets?" Jake asks. "Where to?"

Bets honks at an aggressive truck. "Oh, we'll just have to take them home, of course."

Home, Eva thinks. She never wants to go back there again.

Eva moves Brigit's head and looks back over her shoulder. The man in the shiny shoes is only one car behind them.

It's too soon. He has to know it's too soon. She's only just stepped off the boat.

Her rotten deal has already gotten worse. Much worse.

And if she doesn't find her father fast, there won't be time to break it.

CHAPTER EIGHT

—— *February 1945* ——

THEY MUST BE going to her father, Inge decides. She watches the passing road from the car window, biting a nail when Mama isn't looking. Papa must have written to them, a letter in that envelope in Mama's purse. Something has happened, and he must have told Mama to meet him.

The thought comforts the nagging twinge in her middle. It will be good to be with Papa. Papa always wants to see her. To know everything she's been doing. Maybe he will answer some of her questions.

Sometimes, if she's been good, he will answer.

So he'll just have to think she's been good.

But Kurt doesn't turn northeast, toward Berlin and Papa's camp. He turns southeast instead, like they're going to Grandpapa's summer lodge, for vacation. Only it isn't summer. It isn't even spring yet. The car rattles down the road until the shadows stretch and the sun dips down, a pale, cool blaze over the horizon.

They've been driving for three hours.

Adolf is complaining in the front seat, Helga shushing and consoling while Mama tells Kurt to go faster. For once, Inge and her mother are in agreement. A visit to the toilet was not something she'd thought of during her fifteen minutes of packing.

They pull over to the side of the road so Kurt can refill the gas tank with the spare can in the trunk, and Mama lets Erich and Adolf step away from the car and relieve themselves. Mama would never allow her to do that. And there's nothing but the dusk and a fence post for privacy, anyway. Inge hums, rubbing her hands together in the chill, trying to distract herself. Keeping her thoughts exactly where they should be.

She should have given one of the maids a note for Annemarie.

Kurt starts the car, and they're off down the bumping road. When the light is completely gone, Erich takes out a flashlight and starts to read, the very thought of which makes Inge sick, and then, finally, Kurt turns. Inge sits forward. She knows this road, even with no lights. He turns, and turns again, and the car changes its direction. This time to up, pushing Inge back against the seat, the road dark beneath the shadows of the evergreens.

This is the way to the summer lodge. She knows it exactly. But why? Why hadn't Mama just said? They hadn't been at all in the last two years, because of Papa's work with the war. So why would he want to come here now? At the end of winter? Inge turns, opens her mouth to ask, and then closes it again.

Mama is staring straight ahead, her ivory face weirdly lit by Erich's flashlight. Mama is always beautiful, even with her silvery hair. Her skin is smooth. Striking. A blank and perfect piece of paper that now, in the electric light, might as well have been written over with ink. Inge can read it plainly. Like the words of a story.

Anger, pride, derision, disappointment. Determination.

And fear. So much fear.

She drops her eyes before Mama can catch her looking. Before Mama knows what she has seen.

Is Mama a good person?

The question makes Inge's stomach ache. She closes her eyes.

I am Inge von Emmerich. I love Papa, and . . . Mama . . .

The engine roars and whines in turn up the steep road. Tree branches scrape the car roof, and then they are circling into the drive of a timber house with steep gables and rough-sawn furniture on the covered porch, pearly in the light of a rising moon. The windows are boarded up.

Inge shoots a glance sideways, but Mama looks like Mama again. Kurt turns the key, and the rattling engine sounds grateful to die. He rubs his neck.

Mama hadn't given Kurt one direction while he was driving. So she must have told him where they were going before they left. Maybe Mama told him something else, too. Inge needs to get Kurt alone, to ask him.

But Mama is already out of the car, giving orders. Kurt goes to pry the boards off the kitchen door so they can unlock it, and Helga gets the suitcases for the boys. Patches of snow and ice still dot the ground up here, clumps beneath the trees and in the shadowed places on the roof. Inge carries her own suitcase, stepping over the slush, dancing on the balls of her feet until the kitchen door creaks open. Then she hurries through the dark, threading her way through the familiar furniture to the little bathroom in the servants' wing.

When she creeps out again, the lights are on in the kitchen. The room is dusty, damp, and smells like it. Papa isn't here. There's nobody in the house but them.

"Mama," whispers Inge, "the toilet isn't working. It won't flush."

"Kurt can help you," Mama snaps, "since you have so little control."

Kurt moves toward the back hall. "The water valves are probably off," he says in passing, and Inge starts to follow him, to ask her questions. Then she wishes that she'd thought to shut the toilet lid and stays where she is.

"Unload the car," Mama says to her, turning to check the faucet at the kitchen sink. Her purse is on the table, the corner of the envelope peeking out. Inge takes a step forward, but then Mama turns back and snatches up her purse.

Inge nips out the door into the sharp air and starts emptying the trunk. Boxes and baskets. Bread, eggs, vegetable cans, dried fruit, and tinned meats. Sacks of flour. Much more than their rations. More food than they could eat in three days.

They'll be gone longer than three days.

There's enough food here for a month.

I am Inge . . . I am Inge von Emmerich. I love Papa . . . I love . . . Mama . . .

But her mind won't let her think the words.

If Mama is this afraid, then there's something to be afraid of.

They hook up a bottle of gas to the stove, and Helga warms milk mixed up from a powder. There's no chance to speak to Kurt, because Mama has him checking the house, making sure the doors and windows are secure, that the water valves are on in the other sinks and bathrooms. There's a boiler in the cellar, but only a little coal in the hopper. Mama says they will do without, since the weather will be warming up, anyway, and everyone is to go straight to bed. The boys are not ready for this, not after their long ride in the car, but they would never say so to Mama. It's Helga who will have to deal with them.

Helga hands Kurt a mug of cooling milk on her way out with the boys, and Kurt looks at Inge over the rim. He wants to say something to her. She can see it straining at the edges of his eyes.

"Come, Inge," says Mama.

Inge picks up her suitcase, looking back again at Kurt.

"Now, Inge!"

Kurt's gaze drops into his milky water, and so she follows Mama, circling through the cold house. The stairs creak beneath their feet, and at the top, Inge turns automatically to the third room on the right, the bedroom that has always been hers. But Mama has followed her. Instead of taking the big, front room, Mama is opening the little door next to Inge's instead. A small bedroom, almost a closet, plain with a single-size bed, meant for a maid or the nanny. Mama stands in the doorway, waiting until Inge pushes her own door shut with a click.

Inge can't leave her room now. Not without being heard.

The bulb isn't working in the overhead light, so she sets down the suitcase and feels her way through the dark to the lamp beside the bed. The glare makes her blink. The room looks dingy without the rugs and the ruffled curtains, no blankets or even sheets, the windows a blank wall of boards on the other side of the glass. It feels like a cage. And then she hears noise. On Mama's side of the wall. Muffled. Static. Low and humming.

Inge reaches down and slips off her shoes. She creeps to the wall she shares with the bedroom next door, toe to heel, and leans toward the peach-flowered wallpaper. A voice is crackling on the other side.

A radio.

There's a radio in the room next door. There's one downstairs, too, a big one, in the living room, but Mama doesn't seem to want it. Inge presses her cheek against the wall. She can't hear what the voice is saying. But Mama can. Inge listens, hard. She listens to what she can't hear for a long time.

And when she wakes up in the morning, chilled on the bare mattress beneath her coat, crumpled in her League of German Girls uniform because she'd forgotten to pack a nightgown, there's a note on the floor. Slipped beneath her door in the night. It says:

For when you need it

No signature. No other words. But on top of the note is a key.

The car key.

And Inge thinks she knows what it means.

Kurt is gone.

CHAPTER NINE

—— *August 1946* ——

FOR A LITTLE while, Eva thinks the man in the shiny shoes is gone.

And then she catches a glimpse of him over Brigit's brown hat, still crammed sweaty against her cheek. He's beside them in his rusting beige car, then a little behind as Bets muscles through the traffic, and then beside them again. There's a small blue feather in the band of his hat. He turns his head, and for one brief second, two dark eyes lock onto Eva's. Then Bets zooms through a yellow light and leaves the beige car behind in a burst of exhaust.

Eva hasn't seen him since. But they haven't turned, either. So he is back there, somewhere.

Coming.

She needs more time.

The traffic thins, and Bets slows the car, easing it into a parking space on a much quieter street.

"Home sweet home!" she says.

Eva has the car door open before the engine is off, purse in hand, urging a dazed Brigit out onto a neatly swept sidewalk. Her hat is askew, but Eva doesn't have time to straighten it. She looks up and down. The buildings here are four and five stories tall, of stone and brick, running one into the other, with tall bay windows. Wide, clean steps, lined with pots of roses and ivy and geraniums, leading up to glossy doors. Every tree with its own little fence.

It's lovely. Like her life before.

She doesn't belong in her life before. And it will be so easy to be noticed here.

Unless the man misses their car in the endless row of parked cars. Unless they can get inside before he catches up. But she doesn't know which door they're going to. She doesn't know which set of steps.

She doesn't know how to ask them to hurry.

And then Eva spins around. Brigit is off the curb, darting into the street.

"Whoa. Not that way," Jake says, blocking her with an arm. A car honks as it putters by. It's not the beige one. "Hold that harmonica for me while I get your stuff."

Brigit blinks, rediscovering the harmonica in her hand as Eva threads an arm through hers, guiding her back to the sidewalk. Bets is still in the front seat, looking for something in her purse, while Jake saunters around to the trunk, fumbling with the key. Everything today has happened so quickly, and now, exactly when she needs them to be fast, it's like someone put the film on the wrong speed at the cinema.

Eva shifts her feet and breathes. Breathes. Traffic hums and honks in the distance. A scratchy recording of Vivaldi drifts down from an open window. Then the trunk slams shut with the sound of weighty metal.

"Over here," Jake says, a suitcase in each hand. He ducks his head toward a set of steps. There's a pair of bright green double doors at the top, half glass, and a brass sign screwed into the stone that says POWELL HOUSE.

Eva urges Brigit up the steps behind Jake, trying to keep her from stumbling in her hurry. Jake sets down a suitcase, gets a hand on the doorknob, and then Bets comes dashing up, yanking off a glove with her teeth, snagging a note tucked neatly behind the brass sign.

"Well, drat," she says. "Mother Martha had to go put out a fire in the sewing room, and now I'm supposed to be hosting Friday coffee . . ."

Eva looks back over her shoulder, and there it is. The rust-and-beige car. And here they are, standing high and unmissable on the steps. The man with the shiny shoes peers at her as he passes, turning his head until Eva thinks his neck might snap. And when the car motors on down the street, Eva feels calmer.

There's no reason to hurry now. No reason in the world.

Jake is watching her when she turns, his dark brows drawn a little together. But he smiles and opens one of the doors.

"Welcome to Powell House."

She helps Brigit through a little entryway and into a foyer with green walls, heavy white trim, and a parquet floor, a staircase with wrought iron railing sweeping up from one side in a graceful curve. Cups clink in a room to the left, where a crowd of men and women—some nicely, others badly dressed—are milling in front of an ornate marble fireplace. And in a little chair set back beneath the stairs, a woman with curly gray hair, round porcelain cheeks, and a corsage pinned to her jacket sits alone, intent, sewing on what looks to be . . . underwear. Lacy, silky underwear.

"Hello!" Bets calls, breezing through the door. "Hello!" She tosses her purse and gloves on a little table.

"Hello," the sewing woman murmurs, biting her bottom lip. The underwear looks expensive. And large. Very large.

Jake sets down the suitcases and shuts the front doors. But he doesn't lock them. He puts his hands in his pockets. "Everything good over there, Mrs. Thomas?"

"Of course, Jacob," she replies without missing a stitch. "Why do you ask?"

A telephone rings from somewhere below them, and on the other side of Mrs. Thomas and her underwear, coming up a plain staircase neatly hidden beneath the rising curve of the more elegant one, Eva hears a set of brisk footsteps. A head appears, graying threads pulled back into a curling knot, and then a body in a yellow print dress set off by skin that is a deep, shiny brown. The woman smiles. Like she's just about to laugh.

"Mrs. Angel!" says Bets. "We've had a dustup with Mr. Gabertelli, and so we're putting these two nice girls upstairs until we sort it all out. Is the blue room ready, do you think, or should I do a little laundry?"

"The blue room is fine, but you can't do laundry, Bets," says Mrs. Angel, "because you're supposed to be doing the coffee. In the meantime, I've been doing the coffee." She holds up a little bowl and a bottle of milk. And then she eyes Jake. "Mr. Jacob Katz. Are you sick or something?"

Jake steps up and kisses her cheek, making a rude, smacking sound when he does it. Eva feels her eyebrows rise. The woman does laugh this time. Loudly. Then he gives her a real little peck on the cheek before going to grab the suitcases again.

Eva wonders what Hitler would have said about that kiss.

Probably a lot. In Germany, Katz is a Jewish name.

"Blue room, then, Jake," says Bets, unfazed. She glances once toward the stairs, and says, "What's Peggy doing?"

"Mrs. Turgonov's bloomers," replies Mrs. Angel, still chuckling.

"Well, sure she is. Is Olive here?"

"She's answering the phone and washing the cups."

"Right." Bets takes the milk and sugar from Mrs. Angel and sails toward the parlor full of people. "I'll come up and get you two sorted in three ticks!" she calls over her shoulder.

And when Eva looks around, Brigit has reached out a finger, touching the brown skin of Mrs. Angel's arm.

"No, Brigit," Eva whispers, pulling back Brigit's hand, but Mrs. Angel offers up her arm.

"Pretty, isn't it, sweetie?" she says. "Now you go upstairs and take a rest and I'll bring up some milk for you. You like milk, don't you? And cake? I bet you like cake."

Brigit dimples, but Eva knows they can't afford cake. She glances back at the unlocked door. And Jake is watching her again. He smiles and says, "Follow me."

He takes the stairs in a rhythm. Like he has music in his head. They climb the curve, and at the first landing, there are two large rooms, much like downstairs. "Library and music room," Jake says. Up another set of stairs, and there is a little hall with three closed doors. Jake walks to the one at the far end, sets down a suitcase, and turns a blue-and-white china doorknob.

There's a bedroom on the other side. With tall windows across the front of the house and white curtains. A mirror stands on its own in a corner, and Eva catches a glimpse of Brigit in her crushed brown hat. There's a girl holding Brigit's arm, with hot cheeks and hair blown wild by the wind. The girl is thin, very thin, her skirt shabby against the bright blue cornflowers of the wallpaper, her eyes dark and much too big for her face.

Eva looks away. She doesn't know that girl. And she's left her hat in the car.

She might just leave it there. It was an ugly hat.

The room has a chest for clothes, a wardrobe for clothes, and a bed big enough for two with a thick mattress and a soft rug on the floor. The tiny cabin on the boat had seemed like luxury, and this room makes the cabin look like a prison.

She won't be able to pay for it.

Then Brigit tugs herself free from Eva's arm. She trots forward, leaving one shoe, then the other in a trail along the floor. She pulls back the blue-stitched quilt and gets in the bed, eyes closing as soon as her head settles on the pillow.

"Time for a nap, then," Jake observes. He sets down the suitcases. "Bets will be disappointed not to do the laundry."

Eva turns. "You say strange things." The dark brows go up over his lovely eyes.

"Do I? You don't say much at all."

Eva doesn't reply. She goes to Brigit and unpins the brown hat, easing it off her head. The scratches on her hand are thin and a little angry, her breathing already slowed. She looks like a child with her blond hair spilling all over the pillow. Or a fairy. She still has the harmonica. Eva glances back at Jake, and he shrugs.

"She can have it for as long as she wants it."

It's like the drinking tab at a restaurant. When you only have so much to spend, and the people just keep ordering and ordering. The feeling is tight. Sickening. What will happen when they find out that she can't afford this room? Or much of anything at all?

She brushes a strand of hair from Brigit's cheek and pulls the quilt over her legs—it's too hot to cover her any more—careful not to let her skirt rustle, and picks up her cast-off shoes. Jake goes to a window and starts working it upward.

"So you're from Berlin?" he asks.

"Yes."

"I had a grandfather in Berlin. But he came to America a long time ago."

That was probably wise of him, Eva thinks. Jake moves to the next window, and Eva peeks around the edge of the curtain now moving with the barest breath of a breeze. She can see the street, but no shiny shoes. Not yet.

But they are coming.

Why didn't someone lock the front door?

The next window squeals as it moves up its frame. "How's your English?" Jake asks. Eva turns.

"It is not . . . correct?"

"Oh, no. You seem like you're doing great, from what I've heard. Lots better than most that come. But you said I say strange things. We have a class for that. For all the crazy things Americans say that don't make sense when you think about it. Like 'dry up' or 'hit the road' or 'this is a swell joint.' Things like that."

Eva bites her lip. She doesn't know what any of that means.

"You can take it if you want to. It's called Slanguage. They meet on Thursday nights in the library." The last window slides up with ease. Jake turns around and puts his hands in his pockets.

"So, I've been assigned to be your friend," he says. "It's my job to help you with anything you need, so all you have to do is ask."

"Your job? You are paid to help me?"

"No, not paid, exactly. I'm a volunteer. I answer questions, point somebody new to this country in the right direction. It's a job I want to do, but I don't get money for. A volunteer."

Eva can't imagine being able to work for no money just because you want to. But what does he get in return? If this was Germany, she would know how it works. Like getting an aspirin on the ship.

Jake shrugs. "So, whatever you need, that's what I'm here for. Do you . . . need help . . . with anything?"

He's looking at her very intently with those pretty eyes.

"No," she says, turning back to the window. "Thank you."

"You're sure?"

What she needs is to be careful.

"Okay," he says. "I'll just go down and grab some coffee, then. Let you settle in." She hears the doorknob turn. "I'll see you later."

She waits for the door to shut. For the sound of Jake's feet to fade away down the stairs. Then she moves. To the smaller dresser drawers first, opening one, two, and then the drawer of the bedside table. She finds handkerchiefs and some sewing scissors. She hides the scissors. Brigit sighs in her sleep. Eva drags a chair to the doorway and climbs up, running her fingers along the little ledge of wood trim framing the top.

And she smiles. Her fingers come away dusty. And with a key.

Off the chair, a quick look at a peaceful Brigit, and she turns the china knob. There's no one on the landing.

Eva slips out of her room, puts in the key, and with some jiggling, turns the lock. She'd heard the telephone from somewhere downstairs, from the lower floor where Mrs. Angel had come from, and the man in Berlin had said there would be a directory. A book, with names and addresses and phone numbers. He'd said she should look for names.

This book would be near a telephone, wouldn't it?

She thought she'd have more time. She'll have to buy some time.

She goes silently down the steps. If she meets someone, she'll ask for water. If they find her with the book, she will say she is looking for . . . her aunt. She will think of a name. And now she can hear the conversation, the clinking cups. Around the curve in the stairs, and there is Jake's back, leaning against the doorframe to the room with the fireplace, talking to a girl.

Eva tiptoes across the creaky parquet. Jake doesn't turn. The Mrs. Thomas who sews silky underwear has disappeared. Eva flits down the stairs beneath the stairs and at the bottom finds a dim, cool hallway running the length of the house, a door at either end, one stepping up and out to the back, the other stepping up and out to the street. Two more doors in between, the one near the front standing open. Eva can see a desk. A filing cabinet with a menorah on top. And a telephone.

She hurries down the hall, and someone moves across the light from high windows, making it blink. She hears a drawer shut. Feet walk across the foyer above her, sharp heels coming across the ceiling toward the stairs, and Eva skitters through the other door.

It's a kitchen with cream-painted cabinets, little roses and fleur-de-lis stenciled on their fronts, a big old-fashioned stove, and black-and-white linoleum. There's a sink full of dishwater and a percolator plugged into an outlet that dangles from a wire hanging down from the ceiling. The room smells deliciously of coffee. And aftershave. The room smells like a man's aftershave.

A shadow moves in the corner.

And the shadow becomes a person, stepping out into the light of the arched windows. But it is not the man with the shiny shoes.

It's not him at all.

This man is small, wiry, with dark-rimmed glasses and a smile that stretches his face a little too wide.

"Well, well," he says, pushing up the brim of his hat. "Have a nice trip, Bluebird?"

CHAPTER TEN

—— *May 1945* ——

INGE SLIPS ACROSS the kitchen, lifting the door latch with only the smallest sound of scraping metal. Mama is in the dining room, drinking the last of the coffee they'd brought with them to the lodge. In a few minutes, she'll switch to the wine bottles, taking two or three up from the cellar to her little bedroom with the radio. The wine will be gone soon, too. Helga, who has become housekeeper, maid, and nanny all at once for the past two and half months, is thin and dreary, washing out the coffeepot while the boys are at their lessons. She pretends not to see Inge going out the kitchen door.

Helga pretends not to see most things. Inge doesn't blame her.

There have been no letters. No messages. Not one word from Papa.

Inge had found the courage to ask. Finally. Seven days after Kurt left. They'd all been around the dining table, straight-backed, napkins in laps, even though the windows were boarded up and dinner was canned salmon and beans and Helga was no cook. The bread they'd brought was already gone, thanks to Adolf, and what Helga had made was flat and a little tasteless. Jewish bread, Mama had said, pushing it aside. But it wasn't Helga's fault that no one had brought yeast. Inge set down her fork.

"Mama, why are we at the lodge? Is Papa coming?"

Erich had stared down at his plate, the part in his hair a perfect white line down the top of his head. Even Adolf knew better than to speak. But Inge hadn't felt cowed. Not this time. The question was not unreasonable. She had every right to ask it. She'd missed two of her club meetings by then, when Frau Koch had said no absences, and she hadn't seen her tutors. Latin, English, racial theory, history of Germany. Papa had said if she did well with her examinations, she could study music, really study, maybe even in America. He had a colleague there who could arrange it. But how would she be ready for examinations without her tutors? And Erich didn't have his violin. Adolf had no trains. Mama owed them an explanation. It was only fair.

And she could clip back her hair—or not clip it back—any way she wanted to.

Mama stood. She'd been wearing her pearls and her heels that night, so she was tall as she moved around the table, chair by chair, to stand behind Inge. And then Mama had put her hands in Inge's hair.

Inge sat. Frozen. Mama never deliberately touched her. Never. Especially not her hair. Mama's polished nails ran sharp across her scalp.

"Do you miss your sweet Papa?" Mama said. "Ah, my poor girl. Your Papa's precious *Vögelchen*."

Her nails pulled through Inge's curls, tearing out the snarls. Inge kept her eyes straight ahead. Why did Mama make her feel so ashamed?

"Well, Papa is busy just now, darling. He doesn't have time for his favorite girl. Papa has a war to win. He's making sure we all know how to be useful. Productive. He's making a new world. Won't that be lovely? The new world?"

I am Inge von Emmerich. I am Inge . . .

But she couldn't say the words. Even inside her own head.

"We must all be ready," Mama said, "to take our place in the new world. Boys, you will read every day. You will exercise twice. Helga, you will see to it, and you will make sure they are neat, clean, and do not complain. If they complain, you have not performed your duty. And Inge . . ." Mama grabbed two handfuls of her hair, tight. "Inge will give her husband a beautiful German baby. Wouldn't you like that, Inge?"

One, two, three hairs snapped free from Inge's scalp.

"See, we all have our function. The Führer expects no less of us. He requires no less. Everyone should *know their place.*"

She'd said the last words right in Inge's ear, holding out a hand. Inge placed the barrette in her waiting palm.

I am Inge. I am Inge . . .

"When you have finished your dinner, my sweet," Mama said, clipping back her hair, "you can write a letter to Rolf. Come and read it to me when you're done."

But Inge hadn't written to Rolf. Because that was the day that someone dropped Mama's pearls in the toilet. That was the day Mama started in on the whiskey in Papa's cabinet. And that was the day that Inge had first snuck out the kitchen door, taken a crowbar from the garage, and gone half a mile down the mountain to pry the boards from the side door of the Kleinmanns' empty lodge.

And two months later, with examinations and Hitler's birthday performance having passed her by, with her hair grown long and all the nuthatches nesting without her, she's still sneaking out. Gently lifting the latch of the kitchen door, while Helga washes the coffeepot and pretends not to notice.

Inge tiptoes along the porch. The window boards have never been taken off the house. It makes it dark inside, nighttime during the day, but she's glad of it. Because Mama can't look out and see where she's going. As soon as her feet hit the muddy yard, Inge runs, unsnapping the tight barrette, flying down the firmer edges of the road.

She likes the speed. The dripping branches and the softness in the air, the baby green leaves brushing against her skirt from the tips of the bushes. A bird is singing. Singing and singing. The car key, on a string tucked beneath her sweater, bounces against her chest.

If Papa doesn't come, or someone to deliver supplies, she'll have to tell Mama about the car key. They're down to their last cans, and the last of the last sack of flour. Mama doesn't know how to drive, and Inge doesn't know what will happen when Mama finds out that she does.

It might be worse than starving.

Or maybe it wouldn't be.

But even Mama wouldn't want them to starve.

Would she?

Inge veers onto the track that leads to the Kleinmanns' and then stops on the path. Listening. There's a rumble in the air. Planes flying somewhere close by. There have been a lot planes lately, but this time, there's a rumbling beneath her feet as well, a faint shake traveling through the ground.

She didn't know low-flying planes could shake the ground.

She hurries on and props the loose board from the Kleinmanns' door against the weathered cedar walls. Inge reaches in, turns the knob, and squeezes through the tiny opening between the boards. She makes her way to the dark, dust-draped living room, and there, against the wall, is what she came for.

The piano.

Papa used to listen to her play, sometimes, before the war. "It interests me so much," he would say, "that you play that so well. You emphasize emotion, rather than the perfection of technique . . ."

She'd practiced her technique incessantly after that, doing the exercises over and over until they were flawless. She sits down at the bench, nose wrinkled.

For just a moment, she could smell Papa's tobacco.

She runs her fingers over the keys. It's not as nice as her piano at home, and the notes bend more and more out of tune the longer they're held. But she'd rather play than not. So she just imagines how it should sound, and because she's alone, she doesn't worry about her technique. She plays songs from her head. Like she isn't supposed to. Melodies that come and go. Then she shakes out her hands and plays the first notes of "Clair de Lune."

The beginning is peaceful. Like falling asleep. When your thoughts swirl and merge into one, formless feeling. Never the same way twice. Then comes the middle section, the dream. Sometimes she plays this fast, and the dream is about waterfalls, streams that splash over your feet. But today, she plays it slower, much slower, and the dream is about something different. A sound she has forgotten. A mist she can't quite catch in her hand.

Something about violets. She can see violets.

Inge stops in the middle of a phrase, jolted back into the reality of the Kleinmanns' musty room. She feels sick. Maybe the last of the food is spoiling. And then the tarnished picture frames on top of the piano shake, violently. When she wasn't even playing. She listens.

Planes. And something else. Something whistling in the air.

Light shoots between the cracks of the boarded windows, a sudden glare, like lightning, and there is a boom. An explosive boom, an attack on her ears, rocking her body and the floor. If she screams, Inge cannot hear it. The pictures topple over and a vase teeters, shattering on the floor. The front windows have cracks, even behind the boards.

Inge staggers to her feet and out of the living room, scraping her back as she climbs between the boards without bothering to shut the door. The birds have stopped singing. And there's nothing to see, nothing to hear. Except for the planes. Far away. Rumbling.

She runs back up the road, out of breath, splashing her shoes with mud. There's a plume of smoke now, rising into the air a little farther down the mountain. Maybe one of the Luftwaffe has accidentally dropped its bomb. Maybe it crashed.

Inge takes the porch steps two at a time and bursts through the kitchen door.

"Mama! Helga?"

The kitchen looks exactly as she left it. The coffeepot is turned upside down, drying on a towel. But the lodge is quiet.

Not just quiet. It's silent. A thick silence. Dark and deep. A silence that has to be pushed through. Inge creeps across the kitchen.

"Helga?" she whispers. "Erich?"

She walks through the dining room. Mama's coffee cup is cold, half-full on the table, the living room dark, empty like it always is. And then she steps into the front hall and turns the wall switch. Light leaps out across the floor.

And Inge stops. Covers her mouth.

Helga is on the rug at the foot of the stairs, her legs twisted this way and that, a spilled glass of water near her outstretched hand. And there's a hole in her forehead, a perfect little round hole, a stain spreading beneath her head like a halo.

It doesn't make sense. What she's seeing does not make sense. Inge pants through her fingers.

And then she scoots, sidestepping Helga, feeling her way down the wall until she gets a foot on the stairs. She stumbles, rights herself, and the silence is loud. So loud. She steps up, and up, ricocheting from the rail to the wall to the top of the stairs, staggering to the boys' room. Inge throws open the door.

They're both there. They're right there. And they're the same as Helga. Only there's a table knocked over. A lamp broken on the floor. Erich seems to have put up a fight. But they are the same. Still. With no breath to break the horrible silence.

Gone.

Inge fumbles for the knob and shuts the door again. She stands in the hallway. Something has happened to her. Her mind is humming, buzzing, but she can't think. She can't think at all and her lungs have stopped working, no matter how much air she puts in them. Then she lifts her head.

There's a soft noise inside the silence. Just on the edge of hearing.

She walks slowly down the hall. Quiet along the rug. To the little bedroom beside her own. There's a voice, crackling with static. Inge stands with her hand on the knob for a long time before she turns it. The hinges groan, squeak as they fall open.

The room is in disorder. Unimaginable disorder. Not because the bed is unmade or because there are clothes on the floor. Because what was inside Mama's head is now all over the wall. Mama is slumped across the mattress, staining the blankets. She has a gun in her hand.

Mama has a gun.

A leather holster lies dropped on the floor beside the bed, with Hitler's eagle embossed in gold, and the man on the radio is saying that the enemies of Germany have reached Berlin. The Führer is dead, and the enemy is in Berlin.

Hitler is dead.

Everyone is dead.

German girls do not cry.

Inge shuts the door to her mama's room and she screams. She screams and screams.

CHAPTER ELEVEN

August 1946

EVA DOESN'T MAKE a sound. But she does take a step backward. Toward the door. Her skirt makes the faintest rustling noise.

"What's the matter, Bluebird? Got nothing to say?"

The man from the shadows of Powell House pulls out a chair and sits on it, elbow nudging aside a stack of unfolded papers and envelopes littering the wooden table. His pants cuffs have been ironed at an angle, his skin pale and waxy, and the first three fingernails on his right hand are stained yellow, probably from smoking his cigarettes to the stub. She can't see his eyebrows for the heavy-rimmed glasses.

"Well, well," the man says again, crossing one leg over the other, setting his hat on his knee. He glances at the tin ceiling and at the percolator emitting a soft *pufft* of steam. "You've landed well. Nice work. How's your friend? She manage to make the crossing without a straitjacket?"

"What do you want?" Eva snaps.

The man tsks. "Now, is that any way to talk? Good thing I'm not the sensitive type. I'm giving you the deal of a lifetime, buttercup. You do remember that we have a deal?"

This man, Eva thinks, is the embodiment of her deal. Because he is rotten.

"So let's talk about Daddy. And you'll have to be quick. We were supposed to be having a nice, long gab in that apartment these dames worked out. I had the one across the hall. But the greedy landlord wins again. Ain't that always the way?"

He grins. Eva doesn't.

"I told everything to the man in Berlin."

"I read the report. Any clue on where to start?"

"I have only just arrived."

She thinks of the man with shiny shoes, nearly breaking his neck to gape at her as he drove past. They've been watching since she stepped off the boat. She hadn't thought they would come this soon. She hadn't thought they would watch this close.

Breaking this deal is going to be much, much harder than she thought.

"Hmmm," says the man. His stained fingers drum the wooden table. But not like Jake's had in the car. Not music. This is a rat-tat-tat.

Rat-tat-tat-tat.

Eva actually smells the stink of hot bullets.

The man stops drumming, reaching out to take one of the printed papers stacked on the table. He looks it over, folds it in two, and tucks it into his jacket pocket. Then he puts his hat on his head again, leaning back in the chair until the legs groan.

"You know, Bluebird, it would be easy as pie to have you arrested. To find you a nice, big field somewhere in France with about five years of potatoes to dig. Or whatever else that needs doing. They love your kind over there, you know? Love you to death. So don't mess with me. You mess with me, you're a potato digger, and we park your crazy friend in an institution free of charge. I won't lose any sleep."

Eva says nothing. Because he hasn't said anything new.

"Glad we're seeing eye to eye. And here's the next topic." He lowers his voice, eyes narrowing behind the glasses. "You do all your talking about Daddy to me. Nobody else. That's the deal. Daddy's got stuff in his head, and we want it. But other people, they're going to want it, too. Want it bad. So somebody comes creeping around, asking questions, you have to give them the air, Bluebird."

She doesn't know what "give them the air" means. But she doesn't have to. The chair legs hit the floor with a thump and the man stands, walks forward, peering into her face.

"You," he whispers, "will not talk about Daddy to another soul. Have you got that?"

Eva wipes her sweaty hands on her rustling skirt.

"There's a lot at stake. Bring us Daddy, and there might never be a war again. You could make that happen. The United States government is counting on you. We're watching you."

Eva nods. And then she moves to the sink, like she's going to get water. She can't let him be so near her skirt.

"Glad we're straight," he says. "Now we need results quick, so hop to. I've got a list of names for you to start with. People your Daddy might have written to, that might be . . . sympathetic, shall we say. Go say hello, let slip who you are. See what shakes out. And you make contact with me every night, to check in."

Eva wets her hand at the faucet, and puts it to her throat, letting the cool water trickle down her neck.

"And one more thing, Bluebird. What do you know about a girl named Anna Ptaszynska?"

Eva keeps her eyes on the dirty dishwater. "Anna Ptaszynska is dead."

"Yeah, well, we've got info that says that ain't so."

Eva turns from the sink. "What kind of . . ."

The little man smiles, and it is much, much too wide. "Never you mind. But we want her. So keep your eyes peeled. And keep an eye on that crazy friend. We don't want our Bluebird getting. . . ."

Then the kitchen door bursts open. A willowy young woman with light brown hair takes two giant strides across the linoleum before she looks up and starts, ears and neck blushing peach-pink in surprise.

"Oh, hello! Just coming through for the coffee." She moves toward the percolator, then pauses, looking back and forth between the two of them. "Can I help you find something?"

The little man pulls nervously at his jacket. "I . . . am looking . . . for the . . . work?"

Eva only just keeps a brow from lifting. His accent has become something vaguely Eastern European.

"Oh!" The young woman clutches at a pair of glasses hanging from a chain around her neck, ready to pop them on and get instantly to work. "Oh!" she says again. "We'd be happy to help! I'm Olive, and the Refugee Office is just down the hall. Only I've put the files away. We close at five o'clock, you see, though I suppose I could . . . I'm supposed to be taking up the coffee." She looks suddenly at Eva, brightening.

Eva does not want to deliver coffee.

"No. No." The man waves his stained fingers, then rushes up to Olive and pumps her hand. "I come back in morning. Okay? Morning?"

"Certainly," says Olive. "Nine o'clock. And do bring your paperwork!"

But the man is already rushing for the door. He shakes Eva's hand briefly, and she feels a piece of paper slide into her palm. Then he's gone, and Olive is looking at Eva in surprise. As if she'd thought the two of them were together and was only just learning her mistake.

In Powell House, evidently, even a stranger wandering in from the street might do to serve up some coffee.

Eva's fingers curl around the paper.

"I am Eva," she says. "Eva Gerst. I came with my friend, from . . . I was upstairs. She is sleeping and I . . ." What had she been doing? "I was looking for water?"

"Are you one of the girls Bets and Jake were picking up today? Why aren't you at Gabertelli's? Oh, you don't have to explain." Olive grabs an empty coffeepot and starts filling it from the percolator. "I'm sure I'll hear about it from Bets. There are cups and glasses in the cupboard. Chip off a piece of ice from the Fridgidaire if you'd like. It must be hot as blazes up there. Ice pick is in the drawer."

Eva turns her back to open the cupboard, sliding the piece of paper from her hand into the waistband of her skirt.

"So which room are you in?" Olive asks. "Blue or patchwork?"

Eva gets a glass and takes it to the sink. "Blue."

"The nice one! We're practically neighbors. I'm just above you. If you need anything, holler!"

Olive finds the lid to the coffeepot and claps it on. She takes three long strides across the kitchen before she turns. Her eyebrows are soft, nails unpolished, and her hem has been let down twice.

"We're knocking sandwiches together later on. Bring your friend down and we'll make sure you don't starve or anything, okay?" Then she bumps the door open with her backside and disappears.

Eva sips her water, and as soon as the footsteps have gone up the stairs, she sets down the glass and lets her fear settle. Then she picks up one of the papers from the stack on the table. Big, black printed letters say THE POWELL HOUSE CRIER along the top, then a few short articles, and a calendar.

SQUARE DANCE, Saturday night, 8 p.m.
Young and old!

PHILOSOPHIES OF MODERN EUROPE,
lecture series with Dr. Gruber, Monday at 7 p.m.

TUESDAY LUNCHEON CLUB, all ladies
welcome, even if you're not a lady, 11 a.m.

CONTEMPORARY ART EXHIBITION,
Featuring the work of White and Negro Artists,
open to the public every day, 9 a.m. to 3 p.m.

ENGLISH TUTORIALS, 3 p.m. to 8 p.m., Monday,
Wednesday, Friday,

HELP OUR BELOVED HAPPY ANGEL!
Our stairwells could use a scrub!

All the activities listed. And no one locks a door. That little man will be able to come inside Powell House whenever he wants.

Eva takes the paper from the waistband of her skirt. There's a card folded inside, with the name *Mr. Cruickshanks* printed in the center along with a telephone number, and below that, the words *after 8 p.m.* On the paper, there are names, places, some addresses. Her eyes go to one in the middle. "Dr. Herman Schneider, Columbia Presbyterian Medical Center."

She knows that name. She knows it well. And she had not planned on sharing it with Mr. Cruickshanks.

She turns over the card, and on the back, in bright blue ink, is a crude drawing.

A bluebird.

Nobody, Eva thinks, is actually named Mr. Cruickshanks. Her father won't be using his real name, either. And of course the United States government wants Anna Ptaszynska. They always have.

Because Anna Ptaszynska is a killer.

And then Eva starts, looks up, eyes sharp to the ceiling.

Someone over her head is screaming.

CHAPTER TWELVE

—— *May 1945* ——

INGE STOPS SCREAMING AND STARTS RUNNING.

Out of the room where the radio blares that Hitler is dead. Where the announcer explains how death is more honorable than living in defeat. Away from what is left of her mother. Past the door that hides the still bodies of her brothers. Down the stairs, around Helga and her halo, and out. Out the door and into the sunlight, startling the birds.

Papa.

Where is Papa?

The plume of smoke from the mountainside has risen high, a sooty, billowing column. Inge throws open the garage doors, fumbling with the key around her neck.

She has to find Papa.

She can't get the key into the ignition. She pants. And then she screams. And the key slides in.

And the car does not start.

Inge turns the key again. She can't flood the engine. Kurt taught her to never, ever flood the engine. She turns the key once. Then again. The engine roars.

She throws the car into gear and it surges forward, knocking over a rake, some old skis, and a few tins of paint. Into reverse this time, and Inge stomps the gas, hitting one garage door that has swung partially shut again, smashing it right off its hinges. She hears the glass of the taillight shatter and the car whips around. She shifts the gear and goes hurtling down the mountain, wind from the open window tearing at her hair.

The slope is so steep she can see over the steering wheel even without a book, the curves so tight there is no time to wipe her eyes. German girls do not cry. But she is crying. Tears dripping off her chin. Misting her vision. Making everything blurry.

Not blurry from tears, she realizes. From smoke. Wafting through the trees. Acrid, stinking in her nose. Hiding the sky. Hiding the branches. So thick now she can barely see the road.

And then a huge chunk of twisted metal leaps out at her from the haze.

Inge gasps, twists the wheel, bounces through a ditch and swerves again to miss a tree, wood scraping down the side of the car like giant fingernails. She finds the road again, only now it is orange, angry, glowing hot against the blackness.

Fire, Inge's mind says. The road is on fire.

But there's nothing to do about it. There's no time to stop. A burst of heat singes her left arm and cheek through the open window, smoke charring her lungs. And then she's out the other side, sputtering and coughing down the mountain road, leaving the smoke behind, rattling with the ruts and the downhill speed. She glances back in her rearview mirror. A plane. That's what it had been. A plane hanging from the trees, its fuel burning behind it.

The boom hits her body like a blow. A fireball shooting straight upward and into the sky behind her, light piercing the back window of the car. When she looks back again, the tops of the trees are blazing.

Maybe the whole mountain will burn. The house. Erich. Adolf, and Helga. Mama. Nothing left but ash.

She has to find Papa.

And then the front bumper of the car knocks hard against the suddenly level ground, screeching against the gravel road. Inge's chin smacks the wheel. She swerves left, rocks spitting behind as she puts her whole weight on the pedal. She tastes blood in her mouth, but she's off the mountain, tearing down the road toward home.

What kind of plane just crashed on the mountainside? Soviet? American? German?

Maybe it was Rolf in the exploding plane. Maybe Rolf is dead, too. Like the Führer. Like everyone.

Inge cries again. Mama killed Adolf. And Erich. She killed everyone she loved.

Except her.

Mama didn't shoot her. She shot Helga, but not her.

It's too hard to breathe. She can't breathe.

Inge stretches, gas to the floor, pushing herself up and back so she can see over the dash. There's a crack across the windshield. The engine roars and the steering wheel wobbles. And her mind is static. Humming. Buzzing like the radio. Thoughts blaring, then fading, then blaring out again. Only one stays constant above the noise.

Papa needs to know that everyone is dead. She has to find Papa.

She has to go home.

She drives for an hour without seeing another car.

But she does see people, hurrying along the deserted road from farms and little villages, carrying bundles and pushing carts. Inge passes them like the wind, before they can do more than turn a head, losing sight of them to the curves and rolling hills. And she sees planes, lots of planes, flying in groups high with the sun, shaking the sky again and again, until the road crosses through a patch of damp forest and the trees soften the air. Until Inge breaks from the forest into a long open field, lush with spring.

Where a single plane flies in a different direction. Low. Coming straight down the road. Coming straight toward her. It doesn't look German. It doesn't sound like it.

Inge hears taps. Like fingers on a table. Short bursts of sharp sound. Little clouds of dirt jump up from the road in two perfect lines.

And the windshield explodes, bits of stuffing leaping out of round holes that have suddenly appeared in the passenger seat. Inge cries out, jerks the wheel, but the plane has long passed her by, skimming the tops of the trees, following the road. It doesn't turn around. But she can hear the noise. *Rat-tat-tat. Rat-tat-tat-tat.* She grips the steering wheel, knuckles bloody, nicked by flying glass.

They shot at her. She's not a soldier, and they shot at her.

And then the car lurches, throwing Inge forward. The engine sputters. She pushes the gas pedal. And the engine stops, tires crunching the dirt as they slow. Inge stares through the missing windshield, at the pretty pasture that is no longer whizzing by. She turns the key. The engine whines, but doesn't start. There are no bullet holes in the hood. She looks at the gauges.

She's out of gas.

Inge yells, slams the steering wheel with her fist. Her face stings, and when she wipes her cheeks, the tears come back pink. She stares at her hand, then up into a sky that may not be empty for long.

Something balloons inside Inge's chest. A mass. A writhing, leaden, swelling pain that weighs her down even as it tries to rise up and choke her.

But she does not cry. Not anymore. The tears won't keep her alive.

Inge jumps out of the car, taking the key with her, one eye to the sky. She pushes open the trunk on her tiptoes. And there are two gas cans. Both on their sides, one of them leaking a little. The other is heavy. Full. And there is a thick blanket, folded. Perfect for sitting on.

Kurt. Where did he go that night? What happened to him?

Maybe he's dead now, too.

She fills the tank, spilling gas down the side of the car and onto her shoes. The blanket stinks of gas, too. She opens the hood, lets the air out of the gas lines and primes them. Like Kurt taught her. Planes zoom overhead. No one shoots at her. But the ground shakes, little earthquakes that make the grass tremble. She carefully pumps with the pedal. Tries the engine. Ginger, easy. It hiccups, and then it roars.

Inge speeds down the road, driving better now that she's sitting high enough to see, the wind so strong in her face through the missing glass that it's hard to hear the planes.

Papa will know what to say. He'll know how to make it better.

Maybe he will tell her what happens, exactly, when you lose a war.

Slowly, the woods and fields become her woods and fields. She knows the fences. She knows the lanes and side turns that lead to her neighbors. She does not know the columns of smoke in the sky. She does not know the occasional ugly pockmark of dirt and scorched earth that mar the grasses.

She ignores them. If a plane flies too low, Inge swerves beneath the cover of a tree. Like a rabbit diving for its hole. Then she pushes the gas and makes the tires skid.

She's nearly there.

Around the curve, and she passes another car. A military truck, bristling with soldiers and guns, both of them going so fast in opposite directions that they can only turn their heads for a glancing stare. A thought jumps out of Inge's static.

Those men are Soviets. Communists. Russians. The Russians are here.

She hears a shout. A squeal of brakes from around the curve behind her. But she's skimming the tall, neatly clipped hedges that shield her house from the road now. She can nearly see the gate. Smoke is rising with the wind on the other side of the hedges. The house is on fire.

And there is a figure running through the opposite field, mouth moving with words that are much too far away to hear. Long blond hair loose and flowing. Arms in the air, trying to wave her down.

Not now, Annemarie, Inge thinks. My house is burning down.

Inge swerves into the open gate and cuts the engine, coasting down the drive. But there are no birds in the trees. The horses aren't in the stables. And the house is not on fire. At least, not anymore. The servants' wing is just missing, like someone sliced it away with a knife, leaving a giant smoking hole filled with its own bits and pieces. The garage is gone, the toolshed a heap of wood planks and brick. Inge slides the car between the rubble piles, puts it in park, and steps out the door. As if Kurt will appear any minute to polish the hood.

Where is Papa?

She runs through what had been the garden, leaping over the water gushing from a broken pipe, and through the back door. The kitchen is covered in dust, all Frau Kruger's pans in disarray, but she doesn't stop. She goes straight for the back stairs, finding the quiet path among the creaks.

But everything is creaking. Squeaking. Groaning. There's light in the upper corridor, daylight where it shouldn't be, from a great, new hole in the roof. And because the other end of the hallway isn't there at all. Inge's room is a floor and some scattered bits of curtain and cloth with only two of its walls. But Papa's study is whole, on the left, the door a little ajar. Just like she left it. She slips inside.

And Papa isn't there.

Of course he isn't there. He'll be at his camp. In Berlin. But the shock of it feels like a wound, anyway.

The books are covered in dust, a thick, yellowish layer of it, bags and bundles she doesn't recognize piled in the corners. Instead of Papa's pipe, she smells cigarettes. Inge creeps to the desk and runs her hand along its edge. It's dirty, but solid. Unmarred. An anchor. And there is Papa's telephone. And the radio. And his papers.

There was a file here once. A long time ago. A file with her name on it.

Inge searches through the papers. They're in more disarray than Frau Kruger's pans, the pages dirty and askew. But there is the file. And there is her name.

And there are footsteps coming up the stairs.

Inge's hand freezes on the file. The steps are heavy. Booted. Not Papa. Not a maid. And there is a man's voice, babbling words she can't quite hear or understand. Inge ducks beneath the desk, squeezing in the space where Papa's knees belong, hugging the file to her chest. The door is thrown open, thudding dully on the wall behind it, and the voice is loud now, booted feet coming across the study floor. Inge remembers the bags and bundles.

The Soviets. Communists. Living here. Camping in her ruined house.

The boots leave the study. They don't shut the door.

There are many men's voices, downstairs. Laughing. And she hears another voice. One she recognizes. And doesn't recognize. One she understands.

Annemarie.

She's down there somewhere, pleading. Then she is crying, loudly. She's calling for her mother. Inge has never heard Annemarie like that. She closes her eyes beneath the desk.

And the writhing mass of pain inside her intensifies. Solidifies. Swells. Pins her down even as it engulfs her throat. Suffocating. Gagging her so that she has to cover her mouth.

Annemarie screams. And she screams. Until she doesn't scream anymore.

And this, Inge thinks, is what happens when you lose a war.

CHAPTER THIRTEEN

—— *August 1946* ——

EVA RUNS UP the stairs, tucking Mr. Cruickshanks's paper and card back into the waistband of her skirt. She knows who is screaming. She's heard it many times. And she will hear it again. It's a noise that hurts. That makes her sick inside. That she will do anything to stop.

Because it is her fault. Always her fault.

There's a commotion in the foyer, a crowd of conversations and murmurs of concern. All backs and shoulders and the napes of necks and hats heavy with artificial flowers. Eva pushes them aside and finds an open door with a little washroom and Brigit behind it. Brigit is sitting on the toilet lid, eyes closed, face red, drawing in breath after screaming breath.

Mrs. Angel and Bets have their hands on her shoulders, her hair, her forehead, prodding and stroking, Olive hovering behind, trying to hand through a wet cloth. Eva muscles them out of the way and pitches her voice low. Steady. Calm.

"I'm here, Brigit," she whispers. *"Ich bin hier."*

Brigit's shrieks soften a little but don't ease. They shouldn't be touching her. But Eva can't think of the English words quick enough, so she settles for "Stop."

It doesn't work.

"Stop it!" she shouts.

The hands drop away from Brigit.

"Touch only her hands," Eva says over the noise, holding up Brigit's hand in one of hers. It's the one with the cat scratches, now with a brown smear spread across them.

"It was just a little iodine . . ." says Mrs. Angel.

Brigit's screams are going hoarse, like she's sucking in air instead of expelling it.

"Let's back up, everyone," says Bets. "A little room, please."

Eva turns her head and finds Jake beside her. "A bag," she says.

He's off, disappearing through the ogling group, and Eva calculates a fifty percent chance that he will come back with a suitcase. She turns to Brigit.

"I'm here. No one is going to hurt you. They cannot hurt you . . ."

But Brigit can't breathe.

Jake comes back, and he does not have a suitcase. He has a small paper bag. Eva snatches it and puts the open end over Brigit's nose and mouth. Brigit knows how to do this. The sides of the paper bag suck in, then blow out. In and out. She's only making a little noise now.

"Let's go finish our coffee, everyone," Olive says. She has long arms, excellent for corralling. "Nothing to worry about . . ."

Bets leans down. "Do you need a doctor?"

Eva shakes her head.

"Tell us how to help."

"She needs to sit. To be quiet."

"Back upstairs?" asks Bets.

Eva nods, and starts gently moving Brigit forward while still trying to hold the bag and Brigit's hand. Mrs. Angel takes over the bag, an arm around Brigit's shoulders, and to Eva's surprise, Brigit does not object to this. They move together toward the stairs, one or two of the curious still watching.

Brigit is beautiful even when she's sweating, barefoot, and breathing into a bag.

"Come, Brigit. *Ist schon gut . . .*"

They make their way, Brigit's breathing slowing with each step up, and by the time they reach the door of the blue room, she's only shuffling her feet. The door is open, Eva sees, with a key in the lock. On the outside.

"She was running around in there," Mrs. Angel whispers, as if maybe Brigit won't hear. "She was kind of frantic, and I thought maybe she had to go, and I had a key. But there was somebody in the upstairs toilet, so I took her down, and then I thought we'd better get something on that scratch . . ."

Eva feels the tendrils of guilt crawling up her throat. "I should not have left her."

Mrs. Angel shakes her head. "Poor lamb."

Eva doesn't know which one of them she means.

They get Brigit settled back on the bed. She can breathe without the bag now. Bets comes in with a water pitcher, and Mrs. Angel helps Brigit drink while Eva bathes her face.

"A nightgown?" Bets asks.

Eva points at Brigit's suitcase, and then adds quickly, "I will dress her." They do not need to touch Brigit's skirt.

In five minutes, Brigit is back where Eva left her, now in a much cooler nightgown, her breath slowed, hair splayed on the pillow, the harmonica back in her hand. Eva takes Brigit's skirt with its rustling hem and hangs it carefully in the wardrobe. The sun has lowered behind the buildings, a breeze pulling through the open windows, and she can hear the front door of Powell House opening and closing, voices chatting and saying goodbye. The air in the wardrobe smells like cedar.

Had she had cedar chips in a wardrobe, once?

The thought gives her a quick, sharp pain.

"You must be starving," says Bets. Eva jumps. She'd almost forgotten she wasn't alone. "Let's go downstairs and make you a sandwich."

She can't afford to pay for anything too expensive. And she can't leave Brigit. But Mrs. Angel has already pulled up a chair beside the bed.

"I'll just sit right here for a bit. My shoes are too tight, anyway." Her smile is soft. Butter in the sunshine. She waves a hand. "You go on. If she wakes up, I'll come and find you."

"I'll make you a sandwich and bring it up," Bets says. "Chicken all right?"

"Put some pickles on it," says Mrs. Angel.

"Right. Come on, then, Miss Gerst," says Bets. "Downstairs to be fed and watered. And then we can chat, yes?"

Bets has brown eyes that are wide and intelligent. And so sincere. She could fool anyone into buying a sandwich. Maybe she would have done well in Berlin after all. Eva wishes they would just say what it's all going to cost, but maybe it doesn't matter. She'll have to eat. And there's probably a beige car out there. And Mr. Cruickshanks.

Brigit is still, serene, Mrs. Angel bringing out a yellow ball of yarn and two long needles from a voluminous apron pocket. Bets beckons, and Eva steps after her, letting her softly shut the bedroom door behind them.

Jake is waiting in the hall, slouched against the wallpaper beside a blue-and-white vase on a stand, hands stuffed deep in his pockets. But his toes had been tapping. "Everything okay?" he asks.

"Sandwiches," replies Bets, making a beeline for the stairs.

He nods, peeling himself from the wall to follow her, and Eva's fingers brush across something in the waistband of her skirt. The paper, wrapped around a card.

A card with a bluebird drawn on it.

She looks back to the closed door of the bedroom, eyes roving fast across the little hall. Then she darts to the vase, and drops the paper and card inside it.

Jake is just around the corner and two steps down. He has a brow up. "Coming?" he asks.

Eva smooths her skirt. His eyes are pretty. And they are also sharp.

She doesn't need to be careful. She needs to be very careful.

The kitchen is crowded, noisy, and hot. Someone has set up an electric fan, adding to the hum, the stacked papers now all to one side of the table with plates on top of them, their edges rippling and fluttering. On the other end of the table, a small, round woman with an enormous bust and tiny glasses is busily slicing up a chicken.

"Oh, hello!" Olive calls from the sink, craning her neck forward and back around the milling bodies. "Is your friend okay? We've got cold chicken and . . . oh! Hi, Jake."

"Hey, Olive. Got any lemons?" Jake heads straight for the icebox, and Olive watches him pass, her fingers dripping dishwater, mouth held slightly agape.

Bets, Eva decides, might survive Berlin. Olive would not.

"Everybody," Bets shouts, "this is Eva Gerst. She and her friend, Miss Heidelmann, will be staying here at Powell House until we can get them sorted or until Mr. Gabertelli has an angelic visitation. Eva, this is Martha, otherwise known as Mother Martha. She's in charge of us . . ."

The woman cutting chicken smiles and waves her knife.

". . . and this is everybody else!"

Eva is greeted, seated, patted, and pushed up to the table. Someone drops a napkin in her lap, and someone else sets a plate of crackers and sweating cheese in front of her. And it's nothing like the picture she'd been given of America. With the different skin colors kept separate. Here the faces are brown, peach, ivory, black, and most things in between, all of them women except for Jake, still bent over the icebox, and one other man, sitting in the corner and fanning himself. The hems are just as varied, and so are the eyebrows. Every shape and size with only one thing in common. Cheerfulness. All the eyebrows are cheerful.

Eva relaxes, just a little. They don't seem like people who would hate her for being German.

Even if they probably should.

Bets plops down into a chair across the table, and then Eva notices who is slicing bread beside her. Mrs. Thomas with the fancy underwear. She still has the corsage pinned on her jacket. Bets's eyes crinkle.

"And how's your day been, Peggy?"

Peggy lowers the bread knife. "Mrs. Turgonov thinks that I have been provided by Uncle Sam for the sole purpose of putting new elastic in all her best bloomers. Our government, Bets, they think of everything."

Bets laughs. And Peggy laughs.

Their laughter makes Eva feel lost. A minnow in the ocean.

Bets picks up a knife and starts smearing butter on Peggy's bread slices. She smiles at Eva. "So you've known Miss Heidelmann a long time?"

Eva nods.

"Not to pry or anything, but do you know what her trouble is? Did she see a doctor in Germany?"

Eva nods again, but she can't say what happened to Brigit. Not in this happy kitchen where the war is a bad dream no one seems to have had. The doctor in Berlin had looked Brigit over, ticked a box on his form, and shaken his head.

"Well, frankly, I'm surprised they let her in this morning, Eva. Is it okay if I call you Eva?" She pronounces it with the *e* sound long, like *evening*.

"Eva, as in 'ever,'" she says, and Bets nods.

"Your English is very good. I really think you're going to do well here."

This makes her smile. She'd practiced so hard in the camp. And on the boat. Someone starts laying chicken slices on the bread Bets has buttered, while Peggy pretends not to listen.

"There are some pretty strict rules about immigrants with . . . well, difficulties," Bets goes on. "People who might not be able to earn a living. Does Miss Heidelmann's sponsor know about her . . . condition?"

Eva bites her lip. She doesn't know their sponsors. Mr. Cruickshanks probably made them up.

"Hmmm," says Bets. "What would you say to arranging for Miss Heidelmann to visit a doctor here? See what they might have to say . . ."

And Eva's mind shifts into gear. There's nothing to be done for Brigit. She'd been told in both Berlin and Lisbon. But there had been a doctor. Dr. Schneider. At a hospital called Columbia. Exchanging letters with her father, comparing ideas and research. Her father could have gone to Dr. Schneider for help. Dr. Schneider could have even gotten her father a job. It's where she had planned to start looking. And now it's a name Mr. Cruickshanks has, too. On the list she dropped into the vase.

She has to find her father before Mr. Cruickshanks does. Or there will be no justice.

She has to keep both of them from finding Anna Ptaszynska.

Jake slides into the empty chair next to Eva and sets a glass of pale liquid and ice in front of her.

"Hey, aren't you supposed to be home on Friday nights?" Bets asks him. Jake grins and shrugs, and Bets points her butter knife. "Do not get me in trouble with your mother . . ."

But then, Martha, the woman with the chicken and the bust and the glasses, claps her hands, and all at once, the room goes from noise to silence.

Eva looks around, startled. Peggy's eyes are closed. And Olive's. Bets has her head bowed. Every head around her is bowed. Except Jake's. He winks. The electric fan whirs and the paper edges ruffle. Then Martha looks up and smiles, and everyone starts chatting again.

Jake leans over. "They're Quakers. It's what they do. Want a sandwich?"

He makes a plate for her and one for himself. Bets is fishing pickles from a jar for Mrs. Angel. Eva sits forward.

"A doctor," she says. "Brigit, she would need . . . a special doctor. For the mind. A psychiatrist."

Bets tilts her head. "Yes, I can see that."

"He should be older, to not upset her as much. More than fifty."

"Would she do better with a woman? It would be harder, but . . ."

"No, no," Eva replies quickly. "But he must speak German. It is . . . difficult to know how much English Brigit has learned. Maybe someone from . . . Columbia?"

Jake throws Eva a sideways glance.

"That's a very good hospital, of course," Bets says. "But getting someone there could be a tall order . . ."

"Uncle Paul might be able to help," Jake says.

"Oh!" says Bets. "That's a good idea!" She turns to Eva. "Jake's uncle is a surgeon at Columbia, not a psychiatrist, so different departments. But he might be able to point a finger for us." She looks at Jake again. "Could you ask?"

"Sure. I'll do it tomorrow."

Eva nods. If this doesn't bring her to Dr. Schneider, it will at least bring her to someone who knows him. It could even bring her to her father. How many German-speaking psychiatrists could there be at Columbia? Then she bites her lip again. Dr. Schneider is the best plan she has. Her best path to justice. But doctors cost money. And she has to eat. And so does Brigit. Which is a need more immediate than justice. How far can fifteen American dollars stretch?

Not far enough.

"I cannot pay," Eva blurts out. "For the room."

Bets's neat little eyebrows pop up her forehead in surprise.

"Pay?" Jake says. "Who said anything about money?"

Bets reaches over the table. "Dear, there is no charge for anything at Powell House. Here's your American phrase for the night: No strings attached. It means you don't owe us a thing."

Eva opens her mouth and closes it. It doesn't make sense.

Jake grins from one side of his mouth. "You have a frown on your face, Miss Gerst."

"It is not . . . it does not seem . . . fair."

Bets laughs and pats her arm again. "Oh, we could all use a little unfairness sometimes. Both in the giving and the getting. We shan't pass this way again, you know."

Eva has no idea what she's talking about. Bets gets up to take Mrs. Angel her sandwiches, and Jake nudges Eva again.

"I'll check with my uncle, and they'll work out something for the doctor. You'll see. And I went over there and squeezed you a lemon with my own hands, so you really should drink that."

She'd forgotten about the glass. The lemonade is sweet, tart, and ice-cold. She eats a chicken sandwich. And a boiled egg and some cheese. The little man in the corner tells a joke Eva doesn't understand while Olive bravely starts a conversation with Jake. Eva watches it all. A world she hadn't known existed. A world where you do work without pay. Where Jewish boys make you lemonade and people sew your underwear just because you ask them to. Maybe they deserve a world like that.

She doesn't.

Fair is fair, no matter what Bets says.

And in her world, there's no one else to make sure of that. No one but her.

She says the names in her head. Twenty-seven names.

And she waits, patient, careful, until Peggy has disappeared and Bets is washing the dishes and Olive is rapt, listening to Jake talk about the classes he takes at a university. She chooses her moment and reaches out a hand, sliding the bread knife over the edge of the table and into the napkin in her lap.

CHAPTER FOURTEEN

—— *May 1945* ——

INGE CROUCHES BENEATH Papa's desk, waiting, careful not to move. To keep her breath from making the tiniest sound. Annemarie hasn't made a sound. Not in a long time. Inge had been stuffing her fingers in her ears, begging her to stop, and now, she just wants her to make a noise again. Any noise.

She's afraid Annemarie can't make a noise.

The heavy boots still tromp. Laughing. She can hear crashes. Glass breaking. Then the soldiers are back inside the study, and someone finds Papa's whiskey in the cabinet. They shout. Celebrating. And now, Inge thinks, it is her turn. They'll turn over the desk. They'll notice the car.

They are going to find her.

A pair of feet comes behind the desk, so close Inge can see dried mud on the boot heels. She hears words she can't understand, paper tearing, pages ripped from the books, floating down into a pile near her aching knees. Then someone fires a gun and she has to cover her mouth, clutch her own throat to silence her scream. But she is not bleeding. The men are still laughing. While the airplanes fly and the earth shakes and faint in the distance is the constant staccato of bullets going *rat-tat-tat*.

Inge closes her eyes, and she can feel herself fracture. Split into pieces. One piece is the Inge who feels pain. A swelling, leaden weight. Ice-cold and aching. And beside that is the Inge who is afraid. Who buzzes and shivers like she's just put a finger in a light socket. The Inge that might leap out from under this desk and run and run and run until someone shoots and makes it so she can't run anymore.

Is this the world? Where nothing is fair? Where it is impossible not to cry? Where wars are not glorious or noble, just dirty and blood-soaked?

Paintings are coming off the walls. She can hear the rip of canvas. The deep, satisfied bellows of destruction from the men.

And Annemarie is silent.

Inge breathes. And breathes. Her pain is cold, her fear electric, but rising above them both is another Inge. A different piece. And this one is fire. A silent inferno.

This is the Inge she chooses.

She opens her eyes. The soldiers have left the study. Taken their heavy boots down what is left of the stairs. Their shouts are moving outside. She raises one eye carefully over the edge of Papa's desk. The study is ransacked, curtains hanging by threads. But it is also empty.

She stands, and underneath her feet is a file. The file with her name on it. She'd forgotten it was there. Inge unbuttons her blouse and stuffs the file inside, buttoning it back up again. Then she slides open Papa's desk drawer and takes out his letter opener.

She's going to find Annemarie.

The shattered house groans, but there's no one in the hall. She hates the front stairs. There's a space underneath them. But this Inge goes straight down, shirt bulging, letter opener in her hand. The front door is standing open, the dining room a shambles of broken furniture, and in the parlor some of the ceiling plaster has fallen, the windows blown out, and the piano is riddled with bullet holes. And no one is there.

No one except Annemarie.

She's lying on the floor, still, skirt twisted and legs sticking out, arms splayed over the rug. Her hair is streaked red. Like Helga's had been. Like Mama's. And the Inge that knows pain feels the cold rising, swelling, freezing her into place. She can't move. She wants to scream.

And then she sees Annemarie's chest move.

Inge runs. Drops the letter opener. Drops to her knees. Touches Annemarie's face. "Can you hear me?" she whispers. "Can you hear me?"

She can't hear her. But she's not like Helga, Inge sees. She doesn't have a hole, she has a cut, just behind her ear. Someone has hit her with something. And more. They've done much more. Inge can see that, too.

And the fire inside her explodes. Blazes. Like the plane on the mountain. She couldn't do anything about Adolf. She couldn't help Erich.

But those men will not touch Annemarie. Not again.

Inge buttons Annemarie's shirt where it isn't torn and pulls her skirt down. Then she yanks Mama's blanket—the big one she would put over her knees in the wintertime—out from beneath a pile of plaster dust and spreads it beside Annemarie. She rolls Annemarie onto it, trying to get her in the center, grabs the two corners of blanket near Annemarie's head and pulls.

She grunts, dragging Annemarie through the ruined house. Over glass, through dust and rubble, knocking furniture out of the way. She's forgotten the letter opener. But no one tries to stop her. There's no one inside. The gunfire is outside. Close. Near the front. Shouts and short *pop, pop*s. In the kitchen, Annemarie slips off the blanket. She's left a bloodstain, but Inge ignores it. She rolls her back on and drags Annemarie until her muscles burn, until her breath is gone. Across the courtyard, through the mud from the burst pipe, around the rubble pile that used to be the garage. Where she left the car.

The blanket rips. And the shouts are coming from inside the house now.

She opens the back door of the car, thrusts her arms beneath Annemarie's and tugs backward, across the broken drive, heaving Annemarie through the car door, scooting across the back seat, pulling her in. Someone is speaking fast Russian in the courtyard, on the other side of the rubble. They're going to see. They're going to find them. Inge yanks one last time, crawls over Annemarie, pulls her legs inside, shuts the car door with a click, and scrambles over the seat to the steering wheel.

Where is the key?

Where did she leave the key?

It's in the ignition.

There are many voices beyond the rubble now. Low. Angry. That can't be helped. Inge breathes. Breathes. And turns the key.

The engine explodes into life. She throws the gear into reverse, switching to drive just as the first startled soldier comes around the rubble. He lifts a gun and shoots once, jumping out of the way as she passes. If she'd still had a windshield, it would be shattered. But wherever it went, the bullet hasn't touched her. She doesn't think it's touched Annemarie, either.

More soldiers come pouring out into the drive, shooting, but Inge is already up the slope, making the turn into the road.

She has no idea where she's going.

She thinks they'll be coming after her.

She drives with her foot to the floor, swerves at the last second, skids her turn, and takes the lane to Annemarie's house, where the trees can hide her from the air. Annemarie needs her mother. Someone. But halfway down the lane, Inge smells the smoke. Sees the haze. She passes the path to the farm, looking instead for the long metal gate that leads to the pastures, where Annemarie's father keeps their cows. It's open, and the cows are gone, so she drives through, pulling to one side along the tree line. She leaves the car running and jumps out.

Annemarie has fallen into a heap on the floorboard. Her head is still bleeding. But Inge leaves her there. Out of sight. She climbs the pasture fence and runs through the woods, letting branches rip her clothes and tear at her face. The smoke is thick, choking, and when Inge gets close to the little farmhouse, she doesn't even come out of the trees. There are six piles of what looks like limp clothes in front of the burning house. Only there's an arm sticking out of a sleeve. An ankle just showing beneath a trouser leg. Inge turns and runs back to the car.

Annemarie doesn't have a mother. Or any family at all.

Maybe this is why Annemarie was running through the fields.

Inge tugs Annemarie back up onto the seat. Her eyes are closed, one side of her face swollen and bruising, the streaks in her hair turning dark. But there's a pulse at her wrist, a little wheeze coming from her mouth. Inge jumps into the driver's seat.

A truck comes roaring down the lane, on the other side of the trees, but it doesn't stop. It doesn't even slow down. Inge closes her eyes and sees Annemarie's hair flying, her mouth open, shouting what Inge couldn't hear, waving her arms at the car.

And she hadn't stopped.

She drove right past her.

Another piece of Inge fractures. Breaking away from cold pain and fiery anger and the buzzing fear. Guilt, sick and venomous, spreading up from her depths like a poison.

Inge chooses the anger.

She opens the glove box. There was a map there once, and there still is. She spreads it out on the seat and traces the roads with a finger.

Papa must be at his camp. And there will be soldiers there, won't there? German soldiers. And Papa's camp has a hospital. Where he works. She'd been there once. Through the big white building with an iron gate built inside it. Papa had been in his office, in his doctor's coat, smoking his pipe, and Rolf, too, nodding and smiling and patting her knee.

She needs a back way. Little roads. Where big trucks and tanks won't move as easily. Around Potsdam, around Brandenburg, to Sachsenhausen, north of Berlin. There might be Soviets. And British and Americans. Maybe all the roads will be blocked.

It doesn't matter. She has to find Papa. She has to tell him about Mama. He has to help Annemarie.

A plane flies overhead. But it doesn't shoot at her.

She takes the file out of her blouse and throws it in the floorboard, then runs to the stream on the other side of the pasture, grabbing an old milk bottle that Annemarie's father had kept there, tucked between the rocks. She fills it and bathes Annemarie's cut, then tips some into her mouth. Annemarie chokes, but doesn't wake. Inge drinks, fills the bottle again, and relieves herself behind a tree. She squishes the bottle between the seats, hoping it won't spill, and pours a can of gas into the car.

And she drives. Slowly this time. Listening for planes. For

trucks. Bouncing through the ruts. When she comes out of the trees, the sun is beaming low through the haze, and she zips down a bigger road, still smooth and unbombed. The wind blows hard in her face, drying her eyes and parching her mouth. She passes a wrecked train, cars piled as if Adolf has left his toys on the rug. The dark comes down.

And there are lights in the distance. Headlights. Coming toward her.

Inge swerves hard into the ditch beside the road, rattling down and up and across the uneven earth, speeding through a field until she finds a little copse of trees to hide behind. It's not a good place. But there are no places. She cuts the engine.

There are dozens of trucks. Hundreds, maybe; she loses count. And tanks. They are not German. If they shine a light, they'll see her. But they do not shine a light. They're looking for armies. Not little girls driving their mother's Mercedes.

Annemarie makes a noise in the back seat. A little moan. Inge is glad to hear it.

She waits half an hour after the army passes and drives on. The moon rises, huge and bright. Inge turns off her headlights, chin forward, peering at the road. She hides one more time during the night while trucks pass, this time behind a rubble pile that had once been a barn, and then misses her turn twice in the dark. She has to consult the map and double back. Past ruined buildings and places that look like the war hasn't happened. There are no lights anywhere.

And as the sun comes up, she begins to pass people, lines of them with carts and suitcases and packs, all going in the opposite direction from her. Inge drives faster. She wants to get away from them. People make the planes come.

She takes her last turn, to the west, and the air becomes dull. Dusty. The sun is a color of orange she's never seen. And then she has to stomp the brakes. There's a crater across the road. A crater you could drop a house into. Inge drives carefully around it, bumping over a fallen fence, squinting through the unreal, red-yellow light. There's another crater. And another. And another.

So many bombs.

She picks her way through like she's exploring the moon, veering toward some sort of warehouse with a chunk missing, a bite taken out of one wall. The maps says there's a bridge over a river, but the bridge isn't there. She drives behind the warehouse, looking for a way through. Over bricks, crunching broken glass.

And then the car lurches, bumping violently. Inge hangs onto the wheel, steering into a space between a pallet of crates and a truck blackened by fire. She stops. The car is listing heavily to one side, and she knows what she will see before she looks. A punctured tire.

There is no spare.

Inge kicks the tire. There's blood on the toe of her shoe. She doesn't know whose blood it is. Her hair is tangled, her knuckles scabbed, and she can feel the crust of her own dirt. And she knows that she is tired. So tired her knees are close to buckling. So tired that the angry piece of herself is nearly smothered.

Then Annemarie moans once from the back of the car. And Inge remembers why she is here. She snatches up the map and spreads it out. Papa's camp is only a kilometer or so away. But she can't get the car there.

So she'll walk.

Inge looks around. The blackened truck stinks, its tires still smoldering, and on the other side of her, some of the stacked crates are also singed, one or two broken and spilling out their contents.

Boots. Soldiers' boots. Inge had hoped for food. Half the crates are still covered with charred canvas. She yanks the canvas, tugging and pulling from different angles until it's off the crates and covers most of the car.

Maybe the planes won't be able to see the car. Maybe they won't care about a warehouse of shoes that has already been bombed. Maybe no one will come here, and Annemarie will not decide to wake up. Or make any noise.

Inge starts walking.

She is almost to Papa.

The river is a canal, not too deep, and she can see where the bridge was. Chunks of concrete with sharp metal bars sticking out of the water like giant stepping-stones. She jumps from block to block, rubble to rubble, and keeps following the road. And there's more water to cross, only this time it's a river. Slow and maybe twelve meters wide.

"Twenty-five laps," Papa would say, sitting in a beach chair with a book. Other fathers played with their children in the sand, but Papa had his necktie on. "German girls must be fit and healthy. You want to bear healthy German children, don't you, my *Vögelchen*? Do you? Tell me who you are . . ."

I am Inge von Emmerich. I am Inge . . .

Inge takes off her shoes, ties them together around her neck, and swims the river. It isn't nearly as cold as the Baltic Sea. She walks down the road, panting, dripping, holding her shoes in her hand.

There are houses now, on either side, a few missing, more craters, and the road is littered with the empty shells of burned cars. A woman calls out to her. A dog barks and chases, but she keeps walking. She can't stop walking. She's almost to Papa. And then she comes to the railroad tracks.

There had been a train near Papa's camp. She remembers hearing it. That day in his office, with Rolf there, patting her knee. Papa had shown her the infirmary, white-tiled and shiny, where he helped the prisoners who had difficulty understanding how to be loyal to Germany. One of them brought wine for Mama in his striped uniform while Papa smoked his pipe. Then the train whistle blew, and Inge slid away from Rolf and asked Mama why they'd driven the car all the way to the camp instead of taking a train.

"That train," Mama had replied, "is not for us."

And Rolf had chuckled. And Papa chuckled.

She'd always wondered why they had chuckled.

Papa might be there. Waiting for her at his desk.

The train tracks are a long way behind her now. She's in a field dotted with trees. Inge catches a glimpse of bricks. A brick wall behind the branches. The wall to Papa's camp. Tall and thick with a watchtower to one side. A wall that would keep everything safe inside it.

She runs, shoes dangling, knocking against her leg, and she doesn't even feel the rocks tearing at the soles of her feet. She has to find the gate. The iron gate in the big white building. And then she finds a place where the top of the wall has tumbled, like something struck it, leaving a pile of rubble along its base.

Inge climbs the rubble. She drops her shoes and uses her hands and feet. She scrapes her knee and doesn't care. She gets to the broken place at the top of the wall and she stands.

And looks down.

Into Papa's camp.

CHAPTER FIFTEEN

—— *August 1946* ——

EVA HOOKS A finger around the edge of the curtain, looking down into the street outside Powell House. There's no man with shiny shoes and no Mr. Cruickshanks.

Not that she would be able to see them.

She hasn't called the number on Mr. Cruickshanks's card, rescued from the blue-and-white vase. Because there's nothing she wants to tell him. Not yet. This place is not like Germany after the war.

Crimes here will not go unnoticed.

So she is going to need a plan. A good plan. And she might have one. By the end of the day.

Eva looks at the little clock on the nightstand. Twenty-five minutes until two.

When Jake came back to Powell House on Saturday, he'd told her that his uncle Paul wanted him to bring Eva by the office on Tuesday at three. That he knew a German psychiatrist. Then Jake had leaned on the doorjamb and said there was a dance downstairs. They'd rolled up the rugs. Why didn't she come down?

But Brigit had been behaving badly. Biting. Hitting. Throwing her shoes. This was not the Brigit to be frightened of. This was the Brigit who had realized they were not going back to the last place she'd gotten used to. It took two days, usually, for her tantrums to cool. So instead of taking Eva to the dance on the first floor, Jake had taken Brigit to the second floor, to the music room, where it was quiet, comfortable, with a record player, a radio, and a baby grand with curved legs and polished mahogany.

Eva went straight to the piano, touching the ivory keys. She pushed one, two, three in a row. It was beautifully in tune.

"Do you play?" Jake asked. She'd shaken her head.

Then he showed Brigit a chest full of drums. Different sizes and from all different places. He let her choose one, and Brigit had smiled, dimpling when he gave her a soft mallet to hit them with. Eva curled up in one of the cushioned chairs beside the radio, watching Jake try to play along and keep Brigit on a rhythm. It was funny. And so strange, that Brigit had no fear of him.

Jake was not handsome, Eva had decided. Just very difficult to look away from.

Brigit had a good time, and then she got tired and needed the toilet, and when Eva finally got her to sleep, Jake was outside the door of the blue room again, this time leaning against the wall. "Sixth floor," he'd said. And smiled.

He made it hard to say no.

They climbed all the way to the top of Powell House, up the last little set of narrow stairs, where the attic had been made into a kind of game room with a sofa, some chairs, and a portable record player. There was also table tennis, which Jake called Ping-Pong, and a tournament was underway.

Larry, who was from India, working on a PhD at Jake's college, played against Jimmy, a Quaker, who hadn't gone to the war because he didn't believe in it. Jimmy had just gotten engaged to Colette—his assigned "friend" when she first came to Powell House—a tall girl with short blond hair who'd spent most of the war hiding from the Gestapo in a cellar in France. And when Larry won, he played George, and Marion played Ernst, all of them former immigrants turned volunteer. Jake played the music, shuffling through the records, and Eva found a corner of the couch and listened.

To Marion, who'd lived through the occupation of Holland. Ernst, an Austrian, alone in America with no family. Lucy, who had been sent from Berlin to London for safety, only to just survive the Blitz and never see her parents again. All of them were Jewish, their lives upended by Hitler. Eva listened to their stories. Like she'd always listened. In the displaced persons camps.

It's always better to know. You should always know the things that happened. If you don't know, then you can't understand what justice is.

But she avoided her own story. Like she always had. And when Lucy asked directly, Jake told Eva to stop shirking her duties and come help him choose a record.

She's not the only one who watches. And listens.

It was late before they'd all gone down the stairs. Jake lingered behind, and said he'd pick her up on Tuesday after his classes. At two.

Eva looks at the little clock. Twenty minutes until two.

Brigit is on the floor on the other side of the bed, hair still damp from her bath. She isn't angry anymore, at least not all the time, the room and the people having lost most of their strangeness. But leaving Brigit in one part of a house while Eva goes to another is one thing. Leaving her in another part of the city is . . . risky.

But it has to be done. And it's been such a long time since she really tried to hurt anyone.

Air moves the curtains, and a little girl on the sidewalk is jumping rope in front of the big bay window across the street, pigtails bouncing to the count of her steps.

One, two, three, four . . .

If Dr. Schneider did help her father leave Germany, and if she meets Dr. Schneider today, then she might find her father soon. Very soon.

The little girl misses her beat and starts over again, rope slapping the pavement.

One, two, three, four . . .

"*Eins. Zwei. Drei. Vier* . . ." Eva whispers. She closes her eyes.

In German! Her father's voice comes sharp inside her head, like the edge of broken glass. *Say it in German! How old are you?*

Or what if Dr. Schneider got him a job? What if her father is in that hospital right now, sitting behind a desk, smoking his pipe?

Waiting for her.

Spreche auf deutsch! The voice cuts through her mind.

Vier! Vier! Ich bin vier!

Eva opens her eyes, hand on her stomach. She didn't get sick. Only just a little. And the papers from their skirts are now hidden in a new slit in the mattress, the bread knife concealed in the lining of her purse, along with Mr. Cruickshanks's card.

She's ready.

And then Eva realizes she can't hear the little girl jumping rope anymore. She looks over her shoulder.

Someone has shut the window.

Brigit is sitting on the edge of the bed, her hair bright and almost dry. She's put one shoe on. The little clock on the nightstand says ten minutes until two.

"*Jeden, dwa, jeden, dwa,*" mumbles Brigit, playing with her fingers.

"Very good, Brigit," Eva whispers. Brigit doesn't often speak nonsense when she's awake. Eva turns to push the window open, to let in the air, and there's a soft knock on the door. Mrs. Angel sticks her head in.

"Afternoon," she says. "And how's my girl today?"

Brigit looks up, smiles, and Mrs. Angel tiptoes into the room like she's afraid of her own footsteps.

"Look, sweetie," she says. "I've got a surprise for you."

Mrs. Angel reaches deep into an apron pocket and brings out a kitten, sleepy, with infant blue still in its eyes and scruffy gray fur, wrapped in an old sock. Brigit's eyes go wide and she holds out her hands.

"Easy, now," Mrs. Angel says. "Let him sit in your lap." She catches Eva's eye.

"You are brave," Eva says.

Mrs. Angel laughs.

Eva picks up the curious kitten, already escaping Brigit's lap to explore the room. It's warm and its nose is pink. She puts Brigit's hand on it, gently, and looks back at Mrs. Angel.

"You do not . . . mind? She has headache, sometimes, and will need to be quiet, and she should stay . . . busy."

"I'm the same way myself."

"If she is upset, you can put a towel or a blanket over her head. To make her feel safer. And . . ." Eva hesitates. "She should not have sharp things. Or anything that could . . . hurt."

"I understand." Mrs. Angel smooths back a lock of Brigit's brushed hair. "You sure do a good job with her. Now, go on and find this sweetie a doctor."

Eva hesitates, then picks up her purse. Sweetie, she thinks. Like a candy. A word for someone you like. Like *mouse* or *bear* in German. She thinks of those sheets of paper in the kitchen, asking people to help scrub the stairs. "What is your first name, Mrs. Angel?"

"My name is Happy Angel." She grins. "Only nobody but Martha will use it. Bets says it feels disrespectful, even if it isn't."

"Your mother called you Happy Angel?"

"Oh no. It's what I call myself. I chose it. And I chose it because it's who I want to be." She waves her hands. "Now run on! And don't worry about a thing here. Shoo!"

The kitten mews as Eva shuts the door, purse held tight against her chest.

You can change your name. But it doesn't change who you are.

And sometimes, that is a rotten deal.

"Hey. Ready to go?" Jake says when she comes around the curve of the stairs. He's got a suit jacket on today, no tie, hands in his pockets, while the foyer around him is in chaos. Men in coveralls moving out the couch, passing two others hauling in a heavy wooden crate, the front parlor now haphazardly furnished with easels and small tables, wrapped packages, and more crates. A woman in a red turban is unpacking one of them, Martha sweeping sawdust off the rug.

"What are they doing?" Eva asks, sidling after Jake through the front doors. There's a moving truck pulling up for the couch to go into.

"It's the art exhibition," Jake says. "Opens with a party this weekend, to kick things off. Tea and dignitaries, the works."

Eva's gaze darts right and left as they step down to the street, but she doesn't recognize anyone other than the girl jumping rope. "What are . . . 'dignitaries'?"

"Important people."

"People with . . . dignity."

"You've got it."

Jake is setting a quick pace down the sidewalk, and Eva leaves the mystery of the phrase "the works" for later. They turn right, onto Lexington. Eva makes note of the sign. She likes to know where she is and where she's going, but right now, she's having to trot to keep up.

"Why do they put the art in Powell House?" she asks. "Instead of . . ."

"Instead of a museum? Because it's the work of white and Negro artists shown together, all mixed up and side by side. Museums don't really do that." Jake dodges a deliveryman on a bicycle.

"But at Powell House, they would show art like this? All together?"

"Sure they would." He shoots a glance over his shoulder, and takes Eva by the elbow across an intersection, making a taxi honk its horn. "If we hurry, we'll just make the two-fifteen train . . ."

Eva's heels clip along on the pavement.

"But you know some schmuck will show up," Jake goes on, "just to make a scene or spit on the floor or something"—they dart right again, around a corner—"and Martha will give them a card and ask if she can do anything to help their family, and I'll have to take the jerk outside and sock him one."

"Sock him?"

"You know, hit him. In the eye." Jake grins at her sideways. "Of course, I'd be the disappointment of the century if I did that."

They pass a building with stone dogs, cats, and owls carved around its windows. "So Powell House is . . . different than the rest of America?"

"You can say that again." Jake turns right again, and Eva steals a glance at him. Wherever they're going, it's not very direct. The buildings are taller here, the ground floors all nice shops with dresses. Groceries. Flowers. Jake steers Eva around a man selling watches from a box. They're practically running down the crowded sidewalk.

"Say," Jake says suddenly, "do you want an ice cream?"

And without warning, he pulls her across a street, into the middle of a crowd getting off a bus, then left through a pink door, making a little bell ding.

"Hi, Fred. Scoop of vanilla on a cone, please." Jake looks down at Eva. "Vanilla all right?"

She stares at him. The shop is dim, cool with a fan blowing, an ornate wooden counter, and paintings of cows on the walls. And when Eva looks past Jake's shoulder, just outside the big glass windows, beyond the word SCHRAFFT's painted in reverse pink and gold, a man is hurrying down the sidewalk, pushing past shoulders and craning his neck. Eva can't see his shoes, but she knows they are shiny.

She turns back to the counter. The man named Fred is looking at her, waiting for her answer. She's forgotten the question. She nods.

"Sure thing," says Fred, disappearing to the back. Jake slaps down two coins, and Fred comes back with a round, creamy, pale yellow scoop on a cone wrapped in paper. Fred hands it to Jake, and Jake hands it to Eva.

"Cute," says Fred.

"Mind if I use the back door?" says Jake. "We've gotta catch a train."

Fred shrugs a shoulder. "Go ahead."

Jake takes Eva's arm again, the one without the ice cream, maneuvering her around the counter, through a door, and through a kitchen where a woman with a net around her hair is scrubbing an enormous aluminum tub.

"Hey, Jake," she says. "Who's the new girl?"

And then they are out the back, into an alley, past several cans of stinking garbage, onto the street and around the corner, back onto Madison with the dress shops. Going in the opposite direction from before. They walk two blocks, pushing to the middle of a little milling mass of people. Eva can't see the man with shiny shoes. All she can see are heads and necks, the tops of buildings, and one strip of sky. But she does see a sign with a picture of a bus on it.

She looks up carefully at Jake. "You said we were taking a train."

He checks his watch. "Yeah, we missed it. We'll grab a bus instead." And he puts his hands in his pockets, leaning forward to look for the coming bus like everyone else is doing. He turns his pretty eyes on her. "Hey, your ice cream's melting."

She licks the dripping cone, sweet, cold, and sticky on her fingers. Thinking. She finds a can to throw away the paper, and she watches the street. And so does Jake.

They're watching for the same man.

And then the bus is coming, people automatically lining up at the curb. Jake pays, and they find a seat together near the middle. Jake gets a handkerchief from a pocket and dabs her face with it.

"Ice cream," he says. "On your nose. Not that it didn't suit you." He smiles, giving the tip of her nose one more swipe. He smells very faintly of cigarettes.

Then the bus jolts into movement, jostling them away and down the street. Eva watches the city pass outside the window, clutching her purse. She can feel the knife, hidden in the lining. Like the anger she's trying to hide from her face.

How could she have been so stupid? Because he has pretty eyes? Because he seems nice? When she knows nobody does anything for nothing. Her father had taught her that much.

So who is Jacob Katz?

Someone who knows things. Things he really shouldn't.

And that makes him dangerous.

And she could be setting him straight on a path to her father.

Why can she never, ever see what has been sitting there, right in front of her face?

CHAPTER SIXTEEN

—— *May 1945* ——

INGE LOOKS DOWN, over the edge of the broken wall, down into Papa's camp. She stares. And stares. And her knees buckle. Bruise, scrape hard against the brick rubble, hands clamped across her face to keep the noise from escaping her mouth.

Human bodies. Dead skeletons with sagging skin. A foot, a hand, a glimpse of a shoulder blade. A pile half the height of the wall and spreading just below her, with sunken eyes and buzzing flies, and a stench that brings the vomit straight from her stomach. But she can't look away.

How can human bodies have so many bits and pieces?

Inge wipes her mouth on her sleeve, the blood running from her knee onto her skirt, and the anger that has been her fuel explodes. Hate. Pure. Scorching her insides. Cleansing her of other thoughts.

The Communists. The enemies of Germany. Cruel. Killers. Unworthy of life. Frau Koch had said they were base. Bad. Inge closes her eyes, covers her ears, rocking back and forth on the rubble. Bullets from a plane. Annemarie screams and screams. She smells the smoke of her house. The Communists killed Hitler, and Mama went mad. They killed her family.

And now they've killed everyone in Papa's camp.

Papa could be down there. In that pile.

The world is black in front of her eyes. And then a whistle cuts through her trance, shrill and startling. There's a man standing near the edge of the rubble heap. A wisp of a man, pale, with blank, dark eyes and only a shadow of hair. He is a skull on a body, but he moves.

"You shouldn't be up there," he says. "The concrete will shift. You'll be crushed."

Inge stares at him.

"Are you hurt?" he asks.

She sees his sleeve, frayed and stiff with dirt, but with the faint outline of stripes. She sits a little straighter. "Are you from the camp?"

Then the Communists didn't kill all of them. This man was a prisoner, and he's still alive.

"I'm looking . . . I have to find my . . . I have to find my father . . ." Inge scrambles down the shifting bricks and bits of mortar, sliding and scraping her legs.

"Careful!" says the prisoner. "Your father, he was in the camp?"

She gets to the bottom. Gets to her feet. Nods.

The man shakes his bald head. "Come," he says. "I'll take you to the man in charge . . ."

Someone in charge, Inge thinks. He will know where Papa is. Papa was an important man. If this man survived, then Papa might have survived.

They walk along the perimeter of the fence. Slowly, because the prisoner is carrying a shovel that is too heavy for him, and Inge has forgotten her shoes. The man smells, and he wheezes, coughs, dragging the shovel behind him and bumping it on the rocks. Faint over one side of his chest is a pink triangle.

"Have you been to the infirmary?" Inge asks him. "For your chest?"

The man's cough turns into a laugh, and it's horrible. "When you have been to the infirmary, little one, sickness is not so much of a worry."

He might be mad, Inge thinks. Maybe Papa can help him.

But if he's mad, maybe he's lied about who is left alive.

They come around the wall and she sees the white-painted building, the iron gate in its middle, two soldiers standing on either side of it. She runs forward, to the short tunnel beyond the gate, going right through the white building. Toward the big open space behind it and the long, low buildings arranged in a semi-circle. Somewhere to the left will be the infirmary. Where Papa's office is. The prisoner wheezes, trying to keep up, but she can't slow down.

"I'm taking the girl to Delov," she hears him say.

And Inge's mind is waking. Whirring. Delov.

She stops. Jerks around. The two soldiers are lounging against the wall. Smoking. Their uniforms are not German. Her hands start to shake.

"This way," the prisoner says, still dragging his shovel.

"The soldiers," she whispers. "They're Russian."

"Yes. Of course, they are Russian."

"But . . ." They didn't leave, Inge thinks. They've taken over the camp. "What happened to the Germans?" she asks.

"You mean the Nazis?" The man spits on the ground. "That is what I say to the Nazis."

"But aren't you German?"

"I was. Until they decided I was not."

Inge wants to take a step back. He's one of the men Papa talked about. The ones who are too mad or too stupid to know when someone's trying to help them get better. And he's taken her straight inside a camp full of Soviet soldiers.

All the separate pieces of herself are telling her the same thing now. That she has come all this way. And now she is going to die.

She has to find out what has happened to Papa.

There are other soldiers milling around now. In the open space around the semicircle barracks. One or two glance at them, but they don't say anything. They're dirty. Sweating.

"Digging pits," the prisoner says. "For the dead."

He pulls one of the soldiers aside and asks a low question. The soldier looks Inge over, and she stares at the ground, so he won't see how much she hates him. The prisoner props his shovel against a wall and beckons for her to follow him.

"Delov is busy," he says. "Easier for you to just look. Come with me."

This man really must be mad. Inge whispers, "If they let you leave, why don't you just run away? You don't have to stay here. Waiting . . ."

The prisoner's brows have come together. He peers at her as if his eyes are weak. He seems confused. And sad. Like she's the one that's mad.

Maybe everyone is crazy.

"Listen, little girl," he says, "when did your Papa come to the camp?"

"From . . . from the beginning, I think . . ."

He shakes his head. "No one sent here from the beginning will be alive . . ."

Inge stares. He thinks Papa was a prisoner, too.

"I'm sorry to be harsh, but he will have been shot or starved and fed to the ovens long ago. Unless they sent him to another camp, but they are all the same. I've been in three . . ."

"Ovens?" Inge says. Her brain is trying to turn, to think. "The Communists put their prisoners in . . . ovens?"

"No, no," he says gently. "You mean the Nazis. But the Nazis are gone now. They can't kill us. Not anymore. The Russians have liberated us, remember?"

Inge pushes a hand against her aching temple. The Nazis have killed us. The Russians have liberated us.

The man turns and starts walking toward one of the barracks buildings. She stumbles after him. He steps up two steps and opens the door. And looks back at her.

"You won't find him, little girl. But you should look. If you don't look, then you will never really know . . ."

The Nazis have killed us. The Russians have liberated us.

Inge goes up the steps, and through the door.

It's so dark that all she can do is smell. She gasps, tries to cover her nose with the filthy collar of her blouse, but as her eyes adjust to the dim, she can see wooden platforms, stacked two and three high, and they are packed with the shadows of people. Like the corpses in the pile beside the wall, only these bodies make noise. They move.

"Do not try to recognize him," says the man. "Look at the faces, and see if anyone recognizes you . . ."

Inge follows the man between the rows of platforms. They're supposed to be beds, but there's nothing on them but wood. She does what the man says. She lets them look at her face. There are fleas. Boils. Terrible wounds. Every kind of fluid. And two Russian soldiers, spooning a thin soup into open, eager mouths. Two spoonfuls, and the next. Two spoonfuls, and the next.

"Why don't they feed them more?" she whispers. "It's so cruel."

"Because when you are starved, you are too weak to digest. Food will kill you. You must go little by little, until you are stronger . . ."

Inge looks down into the face of a woman who is twitching. Naked. She doesn't have teeth. So skinny, so grotesque, so delicate that she does not seem real. Only, she is real. How long does it take to starve? Until your muscles are gone, and there is nothing left of you but skin sagging over bone?

Much longer than the Russians have been here.

I am Inge . . . von Emmerich. I am . . .

She lets the tears roll down her face.

The man in the faded stripes holds the door open for her, and Inge sucks in the fresh air. The sunshine.

"I knew you would not see him," he says.

"They were prisoners?" Inge whispers. "Like you? Prisoners of . . . the Nazis?"

He nods.

"Who are they?"

"Jews. People who tried to save them. Anyone who disagreed, or was . . . different. Mostly Jews . . ."

Like Ruth. Who moved away. All of them moved away. It's hard to breathe. Hard to get her words out.

"Did anyone . . . did any Nazi try . . . to help them? The . . . doctors?"

At the word *doctors*, the man grimaces. "Never the infirmary," he whispers. "Better to starve, or be flogged, or be hung by your wrists . . ."

He glances sideways, and Inge sees tall poles, with ropes hanging off their tops, and what is unmistakably a gallows.

"Tell me your Papa wasn't sent to the doctors, little girl?"

Inge shakes her head.

"I got sent to the doctors . . ." He fingers the two remaining buttons on his filthy shirt, and Inge sees the beginnings of a pink scar, not long healed, running longways down his chest. "They don't care about pain there, the Nazi doctors . . ."

"But what about . . . a man named . . . von Emmerich?"

The former prisoner squeezes his eyes shut. "The others . . . they tortured and killed . . . they liked it. But the Doctor, he was . . . curious. He wanted to know what he could make you say. Make you do. How much you could endure. He made sure you were crazy, before you died . . ."

"Who . . . did?"

"Von Emmerich. The Doctor. They just called him . . . the Doctor . . ."

She shakes her head. Where is the air? Why isn't there air?

"But why? Why would he . . . do . . . those things?"

"Lab rats," the man whispers. "We were rats. Unworthy of life . . ."

Her head jerks around to the barracks. Unworthy of life. Like Papa's book.

But who gets to decide? Which people are more and which are less? Who had decided Ruth was less?

Why had she never asked who got to decide?

The man in front of her is still talking. Eyes closed, singsong. "He will give our life meaning, the Doctor said. We will contribute to the noble pursuit of science. Because if the mind of lesser beings can be controlled, we can become productive. Useful. No need for wars and messy camps. We will help him make the world better. We, you see, we could make it all go away . . ."

A glorious war. A scientific pursuit.

We will teach them to be useful, my Vögelchen, productive. And won't that be a better world . . .

The different parts of herself buzz, freeze, flame. Collide in confusion. The world has inverted. Turned inside out. Right is wrong and wrong is right. Nothing is real. Nothing is true.

Except that Hitler was a liar.

Her father is a liar.

Because this is not a better world.

"What happened to him?" Inge whispers. "What happened to von Emmerich?

The former prisoner suddenly opens his eyes. "What did you say your papa's name was?"

Inge takes a step back. "What happened to von Emmerich?"

The man smiles. "They were arrested. The commandant, the officers. They will hang them, I think. For crimes against humanity." Then he frowns. "But the Doctor wasn't here . . ."

Inge backs away, past the barracks, past the poles with the ropes, and the gallows.

"Wait," calls the man. "What is your name?"

She turns and runs for the gate, pebbles biting into her bare feet. Someone calls out in Russian, but she doesn't look back. The anger that had scorched her insides twists, turns. Roars. Finding a new fuel for its hate.

"What is your name?" the man yells.

I am Inge . . . I am Inge . . .

But she isn't.

She doesn't want that name.

Not anymore.

CHAPTER SEVENTEEN

August 1946

"THIS IS OUR stop," says Jake, grabbing the back of the seat. Eva clutches her purse. She can feel her pulse in her ears.

Cruickshanks had said there would be others. Others who will want her father just as much as the United States. And for the same reasons.

She has been so stupid.

They step down off the bus, people already pushing forward to take their place. The hospital is tall, pale brick, with dozens and dozens of glints of window glass winking at them in the sun. Jake takes her down a broad sidewalk, curving around a semicircle drive to double doors beneath an arch. He opens the door for her, then lets it close again.

"Are you okay?" When she doesn't answer, he asks, "Are you nervous?"

She's not nervous. She's furious. Because she's been stupid. Because she knows better than to trust. And because anger is more useful than the fear, or pain, or guilt.

Jake opens the door and this time she walks through, into a waiting room with chairs and benches, the hum of electric fans circulating the smell of bodies and disinfectant. They pass a nurse at a desk, talking on the telephone, her fingernails bitten to the nub in a disconcerting way, and then to an elevator, stepping inside as soon as the door slides open. Jake pushes the number twelve.

"Are you afraid of hospitals?" he asks when the door closes. They're alone, machinery clicking and squawking as the elevator lifts. "There was a man once, Mr. Gravinsky. From Poland. He still shows up for coffee sometimes. He wouldn't set foot inside one, because he'd been in a hospital at one of the camps."

The elevator bell dings, one for each floor, and the question sits between them like an unpinned grenade.

Were you in a camp, Eva?

Yes, Jake, she could say, I was in a camp. For a little while.

She can see Jake in the mirrored reflection of the walls, brows together, hands in pockets. And she can see herself beside him. Small. Big-eyed. And straight-backed.

Oh yes, she had been in a camp.

And that thought incinerates the others.

She will find Schneider. She will find her father and there will be justice. She'll do what she came to do, and she'll do it in spite of this boy standing next to her.

Whoever he is.

The sliding wheel of numbers at the top of the elevator car reaches twelve. The bell dings and the door opens. Eva walks out first, briskly, turning to wait for Jake.

"Hey," he says, "you were right not to say anything. It's none of my business. But if you were in a camp over there, it's nothing to be ashamed of, okay?"

He knows nothing of her shame.

They walk down a bright hall with a shiny white floor, past men with clipboards and lab coats, and rows of closed doors. Jake stops in front of one, knocking once before he turns the knob.

"What?" The voice inside is abrupt. Surly. And Jake waltzes through like he's been invited. "Oh, so it's you!"

"Hi, Uncle Paul." Eva takes two steps into the office. "This is Miss Gerst."

Dr. Greenbaum is big, beefy, with eyebrows that stick out in all directions. But his hands are very clean, soft-looking, and oddly delicate, twirling a pen. His fingernails are perfectly trimmed. He turns his dark eyes on Eva.

"Gerst? Any relation to the Gersts on East Twenty-Third? No? Good. Those Gersts are schmucks."

"Mind if we sit?" Jake asks.

Dr. Greenbaum waves a hand, and Jake gets two chairs.

"So where are you from, Miss Gerst?" Dr. Greembaum asks.

"Germany," she replies. "Berlin."

"So you're Jewish?"

Eva gives her head a tiny shake, and Jake's brows come down, puzzled.

"Hmmm," says Uncle Paul. "Well, Jake told me what you're looking for and I've got him."

Eva looks steadily at Dr. Greenbaum. And there comes her pulse, a little heartbeat in her ears.

"Dr. Holtz," he says. "Psychiatrist. Been in the country less than a year. Think he practiced somewhere near Berlin. Fluent German, of course, and he said he'd be pleased to have a talk." For a moment, Dr. Greenbaum looks just like Jake, handing Eva an ice-cream cone. He pushes back his chair, lifting himself heavily from the desk. "I've got him waiting. Let me grab him."

"Thanks, Uncle Paul," says Jake.

Eva only nods, mute as Dr. Greenbaum leaves, shouting at someone down the hall. The pulse in her ears picks up, pounding in her chest. A German psychiatrist. Here for less than a year. Dr. Schneider had gotten her father a job. It's today. The time is now.

Justice is now.

She gets up from her chair and goes to the window. There's nothing to see outside but another brick wall. She sets her purse on the little ledge and unsnaps the clasp.

She hadn't thought it would be now.

"When the doctor comes," Eva says. "I would like to speak with him alone."

There's a pause, and she hears the wood of Jake's chair creak. "I'll be out in the hall."

The door to the office shuts, and Eva reaches into her purse, finds the slit in the lining, feels the cool blade of the bread knife.

She breathes. And breathes.

She says the names. Twenty-seven names. Quietly. Under her panting breath.

She frees the bread knife from the purse lining, the handle tight in her grip.

Justice is now. It's up to her. And whatever happens next must come.

And then the door is opening, Dr. Greenbaum's voice booming somewhere in the hallway. It shuts again with a gentle click. But she can feel the presence of the man behind her. She can hear the rustle of a trouser leg. Blood rushes hot through her veins. She has her purse in one hand, the knife held inside it with the other. The German voice behind her is strong and soft.

"*Guten Tag. Nett sie kennen zu lernen . . .*"

Eva spins around.

CHAPTER EIGHTEEN

—— *May 1945* ——

INGE RUNS. SHE runs and runs. But how can you escape from what's inside your head?

Moved away, that's what Mama had said. Why had she never asked where "away" actually was? Had they all gone to a camp like her father's? Where "make them loyal" had meant "stop feeding them until they die?" Where "make them productive" had meant using them like lab rats? Worse than rats.

Was Ruth dead? Were they all dead? Were they all put in ovens?

That couldn't be true.

Only, anything evil could be true. And anything good could be bad. The shattered pieces of herself crash, fly, a whirlwind of confusion.

Papa loves her. Doesn't he?

Papa is a monster.

But could he love her, and do all those things? What she'd seen? What she'd heard? He'd said Mama loved her, and Mama had shot her own children.

Except her. Mama hadn't shot her.

Was that love, or not love? Inge runs faster.

You can't escape from your head, and you can't escape from your blood.

Brown water billows her skirt, her cuts and scrapes burn. Sting. She's swimming the river. But she has no breath. Her legs are shaking. Her arms are weak.

The current swirls gently, undulating. Smooth and steady. The river isn't good and the river isn't bad. It just is. And there is no escape.

Inge stops swimming.

And the world becomes cool, dark brown, gurgling. Suspended. Still and quiet with a sparkling surface. Sun streaming down through the murk. Like ribbons of light. Like plaits of yellow hair.

And Inge's body jerks.

Annemarie.

She's forgotten Annemarie.

She swims. Breaking the surface with a sputter and a cough. Pushing herself toward the bank, dragging herself from the mud. She stumbles to the canal, across the rubble bridge, and there is the bombed factory, the crates, the car underneath charred canvas, leaning on its deflated tire. Inge pulls back the canvas. Yanks open the door.

Annemarie is lying flat on the back seat, eyes open, unblinking, staring at the roof of the car. But she is not a skeleton in the pile. Her chest is rising. Little moans coming from her mouth.

Relief pours through Inge's chest. Water on a fire. Inge watches Annemarie breathe and makes a decision. Not everyone is going to die. Someone is going to live. Annemarie is going to live. And there is no one to keep Annemarie alive.

No one but her.

She will splinter into pieces later.

Inge unties Annemarie's shoes. Annemarie has soiled herself, lying there, but it doesn't matter. The shoes are tough leather lace-ups, for working around the farm. Much too big, and much better than nothing.

Inge can't imagine, anymore, leaving behind something as valuable as her shoes. She can't imagine being so stupid.

She scavenges the yard. A tire iron. A can of rusting nails. A chunk of concrete with a bit of metal inside it, a piece that fits well in her hand. She puts this in her pocket, then takes the bottle from the farm and an empty gas can and hauls water from the canal.

Annemarie's eyes are closed now, but she swallows the water. And she swallows more. This is good. Then Inge strips off Annemarie's clothes, washing Annemarie and the seat with a blouse and water from a can that smells of gasoline. Annemarie doesn't like this. She frowns. Cries out, but Inge doesn't mind. She's glad to see Annemarie doing anything at all.

The wound on the back of her head has bled again, and her thighs, belly and chest are mottled with bruises that run one into the other like a vine of ugly flowers. Inge takes her soiled clothes to the canal and scrubs them beneath a sunny sky with no planes. No bombs. A sky so quiet, it's unnerving. Unsettling. Wrong.

And Inge realizes there are no birds. No birds anywhere.

Annemarie's wet clothes get laid out to dry on the dashboard and through the missing windshield onto the hood. Skirt, blouse, socks. She doesn't have any underthings. It's hot underneath the canvas, stale and steaming. Annemarie is asleep again, curled up and naked on the wet seat. And then Inge notices papers, scattered all over the passenger-side floor.

The file. With her name on it.

She gathers them up, shaking off bits of broken windshield. They're wrinkled, out of order. Journaled notes written in her father's slanted hand. Inge finds the first page, marked with the date November 1933, and a name.

Observations: Anna Ptaszynska.

Inge stares at the name. And she throws down the papers.

It's the wrong file. The soldiers knocked the files off the desk. Mixed them all up. Whatever Papa had decided to write about her is gone.

Everything is gone.

Inge leans back against the seat. Her stomach is cramping, empty except for the canal water she drank. The last time she'd eaten or slept, Adolf and Erich had been alive. She is alone. Lost. Hollowed out. Why should she care what her father wrote about her? It doesn't even matter. They will hang him if they catch him, like they'll hang the commandant. For crimes against humanity, like the prisoner had said.

Inge sits up.

What evidence does a court need to bring someone to trial? Her father hadn't died, because he wasn't there. And she'd seen the witnesses piled up against the camp wall. Dying in the barracks. And where would the survivors be, after the war?

She gathers up the papers again, reading.

Race is the ultimate factor in determining the potential of the individual . . .

. . . noble yet misguided intentions, that the subspecies of Jews and Slavs could be improved upon by careful training from childhood . . .

Anna Ptaszynska had been the child of arrested Polish Communists. Taken at the age of four years, four months. And there are two pages of a chart, chronicling her behaviors.

NOVEMBER 11: *Speaking Polish: Beaten.*

NOVEMBER 11: *Speaking Polish: Food Withheld.*

NOVEMBER 13: *Mention of previous parent: Beaten.*
NOVEMBER 15: *Speaking German: A toy*
NOVEMBER 16: *Speaking Polish: Food Withheld*

. . . believe it may be possible to split the human personality, to create a new persona. In this way, previous habits and defects, objectionable traits, can be set aside, or wholly erased . . .

The punishments increase in severity. An emetic drop, given to make her vomit when referring to previous home or parents. Sensory deprivation. And rewards. Cake after a day without food, for saying *cake* in German. A hug for using her proper name. But eventually, Anna Ptaszynska stopped speaking at all. She stopped eating.

And then,

Anna Ptaszynska died July 11, 1934. She is no more.

. . . and while the racial defects of the subject were observed and recorded, there were other areas of interest that arose from . . ."

And there's no more. His notes end there.

Inge throws down the papers. Digs her nails into the back of her neck. And where had she been when little Anna Ptaszynska was dying in 1934? The Baltic Sea, probably, where they'd spent every July before the war. Playing on a beach.

Her father is a man who let innocents suffer by the hundreds. By the thousands. Who causes their suffering. A man who ruffled her hair and tickled her with his beard and kills little girls.

This is her father. And it is not understandable.

She draws her knees into her chest. Curls into herself. Closes her eyes.

She can't bear to say her name.

She doesn't want her name.

And when Inge wakes up, the air has gone chilly. Her neck hurts, propped up unnaturally against the steering wheel. And someone is moaning behind her. She twists around. Annemarie is huddled on the back seat, eyes closed, naked and shivering. Inge shakes out the blanket she'd been sitting on to drive and throws it over her. Annemarie shudders and settles.

Annemarie must not die.

Annemarie needs a doctor.

Annemarie has to eat. Soon.

Outside the canvas, the sky is golden to the east, the littered ground damp with dew. Inge finds a place near the fence for a toilet. Her legs are shaking. There are no people anywhere. Not a voice or a call or the sound of a motor. She checks for the lump of concrete in her pocket, picks her way across the yard and climbs through a hole in the wall of the ruined warehouse.

Not a warehouse, she sees. A factory. An enormous room of broken glass and machinery half-buried by the fallen roof. She can still smell the fire. A plane flies low, shaking the air, and one or two bricks tumble from the broken wall, crashing in puffs of dust. Inge hurries over, under, through the debris, to a door on the far end. She pries it open.

The hallway behind the door looks almost normal, except for dust and the smell of smoke. She passes rooms with offices, filing cabinets. One with bunk beds and cots. And at the very end of the hall, she finds what she was hoping for. A kitchen. Big. Industrial, with metal counters that had been clean before the bombs, a table with a printed cloth in the center where the supervisors could sit and eat.

There must be food somewhere in the kitchen, because it is rotting.

Inge roots through the drawers and cabinets, taking a cooking pot, a kitchen knife, forks and spoons, and a can opener. And in a windowless storage room, standing on a chair, running her hands over the empty shelves, she discovers a prize.

A can of beans.

How long can two people live on one can of beans?

Longer than they can live without them.

The can goes into the pot with her other treasures, and Inge gets on her hands and knees, checking the shadows. The corners.

And then she stops. Freezes. And scrambles back.

There's a foot underneath the table, nearly hidden by the table-cloth. A bare foot inside a sheer stocking.

The toenails are blue.

Inge covers her mouth. Now she understands the smell. And then she crawls forward, because she can't help it, and lifts the edge of the tablecloth.

A young woman is lying on her face. With an orange print dress and light brown hair nicely curled. Inge can't see how she died. She doesn't want to. But she does look at her dress. Her stockings. She looks at the bent end of a hairpin. She'd never thought about things like hairpins and shoes and cans of beans before. In the old world, food and clothes were easy. Endless. They just appeared.

This is the new world.

But she doesn't think she can bear to turn the girl over.

Gingerly, guiltily, Inge reaches for the purse lying near the splayed hand and slides it closer through the dust. She finds lipstick, a pow-der compact, a pen. A half-empty pack of cigarettes and a lighter. Coins and used tissues. And in the inner pocket, a folded card. Inge pulls it out, but she already knows what it is.

Identity papers. Stamped with the red ink of Hitler's eagle. She looks at the girl's picture, her birth date, her Dresden address. She'd been pretty, not much older than Inge. She'd probably thrown flowers at parades and gone home to a mother who loved her. She probably never imagined that she would die so young. Rotting under a table in a factory. Why was she here? No one will ever know. And then Inge thinks about that.

No one has to know.

She finds the lighter in the purse again. And after three sparks, up shoots a little flame. Inge memorizes the dead girl's smile, and then she lets the fire lick the corner of the paper. It smokes, catches, and burns. Hot. Bright.

She turns the paper this way and that, letting the flame eat a path, and then quickly blows it out, flicking away the bits of ash. The girl's face is almost gone, just a hint of a cheek and a chin, along with a good bit of Hitler's red stamp. But the name is still there. In stark, black ink.

Gundrun Eva Gerst.

The burned papers go back in the purse and the purse goes into her cooking pot with the beans. But then she pauses, turns back, and pulls the dusty, debris-strewn cloth off the table and carefully covers the girl with it. Until there's nothing there but a bump beneath printed lilies. So the girl doesn't have to be stared at.

"Well," says a voice from the door. "That was very nice of you, *Vögelchen.*"

Inge spins around.

CHAPTER NINETEEN

—— *August 1946* ——

"**MISS GERST?**" **ASKS** the man called Dr. Holtz. *"Fühlen sie sich wohl?"*

Eva presses her purse to her middle, one hand inside it, fingers tight around the handle of the knife. Dr. Holtz is short, round, with wispy gray hair, a full beard. His shoes are slip-on, sweater a little tatty, and there's a long, deep wrinkle in his forehead, where his eyebrows push together. He closes the door to Dr. Greenbaum's office.

"Miss Gerst, are you all right?"

Eva breathes. Sweat dots her forehead, a trickle running down between her shoulder blades.

It's not him. It's not her father.

Justice is not happening now.

Dr. Holtz comes forward. "Here, please . . ." he says.

Eva drops into a chair, willing her fingers to unwind from the knife. She slides her hand out of her purse and quickly clicks it shut.

"Some water?" asks Dr. Holtz. His English is clear, but the *w* is still German.

Eva shakes her head and his wrinkle line deepens. She tries to smile. Like everything is normal. Like she is normal.

"I am sorry. I thought you were . . . someone else. For a . . ."

"Moment?" asks Dr. Holtz. "Is that the English you want?"

She nods, and Dr. Holtz sits down with a little huff, where Jake had been.

"My wife tells me I have one of those faces. Very unremarkable." He chuckles before he shakes his head. "And we have all been living in such uncertain times and in uncertain places, yes?"

He settles back, fingertips propped beneath his chin.

"Paul tells me you are here about your friend. Is it so, Miss Gerst? Tell me about her, when you are ready. In German, if you'd like."

Eva tells him, in German, hesitating at first, but with her pace picking up toward the end. The wrinkle line on Dr. Holtz's forehead gets longer and shorter as he listens.

"There are too many young girls with this kind of trauma. Thousands, I am sorry to say. But in this case, the reaction seems unusually severe. She has no family?"

Eva shakes her head.

"These types of regressions, they are not my specialty . . . but I may know someone, a doctor, who has done well with such cases. I would like to write and ask his advice, if you are agreeable . . ."

Eva sits back. "You think Brigit could be . . . helped?"

"I do not know. But without more information, it would be wrong to say she could not be."

"But the doctors in Berlin said there was nothing to do for her."

Dr. Holtz waves a dismissive hand. "And I am sure they are very good doctors. But a hospital in a war zone is overwhelmed, and patients sometimes cannot be given the attention they deserve. But before I write, I would like to have Miss . . . what is her name?"

"Heidelmann."

Dr. Holtz brings out a little notebook, bent and crushed to the shape of his shirt pocket, flips to a clean page, and jots down Brigit's name with a stub of pencil.

"Yes," he murmurs. "But before I write, Miss Gerst, I would like for Miss Heidelmann to see a doctor of neurology, to make sure any physical injuries have been addressed."

"What is a . . ."

"A doctor for the nerves and the nervous system."

"But Brigit is not hurt in that way."

"Ah. But the brain is part of that system, and in medicine, I believe it is best not to leave the path unwalked, yes? It's a request I make for many of my patients . . ."

Eva gazes at Dr. Holtz and feels poison creeping up from her middle. It's a familiar feeling. The guilt of knowing something Brigit needs and not being able to give it to her. Like food. Safety. Aspirin on a ship.

"I do not want to . . . take your time," she whispers. "But I do not have money for this doctor."

The line in Dr. Holtz's forehead deepens. "You are staying at Powell House. Is that so?"

She nods, and he leans back in the chair.

"Then let me explain like this. When I came to this country, I had nothing. A medical degree and the clothes on my back. I came as a German Jew, a survivor of the camps, a difference not everyone can understand when their sons have been buried on a battlefield or torpedoed by a U-boat. And the ladies of Powell House, they found me a bed and then an apartment. They sewed me a decent suit. Made the introductions that got me this position. I went for help, but I kept going back for friendship. I became a person again. And now I have a wife, an apartment, and pots to grow tomatoes. And never, Miss Gerst, in all this time, have they asked me to pay.

So today, by finding your friend a doctor, I am paying a little of what I owe. Do you see?"

She does. And it is strangely unfair. But Dr. Holtz survived the camps. He deserves it. She does not.

Dr. Holtz pats her arm and stands up. "I will make a telephone call or two, and I will send word, yes?"

"Thank you," she whispers. There's a sharp rap on the door and Dr. Greenbaum sticks his head inside.

"Are you done? Mind if I use my office?"

His tone is gruff, face smiling. A paradox. Like Powell House.

"A word, if you don't mind, Paul?" says Dr. Holtz. Then he smiles at Eva and gives her a little bow. "Thank you, Miss Gerst."

Eva nods again and slips out into the white hallway. She leans against the wall, purse against her legs, and closes her eyes. Breathes. She'd thought she was going to see her father standing in that office. She'd thought it was time for justice and then it hadn't been.

Was she relieved or sorry about that?

Eva tightens her grip on the purse against her legs. She'd thought she was ready, but she hadn't been. She'd been frightened in that room. Weak.

She isn't sure which emotion makes her more angry.

"So, what did you find out?"

Eva's eyes snap open. Jake is leaning against the opposite wall, fingers tapping another rhythm against his thigh. "You came out of there ready to put your dukes up."

Eva stands up straight, tucking a curl uncertainly behind her ear.

"I just meant you look like you're ready to fight the whole world," Jake says. Then he grins. "Not that it doesn't suit you."

Eva looks at Jake's easy smile. The clever fingers and the lovely eyes.

He is such a good liar.

Dangerous.

Jake pulls himself off the wall and they start back down the hall to the elevators.

"So what did Holtz say?"

"That he will write to a doctor. He . . ." Eva pauses. There's a man coming toward them down the hall, in a pale blue jumpsuit, pushing a wide broom. "First he wants to . . ."

The man glances up, adjusting the trajectory of his broom. And she knows him. She'd know him anywhere.

Eva stops.

She'd thought he was dead.

The man with the broom has his head down, eyes on the gathering pile of dust and debris he's pushing down the hallway. But he's picked up his pace.

Eva's body shifts into gear. She turns in place and walks away. Like someone floored the gas pedal. Down the hall, as if she knows exactly where she's going, heels clipping smartly on the floor tiles, purse swinging. She turns the corner of the hall.

And the corridor stops. A dead end of doors with no elevator. Not even a potted plant.

She can hear the man coming, his broom brushing, a little tune whistling between his teeth. He's going to come around the corner. He's going to see her. And then what?

Eva doesn't know. Only that it can't happen.

She looks left, then right. She chooses right, opens a door, steps inside, and closes it again.

The room is windowless. Pitch-dark. Small. She can feel the smallness. She finds a shelf beside her and puts her back against it, her hand inside her purse, where she can feel the bread knife.

She breathes. Breathes. The space is too tight. And he's coming. There is so much pressure inside darkness.

And then the door wrenches open, blinding before it shuts again. She fumbles for the knife. Someone else is scrambling near the door. A switch clicks, a light comes on, and Eva only just controls the urge to scream.

It's Jake.

"What the hell are you doing?" he whispers.

They're in a narrow closet, with shelves of cleaning supplies, a sink, and a dirty mop bucket. Jake takes a step forward. He's not smiling. He's not moving to some music in his head. He grabs a shelf on either side of him, arms spanning the width of the closet. Blocking her way out.

"Who are you?" he says.

She steps back along the shelf.

"You going to answer the question? Or would you rather stab me with that knife you've got stashed in your purse? Who are you?"

"My name," she whispers, "is Eva Gerst."

"You sure about that? Because I thought some people called you Bluebird."

Eva takes a deep breath, and then she straightens. Relaxes. It's always so much better when you know. She narrows her eyes. "That," she says, "is not my name."

"Fine. It's not your name. Then who's outside?"

Eva glances at the mop and bucket. She's walked through the one door a man cleaning a hallway just might decide to open.

"Come on!" Jake yells. "Who is the man outside?"

She levels her gaze at his pretty, lying eyes.

"A Nazi."

CHAPTER TWENTY

—— *May 1945* ——

INGE SCRAMBLES AWAY from the voice at the door and she screams. An eruption of fear she has no control over. Back and back, away from the dead body, banging hard into a set of cupboards. A shadow is in the doorway. In a uniform. An SS uniform. He steps into the kitchen.

"Rolf," Inge whispers.

"Yes, hello." As if he just happened to stop by and stick his head inside her father's study. He's thinner now, with an untended cut running along his cheekbone. "I'm sorry to have frightened you. But I always did frighten you, didn't I?"

He walks to the body under the table, gives the cloth a prod with a toe. "Poor Eva. She was so stupid."

Inge sidles along the edge of the counter, toward the door, but Rolf blocks her way. Holds out a hand. "No, no. Don't go, Inge. You shouldn't go outside. The Communists are here, you know. And the Americans, the British, they will all be here soon. There isn't much time."

He smiles, and starts opening drawers, like she had been doing. She stands a little in front of her cooking pot. It's going to be hard to run away in Annemarie's enormous shoes, and she doesn't want Rolf to notice her beans.

"What are you doing here?" she whispers.

Rolf looks up. "I was a guard here, before the bombs fell. Didn't you know that, *Vögelchen?*"

"I thought you were a pilot."

"Oh, no. I never passed the tests. Your father didn't tell you? Ah, well. He got me into the SS instead, and I was assigned here, to watch the filth from the camp make boots. So we can all have boots. I'm told this was useful. Noble, in fact." He pulls a drawer out from its slot and upends it. "And now I am disappointed. I felt flattered that you came to see me. But life is a disappointment, isn't it, *Vögelchen?*"

"Don't call me that."

"Oh." He looks up. "I am sorry. That was special for your papa, wasn't it?" He rummages through the drawer. "Why didn't we have our own special name? I should have thought of it before. How about *Zuckermaus?* No? Or *Prinzessin?* I am surprised your father did not call you that. Or . . ."

Rolf stops and smiles, showing the little gap between his teeth. It must hurt, the way it stretches the cut on his cheek.

"Or I could be your *Kuschelbär*, and you can be my *Honigbienechen*. Because you are a sweet little bee that likes to sting your cuddle bear so much."

He waves away a fly and goes back to his search, pleased. There's blood on his uniform. It might be his. It might not. Inge reaches inside her pocket, feeling for her lump of concrete.

"So why you have come then, my *Honigbienechen*, if it wasn't for your *Kuschelbär?*"

"I was looking for my father."

"Oh? And where is the rest of the family?"

Inge pauses. "Dead."

"Of course. Yes," he mutters. "I suppose Ilse did it herself? Otto always said she would do the right thing, if the time came. . . . "

Inge watches him sigh and pocket a box of matches.

Do the right thing.

Her anger is a pure white flame. She bites her lip until she tastes blood.

"Ilse was right," Rolf says. "There is no hope. Not without the Führer. Berlin is gone and the war is lost. And we are the criminals now. . . ."

And then Rolf has a knife, much like the one in her pot. He holds it up in the air, examining the sharpness of the blade.

"Your father said it would happen. Otto said if the Third Reich was victorious, then we would be heroes. Gods among men. Architects of the new civilization. But if we lost. . . . Then we would be the worst criminals this world has ever seen. I wrote it down, you see. What he said . . ."

Maybe she is a criminal. The man at the camp would have thought so. And Ruth would, too.

Rolf is looking at Inge. His eyes are glistening. "And now it is true. And you and I are here. Together . . . at the end. It was supposed to be the three of us. And now, they will hang him, just like he said . . ."

Inge shakes her head. "The man at the camp said he wasn't there."

Rolf goes still. "You went inside the camp?"

"They arrested the commandant and the officers, but . . . von Emmerich . . . wasn't there when the Communists. . . ."

Rolf moves, faster than she was ready for, down the length of counter, knife in hand.

"He escaped? Are you certain?"

He has her by the shoulder. He doesn't seem to remember he has a knife. She struggles loose, away from the blade, but Rolf doesn't notice.

"I did not know. I thought . . ." He looks up. "Then Otto will be hiding. Going by a new name. He will leave Germany. It's what he told me to do if . . ."

Rolf paces back and forth in front of the dead girl's feet, the knife swinging dangerously close to his leg. And all at once, the way to the door is clear. She might have to come back for her pot.

"Pretend to be a refugee. A civilian, he said. And there was a place, a ship . . ." Sweat is breaking out on his forehead. "And if Otto is on the run, he will need me. And you need me . . ."

Rolf is a man with a new cause. A new fight.

"You need me. To protect you. We will find him together and start again. The three of us, like it was supposed . . ."

Then he looks up and frowns. "Where are you going?"

She'd made it halfway to the door. Inge keeps walking, slowly, an eye on Rolf's knife. "I have to go now, Rolf."

"What?"

Inge keeps walking. Ready.

And when Rolf runs, she runs. But she's not fast enough in her heavy, loose shoes. He catches her beside the door, jerking her back by the collar, and when he turns her around, Inge goes still. Rolf's eyes are red-rimmed around the blue. He smells like whiskey, and the knife is very close to her cheek. She turns her face away. He strokes her hair with the knife hand.

"Why am I never good enough for you?" he whispers. "I have the papers. All the right bloodlines. And I did everything. Everything he asked of me. You are my reward . . ."

"I have to go now, Rolf," Inge whispers. She looks for her fire, but she can't find that piece of herself just now. She is the Inge with fear sparking through her veins. She's the Inge whose thoughts unravel.

"You are coming with me," Rolf says in her ear. He's pressed against her, the cut on his cheek bleeding onto hers. "You were a promise. Your papa said if I could do what he needed, you would belong to me. And you always do what your papa says, don't you?"

If she had, she doesn't anymore. Inge takes her hand from her pocket.

"You belong to me," he says, mouth against her neck. "And you do what I say now. I will take care of you. You will come with me to find your . . ."

And Inge explodes backward, shoving Rolf so suddenly that he staggers. She sidesteps toward the door, and Rolf nearly flings the knife as he screams, "Why am I never good enough?"

She makes a dash and he comes for her, this time grabbing her by the hair.

And Inge turns and hits him. As hard she can. With the chunk of concrete.

Rolf lets go of her, lurching, one hand to the side of his head. He reaches out, this time with the knife hand, and she hits him again. Harder. Yelling while she does it. He falls flat. He doesn't move.

Rolf doesn't move at all. His feet are just touching the toes of the dead girl.

And she belongs to no one but herself.

CHAPTER TWENTY-ONE

—— *August 1946* ——

JAKE'S BROWS ARE dark, drawn together in the glare of the cleaning closet's light bulb. He stares down at Eva. "What did you say?"

"I said he is a Nazi," she whispers. A Nazi she'd thought was dead.

"Does this Nazi have a name?"

"Rolf," she says. "Steiner."

She has to think. Think.

Jake leans forward. "How do you know he's a Nazi?"

"He was SS. A guard . . ."

"At the camp?"

Eva doesn't break her gaze. Jake thinks she'd been in a camp. As a prisoner. Her shame at the lie is not what it should be. Because Jake isn't what he should be. Because not thirty seconds ago, he had called her Bluebird.

"You recognize him," Jake says. "Are you sure?"

Eva nods and Jake swears.

"So what's he doing here?"

She shrugs, and the shrug is not a lie. And neither is the shake in her voice.

"I cannot see him," she says.

What she really means is, he cannot see me.

"Okay," Jake says. "Okay." He runs a hand through his hair. "Stay here. I'm going to take care of this. But then . . ." He turns back to look at her. "Then you are going to level with me."

Eva doesn't know exactly what "level with me" means. But she can guess.

Jake cracks open the door, peeks out. "Don't move," he says over his shoulder. The door clicks shut behind him.

Eva sags back against the shelf. Rolf is alive. In America, sweeping floors. When she'd thought she'd killed him. And Jake knows about Bluebird. The knife. The man with shiny shoes. Cruickshanks had said others would want her father badly. Badly enough to do what? And now she's just sent Jake after Rolf, and what will happen next she cannot even begin to predict.

But there is one thing she knows. One thing of which she is completely certain.

If Rolf is here, her father is not far behind him.

The door cracks open again, and Jake's arm comes through, beckoning. She slips out, and Jake grabs her hand. So she can't run away.

The dead end of the hallway is deserted. No broom. No whistling. Just the quick tap of their feet over the shiny tiles. At the far end of the hall is a door. And behind the door, there are stairs.

Of course, there are stairs.

They go down fast, together, footsteps echoing against the concrete. Down and down, until Jake pushes open another door, and they walk into another hall. Around a corner, past the elevators, the busy nurse with the bitten fingernails, through the hats, coats, and crying babies and straight out the front doors to the semicircle drive.

"Come on," Jake says.

He's still got her by one hand, pulling her at a trot, her purse swinging, across a wide street of traffic, pausing and dodging the buses and the cars, down a set of steps in the middle of the next sidewalk. Into a tunnel, where he finally lets go of her hand.

He drops two coins in a slot and pushes her through a wooden turnstile. And almost as soon as they're though, the subway train roars into the station, whipping Eva's hair. They hurry, stepping through the open doors just before the conductor can shut them again. Jake points her to an empty seat while he stands, hanging on to a ceiling strap as the train jerks into motion. He holds out a handkerchief.

"Your finger," he says.

Eva looks down. She's nicked her finger. Probably on the bread knife. She takes the handkerchief. At least she hadn't bled on him.

She studies Jake from beneath her lashes. He's thinking, moving with the train's rhythmic sway, staring at a pasted advertisement for hair cream without seeing it. Left thumb hooked in a pocket, the fingers long, with very short nails. Their tips are calloused. She'd felt it when he held her hand.

Dangerous, she thinks. But she's less scared of him than of Rolf at the moment.

Jake wants her to "level" with him. Only, he is going to have to level with her first.

The train lurches and squeals. "This is our stop," Jake says.

Eva stands, follows him through the pushy crowd, across the platform with 135th St. spelled out in different-colored wall tiles. Up the steps, and they are back in the world of buildings, now dimmed by thickening clouds. Children play along the street, in front of the houses and the shops, shooting marbles and hopping in squares chalked on the pavement. Jake puts a hand on her back, helping her keep pace.

Making sure she doesn't run off.

They cross the traffic, down a block and turn a corner, past big churches, a little diner called SNOOKIE'S SUGAR BOWL, more children, a sign that says THE RENAISSANCE and THE YEAH MAN. A woman pauses her conversation on the steps of an apartment house, turning to watch them pass. Other than one strolling policeman, their faces are the only ones that haven't been a shade of brown.

Jake presses Eva to the right, and they turn onto a street that is narrower, shabbier, stopping at a dark door. The knob is black. Even the diamond-shaped pane of glass in the door has been painted black, and there is a heavy-fringed curtain hung across the narrow little window to one side.

Jake knocks. Three sharp raps.

A sign over the door says MONTY'S BURROW. A sign in the window says CLOSED.

Jake knocks again. Three raps. His hand presses firmly into her back. Then the door cracks open, and a woman's bobbed, bleached-blond head is framed in the dark between the door and the doorjamb. And she is not brown. Her face is moon-pale and rouged, shining in the dim, with lipstick that matches her earrings. Bright red.

"Oh," she says. "It's you."

"Rehearsing?" Jake asks.

"Auditioning," she replies.

"Can you do coffee?"

The woman rolls her eyes. Shakes her short hair. Her earrings rattle. But she smiles. "Yeah, yeah, I can do coffee."

"Thanks, Cherry. This is Eva."

"Hi," says Cherry, backing up to let them in. Cherry is wearing pants. And a short, tight top cut away to show a triangle of bare skin above her waistband. Then the door closes and it's too dark to see anything but her hair.

Another curtain, heavy and gold-fringed, hangs over a steep

stairwell. They follow Cherry down, and beyond the second curtain, someone is blowing a horn. Loudly. Up and down the same scale. The wrong scale. Jake keeps his hand on Eva's back. As if she would know where to run.

"Mind if we grab a booth?" Jake asks.

Cherry waves a set of scarlet fingernails. "Take your pick!"

The room at the bottom of the stairs is full of empty tables and chairs, the bright lights pointed at a stage on the far end, leaving everything else in the shadows. The musicians are setting up stands, and drums, wiping down brass, one plucking at some bass strings.

Jake leads Eva to a corner, to a booth with a narrow table and high backs, turned to one side for a clear view of the stage. She slides in, and Jake leans down.

"I'll be right back. Don't run off. And you can't get out anyway, because Cherry locked the door." He smiles and melts away into the dark.

Eva sets down her purse. She could get out if she wanted to. That front window is made of glass. But she doesn't want to. Not yet. She has to know where Jacob Katz stands.

She slides her purse closer. Within easy reach.

A man with his sleeves rolled up walks back and forth across the stage, shouting instructions to the band while they arrange their chairs, eventually settling in at the piano. It seems cheerful. Haphazard. So different from the symphony in Berlin. Her father had taken her to a performance of Wagner. For her birthday. She'd been so happy that day. Living in a world made of lies.

The horns go up, gleaming in the lights. A brief, suspenseful moment, and music bursts off the stage. It's loud. Bright. Brash. The sound of surprise. The pianist is all over the keys.

Then Jake is sliding into the opposite seat. "Still here?" He leans forward on his elbows, talking beneath the music. "I checked on Brigit. She's good. Great, in fact."

Eva lets her guilt bubble and cool.

"Mrs. Angel has her beating rugs in the backyard, after all that sawdust from the crates. She seems to have a knack for it. Having big fun, so Olive says."

They shouldn't have done that. The next time Brigit picks up a stick, the rug might not seem any different to her than the wall or the lamps or someone else's head.

"But the important point," Jake says softly, "is that I have you to myself for a while." She can feel the intensity of his gaze in the dark. "So. Ready to level?"

Are you? Eva thinks. But she doesn't say it. Only Jake seems to think she has. She can just make out the shape of his smile.

"Come on, Bluebird," he says. "Which is it first? Want to tell me about Nazis, or who you really are?"

CHAPTER TWENTY-TWO
—— *May 1945* ——

INGE STEPS AWAY from Rolf's still body. From the blood running onto the floor. She picks up her pot with the beans and the dead girl's purse, turns, and runs from the kitchen in her awkward shoes.

She does not look back.

Out of the factory, back under the canvas, and into the front seat of the car, throwing the purse and the pot onto her father's scattered papers.

She breathes. And breathes. And looks down at her right hand. She still has the chunk of concrete. There's a smear of blood on it. She throws it out the missing windshield, over Annemarie's drying clothes, letting it dent the hood and roll away.

She hadn't known she could kill someone.

Maybe they'll hang her. Like the rest of the Nazis. Like a criminal, like Rolf said. Maybe they should. Only she can't let that happen. Someone has to live. She has to make sure that Annemarie lives.

And then Inge looks over her shoulder and turns, flipping herself around onto her knees, grabbing the leather seat with both hands.

The back of the car is empty. The door is standing open.

Annemarie is gone.

"Annemarie!" Inge screams. She crawls over the seat and out the door. Out from beneath the canvas. "Annemarie!"

The factory yard is just as she left it, dust and bits of trash blowing. She spins in all directions, and then sprints toward the canal. She doesn't know how awake Annemarie is. Would she remember how to swim?

Did Annemarie ever know how to swim?

Clouds are coming, and the air is heavy, rumbling thunder. Or is that bombs? Tanks? There's no one on the bridge rubble. Maybe Annemarie is already beneath the brown water. Like Inge had been.

"Annemarie!" she cries.

And then she spins again. From somewhere close by, a girl is shrieking. Wailing. And all the different pieces of herself slam, smack together, until she is a fiery, freezing venomous ache.

She knows those screams. She will never forget them.

And she doesn't even have her piece of concrete.

Inge runs down the path beside the canal, stumbling in her shoes, flinging herself toward Annemarie. Through a break in the brush, charging around the trees, until suddenly there aren't any bushes or trees, because the land has dropped away like a bowl, open to the sky.

A bomb crater. And at the bottom, dark figures hunch over a girl. Blond hair splayed over the blackened rock, over the scorched, red earth, and she is fighting, kicking and screeching. Inge slides down the steep slope, bringing dirt and rocks and gravel with her.

"Get away from her!" she screams. "Get away!"

The figures stand. Stare. Back away. Annemarie is huddled on the ground, trying to cover her face and fight away the stranger's hands, even though the hands aren't there anymore. She's naked, though someone has tried to cover her with a trench coat.

Inge drops to her knees, puts her arms around her. "It's me," she whispers. "I won't let them hurt you. I'm here. You're all right."

Annemarie stops fighting, but she is sobbing. She uncovers her face. The blue of her eyes is bright against all the bruising. It takes them a long moment to focus.

"Inge," she whispers, tears running down her face. "You . . . you drove away! You left me . . . and . . . drove away!"

The poison seeps through Inge like a sickness. She will always be poisoned. "I'm sorry," she says. "I'm so sorry . . ."

But Annemarie doesn't hear. She's moaning, crying, rocking again. "I don't know . . . where . . . I am! The soldiers came and . . . I don't know . . ."

"I am going to take care of you," Inge whispers. "I take care of you now. . . ."

And she glances up. The people surrounding them are quiet. Watchful. An old woman shaking her head, a child huddled on a rock, staring, with a bloody bandage around his hand. It looks like he's missing some fingers. And two men are standing back, unsure. Inge's gaze stops on the nearest one. Because she knows him.

The prisoner from Sachsenhausen. He's gotten a shirt and trousers from somewhere, instead of the stripes, but it's him. She sees his recognition and he sees hers. The last words he'd shouted sit loud between them.

What is your name? What was your papa's name?

She looks back to Annemarie. Pulls the coat around her shoulders without bothering with the arms and tries to button it.

"Is something broken?" the old woman says. "She's been beaten."

"She's lost her mind," says the other man, turning up his lip. He's tough, wizened, with several days' growth of beard. "Running around like that . . ."

"She's sick," Inge snaps. Annemarie sobs and the man looks disgusted.

And suddenly, Inge realizes she's seeing spots instead of the coat buttons.

The old woman puts her hands on her hips. "You've got to keep that girl away from the Communists."

I know, Inge thinks.

"They're not bad," argues the former prisoner. "The Soviets set me free."

"Well, they weren't so nice to everybody!" says the old woman. "Look at her! And they'll get this one, too, if they can. We have a cart . . ." she begins, but the disgusted man starts arguing.

"No. Just the four of us. I'm not traveling with strangers . . ."

"We were strangers only yesterday!" the woman says.

"We do not have enough for sharing . . ."

"I can share," Inge whispers. "I have . . ."

But she can't remember what she has. Annemarie is crying quietly on her shoulder, the bottom of the bomb crater teetering left and right, left and right . . .

"We do not leave children by the roadside. Who is in charge here? If you don't . . ."

Then there's a hand shaking Inge's shoulder. A gnarled hand. Someone bending down beside her. The old woman. She doesn't remember how the woman got there.

"Have you eaten?" Her voice is something distant. Disconnected. "What is your name, child?"

What is her name? She doesn't know. She just doesn't know.

And the next thing she sees when she opens her eyes is a cart, turned upside down and propped up with sticks over her head. Rain drums down, dripping along the edges, running in rivulets that soak her feet. The world is dark. Hazy. Vague. But she can see Annemarie's yellow hair beside her, her shoulders rising and falling. And a voice whispers, close, the breath tickling her ear.

"I know who you are. And you have blood on your hands."

She dreams of it when she's sleeping. Blood, shiny on her hands.

The next time she opens her eyes, the sun is bright. Someone must have managed to feed her, because she's stronger. Hungry, but not dizzy. She sits up. She's still underneath the cart, and Annemarie is in the same position. On her side. Sleeping. The old woman squats beside a small fire.

"What did you say your name was?" the woman asks, as if their conversation had never been interrupted.

She looks around the little camp. They're away from the bomb crater, in the trees, the smoke the tiniest trickle in the sky. The boy lies still next to the fire with his wrapped hand, and she can see the former prisoner, his head with its shadow of hair leaning against a tree trunk. Watching her. She knows he was the one who whispered.

I know who you are.

She levels her gaze at the old woman.

"Eva," she replies. "My name is Eva Gerst."

CHAPTER TWENTY-THREE

—— *August 1946* ——

JAKE WAITS, LEANING across the table, his collar loose around his throat. She can smell soap, and the heat of a body that's been dragging a girl through a city in the summer. He smiles.

"So, what's it going to be, Bluebird? Name or Nazis?"

That, Eva thinks, is a more complicated question than he could possibly know. She tucks her hair behind her ear. "You should not call me Bluebird."

"Oh? That's too bad. It suits you. What name should I use, then?"

"Eva."

"Well, at least you didn't say 'Miss Gerst.' After getting rid of a Nazi for you, I'd think we could drop at least a few of the formalities."

He leans back, digging in a pocket, and comes out with a pack of cigarettes and a box of matches. He offers one to Eva, but she shakes her head. Yellow-orange light flashes from the other side of the table.

"I didn't know you smoked," she says.

"I don't," Jake replies, making the cigarette glow. He listens, watching the trumpets tap dance up and down. Finally, he says, "You're not much of a talker, Eva Gerst. So I think I'll get the ball rolling. Are you ready to level?"

She doesn't think she is.

"All right. First question. What do you think?" He tilts his head toward the band.

He's playing a game with her.

Eva looks at the musicians—all shades of black and brown—blowing out their jazz. At Cherry in her cutaway shirt, threading her way through the tables and chairs like the lights are on. Nothing in this room would have been legal under Hitler except the coffee that hasn't come yet. She puts her gaze back on Jake and says, "It isn't Wagner."

Jake laughs. "I guess it isn't. But what do you think?"

"That the time . . ."

"The beat?"

"Yes. The beat is not always where it should be."

He points with the cigarette. "Or maybe the beat is exactly where it should be, only you don't expect it to be there."

"And that," says Eva, "is why you like it."

Jake blows smoke and smiles. "Touché. Second question. Do you play?"

Eva shakes her head.

"Liar. Nobody looks at a piano like you did and doesn't play."

She looks away. "That was a long time ago."

"Fingers don't forget. You should try it out. Lunch is a good time. There aren't any classes, and the girls sit in the kitchen or out on the back patio to eat. I go up there, sometimes, to practice."

"You play the . . . *gitarre.*"

"Guitar, in English. Very good. How did you know?"

"Your fingers." She raises her left hand, rubbing the tips. Jake lifts a brow.

"Anything else?"

"You ask too many questions."

He laughs again, though she'd been serious about that one.

It's a game. But she doesn't understand it. Not yet.

Then Cherry's bright hair appears from the shadows. She has a tray balanced on one palm. "I brought you milk and sugar 'cause I don't know what your girlfriend likes," she yells over the band.

"You're a lifesaver, Cherry."

Cherry puts the coffee on the table while Jake puts down two coins. She scoops them up, careful of her fingernails, and gives Jake a little sideways glance. He smiles, and she sashays off with her tray. She looks smitten. And every day of forty.

Jake dips a spoon into the sugar bowl. "Thank God you're here," he says. "She always thinks I take it black."

Eva watches Jake stir the coffee while holding a cigarette.

"You could ask her for the sugar."

"What? And hurt Cherry's feelings?"

Eva wraps her fingers around her cup. She takes it black, because sugar is expensive. She'd learned that, after the war. She'd learned "take it black" from Mrs. Schaffer. On the boat.

The boat seems like a long time ago. But the war never does.

Eva sips her black coffee and says, "What did you do to Rolf?"

"Who?"

"You know who."

"Do you think I stabbed him with a bread knife and left him stuffed in a closet somewhere in the Columbia Presbyterian Medical Center?"

She keeps her eyes on Jake over the coffee cup.

"Fine. I went and told him someone was being sick beside the elevators."

Eva sets down the cup. Bites her lip. Because she wants to laugh. She should not want to laugh.

"Then I slipped you down the stairs and brought you to a jazz club, which makes perfect sense if you think about it." He throws out an encompassing hand. "No Nazis in sight."

She smiles at the irony. But he had chosen well. They were not going to be overheard.

Eva watches Jake. Thinking. Gray-green eyes under dark brows just over the rim of the coffee cup. Clever fingers stubbing out the cigarette. A smile that says he knows things he shouldn't. And just a little, she shivers.

Jake is dangerous. Maybe in more ways than one.

And she can never let him find out who she really is.

CHAPTER TWENTY-FOUR
—— *May 1945* ——

I AM EVA GERST.

She meets the eyes of the former prisoner, leaning shadowlike against his tree. He knows it's not her name. It had been a dangerous move. But she needs the old woman's help, and she can't be arrested or sent away. Annemarie has to live.

And she will never be Inge again.

You have blood on your hands.

She can see the words forming in his head. She waits for him to decide. To tell what he knows. But he doesn't. He just leans against the tree.

"Well, Eva Gerst, I'm Frau Henkel," says the old woman. "This is my grandson, Michael, and that's Mr. Liebermann over there."

No one mentions the disgusted man. He seems to have gone away.

"We need to move," Frau Henkel says. "We've heard the fighting is over, now that our Führer has gotten what's coming to him. A Red Cross hospital has been set up somewhere on the road between here and Berlin. We have to get there. "

A hospital, she thinks. Annemarie needs a doctor and so does Frau Henkel's grandson. She puts a hand on Annemarie's shoulder. Sleeping, though her eyes are a little open. Someone has put her arms in the trench coat.

"I should go get our things. Annemarie has clothes. It isn't far . . ."

Frau Henkel's skin sags, pulled downward by a frown. As if going to get Annemarie's clothes is some sort of pretense. As if she might sneak away. Never come back.

"I won't leave her." She tightens her grip on Annemarie. "I would never leave her!"

Liebermann stands. "I'll go. See if I can find anything to trade for food."

Dangerous. But's there's nothing else to say.

She gets to her feet, creeps away to relieve herself, and searches the undergrowth until she finds a stone that fits well in her hand. She holds the stone in her palm, her hand in her pocket, limping down the canal path with Liebermann, wary, careful to stay behind him and a little out of reach.

But he doesn't say anything about blood or who she is and he doesn't try to kill her. He doesn't even speak. Just glances once at the Mercedes when she flips back the canvas, then goes on to pick through the litter in the yard. She breathes, lets go of the stone, pushes back her hair. And pauses. She's wearing earrings. Rubies and diamonds. From her father, for her fifteenth birthday.

She turns away and takes them out. Quickly, before Liebermann can see. She doesn't want them. But they have to be worth some money.

They leave the factory with what they can take. She has Annemarie's clothes, all their little collected possessions, her father's papers and a dead girl's identity neatly folded and stuffed behind her waistband, the earrings hidden, pinned to her bra. Liebermann drags a crate full of boots.

He never suggested going inside the factory. Neither did she.

She never wants to see the factory or the car again.

She walks upright down the path, Annemarie's shoes stuffed with bits she cut off the blanket.

I am Eva Gerst, she says inside her head. *I have no country, Annemarie is my family, and I belong only to myself.*

She says it twenty times. Until she's sure.

They right the cart and load up the boots, the little boy, a sleepy Annemarie, and a rather nice mahogany side table that had belonged to Frau Henkel's grandmother. No one wants to pull the weight of the table, but Frau Henkel is in charge. The cart wheels groan, the sun rises over their heads, and they maneuver down a track through the trees and onto the main road.

I am Eva Gerst. I am Eva. . . .

The road to Berlin is the apocalypse.

She'd learned that word from one of her tutors. "The end of the world," he'd said. "Where man has ruined everything just before the coming of God." Her mother fired that tutor, but too late, because now, she knows an apocalypse when she sees one.

Craters, burned cars and tanks, bullet casings. Blasted trees. Smoke and stench and half walls rising from the rubble. She pulls the cart with Liebermann like a matched pair of oxen. Past unburied bodies with crows and dogs, rats, beetles, and flies. Around the ones who have fallen because they can go no farther. Down into the ditch to make way for a Soviet truck—averting their eyes, covering her head in a scarf, covering Annemarie, so the soldiers won't take any notice—then pushing, tugging, dragging the cart up and back onto the road again. They are one squeaking cart in a wandering horde, all wounded, desperate, lost, either going to Berlin or coming from it or something in between.

Frau Henkel decides when and where they stop. To find water. To forage for food in the woods or an abandoned house. To trade away a pair of Nazi boots. One pair of boots is worth one day of meals which is two cans of tuna. And Frau Henkel decides where it might be safe to sleep. Keeping them quiet, out of sight, hovering like a brooding hen with the knife and a stout stick she'd found on the side of the road. Watching over her grandson, the girls, and the boots until she can't keep her eyes open.

And when Frau sleeps, that's when Liebermann decides to speak.

I am Eva, she whispers in her mind, Liebermann's words in her ears. *I am Eva Gerst. . . .*

She'd thought a long time about Liebermann, their first day pulling a cart down the apocalyptic road. About sitting clean and pretty in her father's office, with her mother and Rolf, and the man in the striped clothes who had brought them the wine. The man she'd vaguely thought must be there because he should have learned better. That her good papa was going to teach him to be better.

Liebermann looks different from the prisoner with the wine. Maybe everyone looks different. But it really doesn't matter. He saw her. He knows.

And so he comes. Like a shadow. Like a bad dream every night. To tell her about her father and Sachsenhausen.

He tells her about men who were whipped with salt rubbed in their wounds. About hangings, and shootings, and the ovens belching smoke. About experiments, to see if a certain drug might kill you, or make you see things, or just disintegrate your mind. Experiments to see how long a drug could make a man run—with twenty pounds, forty pounds, eighty-pound packs on his back—run and run until his heart gave out.

But it was Dr. von Emmerich who'd said, what an opportunity. Who'd said have these men run in the boots from our factory, to see the different wear on the different kinds of treads. Make them run on different surfaces. Test even more men this way, and with more kinds of drugs, so Germany could make the very best kinds of boots. Wouldn't that make the men productive and useful?

Von Emmerich was just called the Doctor. And it was the Doctor that no one ever, ever wanted to see. Because the Doctor was not even official. He was a friend of the commandant. A friend of Hitler, with no inspections, no records, no reports. You'd choose a hanging rather than an appointment with the Doctor. Because the others would hurt you. Kill you. But the Doctor, he could speak a word and make you do those things to somebody else.

He could make you say things, think things you would never dream of in a nightmare. Cut up this body on the dissection table. Now cut up this man tied to the chair. Piotr, a loyal man, a brave man, went to see the Doctor and told which of his friends had hidden food. Alfred had kicked the hanging stool out from beneath his own cousin's feet. Done it in front of hundreds of witnesses, and then sworn he hadn't.

And Mina, meek and obedient even while she was starving, who during her sessions with the Doctor was given a word. Her special word. To make her obey. The Doctor said the word, and Mina shot a man. He said the word, and Mina shot herself in the leg. And at the next session, when instructed to shoot the other leg, she shot herself in the head, instead.

Liebermann whispers and whispers. He whispers until she is exhausted. Wasted. Scraped out inside. And only once did she ask him, "How do you know?" Nodding when he replied, "I was there."

But she never asks him to stop. She listens to every word. To every story.

Because Liebermann tells her the truth. Liebermann allows her to know.

It is always better to know.

He tells her twenty-seven names. He helps her memorize them. She chants them before she sleeps, while her father's papers rustle inside her shirt.

I am Eva Gerst. I have no country, Annemarie is my family, and I belong only to myself.

She says it twenty-seven times, for the twenty-seven names, until she is sure.

Until Inge is gone.

Inge is no more.

And after three days on the road, Frau Henkel says, "Eva?"

She looks up, startled. She'd been running her fingers through Annemarie's hair, trying to find fleas by the firelight before Liebermann comes. They're safe inside a house, with the back half still intact and doors they could block, and it's the second time Frau Henkel has spoken. She hasn't gotten used to the name.

"Yes?" Eva replies.

"I don't think a hospital will do her any good. I think she's given up."

She means Annemarie.

The first day riding in the cart, Annemarie had cried, huddled, arms tight around her chest. The second day, she'd murmured and she'd slept. And today, Annemarie hasn't spoken. Her swelling has mostly gone, the brilliance of her bruises dulled and fading. But she'd spent the day staring while the cart rocked, wide blue eyes open to a wide blue sky. She ate only what Eva put in her mouth. Walked only when she was led. She didn't take herself to the toilet. A person who's fallen asleep while they're still awake.

Until Liebermann, or a man passing down the road, or a grandfather trading for their shoes happens to stray too close. Then

Annemarie wakes up. And she screams. Like she had in the bomb crater. Flailing. Yelling herself hoarse. She frightens Michael, who lost two fingers picking up a dead soldier's loaded gun. Liebermann used the kitchen knife she'd taken from the factory to carve Michael a soldier. For bravery. To clutch in his good hand when Annemarie screams.

Annemarie has a mind that is leaking. Draining. The person she'd been seeping away to a place that no one can see.

And Eva knows whose fault it is. She knows exactly.

But Annemarie has to live. Doesn't she?

After four days on the road, Frau Henkel says, "Eva?"

"Yes?"

"Michael has a fever."

Eva nods. They have to find the hospital. The waistband of her skirt is so loose she'd tied a rope around it. To keep her papers in. The earrings are still hidden. She'll sell them or trade them before they starve, but she can't get what they're worth on the road. And she will need something to pay Annemarie's doctor. But there's no one coming from the right direction. No one to tell them which way the hospital might be. Just a long, macabre parade on its way to and from Berlin.

On the fifth day, while they're stopped so she can shade Annemarie's eyes with the blanket, to keep her from staring at the sun, Frau Henkel says, "Eva, when we get to the hospital, even if it's the Red Cross, the Soviets might be in charge. They might not let the doctors treat Michael because we're German. The enemy."

"They will treat a child," says Liebermann. He takes his side of the cart yoke, waits for Eva to take hers, and they give a heave together, making the cart wheels squeak and rattle. They are a good team of oxen. Michael whimpers. Annemarie is silent.

"They might not," Frau Henkel says. "It was like that before, in some places, during the last war."

The last time Germany had been defeated. Eva tries to imagine having hell happen twice. "What did you do, Frau Henkel, during the last war?"

"Starved, nearly. And dragged my grandmother's table all the way from the Rhineland after my brothers were killed."

And now, she thinks, I am dragging it to Berlin for you.

On the sixth day, they come to a stretch of road where the going is easier. The wreckage has been pushed off to one side. Mounds rise up by the roadside, the dead people tucked away neatly underneath them. Where the houses that are not destroyed have people trying to nail their roofs. There are more Soviet trucks, and then Frau Henkel shouts, "Stop! Wait! Stop!"

She takes off like a shot.

Eva exchanges a look with Liebermann. She would have never guessed Frau Henkel could run so fast. If they had known, they might have asked her to pull the cart. Frau Henkel propels herself down the pock-marked road, waving her arms at a truck lumbering slow among the potholes and the ruts. It has a red cross painted on its side. Frau Henkel catches up to it, bangs on the metal. Gears grind to a halt.

A woman sticks her head out the window. She has on a nurse's cap.

"Please!" says Frau Henkel. "A hospital. My grandson. He's just a little boy . . ."

Eva and Liebermann exchange another look and start pulling the cart toward the truck.

"My grandson!" pleads Frau Henkel.

The nurse climbs out and hurries to the cart. Her eyebrows are plucked thin, and she's pushing them daintily together, looking up and down the road. They're standing in a thin spot along the parade, and Eva can see the nurse doesn't want anyone else to catch up and ask for help. There probably isn't room.

"You . . . speak . . . English?" she says. In very bad German. She sounds Swedish.

"I speak it," says Eva, in bad English.

The nurse looks beneath the bandages on Michael's hand while Frau Henkel explains things she can't understand, going much faster than Eva can translate. Then the nurse calls out, and two medics jump out the back of the truck with a stretcher. Two young men in caps. Coming fast to the cart.

"Don't," Eva tries to say. "Stay away from . . ." But one of the medics is already reaching over Annemarie to get to Michael.

Annemarie lets out a scream. A horrible, strangled shriek impossible in its length, rolling and kicking and hitting out against nothing.

The nurse turns, mouth open, but the medics know their job and get Michael up and out of the cart. Eva tries to soothe, hold Annemarie's hand, but she's beyond reason. Eva isn't sure she even hears the words. Michael is being put swiftly and smoothly onto the truck, Mrs. Henkel chasing, calling out instructions in German.

And then Annemarie goes quiet. Suddenly, in mid-scream. Like someone flipped a switch. But her flailing doesn't stop. Now it's rhythmic. Her back arching up and down in a way that is unnatural, body beating itself against the cart.

Annemarie is dying. She was supposed to live, and Annemarie is dying.

"Help!" Eva shouts.

The nurse barks a word in Swedish, the medics come rushing

back with the stretcher, and Annemarie is surrounded. Another shout. Someone produces a medical bag, and the nurse turns Annemarie on her side and puts a needle in her.

Eva watches, too stunned to feel any of her fractured pieces. Annemarie relaxes. Her body quiets. Then the medics do the same thing to her as they had to Michael. Up and out, onto the stretcher, and away to the back of the truck.

"Wait," Eva whispers.

The nurse picks up the medical bag and trots toward the truck. The medics shut the back doors.

"Wait!" Eva yells. "I'm coming!"

The nurse turns around. "No," she says in bad German. "Sick only."

"But . . ."

The nurse climbs into the truck. The gears change, the motor chugs, and the truck lumbers off.

They're leaving. Annemarie is leaving. Without her.

And then she isn't stunned anymore. She is the inferno.

The truck lurches forward, moving slow through a pothole, and Eva runs. If Frau Henkel can catch it, then she can, too, even in her stuffed shoes.

She flies down the road, like she's on air, like she has wings. She hears voices calling, but her anger has no time for them. The truck picks up speed, then slows again as it dips down into a rut. Michael's carved soldier is on the ground, dropped into the mud. Eva bends down and snatches it with barely a pause in her stride. The truck pitches downward as Eva grabs the back door handle, just getting a knee on the flattened bumper.

One foot underneath and she's up, hanging on to whatever she can grab. She pulls down the handle. The door flies open and she nearly falls off. But she doesn't. She sways and steps inside, reaching out to pull the door shut again with a bang.

The truck finishes navigating the potholes and shifts to the next gear. The young medic behind her just shakes his head and goes back to work on Michael, Annemarie lying quiet and still on a higher bunk. Eva puts the muddy soldier in Michael's good hand.

And when she looks out the back window, palm flat to the glass, she can see Liebermann and Frau Henkel, standing still beside the cart. Just watching them go.

CHAPTER TWENTY-FIVE

—— *August 1946* ——

JAKE SETS DOWN his coffee cup. She sets down hers.

She hasn't given him an answer about her name or Nazis, because she doesn't have one.

"You're a strange girl, Eva Gerst," he says. "Interesting, but strange."

He lights another cigarette. The music has become a saxophone's slow sway, though she hadn't noticed the moment it changed its mood.

"Want to know why I think that?"

She's not sure she does.

"See, when I get an assignment, usually I take my new friend around town, show them how to use the subways, count money. Maybe take them to a museum or a baseball game. Until they settle in or find some place to move on to. And it's interesting, right? Nobody cares where you come from at Powell House. So I've been assigned to a Catholic and an atheist and others who never said. To immigrants from Latvia, Poland, and Yugoslavia. Older, usually. Grandmother, grandfather types. You wouldn't believe the stories. But you . . ." He points with the cigarette. "I asked for you. Do you know why?"

Eva shakes her head.

"Because you're German. We don't get many Germans anymore. Either Uncle Sam won't let them in or Hitler did his worst, right? And I wanted to talk to a German. Because even though my grandfather came here from Berlin a long time ago, his brothers didn't. And my uncle David, he went back for business, with his wife and kids, back in 1934. So uncles, aunts, cousins, there were more than twenty of them in Berlin, and do you know how many my mother has heard from since the war?"

Eva shakes her head again. The tiniest of shakes.

"Zero. Because they're dead. All of them. That's what we think."

He's probably right. But Eva doesn't say it. She feels sick.

"So I wanted to talk to someone from Berlin. Find out what happened that wasn't in the newspapers. I didn't think they'd know my family, but . . . I just wanted to know. You can understand that, right?"

This time she nods. It's always better to know. She digs a fingernail into her palm.

"So last week, I get into the car with Bets to go pick up this interesting girl. A pretty little thing who looks like she'd just love to knock my block off. And what do you think happens? A greasy guy smoking on the corner at the ferry shows up all the way across town, doing the same thing at Gabertelli's. Then he follows us to Powell House in a rusty car. And then again, right out of the front door, and I have to lose him in an ice-cream parlor. And not only that . . ."

Jake leans forward, face lit by the orange glow.

". . . that same day I pick her up, I'm having a nice time, drinking coffee, and I see this girl sneaking down the stairs like she means to steal the silver. And when I go down to check on her, there's another guy in the kitchen, talking tough and calling her by a nickname, "Bluebird." A guy who changes his accent as soon as Olive walks in.

Then this same strange and interesting girl drops something in a vase outside her room. A card with a bird drawn on it in blue ink, and the name of Mr. Cruickshanks. And when I called that number . . ."

Eva digs the nail deeper into her palm.

". . . the guy on the other end says he doesn't know any Cruickshanks and tells me to get lost. And if all this hasn't been interesting enough, this very same girl—just an hour ago now—goes running off down the hall of a hospital and hides in a closet, because the janitor is a Nazi. Not to mention that I'm pretty sure she's got the bread knife nobody could find in the kitchen—the bread knife that had been sitting on the table right in front of her—tucked away in that purse, on which she has cut her finger."

Eva looks down at the nick on her finger. Jake sits back.

"Okay," he says, exhaling smoke. "I laid it on the table. So where are you going to start? Mr. Cruickshanks?"

CHAPTER TWENTY-SIX

—— *February 1946* ——

"GO ON IN, MISS GERST," SAYS THE WOMAN BEHIND THE DESK. Or at least, that's what Eva thinks she says. Eva has been working on her English, but the woman is difficult to understand behind the scarf wound around and around her head and face. Eva envies that scarf, though she'd give more for a pair of pants. Her legs are bare, and the snow blowing in beneath the door does not melt.

She has no time for her own envy. She is much too busy with fear.

Eva doesn't know why she's in the camp director's office. There's no reason for her to be in the director's office. But she can guess, and that is why she's afraid.

Eva helps Annemarie to stand, an army blanket pinned over her head and shoulders like a cloak. Her eyes are lovely, the way they're framed. Clear blue. And empty.

"No, dear. Just you," says the muffled woman. Eva pauses, and then turns Annemarie around. Like they're walking out the door. "Oh, never mind!" the woman says, waving a gloved hand. She's shivering.

Eva knocks on the office door, smiling steadily at Annemarie. Annemarie does not react well to fear. And then someone says, "Come in," in German and she knows she is in trouble.

Inside the office is something wonderful. A heater, with a few glowing coals. The room is deliciously warm, and a stranger sits at the camp director's desk. A thin man, with a thinner, black mustache, wearing a civilian suit, his heavy wool coat and gloves thrown unneeded over the chair behind him.

Eva turns Annemarie's back to the desk, quickly pulls a chair close to the heater.

"Annemarie," she says calmly. She waits for the empty eyes to make contact with hers. "Sit here."

Annemarie sits, her back to the man, and she opens her hand. Eva lays three buttons on her palm. Annemarie looks at the buttons, and when Eva turns her attention to the man again, he is watching with amused interest. He smiles, stands.

"Miss Gerst? Can I offer you a seat?" The German is formal. Official. Fear jolts through Eva's veins in tiny shocks.

"No, thank you. It would be better if I stand here."

"I see. Annemarie, is it? You take your friend everywhere, do you?"

Annemarie whimpers. She doesn't like the man's voice, but she concentrates on her buttons, like Eva taught her.

He looks at his papers. "Has she been to a hospital?"

"Yes. At a Red Cross camp and in Berlin. They said she has had a bad war."

"Did she see the doctor here?"

"Yes."

"And what did he say?"

"That she has had a bad war."

"Ah." He consults his papers one more time and says, "My name is Mr. Cruickshanks. I am an American, here doing special service for the United States government, working with the German people."

He smiles, stretching the thin mustache. She was right to be afraid. This man is hunting Nazis.

"And where were you before the Düppel Center?"

"With the International Red Cross. Until the field hospital was closed."

"And before that you were in . . ."

"The hospital in Berlin. With Annemarie."

"And before?"

"Dresden," she lies.

He holds out a hand for her papers, and Eva takes them automatically from the pocket of her coat. Her identity papers are brand-new. Crisp. With a photograph of herself. There was an office here for such things. She is Eva Gerst now.

Sometimes, when Eva glances at her new photograph, she thinks it could be Inge. Then she doesn't know the girl in the picture at all. Mr. Cruickshanks barely looks at it. He smiles pleasantly.

"And you have been doing well here in Berlin, in the American Zone?"

Since Annemarie left the hospital, Eva has learned how to scour pots, fumigate clothing, sew a hem, and comb lice from children's hair. She can disinfect medical equipment and knows how to erect a quonset hut. And she has done it while managing Annemarie at her side, working among the survivors of the concentration camps, the slave labor factories, people whose families and villages were obliterated by Nazis who believed they had no right to exist. People who would happily see her shot.

She doesn't make friends with them. They should not be her friend. But she listens to them. All of them. Every story.

And she gets two meals each day—including one cup of milk and one tin of meat—and the room she shares with five other women has walls during the worst winter anyone can remember. Some are in tents. Others are dead.

"Yes, I'm doing well here," Eva replies.

"What can you tell me about your parents?"

She tells a noncommittal story about living with grandparents, about not knowing much about her parents, in case Mr. Cruickshanks knows something she doesn't. Which is likely, since she doesn't actually know anything at all.

"Hmmm," he replies. "And you are sure this is correct?"

He looks her in the face this time. Straight into her eyes. Eva tilts her head. Looks right back at him. Lies don't make her flinch anymore. Especially when the truth will not help you survive.

"Yes. Very sure."

"I have information," he says, "that the daughter of a prominent Nazi family is using the name Eva Gerst."

Annemarie whimpers. She has heard the change in tone. Eva puts the fourth button—the blue one, held back for this purpose—into Annemarie's palm. But she doesn't take her eyes off Mr. Cruickshanks.

"Then you must have the wrong Eva Gerst. I would think there's more than one."

"Yes, yes," says Mr. Cruickshanks. "I imagine we do. But you can understand why we are interested, of course. Dr. von Emmerich . . ."

"That is his name?" Eva asks. "The Nazi you are looking for?"

"Correct. He is a man my government would very much like to find. You are familiar with the trials at Nuremberg, of course. There will be a trial for the Nazi doctors as well. For crimes against humanity."

And that is where her father belongs. On trial. She would give him to Mr. Cruickshanks if she could. Only she can't. And she knows what has happened to the other families, the ones whose mothers didn't kill themselves. Arrested. Exiled. Farm laborers in France.

Annemarie is quiet now, focused on the new button. Eva is quiet, too. Without Eva, Annemarie will not eat. And they will put her somewhere. A hospital. An institution.

She knows what the Nazis did to people in institutions. They murdered them. Because they were useless. That's what people like her father said. A waste.

She will not let Annemarie go to an institution.

"We are also looking for someone else," Mr. Cruickshanks says. "Anna Ptaszynska. Do you know anyone by that name?"

He's staring straight at her again. Looking hard into her eyes. And Eva knows that this time, for a moment, she flinched. She blanks her expression, replaces it with curiosity. Shakes her head.

"Who is she?"

"A long-term patient of von Emmerich's, we believe. Someone with whom he had fairly regular contact. A faithful Nazi. The daughter and Miss Ptaszynska, they would have the best information for finding him, you see."

Eva nods. Innocent. Wide-eyed. Mr. Cruickshanks is observing every move of her every muscle.

"Well, that's all for now, Miss Gerst. Thank you for coming."

She gathers up Annemarie and is not sorry to go even if the office is lovely and warm.

Liebermann. He's the only one who knows, and he has been talking. She doesn't blame him for talking. He wants the Doctor to pay. But he is going to ruin everything.

She needs to think. Think.

She waits. Does her turn in the kitchen. Breaks the ice in the washing bucket and warms it for Annemarie. And three hours before dawn, while the moon shines down through the frost on their window, while the other women are sniffling and shivering in their cots, Eva sits on the freezing floor and carefully rips out the lining stitches of her duffel bag. She'd been given the duffel bag at the hospital, and she likes it. She'll have to sew it back, and that will mean finding thread. But for now, Eva reaches between the lining and the canvas and pulls out her father's papers.

She's read these notes many times now. Every word. Sometimes she needs to read them. When she is sore inside. Missing the feeling of having a papa who loves her. When she needs to remember.

Anna Ptaszynska died July 11, 1934.
She is gone now. She is no more.

Cruickshanks is mistaken. Her father had killed Anna, trying to train her to be someone "better." To make her mind forget who she was. To make her do things she would never do. Like what Liebermann had said about the prisoners. Controlling them. It is cruel to read, unbearable, but it's all here, written in her father's slanting hand. She pulls her feet underneath her, trying to stay warm. What could Cruickshanks think he knows?

Eva reads the papers again. "She is no more" is a strange thing to say for a scientist, lacking her father's usual precision. And he doesn't say how Anna died. Eva had assumed starvation, because the notes said Anna had stopped eating. But, then again, she doesn't have all the notes.

Someone her father had regular access to, Mr. Cruickshanks said. That must be true. These were personal observations. And "faithful Nazi." Even the best of German four-year-olds could not have been called that. Had Anna survived? Had she survived as . . . someone else? Is that why she was "gone"? No more? Like Inge?

A faithful Nazi.

Anna Ptaszynska.

Annemarie turns in her cot, shivering beneath her coat and blanket, the moonlight shining on her hair. Eva tucks her in more tightly. She is so cold sitting on the floor that her toes have gone numb. There's ice on the inside as well as the outside of the glass, despite the bodies and breath in the crowded room, and all the other cots are pushed to the opposite wall. As far from Annemarie as they can get.

Because they are afraid of her.

The day Inge drove the stolen car, Annemarie had said Dr. von Emmerich was the "nicest man." How had she known that? When had Annemarie ever even met her father?

Anna.

Annemarie. Who looked nothing like her brothers and sisters. Or her parents. Why had she never noticed that before?

A faithful Nazi.

The wind comes right through the walls. But Eva stays where she is. There's something she should remember. Something about violets. Something about a bird. But the thoughts dissolve like her freezing breath.

Anna Ptaszynska. She used to get a stomachache every time she read the name, but she's practiced so many times now, she can think the words without pain.

Anna Ptaszynska.

Eva folds the papers, but she doesn't put them in the lining of her bag. She puts them in her coat, which she wears to bed, climbing into the cot to put her arms around Annemarie.

She doesn't sleep. She thinks, while the minutes tick and the sun moves toward dawn. She warms, and Annemarie warms, and Eva's mind is a roiling mass of thought.

Anna Ptaszynska.

She has to take care of Annemarie.

The next day, when Eva brings Annemarie back from the kitchen tent, nose running and fingers half-frozen, the Doctor's notes still tucked in her coat, her duffel bag is not where she left it. Her cot has been moved.

The day after that, Eva makes arrangements to catch a truck to a camp in the British Zone. She also makes arrangements to ride in a transport on its way to the French Zone. But she only takes Annemarie with her on one of them.

I am Eva Gerst. I have no country, Annemarie is my family, and I belong only to myself.

Annemarie is her fault and her penance. And she will do anything. Everything. Whatever it takes to protect her.

Cruickshanks can go chase Dr. von Emmerich all he wants.

CHAPTER TWENTY-SEVEN

August 1946

JAKE SMOKES HIS cigarette in the dark, and the music is a sinuous dance that reminds Eva of a swaying cobra. She'd seen a film once, with a bare-chested man playing a flute, making a snake dance its way out of a basket.

Where had she seen that? Hitler wouldn't have allowed films like that in the cinema.

Jake smiles. "Say, you wouldn't be stalling, by any chance, would you?"

She's not stalling. She's thinking. She has to think.

Jake had "laid it on the table," and Jake isn't any Cruickshanks. Or one of the others who wants her father. He's just a boy. A pretty-eyed, sweet-tongued, good-natured, dangerous boy, who notices absolutely everything. Who knows more than is good for him. Who's given her very little room to maneuver.

He could help her. He might even think it was justice.

He'd be making a rotten deal.

Though not near as rotten as the one she'd had to make.

Cruickshanks had said no talking. But she doesn't belong to Cruickshanks. She belongs to herself. And what she needs wouldn't be so dangerous. Not more than what Jake already knows.

Cruickshanks just can't find out about it.

And Jake cannot find out about her.

Jake is waiting for an answer, expectant. Watching her think through the dark. She can smell his smoke, but she can't see it.

What Jacob Katz should be doing right now is running for a train. Jumping in a fast car. Hopping a plane across the ocean. Anything and everything to get away from her.

The band goes on with its snake dance.

Eva tucks her hair behind her ear and pushes the coffee cup aside, leaning her arms on the table. She has the full attention of the beautiful eyes.

"You said," she whispers, "that you chose to be my friend."

"That's true."

"You . . . volunteered. To help me with what I need."

"Exactly."

"I need something."

Eva's whisper is so soft, Jake has to lean in close to hear.

"I need you to help me catch a Nazi."

CHAPTER TWENTY-EIGHT

—— *April 1946* ——

EVA IS ANKLE-DEEP in mud when the soldiers come for her. The potato field had been a parking lot before the war, but now the potatoes are a better use. Annemarie enjoys the mud, and they're all so dirty that no one much minds if she is more so. Eva has pushed fifty-six chunks of potato into the soft earth to sprout, when someone calls her name.

She straightens. Two soldiers. American.

She knows she is in trouble.

"Come, Annemarie," she whispers, then to the soldiers in English. "Could you . . . walk behind. Please. Ten steps away."

"Do it," one of the women in the field calls out. "Or the pretty one will have a fit and you'll be sorry!" Only she says it in French and the soldiers don't understand her.

But they must not think the two of them pose much of a threat. They do as Eva asks, walking about ten steps behind to the director's office. Annemarie drags her feet. Whimpering. She doesn't want to leave the field. Eva checks her pockets.

She doesn't have any buttons. Her fingers tingle. They want to shake.

She could lose Annemarie today.

They don't wait outside the director's door this time, and the secretary isn't there. Neither is the director. Just Mr. Cruickshanks. With no greetings. No niceties. No heater. Just two chairs and the mud that she and Annemarie have tracked all over the floor. Eva turns a chair to the side, facing away from the men.

"Sit here, Annemarie," she whispers, and then to the soldiers. "Stay back . . . away from her. Please." Annemarie holds out her hand, but Eva has nothing to put in it.

Mr. Cruickshanks slams down a piece of clean, white paper and slides it across the desk. Eva tilts her head. It's a very nice drawing of her face. Her hair had been shorter then. And were her eyes really that big? She raises her gaze. Gives Cruickshanks a quizzical brow.

He smacks his palm on the desk. And there is another piece of paper. And this is Annemarie. Awake and alive. The Annemarie who squealed when Inge drove too fast.

Liebermann is good. She should have known he was an artist when he carved that soldier. Michael had been so happy to have it before he died. Eva puts a hand on Annemarie's arm. Her breathing has picked up. Short, little rasps.

"A very credible witness," says Cruickshanks, in German so the soldiers won't know what's going on, "has signed a statement saying he saw this girl, Inge von Emmerich, visit her father, Dr. Otto von Emmerich, in the Sachsenhausen Concentration Camp in the spring of 1944. The witness also traveled with this girl, then going by the name of Eva Gerst, for several days in May of 1945. With them was her friend,"—he puts a finger on Annemarie's penciled face—"who is a mental deficient, for whom Miss von Emmerich showed a special care and affection."

Eva ignores the drawings and picks up a paperweight from the desk, heavy, made of swirling blue glass. "May I take this?" she asks in English, putting it in Annemarie's hands. Annemarie stops whimpering.

Mr. Cruickshanks's thin mustache is tight against his lips. "Do you deny it?"

"Yes," she replies.

Mr. Cruickshanks comes around the desk and hits her. A smart, open palm slap on the side of her face. But Eva knows how to be hit. He hits her again, in the same place, and this time her mouth fills with blood. Boots shuffle in the back of the room.

The third time he hits her, he knocks Eva to one side. Almost to her knees.

And Annemarie explodes from her chair.

She tackles Mr. Cruickshanks, knocking him down, pummeling him with the paperweight. She gets a good blow in on the side of his face, raking her fingernails down the other cheek before the two soldiers are on her. Her screams are terrible, and then she is fighting the soldiers, too. Hammering them with the paperweight. Eva stumbles toward the melee on the floor.

"Don't touch her!" she yells in German, trying to shove the soldiers away.

They don't budge, not until Mr. Cruickshanks extracts himself from a shrieking Annemarie and yells for the soldiers to step back.

Eva takes away the paperweight, dropping it to the floor, helping Annemarie to her feet, her back to the rest of the room while she screams. "It's all right," Eva whispers, soothing, wiping at the blood running down her chin. "I'm here. You are all right . . ."

But she is startled. Annemarie would have killed Mr. Cruickshanks if the others had let her. Bashed in his head.

Mr. Cruickshanks wipes his cheek with a handkerchief. "Corporal Pruitt," he yells over Annemarie's noise. "Help Miss Gerst and Miss

Toborentz to the infirmary. Miss Toborentz has been attacking people. She has bloodied Miss Gerst's lip considerably."

The soldiers take them, stoney-faced and eyes forward. Annemarie yells. The doctor gives her a sedative, and dabs something stinging on Eva's cut lip, telling her she will be bruised. Eva sits beside Annemarie's bed while she sleeps, serene. Eva watches the clock.

She can guess what is coming.

A different American soldier arrives at precisely 3:00 a.m., whispers to the nurse, and they both look at Eva. Eva gazes one last time at Annemarie, and then she follows the soldier, dragging her feet through the mud.

The director's office has been put to rights, the mud and blood Eva left on the floor all cleaned away. The paperweight is gone. But the drawings are still on the desk. And Mr. Cruickshanks has a black eye, two angry scratches mottling his cheek. The soldier leaves and shuts the door, and Eva is sorry about that. Witnesses—even soldiers who have to do what they're told—are better than nothing.

Mr. Cruickshanks stands. Comes across the room. Walks around and stands directly behind her. Eva lifts her chin.

"May I take your coat?" he says. In flawless German.

She lets him take it. He beckons her to the chair, and she leaves a perfect set of muddy footprints across the floor. She sees Cruickshanks see it. But he only smiles.

"Fräulein von Emmerich," he says. "We began badly. Very . . ."

"My name is Eva Gerst."

Cruickshanks's smile widens. He looks lopsided with his black eye. "I will be using real names tonight, Fräulein von Emmerich. Not pretend ones." He reaches somewhere below the desk and brings up a bottle and two glasses. "Could I offer you some wine?"

Eva stares at the bottle and remembers that, earlier that evening,

Mr. Cruickshanks had been hitting her in the face. She shakes her head no.

"Are you sure?" He makes a show of using the corkscrew. "So, Fräulein von Emmerich, how are you enjoying life in Biberach? The French Zone is a long way out from Berlin, isn't it?"

He pours himself a glass.

"It took a good deal of time to find you. And let me congratulate you on having a friend like Miss Toberentz. Nazis are not known for their love of the impaired, and I admit it threw me completely off the scent."

Her anger sparks. Flares. But she does not choose it. Not yet.

"We are going to be direct tonight, Fräulein, because frankly, you have wasted enough of my time. If Dr. von Emmerich goes on trial at Nuremberg, he will be convicted. There was enough evidence in his papers at Sachsenhausen to ensure it. If he is not executed, he will spend his life in prison."

He should be convicted. He should be hung. Fair is fair. It would be justice. It would be a relief.

It would also be painful. And that thought sends the guilt creeping up her neck.

Cruickshanks sips his wine. "Your father, however, is a brilliant man. A brilliant scientist. What a shame, to throw away all that potential. What a blow to scientific achievement. Would you not agree?"

He watches. Waits for Eva to look up.

"Do you know, Fräulein, what your father can do?"

She shakes her head. What she does know, she's not going to tell him.

Cruickshanks leans back, his one good eye dreamy on the ceiling.

"Imagine, Fräulein, if the mind was a moldable object. If

memories could be plucked out"—he snaps his fingers—"and replaced. Imagine if we could say a word, and have a captured soldier walk back across the lines and disable his own country's weapons. If an agent never blew their cover, because they were unaware that they were an agent at all? Imagine if a man like Hitler could have been removed years ago with one of his own officials, sent back to do the work of all those armies . . ."

Imagine, Eva thinks, having all those people do exactly what you tell them.

"What if soldiers could forget shell-shock. Forget fatigue. What if we could turn off murderous tendencies? Lock up greed . . ."

You could make them "better," Eva thinks. And who gets to decide who is better and who isn't? Her father had taught her to ask that question. Though he would probably be surprised to know it.

"We could stop wars, Fräulein von Emmerich. Long before the first soldier dies. That is what your father can do for the world."

Mr. Cruickshanks sets down the wineglass. Leans forward on the desk. "All that potential, all that good, lost because a brilliant man goes to the gallows for crimes that weren't even considered crimes by his own country when they were committed. Don't you think that is a little unfair?"

He really should not have said the word *fair*.

"The United States government does not wish to condemn your father. We want to work with him. To see his research continue. But we have to do it quickly. There are others who want this information just as much as we do. And I think you have good reason not to want your father's work to go to the Soviet Union, isn't that so, Fräulein? I believe"—he smiles—"that we are in a position to help each other."

He's played her wrong, Eva thinks. He's played her wrong in every way.

"Dr. von Emmerich is running. His life is on the line. And you can help him. Share information. Tell me about Anna Ptaszynska. This is someone we would like to find almost as much as the Doctor."

"I don't know anyone by that name."

"Are you certain? Anna Ptaszynska is your father's first experiment. His most successful experiment. We believe she has already proven her worth."

She whispers, "I know nothing of his work."

"Ah. But you would know where the Doctor might see patients. Unconventional patients. Outside of a hospital or the camp. For research. Did he keep files at home?"

What Cruickshanks wants is right behind her, sewn into the lining of the coat he hung on the back of the door.

"We believe that Anna Ptaszynska was kept close," he says. "Hidden. She is, therefore, the only survivor of the Doctor's experiments. And we believe she may still respond to your father's orders. She could be put to work. Right now. For the cause of peace."

Eva thinks of Mina, shooting herself in the leg. That's what Cruickshanks wants. In the cause of peace. A killer. A killer who will do exactly as she's told.

Eva lifts her eyes. "Just because this Anna was alive at the end of the war does not mean she is alive now."

"Many things can happen during war, of course." Cruickshanks shrugs. "Do you know where he might have taken her? Do you think he planned his escape?"

"If you think I am a daughter who would know so much about her father, I'm surprised you think Dr. von Emmerich would have escaped without me."

"It is possible that the Doctor believes you are dead."

Cruickshanks smiles, and she raises a brow. Yes. That is possible.

He runs his finger around the rim of the glass. "My government wants to make a deal with you, Fräulein. We have reason to believe the Doctor has escaped from Germany and made his way to America. We propose to take you out of this camp, create the right paperwork, and book passage to New York, where you will help us find Dr. von Emmerich and facilitate contact. Find him, bring him in, and we will set him up with an office, a generous income, and a place to work. A nice apartment for the two of you. A new life, Fräulein, in a country that has not seen war. Not like yours has."

Eva looks around at the empty office. In the middle of the night. "And is everyone in your government offering this deal?"

Cruickshanks smiles like she aced a serve in tennis. "Not everyone can be so forward thinking," he says. "Not everyone has the vision. And we are dealing with secrets here. But rest assured, if the Doctor were to fall into the hands of the British, or even our own side, and be taken to trial, we have ways of handling the situation. The charges will be dropped or he will be acquitted. Watch the trial of Dr. Kurt Blome, and you will see."

So the threat of trial was nothing. Even if another country catches him, there will be no justice.

No justice anywhere. For any of them.

"And what if I dislike your . . . deal?"

Mr. Cruickshanks sighs. "Since I would prefer that no one else knows of this conversation, I suppose you could find yourself very far away. We have prisons where you will never see the light of day again, if you'd like that better."

Eva stands, walks to the desk, and pours herself a glass of wine. Mr. Cruickshanks watches carefully. Smiling with his little mustache. She takes the glass to the window and looks out. Thinking. There's a blush of orange on the horizon, a glow between the land and the clouds, a rumble just on the edge of hearing. It could be a stormy dawn. Or it could be a city burning. She wonders if she could tell the difference.

She tastes the wine. It stings the cut on her lip. And goes straight to her head. Bubbles to the surface while she boils below.

Twenty-seven names. She whispers them in her mind. She remembers the dead bodies at Sachsenhausen.

And they want her father to do it again. And again.

More Annas. More Minas. Shooting. Blowing up trains. Assassinating who they're told. Killers who have no idea what they've done. Cruickshanks says her father's research will stop wars. But it can also start them. It can very easily start them.

And there will be no justice. Fair is fair, and this is not fair.

Lightning flashes in the distance. Eva lowers her glass.

Unless she, Eva Gerst, can make it fair. Unless she is the one who dispenses the justice. She doesn't know if she can do it. But if she doesn't, who will?

No one.

It's a terrible deal. Stinking and rotten. And she is going to take it.

And break it. Because it is justice.

Because she has to protect Annemarie.

Thunder breaks, another wave of sound across the sky. Thunder always gives her a thrill of fear now. Thunder can sound like so many things. The morning is getting darker.

"What do I have to do?" she says. She hears the creak of the chair.

"Nothing, for now. Arrangements will be made, though it may take a little time. You will be contacted, and when you are, you will cooperate. Mr. Cruickshanks will come speak with you every now and again, to see if anything new has occurred . . ."

Eva looks over her shoulder. "Mr. Cruickshanks? But not you?"

"Oh, no. I'm not the only Mr. Cruickshanks."

Of course, he isn't.

"You'll do well, I think. Dr. von Emmerich is smart, but you are not exactly stupid, are you, my dear?"

Eva doesn't answer this. She watches the gathering storm.

"I do not travel alone," she says. "It's both or neither."

Mr. Cruickshanks sighs. "Oh, we know, Fräulein. We know." He takes a pencil and paper from the desk. "How do you come to know Miss Toberentz, by the way? She has been a friend for a long time?"

"No. Just someone I met on the road."

"Someone you will pull around Germany in an oxcart, that you will not travel without, and who most conveniently attacks those who attack you. How fortunate. Annemarie is such a lovely name, isn't it?"

Eva stiffens.

"But she will be getting a new one for traveling. We think it best. Brigit Heidelmann is what we've chosen . . ."

They suspect. Already. But they're not sure, or they would have Annemarie right now. And they've already chosen a new name. They'd known all along she was going to take their rotten deal. How could she have done anything else? And *Brigit* is ridiculous. It isn't even German.

". . . and you may travel under Eva Gerst," Cruickshanks is saying. "You've done such an excellent job with your papers, there's no need to do them over. But we do not write down names in my department, Fräulein. This project will be known as Bluebird, and Bluebird will be you."

Bluebird. A project named Bluebird.

I am Eva Gerst.

And I am Bluebird.

And I am going to kill my father.

CHAPTER TWENTY-NINE

—— *August 1946* ——

JAKE DOESN'T MOVE. He doesn't take his eyes off Eva. The saxophone is running riot through the empty club.

"You are asking me," he says, "to help you catch Nazis?"

"A Nazi."

One side of his mouth lifts. And then the other. He sits back, shaking his head. "I said you were a strange and interesting girl, Eva Gerst. I did say it."

He reaches again for the pack of cigarettes and pulls one out, lights up the dark with a flash. "Don't tell my mother how many of these things I've smoked today. She thinks I should be spending the money on textbooks or something."

Eva agrees with his mother. The two stubs in the ashtray would nearly make a whole cigarette. And in winter in Berlin, a cigarette could buy something. Maybe even a piece of bread.

"So this Cruickshanks," Jake says, "who showed up at Powell House, he's some kind of . . . what?"

"He is . . . interested in Nazis that have . . . escaped."

"And he works for who? Uncle Sam?"

She shrugs. "It's what he says."

"And he wants you to help because . . ."

"I was in a . . . special place . . . to know."

"You mean, back in Germany, you were places where you could recognize someone. Like a guard." His brows furrow. "And today, your first real day out, you see one. Is the whole city infested?"

"What is 'infested'?"

"Like when you have too many of something in one place. Like too many rats."

Infested. An infestation. Of Nazis.

"The hospital was a place . . ." Eva struggles for the word. Why is it so much harder to lie in English? "I had been asked to go there. But it was a . . ."

"Coincidence?"

She nods.

Jake exhales. Brows together. His fingers tap the table.

"You know what? If I hadn't seen you shaking like a leaf in that closet, I'd never have believed you. What about the guy that followed us this morning?"

"They are together. The same," she replies.

They're trying to keep watch. So she won't go off and do things on her own.

Which is exactly what she's going to do.

"And how about 'Bluebird?' Is that supposed to be . . . what? Some kind of secret lingo? A code?"

She doesn't know what this means, but it doesn't really matter.

Jake shakes his head, chuckling. "You've got to be kidding me," he says. But he's not really talking to her. He's thinking.

"So this must be somebody they want. Really want. Somebody that belongs on trial. Like at Nuremberg."

Yes, Eva thinks. Someone that belongs on trial.

"Somebody dangerous." Jake shrugs. "All right. Let's put him away, then. What do you need?"

Eva opens her mouth, and then she closes it again. Jake leans across the table.

"Come on, Bluebird," he says. "You're my assignment. Tell me what you need."

"A name and address," she whispers. "For the man sweeping floors."

"That's it?" He grins. "Easy."

"And the days, the times."

"His work schedule. Sure."

Eva bites her lip. She shouldn't have done it. She shouldn't have brought him into this. She's opening her mouth to say so when the band finishes with a blast of fanfare that is not all that different from the one Jake had played for Brigit. The sudden absence of sound is deafening.

"Let's take off," Jake whispers, leaving the cigarette in the tray. "They'll bring up the lights in a second and Cherry will want to talk about the band."

Eva grabs her purse and slides out of the booth. He puts his hand on her back again, showing her the way in the dark. Through the curtain, up the stairs, and out the black door without seeing Cherry.

And nothing looks the same on the street. The sun is gone, the strip of sky between the buildings the color of twilight. When they turn the corner, the neons are already glowing, and a rumble rolls through the air, a brief tremor through the sidewalk.

Jake picks up the pace. "We should try to make the train before this hits." Then he looks back. "You okay?"

Eva nods, catching up with him, letting the adrenaline work its way through her arms and legs. Thunder can sound like so many things.

They pass people on the street, hurrying, glancing at the sky, turning up their collars, and halfway to the subway station, the rain falls. All at once. Like the sky upended a bucket.

Jake grabs her hand again and they run, dashing past the awnings and doorways where others have taken shelter, over bottles and puddles and wet newspapers, shoulders hunched against the running water. She should have worn the brown hat.

Or maybe not.

Some of the children have stayed out in the rain, squealing and splashing.

They go together down the stairs to the station, feet in time, into the short tunnel leading to the subway. The rain is coming down at the entrance like a waterfall, running into gutters and drains. Eva pushes away the hair plastered to her forehead, Jake shaking his head and slinging water off his hands. He looks like he's been dunked in the bay.

"So how do you like swimming in Harlem?" he says.

She laughs.

On the train, they're not the only people dripping. Jake sits next to her and says, "Still got that handkerchief?"

"I bled on it."

"It wasn't much."

She finds the handerkerchief in her purse and Jake folds it, clean side outward, using it to catch the water still running down his neck. He smiles.

He hasn't shaved.

He is dangerous.

And then the man standing next to them, slouching with a sodden newspaper pinned beneath his arm, eyes Eva and mutters, "Kraut."

Jake gives him a long gaze. "Hey," he says. "Why don't you just shut it?"

The man decides to shut it and stands somewhere else. Jake shrugs once and smiles.

He never did ask why she has the bread knife.

Then the train slows at 72nd Street, and Jake says he bets the rain will have stopped. That they can walk the rest of the way. They dart through the doors and up the steps from the subway, and Jake is right. The clouds are shredding, the pavement steaming beneath their feet. But instead of taking her down the busy city block, he turns into a park. An enormous park Eva hadn't even known was there. Full of wet grass and iron rails and trees dripping with the last of the rain.

They don't hurry down the paved walkways. If one of the Mr. Cruickshanks is following, he already knows where she sleeps. They pass gray squirrels, gray boulders, two old men playing chess on a bench with their umbrellas up. Jake walks close while he talks. About music, and radio shows, and a place called Neil's, with coffee and twenty-nine different kinds of eggs. And he watches. Front, sides, and behind them. He says there is a lake in the park. With ducks. Brigit might like the ducks. They should bring her next time.

Eva can taste the guilt, bitter on her tongue. She picks up their pace.

The interlude in the club is like a jazz-filled dream.

Out of the trees and they're back onto a busy street. Two more blocks, and they're back at Powell House. Inside they find the front parlor transformed into an art gallery, Peggy and Bets having a passionate debate about whether a watercolor of two fairies on flower petals should switch places with an oil painting of an African man sawing wood. The noise from the kitchen downstairs can be heard in the foyer.

"Go on, then," Jake says, tilting his head at the stairs.

Eva runs up the steps, throwing open the door of the blue room, breathless. Mrs. Angel looks up from her knitting, a finger to her lips.

Brigit is in bed. Clean. Hair brushed. In a nightgown, holding a spoon. Her chest rises and falls with the smallest of sighs.

Mrs. Angel chuckles. "Now, don't look that surprised," she whispers. She stands up, gathering her yarn. Eva shuts the door behind her. Quietly.

"I am sorry. I was away too long . . ."

"You were with Jacob Katz, weren't you? You probably ended up in a club somewhere listening to bebop." She's still smiling. "Now don't try telling me I'm wrong."

Eva doesn't try telling her.

"We've had ourselves a day, and my Brigit-girl has worn herself out. No, nothing bad. She's excited about spoons. And did you know this girl thinks the telephone is funny? Every time it rings."

Mrs. Angel does laugh this time, softly.

"She's eaten and had a bath. A long one, because Bets brought in soap for bubbles. There's probably no hot water downstairs now, but our girl here had fun, so I doubt anybody cares. Did you get caught in the rain?"

Eva nods, putting an absentminded hand to hair. It's wild. But Brigit looks like a storybook. And she had a good day. A better day than Eva could have given her.

Her father used to say that kindness made the weak weaker.

Only, Brigit looks stronger.

When she looks like that, it's hard to believe she could ever do anything wrong.

"Will she sleep through the night?" Mrs. Angel asks. She's shutting the wardrobe. Picking up Brigit's milk glass.

"Yes. She sleeps for a long time."

"Then you could probably run on for a while. Jacob is outside the door."

Eva looks back at her, brows pushed together.

"When something's going on, Jacob Katz is always outside the door." Mrs. Angel turns the knob, and Jake turns his head, looking back from where he'd been waiting at the top of the stairs. "See. Told you." She shuts the door again.

"I'll tell Bets to check on her every now and then, and you do the same. Now put something dry on, and I'm going home to rest my feet!"

"Thank you," Eva says. She wants to do something more, but she doesn't know what that something would be.

"Aren't you a funny thing?" Mrs. Angel says on the way out the door. "And you're welcome."

Eva does what Mrs. Angel says, switching to her only other skirt and blouse, taming down her wild hair, turning it with a brush. It doesn't work that well. Jake smiles when she comes out the door. He's down to his T-shirt, which is only a little damp. He tucks her hair behind one ear. "Come upstairs," he says.

Jimmy and Colette are on the sixth floor, and Larry and Lucy, and they've already started a tournament. Eva had been very good at table tennis, a long time ago. It turns out that she still is. She trounces them. All of them. Colette folds a paper crown and puts it on her head.

Jake keeps her at the record player after that so Lucy can't quiz her about Berlin, asking what she likes about this one or that one. And doesn't she think Charlie Parker plays with a lot of soul? Jimmy tells him to put on some Glenn Miller already, he's ruining his game. Eva watches Colette play with Jimmy's long hair, which is probably what's ruining his game, and tries to imagine a young man in Germany not going to war because he doesn't believe in it.

It's actually unimaginable.

She leans close, like she's examining the records. "What did you do," she asks softly, "during the war?"

"Went to school. I didn't turn eighteen until early '45, and I've missed the draft every time since."

"Would you have gone?"

"Yeah, I would have gone." He puts Jimmy's Glenn Miller on the turntable. "Don't get me wrong. What Jimmy did takes guts. But . . ." He shrugs, watching the record spin. "When I was twelve, I was out with my mom—I don't even remember what we were doing—and this parade went by. Hundreds of people, thousands maybe, marching and holding up swastika flags . . ."

"In New York?" Eva asks.

He nods. "And there were people on the street saluting and shouting 'Heil,' and I thought, all of these people, they don't even know me, and they would really like it if I was dead. And when I think about that, and Uncle David, I'm a little sore I didn't go."

He might have come home and spit on her shoes.

And how could she blame him.

He passes her a record. "I thought you might like this one. It's Dizzy Gillespie." But she sees why he's handed it to her. The record label says BLUEBIRD.

"Anything you need," he says, lifting the needle. "All you have to do is ask."

And later that night, when the attic is empty, and the open windows do nothing to bring a breeze, Eva comes up from the kitchen with a glass of cold milk in her hand. She has on a pink, silky dressing gown that Bets found in the charity box, so she "wouldn't have to get dressed every time she wanted the toilet." She sets the milk on the hall table, beside someone's forgotten gloves, and pauses in the doorway of the parlor turned gallery.

A lamp has been left on, and in front of the ornate mantel, on a table draped with white cloth, sits a sculpture. The head and chest of a woman, serene, arms folded, chin bowed, a kind of diadem on her head.

Eva walks forward, peering into the statue's face. She looks at it for a long time.

Asking Jake to help her today was wrong. And unfair. He would despise her if he knew who she'd been. One of those people on the street, saluting the swastikas. He has every reason in the world to despise her.

As soon as he brings Rolf's address, she'll make sure she doesn't see him again. She'll ask Bets for a new friend if she has to. That will be fair.

But for once, Eva isn't longing for what's fair. She doesn't want what's fair at all.

And that, she thinks, also makes her despicable.

A switch clicks, and Eva turns. A woman is standing beside the door in the lamplight, a red turban wound around her head, the cloth bright against a forehead of rich brown. And Eva remembers. This woman had been opening crates.

"Does it make you feel something?" the woman asks.

"Are you the . . . artist?"

She nods. "Mrs. Savage. Augusta."

"I'm Eva." She turns back to the still, bowed head. "It's very beautiful. Does it have a name?"

"Minerva," Augusta replies.

Yes, Eva thinks, very traditional. Classical. Hitler would have approved. Until he knew who sculpted it, and then he wouldn't have. And her mother had thought Hitler was a god. A god worth dying for.

Her mother was a fool.

So was Hitler.

Augusta comes to stand beside Eva, and now Bets has come into the parlor, cheeks smeared with face cream and her hair already pinned up for the night. They all stare at the sculpture, heads turning this way and that.

"Does it make you feel something?" Augusta asks again.

"Reverence," says Bets. "Like prayer."

"I see sacrifice," says Augusta.

Eva whispers the word *responsibility*.

"You mean responsibility like a duty?" Augusta asks. "Or do you mean blame?"

"Both of them," Eva replies. Though she doesn't really think this. She knows the real word for what the statue makes her feel.

Shame.

CHAPTER THIRTY

"*Look at what I have brought for you, my Vögelchen.*"
"*What is it, Papa? What is it?*" *Sometimes, Papa brings her candy. Or a whistle that makes noise. Sometimes, he brings her things she doesn't want to see and asks her about them. She is hoping for the candy. But Papa only puts a plain brown box on his desk. No ribbons or pretty paper.*

"*Come. Sit nicely in the chair, and see what is inside.*"

She climbs up into the chair. Turns and settles, her feet sticking straight out, folding her hands on her pink dress. The smell of his pipe makes her feel still. Expectant. Papa sets the box in her lap and takes off the lid.

And inside, in a nest of soft cloth, is a tiny bird. A nuthatch. It looks up at her with bright black eyes.

"*Do you like it, my Vögelchen?*"

She nods.

"*Are you happy? Do you see how much your Papa loves you?*"

She nods again.

"*Then let us have a little talk together about what it means to obey.*"

CHAPTER THIRTY-ONE
—— *August 1946* ——

AFTER BRIGIT HAS eaten, Eva sits her on the black-and-white floor of the kitchen and puts the mewing kitten in her lap. Eva had nearly forgotten about the kitten. Until she'd climbed into bed the night before and gotten a surprise. Brigit scoops it up gently—Mrs. Angel must have really worked with her on that— holding it beneath her chin.

Eva wishes she had a camera. If the first Mr. Cruickshanks could see this, he'd never believe that Anna Ptaszynska was a killer. Even if she *had* hit him with a paperweight.

If she was, it wasn't her fault.

Then the kitchen door opens and Martha bustles in, adjusting her glasses, a file and a stack of papers crushed against her chest.

"Miss Gerst?" she says. "I have not met thee properly. I am Mrs. Balderston, though thee may call me Martha, or Mother Martha, since that is what everyone else seems to do."

Eva blinks, confused. Martha pulls out a chair, offering Eva the one opposite.

"I was raised a Quaker, Miss Gerst, and that was a long time ago. We stuck to the old way of speaking. Replace 'thee' with 'you' and all will become clear." She reaches out and pats Eva's hand. "Don't worry. It will drive thee mad at first."

She turns to Brigit. "What a lovely spoon, Miss Heidelmann."

Eva looks down. Brigit is rubbing a spoon with the end of her blouse. She isn't sure where the kitten has gotten to.

"We haven't had the usual chat, which is entirely my fault. I'm afraid thee caught us at a busy time. But we would like to know how Powell House can help thee most. Tell me, what goals would thee like to accomplish in America?"

Eva grabs one of the *Powell House Criers*, still in stacks on the table, and folds it neatly in three. Martha would be horrified by what she'd like to accomplish. So she only says, "I do not know."

"That is understandable. But I would like for thee to begin thinking. We are so happy to have thee here. And Miss Heidelmann. Very happy, indeed. But Powell House is only a temporary solution. Are thee interested in a course of study? Training?"

Eva folds a second paper. Carefully. Life after justice is a tall, blank wall. Like the one around Sachsenhausen. She can't see the other side of it. She has no reason to think the other side exists.

And then Olive's head pops in. "The doctor is upstairs."

"Oh, psssht," says Martha. "Thank thee, Olive." She turns back to Eva. "That was to be the second part of our chat. Dr. Holtz rang and told me he had arranged for a Dr. Forrester, a neurosurgeon, to examine Miss Heidelmann, and I suggested that should happen here, if possible, to avoid strain. On her and thee. And now he is very early . . ."

Brigit has slowed the rubbing of her spoon. She's listening, Eva realizes. How much does she understand?

"Is this plan acceptable to thee, Miss Gerst? Or no? Would the blue room be best?"

Eva looks up. "Do you play the harmonica?"

"I do!" says Olive, her head still in the door. "I mean, I can make it make noise."

And that is exactly what Olive does. She makes the harmonica make noise while Brigit screams and screams. It does help a little, giving temporary pauses, seconds of indrawn breath. But even though Bets scurried to shut the windows, Mother Martha is at the front door, having her second chat of the morning, this time with the neighborhood policeman.

Dr. Forrester is a small man, pale and precise, who does his job efficiently no matter what sort of clamor Brigit and Olive are making, and no matter how Brigit wriggles. He takes her pulse and her blood pressure. He asks about all her functions. He presses his fingers along every inch of her head. He's also very good at avoiding Brigit's flailing arms when her hands escape Eva's. And then he steps back, observing.

As soon as he stops touching her, Brigit stops shrieking. She's breathing hard, gasping, eyes closed while Olive blares with enthusiasm.

"Let her hold it," Eva whispers, taking the harmonica from Olive. She wraps Brigit's fingers around it, and the room is suddenly more peaceful.

"I've read Dr. Holtz's notes," says Dr. Forrester, "and I understand the source of the psychiatric trouble is believed to be abuse by soldiers . . ."

Eva winces. She wishes Bets and Olive hadn't heard that.

". . . but there was an injury to her head that has healed. The butt of a gun or a rifle perhaps?"

Eva nods. It could have been. "She had a cut here, behind the ear . . ."

"Was she unconscious? How long?"

Eva struggles to think while Brigit whimpers. How long had they been in that car? "For two days? She spoke at first, and then . . . she did not."

Dr. Forrester unwinds the stethoscope from his neck. "I want Miss Heidelmann to have an X-ray."

Eva looks to Bets. "Taking a picture," Bets explains, "the kind that looks inside your body."

"The trauma could be purely psychological, or physical, or both put together, of course," Dr. Forrester says. "But this type of X-ray will rule some things out. Miss Heidelmann will need to be injected with iodine, to see the blood flow to her brain. It's not dangerous but will require a hospital stay, and I understand that is going to be a difficulty."

He digs around in his bag, coming up with a blue pad of paper to scribble on. Brigit gasps, in and out, turning the harmonica over and over in her hands. Eva lays one of the bathroom towels over her head, so she can't see anyone else.

"A prescription for a mild sedative," the doctor says, tearing off a page and handing it to Bets. "A half dose to get her to the hospital, so she can still walk, the rest when she gets there, so she falls asleep. I'll see what arrangements need to be made. There are some funds for these kinds of situations. Take the prescription to Clancy's and he'll put it on my tab . . ."

Eva straightens. "Why would you do that?" She'd learned "put it on my tab" from the second mate.

Dr. Forrester looks surprised. "It's an interesting case. And Dr. Holtz is a good man who's done me a helpful turn or two."

And Dr. Holtz had been helped by Powell House. The strange, foreign cycle of fairness.

"But you think Brigit could be . . . better?"

"Certainly. One way or another. Though I can't say how much, and it may be up to Dr. Holtz. Now if you'll excuse me, I'm late to the office. My nurse will ring . . ."

Eva stays in the blue room and brushes Brigit's hair after the others have left. Brigit likes getting her hair brushed now. They'd worked on it every day until she did in Biberach. Like they'd worked on her new name. Away from the others, so Brigit wouldn't frighten them. Her father called people like Brigit "useless eaters." Unworthy of life. But no one in Powell House had ever treated her that way.

No one was afraid of her here.

She plaits Brigit's hair into one long braid down the back, like she'd always worn it, then takes the leftover crusts from breakfast and shows her how to spread them along the open windowsill. It doesn't take long for a pigeon to come, and then two, cooing as they peck. Brigit makes a noise that sounds like "dak."

Eva smiles. Maybe she would like to feed the ducks. She watches Brigit watch the pigeons.

When she gets that address, when justice finally happens, even with a plan—a good plan—it could all go wrong. It probably will go wrong. She'll be arrested. Or a Cruickshanks will take his revenge. And there will be no one to know. No one to believe her. She doesn't even know if they hang criminals in America.

But just because Eva's future is a blank wall, it doesn't mean Brigit's has to be. The doctor said that she could be better. Brigit could have a life ahead of her.

Eva gets the notepad from the bedside table and writes a messy version of a letter, correcting her spelling, her grammar, recopying it neatly when she's done. Then she goes to her suitcase in the wardrobe, carefully sliding the handle loose from its slot. The handle is hollow. And it rattles. And when she shakes it, her ruby and diamond earrings fall out onto her palm.

She pushes the stud of each earring through the paper of the letter, screwing on the gold backs. The letter looks fancy. Decorated. And it asks that in the absence of Eva Gerst, any decisions for the care of Brigit Heidelmann should be shared between Martha Balderston, Elizabeth Whittlesby, and Happy Angel.

It's not legal. But she thinks those three will treat it as if it was. And the earrings should be worth something.

Then the kitten appears from nowhere and tries to pounce on the pigeons. They fly away, snapping their wings, and Brigit is startled. And then delighted. And Eva backs up, behind the curtain.

The man with the shiny shoes is outside, smoking in his rusty car.

And he's still there the next afternoon, when Bets knocks on the door, hair tied up in a red bandanna. She digs an envelope out of an apron pocket.

"Jake sent Larry by with that for you a little while ago." She raises her voice. Brigit has learned to blow the harmonica. Not Eva's first choice for a new skill. "It was something you need, he said?"

The envelope has her name on the front in handwriting that is small, very neat. "Thank you," Eva says, setting it on the table. As if it's unimportant.

"Larry says Jake says to tell you that his mother says he probably won't come by tonight. He has a final paper for his summer class, or something like that, but he'll swing by tomorrow." She glances curiously at the envelope, but doesn't pry. Then Eva sees that her nose is wrinkled.

"Is something wrong?"

"Just an unpleasant job. There's a dead bird in the music room. Its neck is broken, poor thing . . ."

"How did it get in the music room?"

"And inside the piano, too," Bets says. "I didn't think we'd had the windows open. Sorry to be a grump. I don't like dead things."

She waves her way out the door, and Eva waits for the silence after her footsteps. Then Eva tears open the envelope and takes out the paper.

There's a drawing of a bluebird at the top. Not crude, like the one on Mr. Cruickshanks's card. This one is in flight, with big eyes and fluttering feathers. She smiles.

She doesn't mind so much when Jake calls her Bluebird.

And Jake has written a name, Kenneth Lutz. An address, days of the week, and times. Rolf's new name and his work schedule. She studies it, thinking. It says Rolf has a night shift three nights a week. Which means if her father is at this address, that's when he's likely to be alone. And Rolf's first night shift of the week is . . . tonight.

She breathes. She should go tonight. Break her deal and be done. Before Cruickshanks comes back, demanding to know what she's been doing. Before he finds her father himself. Because Cruickshanks had Dr. Schneider's name, too.

Last time, she hadn't been ready. This time, she has to be.

And she cannot—must not—be seen.

The sun is slanting when she catches Bets on her way up the stairs.

"I . . . think I am . . . beginning a headache."

Bets's face registers instant concern.

"And Brigit is tired. She will do better with quiet. I was thinking we might lie down early, if . . ."

"Oh, sure!" says Bets. "Could I bring up a couple of plates? You shouldn't skip a meal, you know. There's barely any of you there. And I'll tell the crew to hold it down, so you two can rest. It takes a lot, coming to a new place."

Eva smiles through her guilt. "You are . . ."

What does she want to say to Bets? You are sweet? Naive? You would have had your shoes stolen in Berlin? Or would Bets have given them away, the first time someone asked?

"I mean to say thank you. Very much."

Bets smiles like she's been given a prize. "Be back in a bit."

Eva shuts the door and gets to work. She folds up Rolf's schedule, Jake's bluebird fluttering at its top, tucks it back into the envelope, and puts it inside the lining of her purse, beside the bread knife and Mr. Cruickshanks's card. Then she pulls a chair up to the wardrobe, reaching past her paper crown, and from the very back of the top shelf fishes out the bottle of pills Olive brought from Clancy's. Two pills go into her palm, then into her pocket. The bottle goes back to the top shelf where Brigit won't find it. Then Eva gets on her knees and unfolds the map of New York City she'd snagged from the foyer, spreading it out across the floor.

She makes notes. Brigit helps by crawling on them. Eva finds the kitten underneath the bed to distract her. Then she shoves every-thing beneath the bed when Bets knocks and says, "Room service!" leaving a tray of apples and cheese, rolls and butter, and two glasses of milk on the little table by the window. When Bets has gone, Eva gets the map back out again, finishes her notes, and puts them in her purse.

She coaxes Brigit into eating. Takes her to the toilet. Pulls her nightgown over her head. Gets two pills and pops them into the back of Brigit's throat, following quick with the last of the milk. Eva knows how to get Brigit to take a pill. Brigit sits down and plays with her spoon.

And Eva waits. While the shadows disappear into the twilight and someone has a conversation across the street. While air that smells like a city moves the curtains. While a man in the street sits smoking in his rusty car.

She closes her eyes. She says the twenty-seven names. She says who she is.

And looks for her anger. Her anger is still Inge to her. Inge pulls Annemarie through the ruined house. Inge looks over walls and does not accept what she sees. Inge is a blaze. Inge is a fire wind.

Eva opens her eyes. And someone has shut the window. She opens it again.

Brigit's eyes are heavy-lidded. She drops her spoon. The kitten plays with its tail. Eva puts them both in the bed, adjusts the blankets, and switches off the lamp.

She doesn't feel afraid. Not yet.

She will. But it doesn't matter. She'll choose anger. And justice.

She'll make sure that none of this can ever happen again.

Brigit's breathing is slow. Regular. She shakes her shoulder, but Brigit doesn't stir. And then Eva moves. She grabs her purse and slips out the door. But she doesn't lock it. Not this time.

So they can take care of her. The letter with the earrings is in Brigit's suitcase, her name on the outside. Where they will find it. If Eva doesn't come back.

They will take care of her.

Eva tiptoes across the landing to the bathroom, shutting the door slowly, slowly, until the latch gives the softest click. She puts the lid down on the toilet seat and steps up, balancing. She gets a knee on the sill.

And climbs out the open window.

CHAPTER THIRTY-TWO

"*TELL PAPA, MY VÖGELCHEN. What does the bird feel like?*"

The bird wriggles, cupped gently in her hands, opening and closing its beak. "Soft," she whispers, and gives a little gasp. "And I can feel its heart! So fast . . ."

"Yes. The heart beats, because the bird is alive. Now, tell your Papa why we must obey."

Her smile is gone. But she recites, "If authority is not obeyed, there is no order."

"And only the weak live without order. Do you want to be weak, my Vögelchen?"

She shakes her head. A tiny shake.

"And to whom do you belong? Who is your authority?"

"Papa," she whispers.

"And you want to be good and strong so that Papa will love you, isn't that right?"

She nods. A tiny nod.

"Then Papa says you must squeeze the bird."

The bird looks up at her with bright, black eyes. "I don't want to," she whispers.

"Does it matter what you want? Does it matter what you feel, when you have been asked to obey?"

"No, Papa. Please . . ." She's frightened now. She is shaking inside.

"Then you know what you have been told to do. Obey your papa, and squeeze the little bird."

She closes her eyes. And her fingers tighten.

CHAPTER THIRTY-THREE

—— *August 1946* ——

THE FIRE ESCAPE outside the bathroom window is rusty iron and loud beneath her shoes. She goes down slowly, toe to heel, and at the second-floor window, she pauses. There's music on the other side of the glass. She leans forward, just enough to get one eye beyond the bricks.

Jake is in the music room. By himself. Playing the guitar. He must have come to Powell House anyway, or finished whatever needed to be done. He came, she thinks, to see her. He's rumpled and scruffy and not playing anything like what she thought he would. Just picking out a melody of single notes. The corner of his mouth goes up when he finds what he wants. Brows down when he doesn't. It sounds like he's playing Bach.

He's still difficult to look away from. Because he's rather beautiful.

She wishes she was that other girl. The one who plays Ping-Pong in a crown. But she isn't. She's the girl with a bread knife in her purse.

The girl Jake would despise if he knew her.

He would be right to.

And she would be wrong to let herself forget it.

Eva slips past the window, going quietly down the fire escape. And discovers that the fire escape doesn't go all the way down.

There's a ladder for the last part, pulled up into sections. If she tries to let it down, there's going to be a racket. She'll have to climb down it, as far as she can, and drop the rest of the way to the ground. Eva turns around backward, purse tight in her hand, and steps out onto the first rung.

And the ladder slides down on its own. Suddenly. Violently. With a swoop in her stomach. Jangling and rattling like she's just set off every fire alarm in the city. She hangs on, the ladder hits its full extension and throws her onto her backside in the bushes.

A light switches on inside Powell House.

Eva scrambles up, finds her purse, dashes through a little gate, and she's out of the back yard, picking her way down a dark, narrow strip of weeds and trees growing where the back fences don't quite meet in the middle. There's an iron gate at the end. It's not even locked. A little alley, and then Eva is around the corner on Lexington with the streetlights and cars and NEIL'S COFFEE SHOP lit in neon down the block.

She smooths her skirt. Pulls a twig or two from her hair. Hooks her purse over an arm and walks. Away from Powell House. Away from the man with shiny shoes, watching its front door. Making a beeline for the subway station, where she breaks one of her precious American bills and gets some change.

She consults her notes, the map in her head, and the map on the train, and when she gets off at her stop, she has to step over a drunken man sleeping longways on the steps.

It's a very different neighborhood from Powell House. There's an elevated train, running loud and raining dirt from tracks above her head, darkening the rows of bars and barbershops that will also give you a tattoo. The gutters stink, and police sirens wail from two different directions. She gets a few long stares. But Eva hadn't survived

Berlin for nothing. She wraps her purse straps around her wrist and starts walking.

Some of the street signs are smudged. Or missing, as well as some of the numbers on the buildings. She ignores the women showing too much chest. She'd seen that in Berlin, too, only those women had been skinny, starving. She passes a man pushing a baby carriage, full to the brim with empty beer bottles, and then she turns the wrong way. Has to recross a street.

But she finds it. A corner building of dingy red bricks with a secondhand clothing shop on the first floor, now closed for the night, a sign flashing the word DINER in rhythm directly across the street. There's a narrow doorway beside the shop entrance, a closed passage between the buildings leading to the upper floors. And on the other side, an alley, stretching back into an abyss her eyes can't penetrate.

Eva stares at the building. She gets some catcalls from some passing sailors, but she knows how to ignore those, too. Rolf's address is 2B, but there are no lights showing on the second floor at all. Just the blare of orange neon reflecting in the glass.

And she feels eyes all over her. Even though the sailors are gone. Her father could be up there, watching her from one of those dark windows. Or Rolf. Eva turns and dashes across the street, dodging a car that honks, and pushes open the diner door.

Faces swivel around to look at her. A man in a dirty apron smoking a cigar, something sizzling beside him on an open grill. Men in coveralls and frayed trouser hems. There's a haze of smoke creeping along the ceiling and not another female in the place.

Eva goes to a booth beside the window and sits. The tabletop is sticky. But the menu of the diner is written on the outside of the glass, giving her a little cover from the building across the street. She thinks through the schedule Jake wrote down.

Rolf starts work at midnight. She'd thought he'd be home now, so she could watch him leave. If her father really is living with Rolf, that's when he would be alone. If her father isn't living with Rolf, that's when she could try to get into the apartment and find out where he is.

"What do you want?"

Eva jumps. A woman in a pink uniform is standing beside her.

"If you're not ordering, you need to go." The woman's fingernails are chipped, coffee stains dotting her hemline.

"Coffee, please. Black."

"All right, honey." The woman leans in and whispers. "Say, you know how to get to the subway, right?" Eva nods. "Well, don't wait on me. Just leave a couple of cents on the table before you go."

The coffee comes, weak and a little stale, and Eva watches the apartment. She finishes the coffee, and the waitress sighs and refills her cup while one of the men on stools yells for her. Then the bus pulls away from the opposite curb and Eva sits up. And shrinks back down again. Because there is Rolf.

He's wearing slacks and a white shirt, a paper sack of groceries in his arms. Except for the coveralls, she can't remember ever seeing him out of uniform. He looks like Rolf. And somebody else. His brown hair is thinning, and when he turns to look for his way across the street, she can see the long, jagged scar running down his cheekbone. For a moment, she remembers what it felt like, to hit him with that chunk of concrete. It makes her sick.

She thinks of the knife in her purse and feels sicker.

She should say the names. All the names. Find her anger.

Rolf goes to the little door beside the secondhand shop and puts a key to the lock. He disappears and Eva waits. Watching. And on the opposite side of the building, a curtained window glows on the second story. That is the apartment. If her father is there, he'd been sitting alone. In the dark.

And then she isn't sitting alone, because someone is sliding into her booth.

Jake is glaring at her from across the table.

"What are you doing here?" she says.

"What am I doing here? What are you doing here?"

All the faces are turned her way again. Eva lowers her voice. "I do not need you to take me to every place I have to go."

"And this is a place you have to go, is it? A diner in the Bowery? After dark? Had a sudden yen for bad coffee and a tattoo, did you?"

Now the waitress is glaring.

"How did you find me?"

"It wasn't that hard. Since I gave you the address this afternoon. And after you woke the whole neighborhood with that ride down the fire escape."

"How do you know I did that?"

"Oh, I don't know, Eva. Maybe the fact that you weren't in your room and there was a print on the toilet lid from a really little foot."

Eva bites her lip. "Do they know I am gone?"

"No. What do you take me for?"

"Is Brigit . . ."

"Sleeping like the dead. You gave her those pills, didn't you?"

Eva nods. Jake runs his hands through his hair, jaw clenching and unclenching. A shadow moves briefly across the second story window. "So, spill," he says. "What are you . . ."

"Shhh."

The light in the second story has gone out.

A few seconds, and Rolf comes out the street door. His sack is gone and he has a jacket on now, his hair neatly combed. Jake doesn't say anything. He's seen him.

Rolf walks down the street and turns the corner, heading toward the subway. Eva looks up at the lifeless windows.

Her father isn't there. But Jake is. Why can't he leave her alone? And then she doesn't have to search for her anger, because her insides are going up in flames. She's sick of her rotten deal. If she wants to find out where her father is, her opportunity is now. She turns to Jake.

"Did anyone follow you?"

"Your friend was out front. But I went out the back, like you did. Only I used the door. I didn't see anybody . . ."

Eva grabs her purse, digs into the little pocket with her change, and puts a dime on the table. The waitress could probably use something extra. Then she gets up and walks out of the diner.

"Hey," says Jake, "wait . . ."

She trots over the pavement to the dark alley beside Rolf's apartment. It smells of garbage and worse things, but Eva sees what she thought she might. A fire escape. And the ladder is pulled up high, like it had been at Powell House. She starts scooting a metal trash can, positioning it underneath, a dog barking at her noise.

"Should I even bother asking you what the hell you are doing?" Jake hisses from somewhere behind her.

She steps on a crate, one hand against the brick wall, and up onto the trash can lid. Teetering in her heels. She reaches, but she still can't grab the ladder.

"I need a . . . a . . . *einen Regenschirm!*"

"What?"

"For the rain! To get the ladder."

"What rain?"

She stretches for the ladder.

"You want an umbrella," Jake says. "The word is umbrella! What you're going to need is a lawyer. What am I supposed to tell Martha when you're arrested?"

A man in soiled clothes stumbles out of the dark part of the alley, waving his hands as he staggers away. But no one on the street has taken notice. Yet.

Jake says some words she doesn't know and probably shouldn't. "Oh, stop it before you break your head! Grab my hands and step on my shoulders."

He squats down, raising his hands. Eva takes them, and gets one foot on a shoulder and then the other, trying not to spear him with her heels. He grunts, her skirt half over his face, her purse sliding down her arm to hit him in the head. She reaches up, the balance much harder than she would have guessed.

"Do not look up," she whispers.

"Oh, for God's sake, Eva. Do you know how bad your shoes hurt?"

The ladder is just above her. She stretches out, wobbling. Jake takes one shaky step forward and she's got it, pulling it down slow. Quiet. It goes almost to the ground. She gets two hands on it, gingerly stepping sideways from Jake's shoulders to the rungs, climbing fast to the landing at the second floor.

The window is dark, but when she crouches down, she thinks there's a kitchen on the other side, a smooth surface like a table just beneath the sill. She pushes on the sash gently, and less gently. It's locked. Then Jake is beside her, pulling up the ladder up and hooking it into place. He spins her around by the shoulders. His pretty eyes are narrowed. Hot.

"Spill," he whispers. "Why are you trying to get arrested?"

"There's no one inside. But he will know others. There will be information . . ."

"Information you don't think Cruickshanks will share with you?"

Eva thinks fast. "Cruickshanks will not know what he's seeing. It could be the only way . . . to catch them."

Jake puts his hands in his pockets, his jaw working.

"Go back to the diner," she says, "and I will break the glass."

She's never seen someone laugh while they're angry. Jake looks down at her, shaking his head.

"Do you really think for one second that I'm going to let you do that?"

He lifts his hand between them, and out jumps a little silver pocket knife. Then his head jerks around like someone tapped him on the shoulder.

Across the alley, five small faces stare from the opposite fire escape, only just silhouetted by a covered bulb in the window behind them. Some sitting, some on their knees, hanging on to the iron rails from a bare mattress that fills the landing like an outdoor bed.

"She forgot her keys," Jake says. The oldest girl giggles.

Then Jake takes his little knife and jimmies open the window.

CHAPTER THIRTY-FOUR

—— *August 1946* ——

JAKE CRAWLS IN the window first. Then his arms reach out, helping Eva over the table, lifting her to the floor without noise. They're in a dark kitchen, very small, with a refrigerator that hums. But there's no other sound from the apartment.

"Stay here," he whispers. "And don't turn on a light."

He tiptoes through the kitchen door.

Eva smells disinfectant, and even in the dim light from the window, she can see that the countertops are gleaming. Her father wouldn't accept anything less. Jake comes back, still quiet, but talking a little louder.

"There's no one here. Tell me what we're looking for."

"Letters," she whispers. "Papers." She steps from the kitchen into a living room, where she can just make out a sofa, a chair, maybe a radio on the table.

"Don't turn on the light in here. You can see it from the street."

"He's gone to work," Eva whispers. But she doesn't turn on the light.

Through a second door is an interior hallway, pitch-black until Jake finds the switch. It's white, a little dingy, cracks along the ceiling and linoleum freshly scrubbed. The front door is here, with three extra locks, and three more doors, two on the right, one at the end.

The first door is a bathroom. Spotless. The next a bedroom. Jake finds the light switch, and there's no desk, only a chest of drawers, a side table with a lamp, and a bed, spread up without a wrinkle.

"The guy must be a great janitor," Jake mutters, opening a drawer. "Because this place is neat as a pin." He looks carefully through some socks. "What time did you say he was supposed to be at work?"

"Midnight," Eva whispers. This is Rolf's room. She can tell. Because it's so empty.

"You really think he's gone already? It's only a little past nine."

Eva doesn't answer, because she's opened the drawer of the side table. There's only one thing in it, a single photograph, facedown. And when she turns it over, she sees a picture of herself. She looks a little stern, her hair clipped back, hands folded on her pink party dress, the first one she'd ever worn with the neckline low, a huge Nazi eagle on the backdrop. They'd taken this for Rolf. To send to him during the war.

Eva drops it in her purse, before Jake can see. She can't stand the thought of Rolf lying in bed, staring at her face. And then she can feel her pulse, beating in her temples, in the tips of her fingers.

Because there's another bedroom.

She leaves Jake searching the drawers and walks down the hall. The walk is short. And feels long. And there is a smell. A scent she knows, and for a brief second the hallway shrinks, shrinks, down to the size of a box, pressing, and there is no air to breathe. She can't breathe.

Then there's too much air, and she's gasping, standing at the end of the hall in front of the third door. Eva turns the knob.

The smell of the tobacco is strong. Recent. It's difficult to be ready for a smell. It makes her fear rise, surge, go crackling in her veins. But she is sure now. This is her father's room. She feels along the wall and switches on the light.

And steps back.

The room is empty. Bed neatly made, a chair and a lamp beside the window, a desk on the opposite wall. But it doesn't feel empty, because the walls are covered with faces. Photographs taken close-up. Dozens of staring, haunted eyes. Men, women, children in striped shirts. Over the bed. Even one or two on the ceiling.

They're identification photographs. Prisoners, only in much larger prints. Her father used to say how the night was his musing time. His time to think creatively about his work. He must have had these photographs enlarged. And brought them here. All the way to America. To look at every day.

His experiments.

And there are so many more than the names she recites.

She hears Jake suck in a breath behind her. "What is this?" he whispers.

She feels sick. And embarrassed, somehow, for him to be seeing this. She hurries to the little table beside her father's chair, opens the drawer, leafing through the stack of books. Jake stands still, gazing at the walls.

"Are these from a concentration camp?" he asks.

"Yes," Eva whispers.

"Do you know which one?"

"Sachsenhausen." She can feel him looking at her.

"Do you know any of these people?"

"I don't know," she says. "I can't look at them."

"Okay," he says. And then just "Okay."

Eva knows he's watching her. Like the four walls are watching.

But the photographs have helped her focus. She knows where the Doctor lives now.

Inge's anger is a fire wind. The silent inferno.

She will be coming back.

Eva turns to the bedside table. Finds a pair of glasses. A bottle of white pills. Slippers beneath the bed. She runs her hands underneath the pillow and feels something cool. Smooth. Leather over metal.

"Schneider," says Jake, turning around. He's holding up a letter. "This guy seems to know a Dr. Schneider at the hospital. I bet that's how your guard got his job. Cruickshanks will want to know about that."

Eva nods, and Jake tucks the letter in his jacket pocket before going back to the desk. She pulls out what was hidden beneath the pillow.

A gun. With the gold eagle embossed on the holster. The last time she'd seen this gun, it had been in her mother's dead hand. So the lodge didn't burn down after all. Her father must have gone there. After. And looked at them.

She slips the gun into her purse beside the photo. She hopes it's loaded.

She could turn out the lights and wait, in that chair beside the window, maybe. He has to come home sometime. And she will be here, and justice will be done. For everyone.

Then Jake says, "Look at this." He's pulling out a case from beneath the desk. Like a briefcase with a handle, made of black metal. Fireproof. Eva comes around the bed. She presses a little button with a fingertip, and the latch snaps open.

A file full of neat, thin papers. The way the ones inside her mattress at Powell House had looked, before they got stepped on by soldiers, stuffed in her shirt, sewn into her skirt, and carried across the world.

The name on the file is Anna Ptaszynska.

Eva opens it, flipping through the information. Charts. Punishments. An experiment with a bird. All in her father's handwriting. Jake tilts his head to read, brows down, but the files are in German. She stops on the last page.

When brought the prisoner, a Jewish agitator set for execution, the patient Anna Ptaszynska was given an order and the proper word. She left her dinner, picked up a gun, and shot the prisoner. She showed no symptoms of agitation or distress. She continued her dinner while the body was removed, and later, when returned to her natural personality, claimed never to have seen the dead man. I consider Anna's training to be complete, and ready for whatever use the Führer deems . . .

Eva closes her eyes. What is this "proper word" that makes Anna Ptaszynska a killer? It can't be anything too common. And then she thinks maybe it's good that Brigit is the way she is. Maybe it's better if her memories never, ever come back. All those times Annemarie was away. At the market in Halbersadt, they'd said. With her father. But that's not where she'd been at all. Eva sets the file back in the case, snaps the lid shut.

Cruickshanks can't have this. He can't see it.

Jake frowns. "Who is Anna . . ."

A door slams somewhere in the building below them. They look at each other, breath held, and then the steps on the other side of the wall are creaking with the weight of feet.

"The light," Jake whispers, and he is out the door. Silent.

Eva can hear two voices. One of them a woman. Very loud. They could be going to another apartment. Until she hears a key scraping in one of Rolf's three locks. She snatches up her purse and the black case, smooths the blanket on the bed, and then Jake is back, shutting the door without a sound. She grabs his hand, pulling him toward the closet. He pulls back, reaches out, and turns off the light switch.

The room goes dark, and a bar of light appears beneath the door. Eva hears Rolf's voice, indistinct in the hallway, and a woman's giggle. She steps inside the closet, pulling Jake in after her. Very quietly, Jake shuts the door.

There's not room for two people in the closet. If there were more clothes, or if the shelf was deeper or Eva taller, they wouldn't have managed it at all.

"I'm standing . . . on shoes," she whispers, struggling for balance. She's got the case and her purse in one hand, and she can't let them bang the wall. Jake puts an arm around her, holding her up.

"Do not fall," he says near her ear. And then, "Which bedroom?"

For a second, she doesn't know what he means.

"He's got a girl," Jake hisses.

"The other one." But the wall of Rolf's room is the same as the back of the closet. "*Scheisse*," she mutters.

"Yeah," Jake breathes. He adjusts his arm, trying to find a comfortable way of remaining perfectly still. The dark is stifling, the tobacco smell strong. The muffled sound of music wafts into the closet from the living room. Someone has turned on the radio.

Rolf cannot be here until he goes to work. The walls are clamping down like a trap. Eva breathes. And breathes. The woman's voice erupts into laughter. Jake's hand moves up to her back.

"Shhh," he says.

"I do not like small spaces," she whispers. "I do not like them . . ." Her pulse is racing, a shake starting somewhere in her middle.

Jake puts his hand on the back of her head, pushing her into his chest. "Close your eyes. Pretend you're somewhere else."

She closes her eyes. Breathes deep. Slow. Smells Jake instead of the tobacco.

Footsteps come down the hall, water running in the bathroom. There's a dent in Jake's chest that just fits her forehead. She can feel his heart beating. Fast, like hers. The water shuts off in the bathroom.

She turns her head, like she's lying in bed, and slides her free hand around his side, under his jacket, hanging on. She can feel the muscles of his back beneath her palm, his breath pushing tight against her cheek.

This is wrong.

It's unfair.

He doesn't object. His thumb strokes her hair. One time. Then his hand tightens on her head.

The woman's voice is loud, coming from close by. "You shouldn't leave the window open, Kenny. You'll get cats!"

Behind the other wall of the closet must be the kitchen.

Where they left the window open.

"What?" says Rolf's voice. The *w* is a strong *v*, like Dr. Holtz. There's a small silence. Eva imagines him running a finger along the window, where Jake's knife splintered the wood before it tripped the lock.

"Wait here," Rolf says. "I will only just . . ."

They hear the woman's protests fade into the living room. And then footsteps come down the hall. The door opens in the room behind them, and Eva hears the click of the switch. It's quiet, so quiet.

And then, almost as if it's right next to her, she hears the wooden scrape of a drawer opening.

More silence. And Eva knows exactly what Rolf is not seeing.

The photograph of her.

Why had she taken it?

The drawer slams shut. The footsteps move. Across the room. Down the hall. Jake reaches behind and puts a hand on the doorknob. Ready to keep Rolf from opening the closet if he can. Eva tightens her arm, and the door to her father's room bursts open, the lights click on, shining on their feet from beneath the door. But there are another set of footsteps coming. Not a woman's. These are heavy. Slow. Deliberate.

There's another man in the apartment.

The walls of the closet shrink. Compress. They're pressing on her lungs. Jake turns her head and puts her face back in his chest, holding it there. She breathes. And breathes. And the footsteps are in the room.

They pause, and in her mind Eva can see them pausing. At the desk. The desk that has no metal case underneath it.

And both sets of footsteps move briskly away. Jake lets out a breath. They hear low voices, the woman protesting. And all the noise moves to the other side of the front door. The steps creak and thump, beyond the wall, like feet are hurrying. And the door to the street shakes the floor as it shuts.

Jake opens the closet. They listen. Step out. Eva can't hear a sound in the building. They move fast down the hall, Eva with the case and her purse, and in the kitchen, Jake puts a finger to his lips and takes a quick look into the alley. Then he mouths the word *up*.

She climbs onto the table and out the window, onto the fire escape, going as quiet as she can up the steps, Jake right behind her. The children across the alley hang on to the iron bars of the fire escape, watching from their mattress like a little prison.

When Jake reaches the third-story landing, he digs in his pocket and says softly, "Hey! Kids!"

And he flips a coin down and across the alley, glinting. It falls somewhere in the middle of them, making them scramble. Jake puts a finger to his lips and the oldest girl nods. And giggles.

They go up a ladder, over the edge of the wall to the sunken roof, where little chimneys and vents stick up here and there like pictures of cactus in the desert.

Where had she ever seen pictures of cactus in a desert?

"And here he comes," says Jake. He's on his knees, just peering over the edge into the alley. "He probably parked the girl in the diner across the street."

Then Eva hears Rolf's voice. "Little girl," he calls. "Little girl! Did you see anyone go in that window?"

"Get lost!" the girl yells. She sounds like she's thirty.

Jake snickers, then trots across the roof to the front of the building, watching.

"And . . ." he says, "he's got his girl. She's a nice one . . ." Though he says it in a way that means she isn't. "And they're off to the subway. Or maybe there's a bus down there, not sure."

"Was there anyone else?"

"No," says Jake. "Just the two of them." He turns to look at her. Smiling. "We've got him," he says. "Give Cruickshanks the address and they'll get everything they need."

It's true, Eva thinks. Everything Cruickshanks could want or need. They could move her right in. She could stay with her father while Rolf has his girlfriends over.

"Hey," Jake says. "Are you all right?"

She's leaning against the roof edge, face to the sky. Her father had been in that apartment, just on the other side of the door. For the moment, fear is winning over fire.

Jake comes to stand next to her. "There were two of them in there, and one wasn't just a guard, was he? One of them is a sick bastard."

"They are all sick," Eva whispers.

"Okay, then. Which sick bastard is this?"

She shakes her head. "Just . . . a doctor."

"A doctor. I'm guessing he wasn't a very good doctor."

"Some people would say he was."

"But those are the sick bastards."

She nods, and he puts his hands in his pockets. And when she dares to meet his lovely eyes, she is full of regret. Jake shouldn't be here. He should have run. Fast, and far away from her.

"I need a favor," she whispers.

His brows go up. "You really are something, you know that? Does it involve keeping you out of jail?"

She nods again, and he sighs.

"I think we've established that I have a hard time saying no to you, Bluebird."

CHAPTER THIRTY-FIVE

PAPA TAKES AWAY THE BOX AND SETS IT ON THE TABLE.

"When we cannot obey authority, what must happen?"

"We must be punished. So we can learn to be better."

"And why does Papa want you to be better?"

"Because I belong to you," she whispers. "And because you love me."

Papa picks her up then. Around the waist, like a sack, arms and legs dangling from her pink dress.

"No, Papa," she whispers.

"When you disobey, the punishment comes next. When you obey, you receive your reward. This is simple. It is fair."

And now the door is coming. The little door with the dark behind it. Where things rustle. Where there's no air.

"Please, Papa! Please!"

It's coming, and its mouth is open, and the strong arms push her inside it.

And the darkness swallows her.

CHAPTER THIRTY-SIX

—— *August 1946* ——

SHE TELLS JAKE that Anna Ptaszynska had been a friend. That the file was going to be difficult to read, and she wasn't ready to read it, not tonight. That Mr. Cruickshanks would never let her, and then she'd never know. She would give the file to Cruickshanks after, but in the meantime, she couldn't be seen taking the case into Powell House.

It was an easy lie, because some of it was actually the truth.

Jake takes her to a bus station in the basement of a hotel. The kind with lockers, to leave belongings in during a trip. He rents one, and gives her a key on a long string. The metal case goes in the locker, and when the locker door is open and Jake is on the other side, so does the gun from her purse. She doesn't want that gun in the same room as Brigit. The key goes around her neck and under her blouse. Like a car key had once.

They leave the bus station, and go to an all-night drugstore near their subway stop. It has a telephone booth inside it, where Eva pretends to call Mr. Cruickshanks. She can see Jake through the front windows, smoking a cigarette while he waits on the street, looking at anyone who might be looking at them.

She'll have to give Brigit the pills again and come back tomorrow, while Rolf is at work. She'll take an umbrella. They won't have had time to fix the window yet. And if her father isn't there, then she will sit in his room and wait for him. The photographs will help. And if her father doesn't come, she'll just wait for him again the next day. She'll wait every day, every night until he walks through the door.

And then what?

Justice. Or it all goes wrong. Or both.

She's relieved that she didn't have to kill her father tonight, even if she has to tomorrow. And the relief makes her angry with herself.

She steps outside, and Jake's brows draw in a little when he sees her face. But he doesn't say anything. He tosses the cigarette, and they take the subway. And then he says, "This is our stop."

Eva looks up, frowning. "No, it isn't."

"Yes, it is."

She follows him out of the train and up to the street, confused. The lights are bright, the street loud, busy, like it's daytime, and when they turn the corner, they're in a square with more lights than she's ever seen together in one place. Flashing advertisements for theater shows and newsreels, colas, cigarettes, and peanuts, the bulbs timed to make little moving pictures, like a cinema. There are so many people it's hard to move. More sailors, soldiers, girls in lipstick. A juggler, and a man with a trained dog doing backward flips. Jake doesn't spare any of it a glance. He grabs her hand, picking up the pace, edging their way through the crowd.

"Come on," he says over the noise. "You need cheering up."

"No, I don't."

"Yes, you do."

They turn out of the busy square, onto a street that's still jumping with noise. She's trotting to keep up. And Jake says, "I'm going to teach you to dance."

"No, you're not."

"Yes, I am."

"I don't want to know how to dance."

"Yes," he says. "You do." They bolt across a street before the light changes, opening a door beneath an enormous sign that says CAFE ZANZIBAR.

It's fancy inside, with mirrored walls and chrome rails and two enormous statues that are supposed to be Egyptian brushing at the ceiling. There's a crush of people going in. Black ties, furs, and shimmering gowns in the glow of crystal chandeliers. Jake still has her by the hand, but now he's whispering in the ear of the smartly dressed doorman, who's greeting the guests and taking money.

Jacob Katz, Eva is learning, knows somebody everywhere.

The doorman glances at Eva and winks, then gives Jake a little nod of the chin. He just let them in. For free.

"Jake," Eva says as he tugs her fast up the carpeted steps. "I am not . . . dressed."

"Yes, you are."

"You know what I mean to say."

"Well, if you're not, I'm not," he says. And it's true. He's a mess. And he's grinning. He can hear the band.

He steers her to one side, and they stop at a counter, a girl standing behind it inside a little room full of purses and hats. She has a red cap on her head.

"Jake, I can't leave Brigit . . ."

"Brigit would be sleeping like a baby even if you hadn't slipped her a mickey. Isn't that what you said?"

She isn't sure whether she said that or not.

Jake leans in. "You can't really tell me that you could sleep right now."

They're standing almost as close as they had been in the closet, and through the open doorway beyond Jake's shoulder, the lights are bright on the brass of swinging trumpets. She looks back at Jake and shakes her head.

"I didn't think so. Leave your purse here. They give you a little card to pick it up with later."

The girl behind the counter is chewing gum, watching this exchange with interest. Eva hands over the purse. Jake gives the girl a coin and slides the card into his pocket. Then he takes her hand again, and they walk into a wall of noise.

There's a stage on one end with a full band, black curtain behind, and more mirrored walls, a bar in the back, and the people in the crowd are both white and every shade of brown. Though all the brown people, Eva sees, are at the tables along the balcony instead of on the floor. But everyone of any color is on the dance floor, writhing with rhythm in a way that is wild, frantic, the cigarette smoke rising like a fog in the lights.

Jake finds a stool at the bar where a man sits alone. "Hey!" he yells. "Give a lady a seat?"

The man grumbles, and Jake grabs her by the waist and pops her up onto the newly empty stool. "Are you thirsty?" he yells.

"I am not used to . . ." She waves at all the empty glasses, little umbrellas, half-drunk bottles of champagne.

"Booze?" Jake asks. "Good. Because I don't have any money. Be right back!"

A girl passes by in a little red outfit like a bathing suit with stockings, a tray of cigarettes for sale hanging from a strap around her neck. The floor so thick with dancers that the couples bump into one another. Then the crowd parts and a girl is sliding across the floor between the legs of her partner, only to be slid right back up again and into the air. A few of the other dancers whoop.

She wouldn't mind being tossed around like that girl.

Jake has his elbows on the bar about halfway down, saying something to the bartender, and a man at the far end raises a whiskey glass to her. He's round, bald, pale, sweating, and at least fifty, and must think she's alone. She turns her back to him, and now the dancing girl is being twirled until her skirt flies up.

Jake comes back with two wet glasses of ice water. "I got him to put a cherry in yours," he yells. "So, what do you think?"

"Hitler wouldn't have allowed it."

"The man was up tight."

He downs the water in one. Eva eats her cherry. Jake holds out a hand. They leave the glasses and go to the edge of the dance floor, where they're less likely to get banged into. Jake puts a hand on her waist, like they're going to waltz, then leans down to whisper over the noise. "Start on the right. Forward, back, triple step to the side, triple to the side. Then the other way, okay?"

Twice through, and their feet start moving in sync. A few more times, and it's almost automatic. Jake dips their hands up and down. But it's nothing like the other dancers.

"Are you ready?" he says.

She doesn't know.

"Okay, then! Double time!"

Suddenly, instead of four beats to a step, there's only two. And now they're bouncing, moving fast to the beat of the band. Eva laughs. "What dance is this?"

"Lindy," he yells. "À la Jacob Katz. And . . . turn!" He takes the first step of each pattern in a different direction, and they travel through the crowd, making a pattern on the floor, crisscrossing all the dancers doing the same sort of thing.

The song changes, but the step still works. They find their beat and start again, and every now and then, instead of one of the triple steps, Jake lets go of her waist and spins her one time under his arm, grabbing her back in time to start it all over again.

"You didn't tell me you were good at dancing!" he shouts.

She isn't sure she is. But she's laughing, dizzy with the heat and the lights that spin as they spin and the noise and the beat of the drums.

She's like a girl who doesn't remember the war.

She's like someone she's never met.

The music winds down, and now the beat is slow, and Jake changes their dance to match it. She's against his chest, like she was before, his chin in her hair, their hands held together near her cheek. She doesn't even know how she got there. She closes her eyes and the world is made of music. And movement. Of him.

The song changes. The band changes. One taking over straight from the other. The rhythm sways. They dance until Jake leans down and whispers, "Eva."

She looks up. Blinking. They're still dancing, but the room isn't as loud, and no one is bumping against their shoulders.

"It's three a.m.," he whispers.

She nods, still in a trance, and he leads her off the floor, along a meandering path through the mostly empty tables. Jake hands the yawning girl in the red cap the little card, and they leave the club hand in hand, Eva swinging her purse as they walk down the clearing sidewalk.

Jake looks down at her and laughs. "You're dance drunk." His thumb rubs her knuckles.

They sit together on the train, empty except for a man sleeping full-length along one of the seats, one of his hands scraping the floor. This time Jake puts an arm around her, and she leans against his neck.

"Where do you live?" she murmurs.

"With my mother and Uncle Paul. Upper West Side."

"Do you have brothers? Sisters?"

"Nope."

"Will your mother be angry, when you come home so late?"

"She's probably called the police."

Eva smiles. "Will your father be angry?"

"No. He's dead."

"I'm sorry."

"That's okay."

They rock together, back and forth with the train.

"What do you want to do, for work, when you finish your school?"

"Write for the newspapers. Here, or somewhere else."

"You would not go somewhere else. You love it . . . here."

"Hmmm. Say, Bluebird, you're not sleepy or anything, are you?"

Eva shakes her head and tucks her head in tighter. Her eyes are closed.

Jake smells like dancing.

He takes her by the hand again to leave the train. Outside, the store windows are dark, and so are the ones above them, the street nearly deserted. She can hear a baby crying somewhere, wailing almost the exact the same note as a faraway siren.

Jake lifts a hand to a patrolling policeman, then takes her around the block to the little alley, to the dark strip of trees and blowing litter between the backyards. Through the gate, and she's back in the square of paving stones and grass behind Powell House. There's a light on over the back door, every other window dark. Eva looks up.

"Did they lock the doors?" She hadn't thought of this.

"Lucky I'm the one you decided to get dance drunk with." He holds up a key on a ring of keys and puts it to the lock. The back door cracks open with the softest of squeaks. She's supposed to go inside now, but he hasn't let go of her hand.

She watches him slowly untwine each of her fingers. But he holds on to the last one, lifting it until it's just pressing against his lips. His jaw is scratchy, but his mouth is soft. He closes his pretty eyes. Smiles beneath her fingertip. Then he lays her hand back at her side.

"'Night," he whispers, and walks away, hands in his pockets, out the gate and into the dark.

Eva shuts the door behind her without a noise. She shivers.

The house is in deep peace. Shadowy. She tiptoes up the stairs, wondering how she'd never noticed so many creaks, sliding along the wall to avoid them. Brigit is actually snoring, the dirty dinner dishes Bets brought still on the little table. Eva takes off her clothes, but it's too hot for a nightgown, so she sits in the windowsill in her camisole, and she can't see a rusty car or anyone on the street at all. She puts the finger Jake kissed against her mouth. Closes her eyes.

It is so unfair. To want so much what you should not have. To think he wants you back. When he should not want anything to do with you at all. And she won't be able to do what she'd planned. Walk away. Disappear. Jake will come after her, like he did tonight.

She could tell him. The truth. Or enough of it. About who she's been, who was in that apartment tonight. He would walk away on his own, then.

It's what she should do. It would be best.

And she doesn't want to do it like she doesn't want to do her own surgery.

It's going to hurt.

Her guilt spreads like a venom. Sickening.

She crawls into bed with Brigit and the kitten, a hint of dawn beginning behind the buildings, and when she opens her eyes again, the room is bright, and so is Brigit. She's out of bed, smiling, happy, examining the one shoe she has put on. Eva feels the poison bubble up again. Ebbing and flowing. But Brigit's long sleep doesn't seem to have done her any harm, and the words Eva read in that file last night are like a nightmare that disappears with the sun.

"*Guten Morgen*, Brigit," she whispers.

She swings her feet out of bed, heavy-lidded and sore inside, and goes to hang up the clothes she'd left on the floor. She never leaves her clothes on the floor. She picks up her black heels, and her purse, and sets them inside the wardrobe.

Then she grabs up her purse again, twisting open the little snap.

The photograph is gone.

CHAPTER THIRTY-SEVEN

—— *August 1946* ——

EVA SEARCHES HER purse again, running her fingers through the slit in the lining.

Where could the photograph have gone?

When could it have gone?

She looks at Brigit, still admiring her one shoe. Could Brigit have found it in her purse? Taken it? She checks Brigit's pockets. Under the bed. She hadn't locked the door last night. What if that picture is lying around, somewhere in Powell House? To be picked up by Bets. Martha. A photograph of her, in that ridiculous dress, sitting in front of the Nazi eagle.

It makes her ill to think about it.

She checks the wardrobe. Snatches up her blouse from the floor and stops, hands dropping to her sides.

There's a bird on the rug. Just below the window where she'd been sitting last night.

A dead bird.

She steps back. Throws another quick glance at Brigit. But now Brigit is busy wrapping yarn around a spoon. It's a sparrow, Eva thinks, brown and nondescript, without a wound or a mark that she can see.

And she can feel the pieces of herself. Rising and falling. Crashing, shattering one against the other like waves from opposite directions. Telling her to remember what she cannot remember.

There had been something in that file last night. Something about a bird.

"Knock, knock!" says a voice from the door. Eva spins, and it's Peggy, her curly, gray hair in a frizz. "Sorry for the startlement, and . . . hello there, lovely."

Brigit is sticking out her shoe for Peggy to see, dimpling like a cherub. Eva takes a little step sideways and drops her blouse over the dead bird.

"I've come to strike a bargain," Peggy announces. And she holds up a dress. Sky blue, shiny and slim, with a wide, low collar and covered buttons. "I came across this in the sewing room down on Twenty-Third, where we do up clothes and send them overseas . . ."

Her blouse on the floor had come from an AFSC box. And so had her shoes.

". . . and I thought you might like something a little more formal for this afternoon . . ."

The party. For the art exhibition. She'd completely forgotten it was today. That means Jake is coming.

". . . and it wasn't likely to be anybody else's size, and it's just your color. So I did a little ironing and thought I'd offer it in trade for a mountain of silver that needs to be polished, because Colette was supposed to help but Jimmy's sick."

Then Peggy leans forward and whispers, "Actually, you'd be making a terrible mistake to accept, because I was going to give this to you, anyway. But would you come polish silver?"

This probably means that Peggy has not seen a photograph of Eva as a Nazi.

Eva forces a smile, and says, yes, of course, and thank you, and in ten minutes, she has both her and Brigit dressed and downstairs with their dirty dishes. And no one else has seen a picture of Eva as a Nazi, either, because everyone smiles and says good morning. And as soon as Brigit is settled, Eva slips out the back, finds a trowel in the little potting shed, and buries the bird she'd had in her pocket—well wrapped in tissue—in a back corner of the garden.

She needs to read that file.

She needs to understand exactly what Brigit is capable of.

The pile of silver waiting to be relieved of its tarnish is exactly as Peggy said. Mountainous. Serving bowls, platters, a punch bowl, little tongs, and other things Eva can't see because they're underneath the rest. Peggy is already at the sink with an apron, scouring with salt and hot lemon, while Eva feeds Brigit and the kitten.

Bets and Mother Martha are at the table, too, going over the food deliveries and the guest list. The head of the Jewish Women's Council, the Urban League, members of the Federation of Churches, the Guggenheim, the president of Hunter College, the wife of the former minister to Liberia, others who should have special tours. Dignitaries, Eva thinks. They can hear Mrs. Angel running the sweeper in the parlor over their heads.

Peggy hands Eva a sugar bowl to buff, lowering her voice to keep from disturbing Bets and Martha. "And now, my dear, you get to hear the other part of my bargain for you. Or maybe bribe is the better word. I do a little luncheon here on Tuesdays, and for the past three weeks, we've had some volunteers reading a play, *Private Life of the Master Race*, by Brecht. Do you know it?"

Eva polishes and polishes her bowl, like the maids used to do to Grandmama's silver. She shakes her head.

"It was banned in Germany, being not all that complimentary to Hitler, but it's very provocative, with different viewpoints on life in

Nazi Germany. A Jewish professor in the city, a butcher forced to live as a Nazi, the baker who believes in Nazism, that sort of thing. Jacob is going to come and read one of the parts for us, since Jimmy is sick . . ."

Her mind goes straight to last night. Music. Movement.

". . . and I thought for our discussion, how fascinating it would be to hear from someone who has lived through exactly what Brecht was writing about. Would you come?"

Eva buffs the sugar bowl. Hard. There is not one thing about how she lived as a Nazi that she would ever like to discuss at Powell House. And she's not sure she could actually survive listening to Jake read a play about it.

Or maybe having to listen to him read it would be fair. Maybe it would be justice.

"All opinions welcome," Peggy says. "We encourage different ideas . . ."

But Eva only asks, "What is wrong with Jimmy?"

"Oh, he gets bouts of malaria ever since the war," Peggy sighs, starting on the punch bowl. "Colette is learning to nurse him through it."

"But I thought . . . Jimmy was not in the war?"

Martha leans over and says, "James requested to drive an ambulance, but he was sent to a civilian work camp instead, with other conscientious objectors. To take over a logging operation for the men who had joined up."

"But it wasn't actually about logging," Peggy says. "The army injected all those boys with malaria, on purpose, and did experiments on them, testing different cures. Told them they were being vaccinated . . ."

"Isn't that disgusting?" says Bets.

Yes, Eva thinks.

Peggy shakes her head. "And malaria stays with you, too. Gives you bouts of fever and chills for the rest of your life."

"And all because those young men acted on what they believed," Martha says. "That killing is wrong, no matter what."

Killing is wrong. No matter what.

Eva keeps her eyes on her silver. "But what about . . . justice?" she asks. Bets puts down her pen. "What if the punishment is earned?"

"The problem with justice," says Peggy, "is that in order to dispense it, someone has to be the judge. And who among us is qualified? What person has the right to decide someone else's life or death?"

But sometimes, Eva thinks, judgment is easy. Some things are so wrong, there's no question. Sometimes, someone has to stop the wrong thing from happening.

Peggy sighs, rubbing vigorously with her cloth. "It's . . . complicated."

Eva agrees with her. Brigit is tugging Eva's skirt, clamoring for attention. Eva moves Brigit's hands away and Bets gives her a spoon.

"I don't want you to think all of America is like that," Peggy says. "It's the case of a few bad apples running amuck and getting away with what they shouldn't, that's all."

Eva gives up trying to envision apples running. But she understands what Peggy means to say, anyway.

"The good thing about America," Bets says, "is that when something does run amuck, at least we can decide to do something about it."

"And what about your young men who were made to be sick?" Eva asks. "What are the people doing about that?"

Martha smiles. "Thee have hit upon the problem, dear. People have to know about a thing to stop it, and Quakers are a quiet lot. More than is good for them, sometimes."

Brigit tugs Eva's skirt again. Spoons are not quite as interesting as they used to be. But then Olive comes in with a cookie delivery and when she gives one to Brigit, Brigit's smile puts the sunshine to shame. Peggy laughs, and Eva smiles, polishing her silver with a steady hand.

She feels calmer now. Focused. Someone does know about her father. Someone does know about what the government would like to let him do. And it's her. Justice is up to her. And that is more important than her guilt, her anger, or her pain.

It's probably not the conclusion these ladies would have expected her to draw.

She sets down her shining bowl and picks up another platter, buffing until she can see her face, reflected like a mirror. And with each swipe of the cloth, she says a name. Twenty-seven of them. She says who she is.

The exhibition opens at five. Everyone should be gone by eight. She'll have Brigit asleep by nine and go out the back. She'll make absolutely sure she is not followed. At the bus station, she'll get the file, take it to the ladies' room, and read it. The gun she'll put in her purse. And this time, she won't go into the apartment until Rolf really has left for work. This time, she won't leave until her father comes.

She won't leave without justice. And then what comes will come.

Bets determines that Eva has the prettiest handwriting of the group, so she spends the afternoon writing names on cards. Selma Burke. Palmer Hayden. Ellis Wilson. Every name from Bets's list, gluing each card to a safety pin, so the guests can recognize the artists. She's quiet while she writes, thinking about what she might say to Jake.

She doesn't have the words. But if she can take a gun to Rolf's apartment, then surely she can tell Jake the truth.

His light has no place in her darkness. And he will have to know it.

Maybe it will be pain, after all, that will be her own justice.

Or being alone.

Eva takes Brigit upstairs, out of the last-minute scurry. Brigit looks out the window, wanting the birds to come, but Eva gives her the harmonica instead, and leaves the window shut. She pulls the blue dress over her head, tries to tame down her hair, and then lets it be what it is. And at a few minutes before five, Mrs. Angel comes in, and Eva promises to switch places with her in an hour.

Eva watches her feet in their ankle-strap heels. Down every step. Walking across each landing. Closer. Closer. She doesn't know what she's going to say to him.

Except the truth.

She can hear the people in the foyer before she can see them. And when she rounds the curve of the stairs, Martha and Bets are shaking gloved hands, all the furs and pearls, ties and flowered hats mingling in a little crowd. And Jake is on the bottom step, waiting for her. He's shaved, combed his hair, and is wearing an actual suit and tie, unwrinkled, though not with the jacket buttoned.

He doesn't move. Just watches her come down the stairs. And he smiles.

She smiles back. It can't be helped.

"Hi, Bluebird," he says, very quiet. "Tired today?"

"A little."

"I never slept."

He lifts a hand, like he's going to tuck her hair behind her ear, and just brushes a thumb against the corner of her mouth. She shivers.

And she can't remember what the truth is anymore.

Jake leans against the wall. "Come out with me tonight."

She shakes her head. But she's still smiling.

"I was thinking we could take Brigit up to the music room, she'd like that. And after she's asleep, we could go down to the park. There's this guy I know, he rents the boats on the lake, he said he'd let us . . ."

And then Jake looks over his shoulder. A woman in a little black hat has just come through the door, kissing Martha on the cheek.

"Hey," he says. "Fair warning. You're about to meet my mother."

She takes a quick peek around Jake. The woman is coming straight for them.

"And I wouldn't mention that nightclub if I were you," Jake whispers. And then he's standing up straight and the woman is beside them, nudging Jake with her elbow.

"Is this her?" she asks. "Is this the one? There's nothing to her!"

She has plucked eyebrows, dark brown hair with no gray, tall heels, and two wedding rings strung on a gold chain around her neck. Eva knows now, where Jake got his eyes. Though she's never seen his gaze narrowed at her quite like this one.

"Eva Gerst," says Jake. "This is my mother."

"I have something to say to you," says Mrs. Katz. "I won't have Jacob running around with girls. He's got responsibilities. He's got school to finish, and he won't do it staying out all night. He's going places, and there will be plenty of nice girls for him to choose from. Later. Once he's made something of himself."

And by "nice girls," Eva thinks, Mrs. Katz means any girl other than her. She glances at Jake, rocking on his heels with his brows up, waiting to see where this might go. Eva tries to imagine what it would be like to have a mother like his.

A mother who cares.

She looks back at Mrs. Katz. "I agree with you."

Mrs. Katz would be surprised to know just how much she agrees.

"Last night was my fault. He probably told you it was his, but he's only being nice. I was . . . I have a friend who came here with me . . ."

Jake is tilting his head in encouragement.

". . . she is not well. I needed help, but I should not have let him stay out so late when he has . . . papers . . ."—Jake half-closes his eyes, giving her the tiniest nod—"for his classes. I have always been told that . . . an education should come first . . ."

An image of Frau Koch flashes through her mind, standing beneath the fluttering swastikas, telling her rapt little group that good German girls get married and produce good German babies as soon as they're able. That a German girl would never ruin her blood-line. Would never, ever even think of sullying herself with a boy like Jacob Katz.

When Jake is the one who is too good for her.

Eva leans forward, like Jake isn't there.

"And after his school, he will be able to choose any girl he wants. Any of them. That is true, isn't it, Mrs. Katz?"

And out of nowhere, she feels tears behind her eyes. As if she isn't German at all. She is so jealous of that future girl. Whoever she is.

Mrs. Katz looks her up and down again, penciled brows pushed together. "Jacob," she says, "go get us some punch."

He goes, one side of his mouth smiling.

Mrs. Katz takes Eva by the arm, and they walk into the parlor, where the flowers are in the vases and little groups chat and point, milling around the art. Mrs. Katz wants to know how long she has been in New York. Is she Jewish? Has she ever thought about being Jewish? That's too bad. Where is her family? That's too bad, too. Jacob lost his father two years ago . . .

Eva sees Augusta behind them, explaining how she based her sculpture of a little boy's face on her own nephew. A rotund little man bends down, peering at it through his spectacles. Augusta smiles, and Eva smiles back.

"You were never married over there, were you?" Mrs. Katz is saying. "You're not a widow or anything?"

"Go on, Mom," says Jake, bringing her a cup. "Ask whatever's on your mind. Don't hesitate on our account."

"They do things young over there, Jacob." She turns to look at the painting on an easel in front of them. Three men lined up on a bench at a bus stop, one flicking his cigarette ash to the wind. Eva looks at it with her.

"Do you smoke, Miss Gerst?" she asks.

She thinks of Jake in the jazz club, stubbing out his third cigarette. "No. I'd rather not. Cigarettes are so expensive, and there are so many other things to buy. Like books."

Mrs. Katz tilts her head again. "Hmmm."

Jake leans down to her ear and whispers, "Remind me to kiss you later." Which makes her blush, and Mrs. Katz notices that, too.

"Bring her for cake, Jacob," she says. "We'll bake her a cake."

Then someone thumps Jake on the back. "Hi, Jake. Hi, Eva."

It's Larry, and Lucy is with him, and Colette. Larry sidles up next to Eva and smiles. "Destroyed any enemies lately?"

Eva shakes her head. She thinks he's talking about Ping-Pong. Jake moves a little closer.

"Hey, Larry. This is nice, right?" He barely puts a hand on Eva's elbow, steering her a little away from Larry and his mother. But it's a move everyone notices. Eva sees Lucy's eyebrows rise. "Hi, Colette," Jake says. "How's Jimmy?"

"Sick," she says, tossing her head.

Lucy asks if anyone wants to go to Schrafft's afterward, for cokes and ice cream, but Jake says he has plans. Colette tells her that Eva has plans, too, and gives Eva a little wink. Eva smiles, but she is looking beyond Colette's shoulder at the sculpture of Minerva. And she remembers exactly how it makes her feel.

Jake introduces her to Mrs. Rutowski, one of his previous assigned friends, and then to Mrs. Powell, a smiley, soft-looking woman who lent the AFSC her house, saying how pleased she is to be attending such an exhibition in her former living room. And then Jake is talking to Larry, laughing about nothing in particular, and Eva isn't jealous of that girl from Jake's future at all.

She hates her.

Eva drifts away, to where a pasty woman with cherries on her hat is standing just on the other side of Minerva, cleaning horn-rimmed glasses, whispering to her companion. "Offensive," she says. And "unsanitary." Though not loud enough for many others to hear. She looks right at Eva, lips set in a line.

"Ridiculous. Isn't it?"

"It is," Eva snaps. "They don't have art half this good in Germany."

The woman opens her mouth, and Eva spins on heel, turning her back on her.

And looks straight into the face of Mr. Cruickshanks.

CHAPTER THIRTY-EIGHT

—— *August 1946* ——

"JOIN ME, BLUEBIRD?" says Mr. Cruickshanks.

Eva glances down at the hand on her arm. This Mr. Cruickshanks's fingers are stained, eyes blurred by the thick, black glasses, and she feels something inside her shift into gear.

She's never really afraid once the battle is on her.

He steers her out of the room in a way that looks friendly, but with a grip that isn't. Martha is standing between the front and back parlors, tinging a spoon against a glass, and no one seems to notice them go. Into the foyer, down the steps, and through the door of the Refugee Office, where he gives Eva enough of a shove to make her stumble.

"Have a seat," he says.

The ceiling squeaks with feet above them. Little shuffles while Martha talks. Eva sits in a chair behind a desk, as close as she can get to the door. Cruickshanks is wearing the same suit as the first time she met him in the kitchen, but he's much more angry. He makes himself comfortable on the edge of a desk, wrinkling the papers he's sitting on. She watches his fingers drum.

Rat-tat-tat. Rat-tat-tat-tat.

"So did the Nazis not believe in using telephones, Bluebird? Or have you just forgotten how?"

She doesn't answer this.

"We had a deal," he says. "And you broke it."

"I have not broken our deal." Or not as much as she will tonight.

"Really?" says Cruickshanks. "See, that's funny. Because one of the first things I said to you was, don't be talking to nobody but me. And have I heard a word from you? Not a peep. But your boyfriend, now. I've heard from him, haven't I?"

He leans back, propping his feet up on the arm of a chair, and looks Eva over in an appraising way. "That was quick work. I didn't know you had it in you."

Mrs. Katz had thought the same thing.

"He found the card," Eva says. "I haven't told him anything about . . ."

And then the door bursts open, and Jake is in the room. He looks back and forth between the two of them, then shuts the door and puts out a hand.

"Cruickshanks, right?"

Mr. Cruickshanks doesn't take his hand, but he does laugh. He laughs in a way that is not funny.

"Oh, dear. Oh, deary dear. Take the weight off, son." And he shoves a chair toward Jake with his foot.

Jake shoots a questioning look at Eva. A look she has no answer for. He sits on the edge of the chair.

"So, did you get them?" Jake asks. "Down in the Bowery?"

"Oh, did we get them?" Cruickshanks grins at Eva. "He asks, because he doesn't know anything, right?"

Eva says nothing.

"No, son," says Cruickshanks. "We didn't 'get them.' They've skipped."

Jake sits up. "What?"

"I mean they've taken off. Left town, probably. We lost the guard dog and his girlfriend on the subway. And not a soul's been back to that apartment since you two were there. The window's still open. And what if it rains, huh? What then?"

He laughs in his unfunny way again, but Eva doesn't move. Her guilt and her anger are suddenly at war. She should have stepped out of that closet. She should have taken her mother's gun from her purse. She should have left that photo in Rolf's drawer. And now, she has failed them. Everyone. All the names. All the photographs on the wall.

She's taken away their justice.

Jake is watching her. And it's hard to find air.

Cruickshanks lights a cigarette. Slowly. "So here's the thing I need to know," he says. "Which one of you tipped them off?"

Jake's gaze whips around. Eva shakes her head.

"Don't look so innocent, you two. Somebody did it, and it sure wasn't me. So after the apartment, where did you go? When we lost the guard dog on the subway, we picked you two back up at the drugstore. You were making a call, sweetie. Who were you calling?"

Now the questioning look Jake shoots Eva is a hard one. Because she was supposed to have been calling Cruickshanks.

But she is thinking. Fast. Cruickshanks missed the bus station. He doesn't know about Anna Ptaszynska's file. She looks back at Jake, willing him not to say anything. Then she levels her gaze at Cruickshanks.

"I was calling you. To tell you we had found them."

"But I didn't get a call from you, buttercup."

"They said no one was there with . . . your name, so I . . . left a message."

Cruickshanks blows smoke.

"I . . . must have . . . did I dial the wrong number?"

Jake's brows are drawn together.

"And where did you go after the apartment?" asks Cruickshanks patiently.

"To the drugstore."

Jake's eyes jump back to her face.

Eva puts her elbows on the desk. Makes sure Cruickshanks is looking at her. She tilts her head at Jake. "He was only helping. He brought me the address. Helped me to get into the apartment. To do the right thing. To bring Nazis who have . . . escaped to trial. That is all. Nothing else. Maybe they knew, somehow, that someone had been in the apartment and were afraid."

Cruickshanks studies her face. He studies his cigarette. "Yeah, I think I get it. The whole thing's a crying shame, really." Then he hops off the desk. "Well, we'll just have to start again. Hey, listen, thanks for your help, pal."

He walks over and sticks out a hand to Jake. Jake stands and shakes it. Reluctantly. He's confused. And wary. Eva can see it.

"You'll understand, of course, that the U.S. government would appreciate you keeping quiet about all this. If word gets out, these guys will go so deep underground we'll never nab them, right?"

Jake nods, still shaking his hand.

"And you'll also get that I need to talk to the lady here alone. She still has good info for us. She can be a big help. So, if you don't mind?"

Jake's gaze cuts to Eva, and she nods. "Yeah, okay," he says. "Sure."

He turns, moves slowly to the door. Cruickshanks goes back to the desk. And Eva watches Jake's hand creep up to his jacket pocket, memory lighting up his lovely eyes.

And she pulls in a breath. The letter. To Dr. Schneider. Jake put it in his pocket and she'd forgotten.

"Hey, listen," Jake says, "I have . . ."

His eyes meet Eva's and she gives him one sharp shake of the head.

"What?" says Cruickshanks, turning around.

"Oh . . ." Jake hesitates. "Nothing. I just remembered I know where he works, but you got that already, right?"

"Yep," says Cruickshanks. "See ya."

Jake throws Eva a look, one she doesn't have any trouble interpreting. She has some explaining to do.

As soon as Jake is out the door, Cruickshanks takes three springing steps, watching around the jamb until Jake is out of the hall and up the stairs. The noise from above them is almost deafening with the movement of so many feet. Martha must have finished her talk.

Cruickshanks spins on a heel. "All right, Bluebird. I kept your cover. What's with bringing in the boyfriend?"

"I had to tell him something." She gets up. Walks across the room. "With your man watching all the time, following us down the street. He noticed."

"Wait a second, he didn't notice us, Bluebird. Are you talking about your friend in the rusty car?"

Eva turns. "He's not . . . one of you?"

"Nope. Which you would know, if you'd called in like you were supposed to. Where did the guy follow you to?"

"Nowhere. He lost us before we took a bus. He just sits in front of the house."

"Yeah, well he can disappear when he wants to, sweetie. We thought . . ." Cruickshanks takes the last drag of his cigarette down to the stub, grinding it beneath his heel on the floor. "Okay, leave the man in the car to me, Bluebird. So, where do you think Daddy went to?"

"I don't know."

"And you would tell me if you did?"

"Why wouldn't I?"

"Because I don't think you're being straight with me. Who else have you been talking to?"

"No one."

Cruickshanks sighs, shakes his head. "I hate it when you lie. You keep forgetting that I can have you in a cell"—he snaps his fingers—"like that. It would be easy. One phone call. And you . . . disappear."

She hasn't forgotten.

"So if you haven't been chatting with any other old friends, then where did you get this? Because you sure didn't have it on the boat with you, Bluebird." And he throws a photograph from his jacket pocket down on Olive's desk.

The photograph of Inge, in her pink dress. Eva shakes her head. They'd followed her from the drugstore. Right into the Zanzibar. She remembers the man at the bar, raising his glass to her. He hadn't been flirting. He'd been a Cruickshanks. And he'd probably bribed that girl in the red cap for a peek in her purse. And just how many other times had they searched her things, to know this wasn't on the boat?

Luckily, they'd never thought to search the skirt she was wearing.

Eva sits down. Leans back. Crosses her legs. "It was in Rolf's drawer. In the apartment. My father must have given it to him."

"A keepsake, huh? Likes to look at your picture, does he?" Cruickshanks tilts his head. "Ah! But you don't like that so well. Is this the real boyfriend, Bluebird? Did you have a spat? Or . . ." He tilts his head the other way, grinning. "Maybe this guy was not exactly your idea?"

Eva crosses her arms.

"All right. Then give me something. How'd you find the guy in the first place?"

"I saw him at the hospital. Rolf . . . Dieter."

"Rolf Dieter. That was the German name? Yeah, okay, that might help. You think Daddy and his guard dog are still together?"

"Yes. Or they will be."

Cruickshanks gets out another cigarette, but he doesn't light it. He taps it on his palm. *Rat, tat, tat.* Dull and muffled. "Look. This Rolf doesn't have to be part of the package. Maybe we can take care of it, you know? But you blew it, taking that picture. You tipped them off, and they skedaddled."

Eva levels her gaze. "I didn't want him looking at me."

"Fair enough," says Cruickshanks. "But if you could have let them know it was you, even a little note, they might not be on the lam right now."

He taps a stained finger against his tooth, glancing up at the creaking ceiling.

"Listen, Bluebird. You did a good job finding Daddy the first time, so you're just going to have to do it again. In the meantime, stay here with the turtledoves. This setup is sweet. And get rid of the boyfriend."

He comes and stands next to her. And now he's so close she can see the eyes behind the glasses. Two black holes. "This isn't a game we're playing," he says. "I don't want to put bullets in people, but I don't hesitate. And I don't get so bothered about it, either. It has to be us that gets the Doctor. The United States. Everything is riding on it. I'll take care of the guy that's been watching. You find Daddy."

She nods, and he backs away.

"Check in every night. There's the telephone. You'll work it out.

And don't forget, you need to be useful, Bluebird. Daddy is what we care about. And we've got leads of our own. You get it?"

She gets it.

"What's the word on Anna Ptaszynska?"

"I told you she was dead."

"And I told you she wasn't." Cruickshanks grins. "How's your friend doing? The crazy one? No dead bodies popping up, I hope?"

Eva doesn't reply.

"You know, I heard she was your neighbor, a while back. Known your family a long time. Not much use now, is she? What did the doctor say? Any joy?"

He knows Brigit saw a doctor. Can Cruickshanks listen to the telephones?

"The doctor says there is nothing they can do for her."

Cruickshanks' grin broadens. It is much too wide.

"Do you think that's funny?" Eva asks.

"All right, all right. Keep your shirt on. Keep her close by, that's all. Okay, I'm gone. If you see any other old friends mopping floors or running a street sweeper, you let me know."

And when Eva looks up again, Cruickshanks really is gone. And he's left her photograph on the desk. She picks it up. She should rip it to shreds. Burn it. But there's nowhere in here to get rid of the pieces.

She folds the picture in half and stuffs it in her bra. Gingerly picks up the cold cigarette butt Cruickshanks left on the floor and drops it in Olive's trash can, wiping the ash from the floor tiles with her shoe. She straightens the papers on Olive's desk, then she shuts the office door and walks slowly down the hall.

She's a kaleidoscope. All the different pieces of herself shaken together. Fear. Because the only reason they haven't taken Brigit is that they think she's useless. Anger. Because she lost her father. Guilt. Because there will be no justice. Not tonight.

And there it comes, the relief. Because there will be no justice. Not tonight.

And that makes her angry. And guilty. And scared that she won't be able to do it.

And someone grabs her arm from the dim of the stairs.

Eva gasps, but it's only Jake. Or maybe it isn't. Or not the Jake she knows.

He doesn't say a word. Just takes her out the back door, up the stone steps, and into the little paved courtyard behind Powell House. Out the back gate, into the no-man's-land between the backyards, startling the pigeons.

For a few seconds, the air is full of wings.

He sits her on an old, overturned crate, the last beams of the low-ering sun making the tree leaves glow.

And he is just standing there. Looking down at her.

He kicks another crate over and sits on it, even though it's dirty, and he's in his suit. He stares at her. And then he looks away. He puts his elbows on his knees.

"You know," he says, very quietly. "The funny thing about old houses is they have their quirks. We've laughed about it, how when they put in the furnace and that little toilet under the stairs, that the vent goes straight up from the Refugee Office. And how, if you hap-pen to go at the wrong time, you could have to pretend not to know some pretty personal stuff getting discussed down there. That's funny, huh?"

And Eva understands. She understands everything.

Jake runs his hands through his hair.

"So when," he says, voice rising, "were you going to tell me about Daddy?"

CHAPTER THIRTY-NINE

—— *August 1946* ——

"YOUR FATHER," JAKE says. "That's who you've been looking for. That's whose room we were in, wasn't it? The sick bastard with the people he's probably murdered all over his wall."

Eva breathes. And breathes.

"The 'doctor' who wrote this . . ."

He pulls the letter to Dr. Schneider out of his pocket, shaking it at her.

". . . about how degrading it is to practice the noble art of his medicine among all the . . . wait, let me see how he wrote it. The 'Jew pigs.'" He shakes it again. "So what've you been doing? Finding out what it's like to get dirty? Curious what it's like to roll in the mud?"

Eva looks away. That had been a hard slap, even though he hadn't touched her.

"And here I was, thinking you were the one to have done something noble. To not be Jewish and end up in a camp. That you were . . . some resistance fighter or something. That it was all probably too hard to talk about, that you'd tell me when you could, when you knew you could trust me . . ." His voice breaks, and he has to stop, take a breath. "And you weren't in a camp, were you? Your daddy was running the camp. That's how he got all those pictures. He was running it, wasn't he?"

Eva doesn't answer.

"Wasn't he?" Jake yells.

"Almost," she whispers.

"Which one? Which camp?"

"Sachsenhausen."

"Where was it? Tell me where!"

She almost can't say the words. "Near Berlin."

"So it could have been my family he was murdering." He throws the letter on the ground. Hits a finger against his chest. "My family, Eva!"

It could have been. A tear runs down her cheek. But she doesn't move.

"And you weren't one of those families just trying to get by, were you? Surviving until something changed. You were this man's daughter. You were cheering it on, weren't you? You were a Nazi through and through."

She thinks of pink roses, crushed beneath marching, booted feet.

"It's true, isn't it?"

She could try to deny it. She could try to explain. But she doesn't. This is what needs to happen. It's better for him. Safer for him. This is fair.

And it hurts so much.

Jake lets out a breath when she doesn't answer. Puts his head back in his hands. Looks up again. "You tipped them off."

Eva shakes her head. She will say this much. "I did not."

"You took a photograph! And you lied to Cruickshanks. I heard you. You lied about that file you got me to hide. And you lied about his name. That's not the name you told me in the hospital. Rolf, the first boyfriend . . ." He says Rolf's name like he wants to spit. "Where's the photograph? Did he take it with him?"

She shakes her head.

"Give it to me."

She looks into Jake's beautiful, hostile eyes, reaches down into her dress, and pulls out the photograph.

He takes it. Opens it. Looks at who she had been.

"Quite a little Nazi princess, weren't you?"

She takes that punch, too. This may be justice, but it is brutal.

"All those lies I told my mother. I went on and on, like an idiot. Like a fool. And you let me believe it. You let me believe all of it. While you played in the mud."

He picks up the letter and folds it up with the photograph, and then he stands, towering over her again.

"Do not come near me, Eva, do you understand? Don't speak, don't be in the same room with me." Then he pauses. "Is your name even Eva?"

She shakes her head, and Jake gives one, bitter laugh.

"Right. Stay away from me, whoever you are. Because I can't stand the sight of you."

His feet crunch in the weedy dirt as he walks away, and each step feels like one of her mother's slaps. Stinging. And stinging. Building until the pain can't be borne.

But she bears it.

Eva gets up from the crate, brushing the dirt from her new dress, and walks back to Powell House. Up the stairs, through the party, and up again to the blue room, where Olive has taken over for Mrs. Angel. And Brigit doesn't like it. She's crammed herself into the corner beside the wardrobe.

"I am very sorry to be so late," Eva whispers.

"Oh, that's okay," Olive says, "though I'm sure I didn't do things right. I just hated for Mrs. Angel to miss . . . Hey, are you okay?"

Eva smiles. "Of course. I'm fine. Please go down and . . . have a good time."

"Well, if you say so . . ." She looks past Eva, to where Brigit is crouched, fingers over her eyes. "I hope everyone is all right."

Eva gets Brigit calmed down once Olive is gone. She gives her the harmonica again, which hurts, like she knew it would. It's well after dark when Bets comes up to tell her that all the guests are gone, but the artists are staying, and everyone is going to knock up sandwiches again in the kitchen, and doesn't she want to come down?

"Brigit wouldn't do well, I think," Eva says.

"Well, let me bring a tray up again. I know it's hard to leave her. Did you have a good time? The dress looked so nice. I heard you met Jake's mother."

"Yes," says Eva, turning to fiddle with something on the dresser that doesn't exist. "I liked her. Was your show a success?"

"A rip-roaring one. Art can be such an eye-opener. Maybe we opened some eyes. And our artists sold five pieces, and food on the table never hurt anybody, right? Such a good day . . ."

"Yes," Eva says.

"Okay. Sit tight, and someone will be up with the eats."

It's Peggy who comes with the tray, elated, her manicure a mess from the silver polishing. Eva thanks her for the dress. Then she feeds Brigit and takes her through all their nightly rituals: bath, toilet, nightgown, brushing her teeth, brushing her hair. She clips her nails, both fingers and toes. And when Brigit goes to sleep, kitten tucked in with her, Eva brings out Brigit's clothes from the wardrobe, scrubs a little stain off one of the collars, and sponges everything fresh and clean. The clock ticks. She hears Bets go up the stairs. So she puts on her dressing gown, takes the little bag that has her toiletries in it, and locks the bathroom door behind her.

She runs the bathtub, piping hot. There will be no hot water left, but it's late, and maybe no one will mind. The water is just on the edge of burning when she steps in, sinking up to her chest. Sweat drips down her temples. Into her eyes. Then she takes soap and a washcloth and she scrubs, hard, until she turns pink. And bright red. Until she is sore in places. As if she could scour the Nazi off her skin. Until her pulse is racing and she's sick and dizzy with the heat.

The bathtub drain is slow, loud and gurgling. And while the water seeps away, she sits on the rug, folds the towel across her face and cries. Screams as loud as she dares into the muffling fabric.

She is only one piece of herself now. Pain. Frozen and pierced.

And the next morning, when the sun is just brightening the curtains, Eva opens her eyes to a commotion somewhere below her. Brigit is sleeping undisturbed, but there are voices raised, calling in alarm. Eva puts on the dressing gown and hurries down the stairs.

Bets and Martha and Olive are in the parlor, hair in pins and in kerchiefs and cold cream, Olive with bare legs from her knees to her toes. But they all share the exact same expression of horror. Because someone has taken the fire poker and smashed the sculpture of Minerva into dusty chunks on the carpet.

The sight is wrong. Everything it shouldn't be. It makes Eva feel ill.

She leaves them discussing who went to bed last, who locked the doors. Were all the windows locked, who checked? Hurrying back up to the blue room, softly shutting the door. The kitten stretches, and Brigit sighs, but she doesn't wake.

She hadn't locked the bedroom door last night. She should lock it. Always.

Eva opens the window. The window she was sure she'd already opened, and sits on the sill.

There's no man with shiny shoes. She almost misses him.

But if he wasn't a Cruickshanks, then who was he? And why had a tough-talking American agent, with all his "I don't care if I put bullets in people" swagger, left a man sitting out there, brazenly watching her door?

Unless he thinks the man with shiny shoes is also an American agent. An American agent, but not a Mr. Cruickshanks. Hadn't she asked the first one, in Biberach, if all the United States government was aware of her rotten deal? And hadn't he told her that not everyone had the vision? It had made it impossible for her to go to anyone else, to know who would take her father to trial, and who might put him to work. But a man who watches and that a Cruickshanks leaves alone, maybe that was an American agent who would have arrested her father. Maybe that was the man she should have been talking to.

And maybe now she's waited a little too late to do it.

She watches the police arrive.

At breakfast, Martha says, "I'd like to finish my talk with thee this weekend, Eva, if thee could spare some time. Before Brigit's procedure at the hospital on Monday?"

"Yes," Eva replies. "But would you mind if I went on an errand this morning?"

She tells Bets and Martha that she met a man at the art show who was interested in having some German letters translated. That she might not be what he was looking for. Her English might not be good enough. She looks at her plate while she says it.

"But you must go," says Bets. "And yes, between us, we should be able to watch over Brigit."

Martha nods. "How long will thee be gone?

"Two hours," Eva says. "Not more." Now she keeps her eyes on her cup of tea. "Have you told Augusta about the sculpture?"

"Yes," Martha sighs. "The piece on display was a painted plaster cast. So there is a mold, and she can make another. It is mortifying, of course, to have such an awful thing happen here. We are going to find some funds to replace the materials for her, I hope. Though funds are . . . well. . . ."

"We're scraping the bottom of the barrel," says Bets. "But we'll find a way. Eva, are you okay?"

She looks up. Tries to do a better job with her smile. "Yes, of course."

Eva lets Brigit get settled with Bets. She tells Bets to make sure Brigit doesn't have knives. Or scissors. To be careful with the open windows. And she gets her ugly hat—the one Bets so helpfully rescued from the back seat of her car—Brigit's old sweater and her purse, and hurries down the stairs. She waits until Olive is in the kitchen and leaves one of her two remaining American bills under the paperweight on Martha's desk. For the sculpture. Then she walks out the front door of Powell House, slowly, pausing to look through her purse when her black heels hit the sidewalk.

She's learned that she doesn't easily see a Mr. Cruickshanks. But she's going to let him get a good look at her.

She walks down East 70th, like she had with Jake, turning on Lexington and passing by the subway station. She picks up her pace, walking around the block and down to Madison. Now she pauses often, stopping to look in store windows. And there is the man selling watches on the street corner again, bottling up the crowd. Eva steps into the middle of it, allows herself to get lost in it, the advantage of being short. And when the bus pulls up to the curb and the chaos is at its height, she backs straight up and through the pink door of Schrafft's.

The same man is behind the counter.

"Excuse me," she says.

"Hey! Jake's girl."

"Would you mind if I use your back door? I need to catch a train."

The man scratches his head beneath his paper cap. He shrugs. "Be my guest."

She makes a dash through the kitchen with its enormous aluminum vats, ignoring the same woman washing them, and out the alley door. She turns left again, past the garbage, out of the alley, around the block, back the way she came, and into a fabric store.

Eva waits, pretending to look at satins and prints, holding up the cloth to block her face while she watches the front windows. Three minutes, and a man goes hurrying by, toward Powell House. Not the Cruickshanks of last night. It's the Cruickshanks that had raised a glass to her in the Zanzibar.

She takes off her hat and stuffs it in her purse. Puts on Brigit's old sweater. The gray-bunned clerk of the fabric store is scowling. Eva walks out the door, two blocks in the opposite direction, and catches the subway.

And in half an hour, she is standing in the bus station, pulling out the key hanging from its string beneath her blouse. She puts it to the lock. Opens the door. And stares into an empty locker.

The metal case with Anna Ptaszynska's file is gone. And so is the gun.

Her father is gone. Jake is gone. Even the man with the shiny shoes is gone.

She has lost everything.

How long, she thinks, to translate a file? And what will they do? Will they come for Brigit anyway? Or is she "useless?"

Or will the experiment go on, even without her father?

And then she is tired. Sick of thinking. Fed up with trying to make everything turn out for the best.

It's time to finish it.

There will be justice, or there won't be. She still has a bread knife.

Eva slams the locker shut and turns the key. Walks to the counter of the bus station, and asks the attendant for the address of the *New York Times*.

CHAPTER FORTY

"My Vögelchen," says Papa. "Shall we start again?"

"Yes, Papa," she whispers. She is back in her pink dress, her hair neatly combed, feet sticking out from the end of the chair. But the dress is looser than it was.

"Do you want to learn to be better now?"

She nods.

"Who do you belong to?"

"Papa."

"Do you love your papa? Do you want to make him happy?"

She nods again. Her palms are sweaty, but she doesn't want to wipe them on the dress.

"Then show me, my Vögelchen."

Papa places a cardboard box on her lap. And he lifts the lid.

CHAPTER FORTY-ONE

—— *August 1946* ——

AT TWO-THIRTY ON Monday, they give Brigit her first pill, and at three, Bets says, "Oh, that's working nicely, isn't it?"

Eva had had her little meeting with Martha, who'd said she thought translation might be a good idea for a job, in a small way, even if it hadn't worked out the first time. Then she tries to ask Eva about her background, her education. What did her parents do? What did they intend for her to do? But finally, she'd taken off her glasses.

"Thee are full of worries. Let's make our plans after Brigit's appointment, yes?"

Eva had nodded and slipped upstairs, into the little toilet over the Refugee Office. And clearly through the vent, she can hear Martha say, "there will have been trauma." And "some depression is understandable." And Bets is saying that something has happened with Jake, because he isn't coming to the hospital tomorrow, when he'd gone to a lot of trouble to change his schedule so he could. Then Martha asks Bets if she's had any letters and Bets says no. She'd sounded sad. Not like Bets at all.

Jake could have told them who she is. Eva wonders why he hasn't.

She wonders when he will.

Brigit's eyes are getting drowsy, but she's awake enough to be walked carefully down the stairs. Bets and Eva put her between them in a taxicab, which Martha decided was worth the expense, just this once. And Brigit smiles and laughs and talks nonsense the whole way, completely undisturbed by the cabdriver.

"*Jaden dwa, jaden dwa*," she sings.

The cabdriver looks in the rearview mirror and shakes his head, muttering something about "loonies." Bets tells him he'll drive faster if he pipes down.

At the hospital, they take Brigit straight back to a room with rows of beds on wheels. The nurse seems to know all about her. The nurse has new shoes that match her starched uniform, hands scrubbed pink, and heavy, unkempt brows. She closes the curtains around the bed, and Eva helps her get Brigit into a hospital gown. Brigit is still smiling. Chattering. The second pill goes down. The nurse is as good at this as Eva.

"How long has she been out of Poland?" asks the nurse.

Eva glances up.

"Not Poland," Bets replies. "Germany. She's German."

The nurse turns Brigit's head to the side on the pillow, a frown on her face, and now Eva is afraid this woman hates Germans. That Germans are the enemy. Maybe she shouldn't let her take Brigit.

Bets might be having the same thought. "Why do you ask, out of curiosity?"

The nurse looks at her in surprise. "Because of the Polish."

"What Polish?" Eva asks.

"The Polish she's speaking," says the nurse, her heavy eyebrows up. "Didn't you know she was speaking Polish?"

"You've made a mistake. Brigit doesn't speak . . ." But Eva stops. Thinking.

"I don't think I made a mistake," says the nurse. Now she's offended.

"Do you speak Polish?" asks Bets.

"Every day at home."

"And what is she saying?"

The nurse listens. "Well, she's getting pretty well sedated, but right now, she's singing, '*Kosi kosi łapci, pojedziem do babci,*' which is a little song my grandmother used to sing to me. And earlier she counted to five and said, '*Moje włosy są żółte,*' which means 'my hair is yellow,' and, well, her hair is yellow. And . . ."

Brigit mumbles, and the nurse straightens up and says, "Bird, bird, little bird . . ."

Eva blinks. And there's something. Something that she can't grasp. The pieces of herself clamor. Like Brigit, begging for attention.

"All of it is what a child might say," the nurse goes on, "but I don't think she could do that by accident. Do you?"

"Huh," says Bets, looking sideways at Eva.

"You really didn't know?" asks the nurse.

Brigit's words are slurring. "*Ptak, ptak, ptasik.*"

Bird, bird, little bird.

And suddenly, Eva is wobbling as she stares at the floor.

"Uh-oh," says the nurse, and grabs a bedpan for Eva to be sick into.

When she's done, the nurse gives her a bed to lie down on until she feels better, and they roll Brigit away. Bets closes the curtain.

"I'm sorry," Eva whispers.

"Not a thing to apologize for." Bets rubs Eva's back. "Lots of people don't like hospitals. Makes you queasy."

Queasy. Eva commits the word to memory. She doesn't want to tell Bets that while Annemarie was being treated by the Red Cross, she'd cleaned the hospital tents in trade for food and a bed. She'd emptied bedpans. Scrubbed the cracks of the foldable floors after surgery. Washed the bloody sheets. And she's seen more dead bodies than she can count. Hospitals do not make her sick.

The wrong thoughts make her sick.

Bets brings her an orange fizzy drink and a magazine. Eva wishes she'd brought a copy of the *New York Times*, though she doubts her advertisement will have had time to appear. She wonders who Bets hasn't had a letter from. The nurse sends them to the waiting room, and after a long time, the nurse comes back and says Dr. Forrester would like to see them in his office.

Dr. Forrester's office is a clutter. Books, filing cabinets, files that should be in the filing cabinets, loose pens, and a full ashtray. But he is neat and tidy. Efficient. Like before. He flips a switch, and a light board comes on behind his desk. Eva doesn't like the look on his face.

Bets whispers, "Tell me if you're going to be sick, okay?"

Dr. Forrester puts two X-rays up on the board, and in pale white shadows, Eva can see inside Brigit's head.

"This," says Dr. Forrester. He points to an area of Brigit's brain that is a different color from the rest, a solid mass. "This is the head injury that Miss Heidelmann sustained back in 1945, a subdural hematoma. It probably should have killed her, except the bleed into her brain was slow rather than fast. The pressure built up, compressing the brain, and that pressure is still there, resulting in the behavioral changes you've described."

Eva takes a moment to process all the English. "Brigit is the way she is . . . because of an injury? To her brain?"

"All I can say is that some of the symptoms, if not most, are certainly physical."

"So, what is the treatment for that condition?" Bets asks.

Dr. Forrester sits down at his desk. "Surgery. Immediately. The hematoma hasn't killed her yet, but it still could. Anytime. But it means opening her skull. And I have to be honest with you. There are no guarantees."

"You are saying"—Eva sits forward in her chair—"that the . . . surgery could kill her?"

"That would be more likely with a bad surgeon, and I am not a bad surgeon. But it is delicate, and I cannot say what the outcome will be. It's possible that Miss Heidelmann could have memory gaps, or won't remember anything at all, or that her brain will not expand correctly after being under pressure for so long."

Bets puts a hand on Eva's back. "But if you are . . . successful," says Eva, "if the . . . pressure is taken away, Brigit could be . . . as she was? Before?"

Dr. Forrester sighs and reaches for a cigarette. "Psychological damage could still be present. Or might be forgotten. Or she might recover completely. The truth is, it could be anything, but she's more likely to be better than she is now. I can't be more straightforward with you than that."

"What is the surgery like?" Bets asks. "What sort of preparation and recovery?"

"I would leave her asleep for a day or two afterward, for the best healing possible, particularly since she has a history of being combative. And then . . . it may be up to her when she wakes up. Her recovery could be almost instant, or it could be very gradual, or not happen at all." He shrugs. "I am sorry."

A silence settles down on the office. Bets is looking at Eva. Dr. Forrester is looking at Bets.

"This is a difficult decision," he says to Bets. "Should you . . ."

"The decision is Miss Gerst's," Bets says firmly. "But, Dr. Forrester, what would you do? If Miss Heidelmann was your daughter?"

"Have the surgery done," he says without hesitation, "and give her the best chance at life. This is no life, the way she's living now. "

But there are worse lives, Eva thinks. She's seen it.

She stands up. The office window looks out to a wall, like Dr. Greenbaum's had, a view of bricks at nightfall. But Eva stares at them. Brigit might wake up and remember things best forgotten. She might not remember anything at all.

She could be someone they should be very much afraid of.

But Eva's mind had been made up when Dr. Forrester said Brigit could die. Anytime. That she probably should have died before. Annemarie has to be protected, and Annemarie has to live. It's always, always been about Inge making sure that Annemarie lives. Eva turns around.

"When will the surgery happen?"

Dr. Forrester nods. "I'd do it tonight if I could, but that's not practical. There's money to be considered . . . No, no, Miss Gerst. This is going to be arranged. There are charities that will help . . ."

"The AFSC might be able to help," adds Bets.

"And there will be no charge from me. But I'd rather move forward whether the money is taken care of or not. The hospital can fight about it later. If we wait, it's possible that we lose her. And frankly, we have her here right now."

Dr. Forrester adds his half-used cigarette to the pile in the ashtray.

"I'm going to keep her asleep, so go home for tonight. A period of rest before the procedure won't hurt, anyway. I'll talk to the nurse. There will be an unbelievable amount of paperwork, but I hope we can get her on the schedule for day after tomorrow."

Eva nods, Bets shakes Dr. Forrester's hand, and they take the subway back to Powell House. Without Brigit. Bets gives Eva the occasional pat on the arm, but they don't speak. Bets is good about not speaking when needed.

Eva is rattling inside. Like an empty train.

What if she's done the wrong thing? What if Brigit is worse than she was before?

What if she's just handed Cruickshanks a killer.

There's an American citizenship class going on in the back parlor when they arrive at Powell House, the art exhibit open to the public in the front, an English class in the library, and a manuscript consultation happening in the music room. Eva goes straight up to the blue room and kicks off her shoes. Brigit's side of the bed is empty. No one is watching from a rusty car.

Jimmy must be feeling better, because she hears him go up the stairs with Colette and Lucy. She listens for Jake, but she doesn't expect him to be with them. He wouldn't risk seeing her face.

It's good, that he wouldn't risk that. She touches a finger to the corner of her mouth.

And sits in the windowsill. Unsettled. Thinking of Polish. What had Brigit been trying to say to her all this time? What could Brigit have told her, if only she'd been able to understand? And there is something. Something. An itch in her mind. A thought she can't grasp.

Something about a bird.

She waits until all the classes are done. Until the feet come down from the attic and Powell House is closed for the night. Until the girls are in the kitchen, because Olive is making spaghetti. Then she creeps to the second floor, into the music room, and sits at the piano.

She touches the keys. She was Inge the last time she played. While planes fell out of the sky and her mother murdered her brothers. She plays the first notes of "Clair de Lune."

Then the first page, and the first section. And Jake was right. The fingers don't forget. Though they do get rusty. She's not ready, anymore, for speed. Her hands struggle to do what she tells them, and she's afraid to play fully, because of the noise. She hasn't turned on the lights. She uses the lights of the city, shining in the windows, and starts over, playing the first part again, slow, soft, the way Inge always said was like falling asleep. Just before you dream.

And she feels so calm. She's aware of the music, of the streetlights and the rug and the shape of Jake's guitar in the corner. But she sees violets. A whole field of them, with the sun shining down, Annemarie's bright hair dotted with them like purple stars. She sees a doorway, an open door with scratches from the claws of a little dog that yaps and yaps, and Annemarie is chubby round, with violets in her hair and violets in her hand and there is music. And a table, so much higher than her head, where red-painted fingernails pick up a knife and slide it into a cake. Yellow-cream frosting dripping, melting in the sun from the window . . .

Eva hears the music from her fingers. She sees the violets. She tastes the sugar. And the world is small. Soft and shiny.

And then it tears. Shreds.

Bangs.

One bang. Two. Three . . . Short, sharp shots.

Eva's body jerks and her eyes fly open. The last dying sound from the piano is sour. Her hands are shaky, and she is sweating. Sick.

The wrong thoughts make you sick. And so do the wrong memories.

She breathes. And breathes. And puts her fingers back on the keys.

She plays. And she sees the bird. Cupped in her hands. And her hands are so small the bird fills them with its softness. Warm. Looking up at her with black eyes shiny in lamplight. Air hazy with tobacco smoke. She can smell the smoke. Feel the heartbeat flutter, a tickle in her palm. And her fingers squeeze . . .

And Eva's eyes fly open again.

She remembers the bird.

She knows.

She scrambles off the piano bench, banging her knees on her way out, across the landing and into the library, fumbling to find a switch or a lamp. She finds it, knocking a stack of children's books written by Peggy onto the floor. The shelves are floor to ceiling, she has to slide a ladder across to reach what she wants. Until she has the book in her hands. A dictionary. A Polish-English dictionary.

Bird, bird. That's what Brigit had said.

And the Polish word for bird is *ptak*. Like Ptasynzska. Little bird.

And the German word for bird is *vögel*. *Vögelchen*. Little bird.

She sets down the dictionary. She sits on the floor. Forehead on her knees. She closes her eyes. Bits and pieces of herself are flying, spinning, a tornado of confusion. A dizzying tumult of memory and thought that whirl, reel, and eventually calm. Slow. Like a film running backward. Pieces floating and falling gently back into their place. Pieces that become something whole again. Repaired. Glued back together.

Eva opens her eyes, and she knows who she is.

She knows her name. She knows why birds die and windows shut. She even knows why Mama hated her so much.

And she knows Brigit is not who Cruickshanks wants. Because Brigit is not a killer. Brigit has never been the person to fear.

The person to fear has always been herself.

CHAPTER FORTY-TWO

SHE PUTS THE lid back on the box. Carefully. Just so.

The bird has gone away. It's gone now.

She wipes her hands all over the pink fabric. She doesn't care if there is blood on the dress. She doesn't like the dress.

"Here, Papa. You can have this."

She puts the box in Papa's lap. She holds up her head. And she waits.

The clock says tick. Tock. Tick.

And Papa laughs. He laughs and laughs.

CHAPTER FORTY-THREE
—— *August 1946* ——

WHEN MARTHA KNOCKS on the door of the blue room the next morning, the sun is high, and Eva is in bed in her camisole. She hadn't bothered with a nightgown. She hasn't even bothered to get up.

But she is calm. She knows who she is now.

And isn't it always better to know.

Even when it's a rotten deal.

Martha smiles, taking no notice of her dishevelment, and comes to sit gently on the side of the bed. She has her hair newly marcelled, like the last twenty years haven't gone by. "Good morning, dear," she says. "I hope thee were able to sleep a little."

Eva sits up. It must be time to go to the hospital. She reaches for her blouse, but Martha puts a hand on her arm.

"I have a proposal for thee. But first, I need to say . . . I have been speaking with Dr. Forrester's nurse, and I don't know if thee has considered, but Brigit will be taken to a unit for intensive care, and they will not allow any visitors to stay with her there. Not even family."

Eva frowns. "But I have to be there for . . ."

"I'm afraid it is their policy."

Eva goes still. Maybe she shouldn't be there. Maybe she should stay away from other people. Even Brigit. And then she finds those tears coming again, like they'd been ready, waiting, just below the surface. Primed and poised to betray her.

"I knew this would be upsetting," Martha says. "But there would be nothing for thee to do there, other than to sit and to worry. And when Brigit shows signs of waking, the nurse has promised to send for thee, right away. She can see the wisdom of bending the rules a little then."

Probably because Martha made her see the wisdom, Eva thinks.

"But that brings me to my proposal. We have a house—another house—outside the city, also lent to us by Mrs. Powell. Sky Island. A lovely place. Some of our young people run it through the summer, for our new arrivals who might like a little vacation. Many of our friends from Europe are in need of quiet and rest after such difficult times. I'm sure thee can understand."

Eva nods.

"Sky Island will close soon for the summer, but we still have a few guests, and one of our girls had to leave to attend a sick mother. Could I ask thee to take her place? It would only be helping to prepare the meals or a little light housework."

Eva starts to protest, but Martha holds up a hand.

"A car or a bus from Sky Island can reach the hospital quicker than a train in the city. And . . . well. . . . we have guests coming tomorrow. I am sorry to say that if thee doesn't go to Sky Island, then sharing with me becomes your lot."

Martha seems to think a girl like Eva would find sharing a room with her terribly objectionable. As if Eva had never slept in sludge beneath an oxcart.

"I don't mind sharing," she whispers. "But of course, I will go. If that helps."

Maybe it's better for everyone. Safer.

At the door, Martha says, "I thought thee might like to know we found a little windfall in our budget, and that Augusta will remake her sculpture."

Eva nods again, eyes on the rumpled sheets.

"Come downstairs, and I will make thee a cup of tea. And there are pastries which would very much like to be eaten." Martha smiles and shuts the door with the softest click.

Eva doesn't go downstairs. But she does swing her legs out of bed.

She doesn't know how long it will take the Americans to get Anna Ptaszynska's file translated from German. She doesn't know what the file might say, if anything in it will lead them to the truth. But being out of Powell House might be a good thing. Especially if she can get out without being seen.

Being alone. It will be her justice.

Eva takes the papers from the slit in her mattress—the papers from her father's desk, from the file that had the right name on it after all—and sews them back inside her skirt. Where they belong. And then she cleans. Shaking out the curtains, knocking spiderwebs from the corners, polishing the tables and the chest and the wardrobe. She runs the sweeper over the rugs. Nips downstairs and gets an envelope with directions and money for a bus ticket that Martha has left on her desk.

She packs the suitcase Miss Schaffer gave her. Neatly. She takes out Brigit's suitcase and packs it. Neatly. Making sure the letter with the earrings is lying prominently on top. Just in case. The pink dressing gown and the blue dress she leaves hanging where they are, so someone else can use them. But the key to the bus station locker she keeps around her neck. Jake had given that to her. And she has a vague idea he can't get his money back without it. Then she picks up the suitcases and walks to the door, the ugly brown hat on her head. And looks back.

She's not sure she knows the girl who lived in this room. She's not really sure who's leaving it.

She'd forgotten what it sounds like, to rustle.

Eva slips out the back without seeing a soul, past the place where she last saw Jake, taking her purse and the two suitcases on a circuitous route to the subway and to the hospital.

She fills out Brigit's paperwork, every blank correct except the one with her name. And they let her see Brigit, for a few minutes. Eva sits beside her bed and watches her. Peaceful. Perfect in her sleep.

After driving Annemarie across a war zone, hauling her to Berlin, moving her from camp to camp to camp and across an ocean, it's hard to believe that now, it's time to let her go. That someone else will be taking care of Brigit. For a little while.

But at least Cruickshanks wouldn't dare to bother her here. He's a man of the shadows, not the newsreels. Eva tells herself these things as she walks away.

She might be telling herself lies.

Her mind has been well practiced, it seems, at telling itself lies.

She finds the bus station and buys an early ticket. Makes a call to Sky Island and tells them when to expect her. And then, she's on a bus, hurtling down a highway.

It's not what she thought she'd be doing today.

Nothing is the way she thought it was yesterday.

The city of New York is huge at first, filling the skyline. But she watches the buildings get smaller. And smaller. And when she turns to watch it disappear behind her, there, in the very back of the bus, sits Mr. Cruickshanks, with his black-rimmed glasses, smoking a cigarette. He doesn't smile.

Eva faces forward. She almost wants to laugh. Almost. Then she borrows a newspaper from the man across the aisle. He frowns at her accent, looks her over from ugly hat to her heels. But he gives her the paper.

She turns the pages carefully, so they won't wrinkle. She reads each advertisement. Until she's a little sick from the rocking of the bus. Until she finds:

Little bird misses her Papa. Ask for Eva.

And the address of Powell House.

That will bring him.

She'd chosen her words well. And she'd left a note on Martha's desk, saying if a German man inquired, for translation, to please send him to Sky Island. Not that it was needed. All her father has to do is ring the doorbell and anyone in Powell House will tell him where she's gone.

Let him come, Eva thinks. Let him. And Cruickshanks can come, too. She's still got a bread knife. And she's not afraid. Because now, she knows she's done it all before.

And this time, it is justice.

The town around the bus station is tiny, with low buildings, unpaved streets, and tall hills, leafy-green. Like she's traveled five hundred miles instead of fifty.

"Hello, hello! Is it Eva?"

A young woman with short, curly brown hair and a sunburned nose leans out the window of a car that must have been running well before the last war. It has a high top and big wheels, like a buggy, idling in a way that makes the girl bounce gently up and down. Eva lifts a hand.

She's lost sight of Mr. Cruickshanks.

"Oh, good," the girl says. "Hope I'm not too, too late. Had to borrow the jalopy from a neighbor. Throw your suitcases in! And shut the door really well. Don't want you falling out, we're going uphill!"

Eva shuts the door, holding on to the handle as they putter away from the bus station. There's a seat spring sticking into her back.

"I'm Patricia," the girl says. "Usually, I room with Bets, but I've been up at Sky Island all summer. Bets is the best, don't you think?"

Eva smiles. Nods. They're out of the little town already, passing woods and a farm with a red barn.

"She told me about your friend. We're all really hoping the surgery goes well. But maybe you can relax in the meantime. Have a rest. It's good for the soul."

"I thought . . . that you needed my help," says Eva. Her teeth are rattling.

"Oh, everybody helps! Now the gang of us that've been up here all summer, we might do most of the helping. But the guests pitch in, too. Makes us one happy family."

Patricia grinds the car into another gear, and they start upward.

"But nobody helps their first day. House rules. Do you have a swimsuit? No? Lots of people don't. We keep a box of them upstairs. Not that they're lovely or anything. But there's lots of nice walks, and a library full of books . . ."

The road is winding up a wooded hill, and through a break in the trees, Eva sees a river snaking through a valley, little patches of the sunset glistening on the water like scales. Then the road levels, skirting the edge of a ridge, and Patricia turns the rickety car through a set of iron gates.

Eva thought she'd be going somewhere rustic. Somewhere that fit with the bumpy road and the dungarees tucked into Patricia's boots. But Sky Island is elegant. Storybookish. With gables and leaded glass and a tall round tower that has ivy crawling up its stones. Grandpapa's entire lodge could fit inside one wing.

They pass trimmed hedges, an overgrown summerhouse with glass walls, pulling around to a patch of gravel for parking in the back. Patricia lets the car die with a gasp.

"Shew," she says. "Made it. C'mon and meet the gang and get a tour."

Patricia gets one of the suitcases, leading Eva through a back door into a long hallway and straight into a huge kitchen. The room smells spicy, steamy with something boiling on a range, a young woman with bobbed blond hair chopping potatoes and singing "Boogie Woogie Bugle Boy" loud enough to make the room echo.

"Hey!" yells Patricia. "New arrival! This is Eva Gerst. From Germany. Not so long off the boat. Eva, this is Greta . . ." The blond singer waggles her knife. "And back there is Mick . . ."

Another young man, also sunburned to a fiery pink, an apron tied over his T-shirt, waves from around the corner.

". . . . and over at the table are Mr. and Mrs. Kushner, from Ukraine, in America about six months now, and this is Valentina, from Russia, fresh off the boat like you . . ."

Valentina raises two doe-soft eyes and manages a smile.

". . . and you don't have to remember any of this, 'cause we'll all remind you when you need it."

Patricia leads her back into the hallway, where there's a little office and a butler's pantry, through into a dining room with a fireplace and a gleaming mahogany table, then into a larger hall at the front of the house, two stories high with a tiled floor.

"Through there is the main living room, and here's a smaller lounge, where we mostly gather right now, since we're not a big group. But your room is up this way . . ."

They go up a wide set of stairs, across a balcony and into a smaller corridor, where Patricia opens a door at the end of the hall. Behind it is a bedroom with bold-flowered wallpaper and a fireplace, two big windows, one with a window seat overlooking the back garden and the lawn and the glints of glass from the half-hidden summerhouse. Beyond that is tree-clad hill after hill.

"You got the prime real estate," says Patricia. "We usually keep this wing for families, but you can have the whole thing to yourself, since it's empty. And you've got a bathroom!"

It's good, Eva thinks, that she'll be off by herself. "The room is beautiful," she says. "Thank you."

Patricia beams. "You're welcome. Come on down when you're ready, but don't wait too long. Mrs. Kushner made goulash."

She shuts the door, and Eva goes to look at the sunset from the window seat. Sky Island is such a nice place. And when her father comes, she's going to ruin it.

Eva unpacks, changes her skirt, hanging the rustling one in the back of the closet, taking her purse with her to dinner. Besides the first group, there are the Petrovas from Yugoslavia, with three young teenage girls, their father, mother, and grandfather, all of them just learning English. Eva sits next to Valentina, because she seems the least likely to talk.

After dinner, Patricia takes them all to the lounge, where there are sofas and upholstered chairs, and Mick and his friend Tony—a young man with dark brown hair and dark brown skin, just back from doing relief work for the AFSC in Finland—start a game of charades. It's a good game for learning English, and the boys are funny. A huge hit, Eva sees, with the Petrova girls.

Eva likes watching the girls, hiding their giggles behind their hands and getting corrected by their grandfather. Sisters, with both their parents. How lucky.

Patricia brings everyone cocoa and crackers. It's much cooler here at night than in the city. And there are clouds blowing in, with a high breeze from the hills. They all chat, but Valentina cups the warmth of the mug, looking deep into its contents. And Eva knows that stare. She saw it many times in Düppel Center. She saw it with Mr. Leibermann. It comes from the concentration camps.

Everyone says good night, going their separate ways, up the stairs to the bedroom wings, Mick and Tony out to a little apartment set up over the garage at one end of the house. But Eva lingers. Looking at a bookshelf, letting the others move ahead of her. Waiting for Patricia and Greta to finish washing up the mugs in the kitchen. Then she tiptoes to what Patricia had called the main living room and creaks open the door.

It's a large space, with a sunken floor, rounded plaster walls. and a massive stone fireplace, windows ceiling to floor overlooking a stone terrace. And at the far end, in the dim, is what she'd thought she glimpsed when she arrived. A full-size grand piano.

Eva shuts the door, moving silently across the carpet, and plays three soft notes in a row. It's in tune. She decides to lay down the prop so she can lower the lid and muffle the sound. And then she pauses. Walks slowly to the windows. The clouds are blowing past the moon, making the light come and go over the garden around the terrace. And there's a shape to one side of the lawn, where the land rises up, wanting to become a hill again.

The shape in the moonlight is a man.

And Eva thinks, Jacob has come. But the shoulders are wrong. And then she thinks it's her father. Only, her father is not that tall, and he would never wear a hat like that. She only knows one man who wears a hat shaped like that. And his shoes are always shiny.

She'd thought he might be dead. That Cruickshanks had "taken care of it." But if the man with shiny shoes really is American—an American who isn't part of Cruickshanks's plan—then he might agree that Dr. Otto von Emmerich is a war criminal. He could put her father on trial.

The man with shiny shoes could mean justice.

He could make all of this go away.

The window in front of her is actually a door, with a lock on the heavy iron latch. She turns it, opens it, and the air is cool. Resin-scented. Her heels click on the flagstones. Across the terrace. Into the damp grass. And the man stands still. Watching her come.

She looks behind her, but there's no one else here, the back side of the house curtained and dark. She climbs the little rise in the lawn, and she can see the feather in his hat now. The deep shadow that is the crease between his eyebrows. The moon is covered, and there's something dark on the ground, hunched at his feet.

Eva stops halfway. Out of reach. "Who are you?" she whispers.

But he only says, "You are . . . Ptaszynska?"

She takes a step back. And another, hand creeping up to her mouth. He's speaking German. And the still shape at his feet is Mr. Cruickshanks, glasses and neck sitting oddly askew.

"You cannot trust . . ." the man says. "Do not trust. Give the doctor . . . to me."

The words are German spoken badly. But the accent is Russian. The man in the shiny shoes is not American, he's Soviet.

And he has killed Mr. Cruickshanks.

"I am . . . watching," he says. "I will watch . . ."

But she has become Inge. Inge in a bombed house full of soldiers. She runs. Fast. Getting back inside the door and turning the lock behind her. She grabs her purse and flies through the murky house, up the stairs, all the way down the silent corridor to her bedroom on the end. There's a skeleton key in her lock and she turns it.

He knows about Anna Ptaszynska. And a glass door and a skeleton key are not going to keep him out.

She looks out the window, but there's not a shape on the lawn anymore. The man is gone. Or inside the house. She doesn't switch on a light. She goes to her purse and gets the bread knife, then to the closet to grab the hanger with her skirt. She listens at the door, turns the lock, and dashes across the hall, to the bedroom opposite, where the room is ghostly with dust sheets. She hangs the skirt in the empty closet, runs back to her own room, and turns the key again.

Anna's papers are safer where she isn't.

Eva sits on top of the blankets in the dark, back to the headboard, knife in her hand. Tense. Curled. Knees to her chest.

Soviet. Not American. And at least one Mr. Cruickshanks is dead. If that Cruickshanks had Anna's file with him, then the Soviets will have it now.

She waits. Through the creaks of a settling house, clock ticking monotonously, incessantly on the nightstand. And there's no other breath to listen to. No one to care if a Soviet agent in shiny shoes bursts through her door.

She's not even sure if she would hear the footsteps.

And when Eva opens her eyes, she is in the exact same position, curled up on the bed, the bread knife tight in her hand. The sun is well up, the rose-flowered wallpaper glowing and a little garish. She creeps to the window. A pristine lawn with the dew burned away. Someone is drinking coffee on the terrace.

There's no dead body on the rise, and the man with shiny shoes didn't come.

She wonders why. And then she looks at the clock.

Brigit is having her surgery.

She goes down to the kitchen, nervous and jumpy, and Greta smiles and says sure, no one minds if she makes her own breakfast. She doesn't ask why Eva would bring a purse with her, either. And when she tries to wash up, Greta takes her dirty plate away.

"Oh, no! House rules! Now you go on and enjoy yourself."

Eva doesn't know what to do with a day to herself. She doesn't want to be alone, and probably shouldn't be with the others. She takes her purse to the living room. The lid is still down on the piano, and then Patricia sticks her head in the door.

"There you are! I brought you this." She tosses two bits of cloth over a chair. "Bathing suit! And hey, listen, careful if you decide to go for a walk, okay? Some of the roads have a really steep drop-off, and we got the most awful news this morning. A tourist must've gone out in the dark and walked right off the cliff down the road last night. Broke his neck. The police were down there this morning and . . ."

"I think I will stay in here today," Eva says. "Will I . . . bother anyone?"

"Oh, no! There's English classes, but they could probably do with a little entertainment. There's music in that cabinet over there. Have fun!"

And with that, Patricia is gone. Probably to do something nice for somebody.

Eva stands alone in the quiet room. Wondering about Brigit. About when her father will come. Wondering why she should feel sorry for Mr. Cruickshanks. She sets her purse close beside her and decides to look in the cabinet.

It's a treasure trove. Books. Stacks of sheet music, some of them silly ones from before she was born. She finds a complete volume of Chopin and plays etudes until there's a pain between her shoulder blades. She sees violets. And a scratched door. Red fingernails on the piano keys. And she hears a voice this time. Melody and resonance. A voice like music . . .

When Patricia comes back, the shadows have stretched. "Have you been here all day?" she asks, seeing the bathing suit where she left it. "Well, don't forget to eat. I came to tell you we had a call. Mother Martha says the surgery went well. As good as it could have. The doctor says he's really pleased."

Eva blinks at the piano keys. There come her tears again. Where do they hide?

"Is she awake?" Eva asks.

"No. They'll keep her sleeping. Martha says they'll call at the first sign. Say, I'm really glad it's good news."

"Thank you, Patricia," Eva says. She breathes. "Thank you very much." She starts to play again, and she tries to remember.

Who is Annemarie?

And what happened to the bird? The bird on the rug. The bird in the piano. The bird on the seat of her mother's Mercedes. The bird she had cupped in her hands.

She plays until it's time to go to bed and everyone lets her. And outside the window, deep in the shadows at the edge of the lawn near the summerhouse, she can see the glow of a cigarette.

Watching.

She turns the skeleton key and sleeps with the bread knife.

Eva takes her purse to breakfast. Everyone is eating muffins, and Greta is painting Valentina's fingernails a cherry red. She does Eva's next, and then the three girls', over the mild protests of their grandfather. Eva holds up her hands and smiles. It's what her fingers should look like. She goes back to her room and tries on the bathing suit.

It might have been a child's once. But it's in two pieces, so there's room for her in between, a little navy skirt with a polka-dot top that ties around her neck. She finds a towel, pins up her hair, picks up her purse, and goes to the opposite side of the lawn from the summerhouse, where the tree line reaches in close from the hill.

The pool is huge, irregular, surrounded by trees and rhododendrons, two sides formed by natural rock. A hidden pond of still water, dark blue in the shade, dappled with floating leaves. Eva tosses down her towel and dives.

The cold is a blow. But she'd grown up swimming in the Baltic Sea. Three strokes below the surface and the discomfort becomes a pleasant rush of water over skin. She comes up for air, pushes off from the side, and swims to the other end. Back and forth, until her arms are tired. Until floating feels good.

She holds her breath and sits on the bottom, looking up at the sun, at the strange waver of the tree limbs. She'd done this before. In brown water. Only she'd been sinking then. This time she relaxes, letting her arms and legs go free, body rising up, and up, to a shadow at one end of the pool. A shadow that wasn't there before. The shadow of a man. Standing with the sun behind him.

And Eva shifts into gear. She changes direction and swims, fast, breaking the surface at the other end of the pool. She turns, gasps a breath, hands on the rocky edge, shaking the water away from her eyes.

The shadow puts his hands in his pockets.

And this time, the shadow is Jake.

CHAPTER FORTY-FOUR
—— *August 1946* ——

EVA SWIMS SLOWLY to the steps of the pool, and Jake doesn't say anything. Just watches while she climbs out, dripping. She picks up her towel and holds it to her chest. His clothes are wrinkled. He hasn't shaved, and his beautiful eyes are wary. Unreadable. The breeze blows and Eva shivers. She's not sure if she's cold.

"Take a drive with me," he says, and walks away from the pool.

She watches him stride across the lawn, kicking at the leaves, and there's no music to it. Not today. She picks up her purse and follows, across the back of the house, to where a car is parked beside the jalopy. A big, dark green convertible with whitewall tires and the top down.

Jake gets in and the engine purrs. Eva tiptoes across the rocks, lays her towel down on the leather seat, and as soon as she has the door shut, he puts the car in gear, spitting gravel. He turns left out of the iron gates, driving farther up the hill, eyes narrowed, concentrating on the winding road. The wind snatches at her hair, pulling pieces from the pins as it dries.

They come to a break in the trees, where parking places line up along a cliff edge with an open vista to the valley and the hillsides beyond. Jake pulls the car into a spot on the far end and turns the key. A town nestles in the bank of the river below them, while above, an enormous boulder, dropped there from the beginning of time, maybe, hangs impossibly over their heads from higher up the mountain. There's a family having a picnic on top of it. Eva looks out the windshield. At all those lovely, unbombed roofs.

Jake lights a cigarette. He studies the sky, the clouds, and the nearest tree branch. Eva pulls her knees up to her chest, bare feet on the damp towel. Now she's cold.

And then Jake asks, "Why did you take the bread knife?"

It's not the question she expected. It's not a question she wants to answer.

"Things have gone missing from Powell House before," he says. "Food, usually. But a lady one time, she made off with the fire poker. It's hard to trust, I guess, when you haven't been safe and you haven't been fed. But that's not why you took the bread knife. Is it?"

Eva turns her face away.

"You were going to kill him."

She tightens the grip on her knees, listening to Jake's breath blow smoke.

"See, something just didn't sit right with me, after I walked away that day. The whole thing stuck in my throat. Because either Hollywood needs to hand you a trophy, or when you saw . . . him, that man, in the hospital, he was not somebody you wanted to see. It was the whole reason I believed the crazy story you spun me in the first place. And when you went in that bedroom, saw that stuff all over the walls, that was not a girl hoping to be with her precious daddy. You were scared sick. I saw it. I felt it, in the closet. But then you lied to Cruickshanks. You took that file."

Eva stays still on her towel.

"And so what gives, I ask myself. Why would a girl want to get in that apartment so bad she'd risk a jail cell, if not to see her father? And if it wasn't to see her father, then why not give him to Cruickshanks? Whose side were you on? I couldn't get it out of my head. So you know what I did? I went down to Martha's office and got the AFSC's reports on their relief work in Germany. They send them out to all the programs. Crazy detailed. And what do you know but a Miss Schaffer of the Berlin office sent in a report on a visit to the Sachsenhausen Concentration Camp in June of 1945 . . ."

Eva can see Miss Schaffer at her desk in Berlin, in her brown jacket with the starburst patch on its sleeve. *The AFSC will work with Germans who are not Jews,* that particular Mr. Cruickshanks had told Eva. *So it will look right. Legitimate . . .*

What would Miss Schaffer have done if she'd said her father was the Doctor of Sachsenhausen?

Offered her some help, probably.

"And when I'd read enough of what went on in that place to make me sick for a lifetime," Jake says, "I went and got this . . ."

He throws his cigarette out the window, reaches into the back, and brings up a black metal case, dropping it on the seat between them.

Anna Ptaszynska's file.

Cruickshanks never had it. Eva takes a long breath. "How did you . . ."

"They give you two keys when you rent those lockers, Eva. I took the thing home, walked over to Mrs. Schumaker's, and she read me every word. She's eighty years old and it took a while. I told her somebody was writing a novel . . ."

He runs a hand through his hair, grabs the steering wheel.

"Can he really do it, what it says in those files? Say the word and make a person do things? Make people kill their best friend and not remember?"

Eva thinks of Liebermann whispering stories in the dark. "There are people who say he can."

"And you were going to kill him. That's what the knife was for. That's why you were looking for him."

She listens to the happy family, the children laughing on top of the rock. And she says, "Yes."

"And you still plan to. To kill him."

"It is justice."

"A knife is not justice, Eva. Nuremberg is justice!" ·

She shakes her head.

"You have to give him to Cruickshanks."

She shakes her head again.

"Give him to Cruickshanks," he says. "Please."

"And where is the justice in that?" she snaps. "Do you think your government isn't interested in what my father can do? That they don't want to control their enemies? Cruickshanks doesn't want to put my father on trial. He wants to give my father a job. A place for research. To continue his experiments . . ."

Jake is shaking his head. Like she's crazy. "That's just not true . . ."

"It is true! They want spies, assassins who don't care who they kill or if they die. And this, they tell me, will stop wars. Anna Ptaszynska and Sachsenhausen are going to happen all over again . . ."

"But you're talking about war criminals here, Eva! Nazis, in the United States. Experimenting on American citizens like they did in the camps. We just don't do that . . ."

"Like they did not do it to Jimmy?"

Jake goes quiet.

"They brought me here to lure my father out of hiding. So they can make sure no one else catches him. So he will not go to trial. So he can do his work. For them. They think I am . . . loyal."

"So go to somebody else, then. Not Cruickshanks."

"Who? Do you know who in your government is giving the orders? Who will take my father to trial and who will not?"

Jake doesn't answer. Because there isn't one.

"Cruickshanks said if my father is caught, even by another country, even with all the right evidence, that the United States will make sure he is not convicted. Dr. Kurt Blome, from Dachau, he will be put on trial next year. In Nuremberg. And Cruickshanks told me that he will be acquitted . . ." Eva sits up, looking in the side mirror. "He will be acquitted before the trial has even . . . begun . . ."

A black car is pulling into an open space of the overlook. And Eva knows the man in the driver's seat. She knows him at a glance. The Cruickshanks from the Zanzibar.

And Anna's file is sitting between them on the seat.

She turns to Jake. "Move."

"What?"

"Move. Now!"

She looks back. The door of the black car is opening. And Jake is just staring at her.

She crawls over the file and over him, shoving him out of the way.

"What the . . ." He spots the man getting out of the car. Eva turns the key, and the engine roars.

"Do you even know how to drive?"

She throws the car into reverse and hits the gas, whipping it around, timing the gear change to spin the wheels forward again with barely a stop. The pedals are easier to reach in this car. Or maybe she's grown.

The new Mr. Cruickshanks is already back in the driver's seat, getting his engine going. Eva stomps the gas and they fly up the mountain road. The metal case is in the floor with her wet towel and her purse, Jake sliding around on the seat.

"Watch it!" he yells. "This is Uncle Paul's car!"

She skids in the dirt around a curve. They're going up and up, a steep drop off with trees to one side. The car is more powerful than her father's. It accelerates quicker.

"Where does the road go?" she asks.

"How the hell should I know where the road goes!"

"*Scheisse*," Eva hisses.

They take another hairpin turn. What the road does is wind its way up a ridge, and then start back down again. They hurtle down the hill, and ahead, to the left, there is some kind of track, two wheel ruts through low-hanging trees. Eva takes it, and now pine needles and the ends of branches whip the windshield. As soon as enough branches are behind them, Eva brakes, and Jake has to catch himself from being thrown into the dash.

"I don't know who's going to murder me first," he says. "You or Uncle Paul . . ."

"Shhh!" She turns in the seat and kills the engine. Listening.

And faint through the trees, she can hear another motor. Seconds later, and the black car passes, rushing down the hill. Eva holds up a hand, and Jake stays quiet. The motor sound doesn't stop. It fades. But it won't be long before he figures it out. Eva starts the car, throws it in reverse, and hits the gas again.

Jake says something she doesn't understand and probably shouldn't. The twigs and leaves are hitting them now as well as the leather seats. She spins the wheel, turning them backward into the main road, changes gear, and now they're driving up the mountain again, around the hairpin turns, as fast as she can take them. Jake doesn't say anything more. He just hangs on.

They pass the scenic spot with the family on the boulder. The gates of Sky Island flash by, and at the bottom of the hill is the farm she'd passed with Patricia, the big red barn sitting not far from the road. The gate is open. Eva pulls a sudden left through the gate, down a bouncing, muddy drive, around behind the barn, stopping just before she hits a fence post. She puts the car in park and turns the key.

And suddenly, she can hear the breeze blowing. Birdsong. They're hidden from the road, and there isn't another car or even a tractor in sight. Just green fields with the hills rising, and one uninterested cow. Jake sits back. He looks at the cow. Then he pulls out a cigarette and lights it.

"So, where did you say you learned how to drive?"

Eva turns her head, gazing out the open window.

"Oh, no," Jake says. "No. Whatever answer it is you have to spill, it cannot be worse than what you've already told me."

She looks him right in the lovely eyes. "The chauffeur taught me."

"Right. The chauffeur taught you."

"I would . . . Sometimes I would steal my father's car."

Jake tilts his chin. "I bet you enjoyed it."

"Why do you say that?"

"Because you had one hell of a time, just then."

She turns her face away again. Her pulse is still racing. Her hair blown wild. And she's on a stranger's farm. Barefoot. In a bathing suit. Jake stares out the window, smoking.

"So, who was he? In the black car."

"A Cruickshanks. He was with us in the Zanzibar."

"'A Cruickshanks, you say? There's more than one?"

"I don't know how many there are now. The one you met is dead."

"Did you take him for a little drive?"

He isn't funny. And he doesn't seem to think he is, either.

"So what did he want?"

"This," she says, touching the metal case. Or it could have been her that he wanted. Or Brigit.

"And how did you say the other one died?"

"The man in the rusty car. He's an agent. Only . . . Soviet."

Jake breathes. Heavy. "And you've been sitting up here by yourself with a bread knife in your purse, have you?"

She doesn't say anything. He blows smoke into the breeze. The cow watches, swishing its tail.

"All those things I said to you that day. You took it on the chin. Like you've taken a beating or two." He pauses. "Have you, taken a beating or two?"

Eva doesn't want to answer that. She doesn't have to, because he takes her silence as an answer.

"What about the rest of your family? Do you have brothers, sisters?"

"Stop," she whispers.

"And what about Brigit? You know what happened to her, because you were there, weren't you?" He waits through her quiet. "Were you there?"

"Yes."

"Who was it?" She looks away. "Come on, Eva! Who and where?"

"Russians. Soviets. In my house . . ."

"And only Brigit? Or was it you?"

"It was Brigit and . . . stop! You don't need to . . . feel sorry . . ."

"I'm not trying to feel sorry for you, I'm trying to understand you!" He tosses the cigarette out the window, running his hands through his hair again. "This is all about Brigit, isn't it?"

She bites her lip.

"Because you already know what's in that file, don't you? What he did to Anna. Playing sick games with her mind. Giving her little things to kill, just because he said so. He ruined her . . ."

"He didn't ruin her."

". . . and you think they'll lock her up or something. That's why you think you have to kill him. Because you know that Brigit is Anna, don't you?"

She shakes her head.

"I heard what Cruickshanks said. He thought she was, and Bets said Brigit was speaking Polish . . ."

"Brigit is not Anna."

". . . and it says right there in those files that Anna was taken from Polish political prisoners. This is you taking care of Brigit, like you always do . . ."

"Stop it . . ."

"You stop! Stop playing with me, Eva."

"Brigit is not Anna!"

"You know she is! You just won't . . ."

"Brigit is not Anna, because I am!"

She watches the words sink into Jake like a stone.

"I am Anna Ptaszynska."

CHAPTER FORTY-FIVE

"ANNA," THE VOICE SAYS. And it is a melody. Like music.

She crawls toward the voice, across the blue rug, thick and squishing beneath her hands. Around the chair. Across the square of warm sun. Under the bench and over the feet. She likes that part.

And the rug is soft beneath her head, while above, the piano strings stretch and stretch, where the music thrums, rings. The music is over, under, around, and she floats and she floats and floats on the sound.

The shoes that play the pedals are black and the fingernails are red. The fingernails on the keys should always be red.

She waves her arms and legs and makes the shape of an angel in the rug.

And the square of sunshine blinks on the floor. A shadow passing the window. The music stops and the little dog scratches and yaps.

And she listens.

There are voices at the door.

They are the wrong voices.

The wrong sounds. Sounds that startle. Sounds that hurt.

Bang.

Bang.

CHAPTER FORTY-SIX

—— *August 1946* ——

JAKE SITS BACK. "No. You're not."

"I am."

He's shaking his head. "I don't believe you."

Eva breathes. Lets her head rest on the white leather seat. There are dark wings up in the sky. High and circling. Riding the air.

"When I was young," she says, "my . . . father brought me a bird. It was a nuthatch. They lived in the trees outside my bedroom window. I liked them."

Jake has gone still, gaze on the floorboard. This must be in Anna's file. He remembers. She can see it.

"He brought it to me again and again. And I can't remember, but I think I . . ." Eva pauses. "He always called me his *Vögelchen*. His 'little bird.' That was his name for me. And I think Ptaszynska means something like the same thing. 'Little bird.' But in Polish."

Jake clenches his hands together, forehead nearly on the dash. "What color are they?" he asks. "The nuthatches. In Germany."

"They're blue," Eva whispers. "Bright blue . . ."

Project Bluebird.

Jake gets out, shaking the car when he slams the door shut. He kicks the tires. Kicks the fence post. Grabs a dry branch from a brush pile and breaks it in half against the corner of the barn. The cow starts moving to the other end of the field. Then he comes to the driver's side and yanks open the door.

"Move over," he says. "You're making me crazy driving around like that." He starts the engine and they leave the farm, turning back up the hill toward Sky Island. Eva slides the towel over her legs.

They drive through the gates without speaking and without seeing another car. Jake parks, picks up Anna's file from the floorboard and a paper sack from the back seat. Eva gets her purse and the towel. When they walk into the back hallway, Tony is coming out of the kitchen.

"Hey! Jake! What are you doing . . ."

"Tony, hi. Listen, I'm going to stay a day or two, if that's all right. I'll put a little something toward food and everything. And maybe, you wouldn't have to say anything to Martha. Or not right away."

"Oh." Tony throws a confused look at Eva in her bathing suit. "Okay."

"Has there been a telephone call for me?" Eva asks him.

"Oh, sorry, no. Talk later, then, Jake?"

Jake nods, shakes his hand, and doesn't look back. Eva follows him through the dining room and into the front hall. They switch places, and he follows her up the stairs, down the corridor, straight to her room, and straight inside it, uninvited, shutting the door and turning the key in the lock. He tosses the metal case onto the bed.

"What?" he says, when he finds Eva staring. "You think I'm going to leave you alone up here for two seconds after what you just told me? Here. Bets sent this. And she said to say that yes, they're yours."

He hands her the sack, and inside is the blue dress and the pink dressing gown. Eva sighs. She misses Bets. She takes out the dressing gown, turns around and pulls it on, flipping out her hair and tying the belt. She hangs up the dress and her towel. Jake throws his jacket over a chair and sits on the edge of the bed. Rubs his face. Then he holds out a hand.

She looks at his hand. And takes it. Pale against his suntan. He sits her down beside him.

"Help me understand," he says. "Please. All of it."

And so she tells him. All of it. Everything. About Inge. The League of German Girls. Mama, and what happened the day the radio said Hitler was dead. About Annemarie. Going to the camp and what she saw over the wall. It's a flood. A torrent of information. Jake listens, and asks questions, but mostly he listens. He opens the window and smokes cigarette after cigarette.

She tells him twenty-seven names, just as Liebermann had. She tells him until he can't stand still and walks back and forth with his hands on his head.

She tells him until she is sick. Exhausted. Curled up on the pillow.

And when she opens her eyes again, it's dark outside. Quiet. The moon a high, pale spotlight among the stars. She has a blanket over her legs, and the water glass from the bathroom is filled and on the nightstand beside her head. Jake is on the window seat, head back, one bare foot on the cushion. The clock says 2:35 in the morning.

Eva sits up, draws her knees to her chest beneath the blanket, watching him contemplate the darkness.

He doesn't turn his head when he says, "The Quakers believe that if a person does something bad, evil even, then you have to consider what pushed them to the act. That they're probably just doing the same evil thing they were taught by somebody else. Violence to violence. And that more violence isn't actually justice, because it only turns the circle. Restarts the cycle. Over and over again.

"But what I don't get about that is consequences. When you do things, there are consequences. And if there weren't, then people would figure out that they can go around doing whatever the hell they want, whenever they want, whether they were taught that way or not. And where's the love, where's the justice, when you don't keep those things from happening to somebody else? Like in the camps.

"So on the one hand, the Quakers are right, and if that's what everybody did, it would be a different world. On the other hand, where's the responsibility? What's the balance? I don't know. I really don't."

She doesn't know, either. She doesn't want to be the judge. Jake swings both feet to the floor, elbows on his knees.

"Look. What I'm trying to say to you is, I'm going to help you. I'll help you kill him."

Eva fixes her gaze on Jake, all the different pieces of herself working in perfect unison. And she says, "No."

"You get to make a choice. So do I."

She flips back the blanket. "No."

"You're the one who convinced me, Bluebird. It's justice."

"It's not your war!"

"Yes, it is." He looks up. "My dead family in Berlin say so."

And there is nothing she can say to that.

Eva gets up, sits back down again. Closes her eyes. Why hadn't he run? Caught that fast train? Stayed away when he had the chance?

"Why did you come here?" she whispers.

"Well, you are my assignment. And I did say anything you need."

"Stop," she whispers.

"I'd also like to point out that you can't actually stop me."

Eva jumps to her feet and goes to the door. She doesn't even know where she's going.

Jake stands. "Your friend is out there."

She turns. "Soviet or American?"

"No idea. He's just sitting back there in the trees. Smoking. I almost asked him for a cigarette. I'm out."

She drops her hand from the knob. Jake puts his hands in his pockets.

"Come on, Bluebird," he says. "You don't have to do everything by yourself."

Eva turns her back on him. Goes to the dressing table and sits on the bench, arms wrapped hard around her middle. He should have found an airplane. An ocean liner. Anything.

He should have run.

"All those things you told me," he says, "and this is what makes you cry."

She swipes her cheek, angry. Jake grabs a chair and sits in front of her.

"Look. Look at me."

She can't look at him. He takes one of her hands instead.

"I've had all night to think about it. I'm going to help you, because there have to be consequences. Because . . . we're in America. We're supposed to be living in the place where people escape from these things. We're supposed to be better than this. And I don't see another way to stop it, and I won't leave you on your own. And . . . there's something to be said, you know, for the punishment fitting the crime . . ."

Eva looks at the fingers around hers, clever fingers with calloused tips, and she thinks of the posters hung on all the street corners of Wernigerode when she was young. Jews were like vermin, the posters said. Jews were like germs. But she is the one. She is the contagion. Infecting everything she touches. Making everything dirty.

She's making him dirty.

Eva takes her hand away from his, wrapping her arms back around her middle. "You said to me, that I wanted to know what it felt like . . . to play in the mud."

She sees Jake wince.

"But that was not me," she says. "It was you."

He has his jaw clenched, gaze on the floor.

"You were the one playing in mud. And now, you're back in it."

He's shaking his head.

"You don't belong there."

"Shut up . . ."

"Get out of it, Jake! Please . . ."

"Shut up!" he says. And he grabs her head in his hands and kisses her. Hard. Once.

Eva's eyes fly open in surprise. Jake's gaze is angry. And beautiful.

And then she kisses him. Hard. Not once. And he lets her. Fingers sliding over the stubble of his jaw, into his hair, nearly coming off her bench to push him back against the chair. He gets both her hands in one of his, holding them still against his chest while his thumb strokes her cheek.

"You are not dirty," he says against her mouth. He runs a finger down her neck, down the edge of the dressing gown, and kisses her once more. Slow. Then he sets her hands in her lap and stands. He walks away to the window seat, arms crossed, looking out into nothing. "But . . . I can't do that again."

Because in the world she'd belonged to—her old, sick world—people like him had always been less. Because people like her had murdered people like him for being less. Because her past and his future are a poisonous mix.

Eva folds her hands. She feels full, and hollow, watching Jake watch the dark. His breath is still coming fast. Shoulders rising and falling beneath his shirt. And she hates that girl in his future. The one who will deserve him.

"I'm going to help you," he says, "because it's justice. It's what I've decided and no regrets. Okay?"

"Okay," she says.

Jake glances back, taking her in. She can tell he wants to come to her, but he doesn't.

"But what if you can't trust me?" she asks. "What if he tells me to do . . . something, and I do it?"

This time when Jake looks back, one corner of his mouth is up. "You seem to do a lot of things your daddy would say no to."

It's true. But it's not the same, and Jake knows it. He goes to the bed and picks up the metal case.

"Here," he says. "Read it. The whole thing. See what it says."

Eva looks at the case. Reluctant.

"I'm not going anywhere," he says.

She takes the case to the bed, curling into her spot, sitting up against the pillow. Jake almost sits next to her, then opts for the window seat. She pushes the little button, and the lid pops opens.

And there is her mother's gun.

Jake knows what she's looking at. "It's only got three bullets in it."

Three, Eva thinks, out of eight. That would be right. One for Mama, one each for Adolf and Helga. Two for Erich.

"I was thinking I could get us a better . . ."

"No." Eva slides the file out from beneath the gun and shuts the case again. "No. I want this one."

She can feel him thinking about that. She can feel the room change when he guesses why she wants it. He leans back, lets out a long breath, watching the tiny glow of a cigarette at the edge of the lawn. Eva opens the file.

The papers are smooth. New and crisp. The first page says *Project Bluebird* with the name *Anna Ptaszynska* just below. And they are almost exactly the same as the pages sewn into her skirt. With more detail. A little more complete. Notes and charts, familiar now not just from the words she's read so many times, but from her memories.

Some of those memories are still hazy, like fever pain. Others are clear. Solid. Like being locked in the little cupboard. The emetic dripped on her tongue to make her vomit as soon as she'd failed to "control a thought." The Doctor had used that one until the wrong thoughts would make her sick anyway. No emetic needed.

And all of it to carefully coax and condition her mind. To make her memories such a source of terrible pain that they were just . . . sent away. To erase the person who had been Anna Ptaszynska out of her own existence.

Because Anna was less.

And when Anna was gone, the Doctor could start making her "more." A good German. Loyal and obedient. Compliant to authority. Even when it went against her own sense of right and wrong. Especially when it did. And this was supposed to save her from weakness. Make her stronger. Better.

Eva reads what she did with the bird in the box.

And then she reads what she did when she got older. When the experiment changed. Because if one piece of a mind could be erased, the memories hidden away, what other pieces could be splintered off, hidden in the same way? And what could these hidden pieces of herself then be made to do? And these are the stories Liebermann whispered on the road. The nightmares she can neither remember nor imagine. But they are all crimes. Cruel, and they all say the same thing.

One word, and she is a murderer. Without even knowing it.

Eva sets down the file. Jake is still, stretched on the window seat, an arm behind his head. Watching her.

"Things have been happening at Powell House," she says. "Things I don't understand."

"Okay, like what things?"

"Like the window being shut when I know I opened it. And I can't remember shutting it again. And . . . Augusta's art . . ."

Jake sits up. "You know Olive left the street door unlocked, right? That the police think some jerk who believes an integrated art show will ruin his nice neighborhood came in from downstairs? And why would you even want to bust up a sculpture?"

Because it had meant something to her. But it's impossible to explain that to Jake.

"And there were birds," she whispers. "Dead. Two of them . . ."

"Does Brigit have a kitten or doesn't she?"

But there had been another bird. In the seat of her mother's Mercedes. She'd thought that was Erich, like the pearls in the toilet. But she'd never been sure.

"And none of that," Jake points out, "is you doing what your father told you to. He hasn't been anywhere near you, right?"

"Just when we were in the closet. I think he was there, in the apartment."

"And you were not exactly murdering me."

She'd been running her hand up his back.

Jake props his elbows on his knees. "I get that in a weird kind of way, it might be . . . easier on you, to be Anna, than to be his daughter . . ."

Eva's gaze darts up.

"... but some kind of cold-blooded killer in a trance who will shoot whoever her daddy says whenever he says it? I don't buy it. I'm not sure I buy any of it. Those people in the camp, he would have chosen them. Just the right ones. But you're not Mina. You're a fighter. You're a fighter every time."

She doesn't want to say what she just read, that "when instructed, Anna squeezed the bird until it died . . ." That she can remember the bird in her hand, and just how much she did not want to squeeze it.

"You get to choose who you want to be, Bluebird, and you get to choose what you do. You're doing it right now, aren't you?"

That has to be a little bit true.

"I think you should burn that file. Get rid of it. We both know what it says."

Eva looks at the papers. At her father's slanted hand. Then she gets up from the bed, turns the key before Jake can say anything, and steps out the door and across the hall. She comes back with her skirt on the hanger, and Jake is waiting, arms across the doorway.

"Do you have that knife?" she asks. "That you used on the window?"

He fishes it out of a pocket while she locks the door again, watching as she perches on the edge of the bed, using the tip of the slim blade to pick out the stitches of her skirt hem. She pulls the papers from behind the satin lining, so wrinkled and dirty they're getting delicate.

Jake has half a smile on his face. Waiting for her to explain.

"They were on his desk," she says. "In Germany. A file with my name on it. My German name. But Anna's notes were inside. They're almost exactly the same as the first pages of the others."

Jake nods, and Eva gathers up both sets of papers into a pile, taking them to the fireplace and laying them in the grate. Jake doesn't say anything. Just pushes open the damper, sits down beside her, and hands her a box of matches.

"I'd thought these would be evidence, once," she says.

"They seem to give people ideas," Jake replies.

Eva strikes the match. Smells the sulfur. And it isn't hard at all to put the flame to the first corner of paper.

They sit, side by side, and watch Anna's life burn.

Eva says, "My father will come to me soon. I put a notice in the newspaper."

Jake's glance flicks once to hers. "Want to know what's in my jacket pocket right now? Dr. Schneider's home address."

Eva smiles. Jake uses the poker to help along the flames.

"Turns out that Dr. Schneider canceled his appointments this week. Because he has guests. From out of town."

"It might not be them."

Jake shrugs. "They had to run somewhere last minute. We could go there, Bluebird. First thing in the morning. Get the lay of the land. It's less than an hour away."

They make their plans while the flames die, while Jake lights one more match, making sure every bit of paper turns to ash.

"You're sure?" she asks him.

Jake smiles. "No regrets. Remember?"

But then he's not smiling anymore. He's looking at her mouth. She can feel him. Smell him. And the longing is a pull that becomes a tug that has to be broken. Jake gets to his feet. Goes to the window seat and stretches out.

Because he can't do that again.

She knows he can't.

Eva curls up on the bed. There's another hour before the dawn. "You can come lie down," she says. "It's only . . . sleeping."

Jake smiles again with his eyes closed and shakes his head.

"I'm in for a talk in the morning as it is," he says. "We didn't go to dinner, and nobody knows where I slept. Either Mick or Tony will pull me aside and mention the idea of leaving a girl in a 'bad position.' Wait and see."

"Will they be angry with you?" Eva asks, hugging the pillow.

"They're Quakers, not saints. And I wouldn't be the first to go creeping around Sky Island after dark. Jimmy and Colette were the worst. But you're new here, and I'm supposed to know better. So I'm thinking the words 'immoral cad' might be used."

Eva closes her eyes. She doesn't know what that means, but she can guess. It's probably wrong, she thinks, to wish that he was.

It's probably wrong to lie there, with Jake on the window seat, remembering what his lips taste like.

Neither one of them really sleeps. And when the sun moves across the sky, they move with it. They take turns with the bathroom, Eva working a few of the wrinkles out of Jake's shirt with a damp cloth while Jake shaves with her razor—which she thinks is unsanitary— brushing his teeth with a finger. She gets out of the bathing suit, into her skirt and blouse, does a little something to tame her hair. Jake puts the gun in his pocket, and she picks up her purse with the bread knife in its lining.

"Chin up, Bluebird," Jake says on the way downstairs. "I have to eat or die, so we get to face the music."

And when they walk into the kitchen, they get a row of hard stares. As if a conversation has just been suspended. Mrs. Kushner frowns beneath her kerchief, the three Petrova girls giggling and ogling Jake until their mother says something stern. But Greta smiles and says good morning, and Eva sees Valentina lost at the far end of the table, staring down into her coffee.

"Good morning," Eva says to her.

Valentina startles, smiling an apology before she's lost again. Jake has grabbed two eggs on a plate, eating them while having a conversation to one side with Mick. Eva catches his eye, and the corner of his mouth just lifts. She has to bite back her smile.

The truth is so much worse, it's laughable.

Eva piles some leftover muffins and two apples on a napkin, quickly, then tells a surprised Patricia that they're off for a drive and she'll see them later. Three minutes, and Jake joins her in the driveway with a thermos of coffee, and they climb into the green convertible.

"So?" Eva asks.

Jake grins. "You're new here. I should know better, and aren't you really pretty."

He puts on a pair of sunglasses and starts the car.

CHAPTER FORTY-SEVEN

—— *August 1946* ——

THERE ARE NO other cars when they leave Sky Island. Russian or American. They drive down the hill to the village first, where Jake stops for gas, a map, and cigarettes. Eva contributes part of her last American bill to the gas, which Jake is amused to see come out of her bra instead of her purse.

"As if I needed more temptation," he says.

They study the map, drinking coffee from the thermos while the attendant fills up the tank, cleans the windshield, checks the oil, empties the ashtray. Jake shows her Dr. Schneider's address—in a suburb that's actually in New Jersey, but not far—and the other places they'd discussed in front of the fireplace. The plan is straightforward. Uncomplicated, unless they are followed by someone. A plan for justice, Jake says. And to keep them out of jail.

Jake pulls onto the highway going south. The top is still down, wind rushing, whipping at their hair under a sky that is bright, but overcast. Glaring. He glances once, then twice, into the rearview mirror. "What do you think?" he asks, voice raised.

There's a black car getting onto the road behind them. Eva can just make out the shadow of the driver's hat in the side mirror.

"It could be," she says.

Jake waits for two exits, then gets off the highway. "Hold up the map," he says. "Like we're lost." She does. He stops at the red light, then drives straight through, back onto the highway. And so does the black car, staying well behind them, keeping pace.

"Yep," he says. "So how do you want to lose him? Movies or my Auntie Joyce?"

"Movies," she says. Riskier, but not involving Jake's family.

"Come over here, then," he says. "We're on a date."

She folds up the map before it blows away, then scoots across the seat, tucking her feet to one side while Jake puts his arm around her. She keeps her head tilted, where she can watch the black car in the mirror.

They turn off toward Englewood, where there are rows of houses, each with trees and a square of grass. The black car stays with them as they drive into a little strip of downtown with a soda shop and a hardware store. The lights of the movie theater are just visible beneath the clouds. Jake finds a place on the street to park. The black car pulls into a space a block behind them.

"Quick," Jake says.

They go hand in hand down the sidewalk, at a trot, like they're late. Jake leans down to the little ticket window outside the theater, where an old man is smoking a cigar. He has a hole in his sweater, a red nose, and hair coming out of his ears.

"Jacob!" the man says. "What are you doing out of the city?"

"Hey, Mr. Nadar. Say, you wouldn't let me kill half an hour in your theater, would you?"

The man from the black car, in a short tie and a pinstripe suit, is coming down the sidewalk at a brisk clip, a newspaper under his arm. Definitely a Cruickshanks.

Mr. Nadar gives Eva the once-over. "Eh, go on, then," he says, chuckling as they head through the door in a rush.

"Do you know everyone everywhere?" Eva asks, trotting past a machine making popcorn.

"Mostly," Jake replies.

"And does everyone you know give you things?"

"Mostly." He grins.

"He's coming in," Eva whispers.

They step inside the dark theater, and there's no time to go straight through, like they'd intended. Jake veers left, instead, to two seats on the last row. Where no one can sit behind them. And then the Cruickshanks is through the theater door.

Jake puts his arm around her, like they're on their date, and Eva gets her head down, not looking as the man passes.

"He's about four rows down, other side of the aisle," Jake says in her ear. "He's seen us. But he'll have to look over his shoulder to watch."

Unless this Cruickshanks is not going to be content with just watching.

"Do you see the door down front, to the left? That's the one that goes behind the screen and to the street."

Only now they can't use it. Now it will have to be Auntie Joyce.

Eva gives Jake a glance. "Do you also know the back way out of everywhere?"

"This is useful information, Bluebird. Should we give it half an hour? I don't think he knows we're onto him."

The theater is nearly empty except for three or four couples, sitting close in the dim light of the screen. "No one is watching the film," Eva whispers.

"You do not bring a girl to a morning double feature during the last week of summer to watch the film."

Jake's arm is warm in the dark. He smells like her own soap.

It would be the smallest thing in the world to turn her face, just a little.

Only she's not supposed to do that.

Then she wonders just how many girls Jake has not watched a film with.

She feels him sigh in her hair. "Watch the movie, Bluebird. It's ironic."

The story is about a female psychiatrist discovering that her colleague is actually a killer on the run who has forgotten his identity. The Cruickshanks doesn't move for a long time.

"I think he's actually watching the movie," Jake whispers. "Let's go."

They slip out without the man turning his head. If they can lose him now, they might not have to go to Auntie Joyce after all. Jake starts the car, but they're not quick enough. Mr. Cruickshanks comes strolling onto the sidewalk in his short, red tie. They're spotted.

"Let him see us go by," Eva says.

Jake drives slowly past the theater, but a different black car picks up their trail. Eva glances once in the side mirror. Now it's the Cruickshanks from the Zanzibar. The one who chased them up the mountain. And he's not being subtle.

"You know, I think that man wants to talk to you," Jake says, keeping a leisurely pace. "Be ready when we get there."

Auntie Joyce lives in a low white bungalow with a picket fence, in a row of other low, white bungalows with picket fences. There are pansies planted around the mailbox. Jake picks up speed at the last minute, throwing the green convertible into park right in front of the house. The black car brakes behind them, finding a space across and a little way down the street, the Cruickshanks just stepping out to the curb when Auntie Joyce answers her doorbell.

Auntie Joyce is in her fifties, what Jake would call a "bombshell" if he was talking about anyone else. She has bleached hair, white pants, a drink in one hand, and smells of perfume when she kisses Jake's cheek. The living room is all white, too, the radio playing a slow dance while Jake spins a tale about a table he's picking up from somewhere. Uncle Paul's nice car. Could they switch for her mother's old Studebaker and switch back tomorrow? Auntie Joyce does not mind having Paul's convertible for the day. Not at all. They trade keys. And is Andy here?

Andy sticks his head out of his room. He's skinny, red-faced, and a little spotted, and more than happy to take some cash from his cousin. In ten minutes, he's opening up the garage, starting up the Studebaker. He yanks it into reverse, Jake lying full-length on the back seat, Eva on the floor. The car grumbles, changes gear, and they're off down the road.

"So who are we avoiding, Jake?" Andy asks over the engine noise.

"Her old boyfriend," Jake replies. Eva makes a face at him.

"Aww, what's with the skulking around? Just duke it out!"

"Shut up, Andy," Jake says, smiling. "You look like you're talking to nobody."

"I thought I already was."

Jake rolls his eyes, hanging on as the car takes a curve. "Anybody with us?"

"Nope."

"Go around the square and make sure. Then pull over somewhere quiet and leave the key."

Andy does what Jake says, and the car jerks to a stop behind a grocery store. Jake takes a peek, and then motions for Eva to come. She jumps out and around and into the front, while Jake removes Andy and gets behind the wheel.

"Take the back way home," Jake says. "Over the fence. You know what to do. If you go in the front, the jig is up."

Andy's hair is flopping down into his eyes. He puts his hands in his pockets, exactly the way Jake does. "Say, you're not eloping or anything, are you, Jake? 'Cause your mom will . . ."

Jake just grins, puts the car in gear, and they putter off, leaving Andy with his mouth open. They're headed away from the strip of downtown.

"Anything?" Jake asks. Eva takes a good look and shakes her head. They've lost him. Then she asks, "What does 'eloping' mean?"

"Running off to get married without telling anybody." Jake chuckles.

He takes the back streets, and this area is more industrial, with businesses and warehouses. They pass a factory being rebuilt. Half the front wall is gone, the parking lot full of trucks, a bulldozer, and a crane beside a big sign that says WILSON'S CARPETS. Jake turns into a side entrance, behind the main building, driving up to a long, low range of offices with cracked windows and weeds poking up through the concrete.

He parks to one side and cuts the engine.

Eva can hear the hammers when she gets out of the car, machinery, the occasional smack of lumber being dropped, but it's muffled here. Out of sight. Everything is out of sight, cut off by the factory's back wall and a wilderness of overgrown fence. There's a green door at one end of the building, locked, but Jake climbs through the window and opens it. Eva steps inside, both hands on her purse.

It's just an empty room. Paint peeling off the walls, concrete floor that might have had a carpet on it at one time, swirls of old, yellowed glue showing through the bits of debris.

"How do you know about this place?" she asks.

"Andy. I spent a couple of summers up here with my aunt. Doing things I shouldn't." He almost smiles, but the feeling goes away. "So, what do you think? There won't be anyone around here at night."

"It will be dark. But that is good, I think."

"We might get a little of the streetlight, if it's working. And there's another room. Back there." He nods toward a dark doorway behind him. "You could wait in there. While I do it."

Eva shakes her head. "No. You know I have to do it."

He looks down at a crack in the concrete. "I've been asking myself all day, if I could really do it. I would've had to, if I hadn't missed the draft. Plenty of the guys I go to school with are back from the war, and some of them . . . they'd have given their front teeth to take out a guy like . . . him. And still, I'm not sure I've got the guts. But I look at you, standing there, telling me you have to and . . ." He shrugs. "I swear, I'd pull the trigger."

He puts a hand in his jacket pocket, takes two strides across the dirty floor, and lays her mother's gun in her palm. The gold eagle shines on the holster. This is different from the heat of battle. This is cold. Calculated. It has to be.

But she thinks she can do it.

Because Anna killed the bird. And other things. She killed other things.

"It's justice," Eva says, and puts the gun in her purse.

Jake nods, jaw set. "So this is the place?"

"Yes," she says.

"Then let's go see what we see."

It takes them about twenty minutes to get to Dr. Schneider's address. Jake circles, makes a few erratic turns, but they don't see any cars following, black or rusty. The streets around Dr. Schneider's look like Auntie Joyce's, only the houses are bigger, the yards wider, everything shiny new. All the trees are saplings. Jake finds a place to leave the car a few blocks away from the house, at a little park with benches and swings. And then they walk, Eva swinging her purse. Like they're on a stroll. Jake slides on his sunglasses.

The wind is cooling, the sky the same color as the sidewalk's unblemished concrete. The hedges are trimmed like somebody used a level. They walk on the opposite side of the street from Dr. Schneider's, and when they reach the right address, Eva has to check it again. The yard is full of children. A herd of them—eight, maybe nine-year-olds—running all over the lawn in suit jackets and big bows. Streamers blow from the little trees, pink balloons dangling from the mailbox.

It's a birthday party. A little girl's party.

"Oh, hell," breathes Jake.

They keep walking.

Another house down and there's a stop for a bus or a streetcar. They sit on the concrete bench, boxes of geraniums on either side, close enough to see, but far enough away to not be noticed, sheltered by the cars parked along the road. The children are playing some kind of game on the clipped grass. Some of them have blindfolds on, screeching and laughing. Jake lights a cigarette.

"What can you see?" he asks.

There's a woman in the front yard, in a green print dress and matching heels, her blond hair curled, stiff with perfection. She's laughing with the children, tottering back and forth awkwardly in the grass, coordinating the game. She calls to a man leaning against the porch rail. He's a little older, with graying temples, heavy, black glasses like the dead Mr. Cruickshanks, watching the fun, and in the corner, in the shadow of a climbing vine, is another man. Seated. A drink in his hand. Smoking a pipe.

Eva looks at him once. Twice.

And sees the man who took her to parades and the sea and to Berlin to hear Wagner. The man who took her memories and her name. The man who makes people to do the unspeakable. After two years, a war, and an ocean.

The Doctor. Her father.

And he's little. Frail-looking. With white in his beard now as well as the gray, wearing a green knit cardigan in a rocking chair. Had he always looked like someone's grandfather?

"Eva?" Jake asks.

"He's there," she whispers. "In the rocking chair."

She can feel the repaired pieces of herself shaking. Threatening to unglue. Splinter. She'd forgotten he was made of flesh and blood.

Jake leans back and smokes, silent.

A little girl with bows on her pigtails comes running up to the rocking chair, opening her hand. Eva watches her father put down his drink, ruffle the little girl's hair like he always has, and set her in his lap. Talking to her. Like she's the most important thing in the universe.

She'd done that so many times when she was Inge. And he hadn't even looked for her after the war. He'd left her behind. In the rubble. It makes her feel small. Less.

And then she's angry that he can make her feel that way. And then she wonders if her father would give that little girl a bird, and Eva wants to go barreling through the birthday party and snatch the child away.

The little girl hops down from the Doctor's lap, off to join the game, and for a moment, her father's gaze lifts, just brushing across the other side of the street. Eva winces. Like she's been slapped.

"Bastard," Jake says, throwing down his cigarette. He offers his hand, and she takes it. Her fingers are pale, nails red against his skin. She breathes, and feels calmer.

"Let's make the call," Eva says.

They walk back to the car, hand in hand. The children are at a decorated table in the yard now, eating cake. The rocking chair on the porch is empty.

There's a drugstore around the corner with a phone booth inside. Jake smiles and comes into the booth with her this time, because he says she can't be trusted. He gives her the number and a nickel.

"What time?" she asks him.

"Midnight?"

She nods, holding the receiver. Jake waits, letting her go in her own time. And finally, she drops the nickel in its slot and dials. The line hums, crackling. And on the third ring, a breathless woman answers, "Englewood 4479. Hello?"

"May I speak to Dr. von Emmerich, please?" she says. In German.

There's a little silence on the other end. But she can hear the birth-day party going on outside. The door must be open. The woman replies in English, though she didn't ask what the German meant. "There's no one here by that name. Who's calling?"

"Tell him it's Inge. And that I would . . . very much like to see him again."

Jake's eyes are such a beautiful color of gray-green. And they are intent on her. It sounds like the woman has put her hand over the other end of the telephone. For a few moments, everything is muffled.

"I'm sorry, could you repeat that please?" she says.

And Eva can see in her mind what is happening. The woman holding out the phone to her father. So he can listen to her speak. So he can know if it's really her.

"This is Inge," she says clearly, still in German. "I have information for my father. The Americans know he is in the country. They are close to finding him. Tell him to meet me in the abandoned offices behind the Wilson Carpet Factory at midnight. Look for the green door. We will not . . . be disturbed there. And I only want to speak to my father. No one else. He should come alone or I'll leave. Tell him . . . I have his file."

Now she can hear snatches of brief conversation. The woman has taken her hand off the phone. "That is much too late," she says abruptly. "He will see you there at four."

And the line goes dead.

CHAPTER FORTY-EIGHT

ONE, TWO, THREE...

The bangs are so loud. She doesn't like them.

Three, four, five...

They're not like drums. They hurt her ears. They make people scream.

Bangs are a bad thing.

Sometimes bad things have to happen. Like brushing out the tangles.
Like taking out a splinter.

Maybe bangs have to happen.

When the wrong people come into the house.

CHAPTER FORTY-NINE

—— *August 1946* ——

JAKE STARTS THE CAR. "I don't like it. Broad daylight. And that crew won't even have finished work for the day . . ." The tires squeal a little as he pulls out. It's twenty minutes past three.

The plan to avoid jail involved never being seen. Jake had argued again and again that her father was a war criminal. In the country illegally. The Schneiders were not going to report him missing. The police might not even be able to identify him, if they made sure there was no paperwork left on him. But none of that works if they are seen.

"I think we have to try," Eva says. "I don't know what else to do."

"Look, if it's not safe, then you don't do it and that's it. We can make another plan. Promise me. We can do this without you ruining the rest of your life."

Or yours, she thinks.

The whole thing always has been a rotten deal.

"Watch for cars for me," he says.

She does, until Jake parks the Studebaker on a street a few blocks away from the factory, like he did in Dr. Schneider's neighborhood. They go in on foot. Past boys playing baseball in an abandoned lot, and then behind the factory. They can hear the construction crew, though they can't see them. The green door is still open.

"Let's both wait in the back," Jake says. "You can go out and . . . do you what you have to. But listen . . ." Jake puts a hand on her arm, making sure she hears. "If you can't, or if you change your mind, you don't have to. I'll do it. Okay?"

She nods, but he says it again.

"Okay?"

"Yes," she says.

They go into the semidarkness of the back room, standing out of view from the window. Jake says, "I never asked if you knew how to use the . . ."

But Eva already has the pistol in her hand, the magazine out. It has two bullets in it, plus one in the chamber, like Jake had said. It's funny, she thinks, when Frau Koch brought in the SS officer to teach the League of German Girls to load and fire a luger, how it had never occurred to her that maybe the war wasn't going so well. They had all been so excited, getting to do something the boys did. Eva pushes the magazine back up into place with a click and switches off the safety with her thumb.

"Let me have the knife," Jake says, "just in case." She gives it to him handle first, and he tosses it on the floor and sits beside it, back against the wall. He holds out his hand. "Wait with me."

She takes his hand. And they wait. Shoulder to shoulder.

Eva closes her eyes. She says the twenty-seven names, slowly, in her mind. And then she searches the pieces of herself, looking for Anna. The Anna who knows how to pull a trigger. But there's nothing there. That part of herself is smooth. Blank. Hidden.

It might be best, she thinks. To have Eva, instead of Anna. Anna might hear a special word and do what her father says.

And when she opens her eyes, the light has dimmed in their little room, the clouds thickening outside the dirty window. Jake has his arm around her. His eyes are closed, head back against the wall, but he is tense. Aware. His wrist hangs near her chin. She watches the hands on his watch go around. And around. Listening to the construction crew go home. To every little noise. Every nonexistent crunch of gravel outside the green door.

At six o'clock, Jake whispers, "I don't think he's coming, Bluebird."

She knows it. He didn't take the bait. Her father will be running now, far and fast, hiding in a hole so deep she'll never find him.

There is no justice. Not today. There may not be any justice ever.

They've lost. And it's her fault.

Jake stands, brushing himself off, putting out a hand, and pulling her to her feet. But before he can let her go, she reaches up on her toes and kisses him once, softly on the lips, lingering only for an extra second.

Jake doesn't move, not one muscle.

"That was for today," Eva says. She turns away. "And I know I can't do it again."

She puts on the safety and drops the gun and the knife back into her purse. They walk away from the dilapidated office and the half-built factory, driving back to Sky Island in the Studebaker. Let Cruickshanks sit out there all night if he wants to, Jake says.

They don't talk much. The relief has come, like she knew it would, because she did not have to shoot her father. And then the guilt comes after that. Because she failed those names. The ones she knows, and the ones she doesn't. And all the names that might come in the future.

The twilight is short, the clouds low and heavy, with the occasional electric flash from the darkness to the east. Over the sea. Jake turns on the radio.

There's a storm coming.

He coaxes the car up the hill, careful on the dark road. The Studebaker doesn't like it, but they make it through the gates and into the drive. Patricia's borrowed jalopy is gone. Eva rolls up the window, while Jake sits with his hands on the wheel. Leaves go skittering over the gravel.

"I'll come up to your room after everyone goes to bed," he says. "You shouldn't be up there by yourself."

There's a heaviness to his words. And Eva wonders if he's changed his mind. About what he will and won't do. If she'd kissed him again in that abandoned office, he would have let her. He would have really let her. And he's barely spoken since. "What will Mick say?" she asks.

"That I'm a lucky guy." He smiles.

She knows he jokes when he's nervous.

They run inside, the wind howling at their heels, and find almost everyone in the warm kitchen, finishing dinner. "Tony and Patricia went down to Nyack to pick up some supplies and the jalopy broke down," Greta says. "We left chicken noodle casserole in the oven. Help yourself."

"Was there a telephone call for me?" Eva asks.

Greta shakes her head and says she's sorry. And no one mentions that she and Jake have been gone all day together. That Eva was supposed to be taking over someone's share of the work.

Jake fills a plate and digs in, starting a conversation with Mick about whether the Red Sox will make the World Series. Which could be spy code, for all Eva knows. She tries, but she can't make herself eat. The women are all chatting about some kind of play Mrs. Kushner and the three Petrova girls have put together for after dinner. An unlikely combination of actors, Eva thinks, but they are all enthusiasm. Valentina keeps losing track of the conversation, and when the wind rattles the windows, she jumps. Eva walks over to the sink, where Greta is up to her elbows in dirty water.

"Go help with the play," she tells Greta. "I'll finish the kitchen."

"Oh, really? That would be great, actually. Thanks . . ."

Eva finishes the dishes and Jake stays to dry while the others go to the lounge with coffee or to set up for the play. They can hear things being dragged down the hall, voices calling back and forth in different languages. Happy. Excited. Their quiet over the dishwater is full of unsaid things.

Jake dries his hands, saying to go on to the living room, he's right behind her. Eva takes her purse, and finds an elaborate sort of stage created in front of the piano, using draperies from somewhere in the house like curtains at a theater, the small audience scattered among the chairs and sofas in the sunken part of the floor. It's hard not to smile at all the effort. At the flushed faces of the Petrova girls.

She finds a spot at the end of the sofa next to Valentina. Jake comes in, leaving a cup of tea at her elbow before finding a chair at the back. Where he can slip out when he wants to. Eva picks up the cup and saucer. The tea is not too hot, with just a little lemon, no sugar. She closes her eyes.

Jake remembers that she likes lemon. He remembers that she doesn't take sugar.

She looks over at his chair, where he's sitting, quiet, hands folded together, elbows on knees. There's no music in him at the moment. But he looks up once, smiles. Eva smiles back and sips her tea.

She would have pulled that trigger today, even if there weren't twenty-seven names.

She would have done it just for him.

Thunder claps, loud and sudden. There are a few gasps, and then laughs. Except Valentina, who is so startled her hands shake. She tucks them under her legs. Valentina, Eva thinks, knows what a bomb sounds like.

And then the play begins.

The draperies open to show an enormous figure of a woman. About seven feet tall, maybe five feet wide, her face painted onto a beach ball. She has a big, pink hat over yellow tassels for hair, wearing a voluminous, old-fashioned dress that might have also once served as curtains somewhere inside Sky Island. And though the English is not always quite right during this play, it seems that the beach ball–headed woman seeks the advice of a Petrova girl dressed as a doctor, to fulfill her lifelong dream of training for the Olympics.

But somewhere under the enormous dress must be secreted another Petrova sister and an open umbrella, because each time the woman follows the doctor's orders, she visibly shrinks as the umbrella closes, which is so silly and unexpected that everyone is laughing.

It's surreal, Eva thinks, to end this day with laughter. Even Valentina laughs, and by the time the umbrella is fully closed, the Olympics have been canceled due to war, and the girls and Mrs. Kushner come out to take their bows.

Eva sets down her cup while the little audience finishes clapping, and then Jake is whispering in her ear that he's given Mick the car keys, to go pick up Patricia and Tony, and that he's going up to her room to take a shower and to give him about twenty minutes. Eva wanders to the window, thinking, and at the edge of the lawn, in the thunder and wind, just inside the tree line beside the summerhouse, she sees the faint glow of a cigarette.

The Russian is here. A Soviet who knows her name is Ptaszynska. And why hasn't he ever come for her?

Maybe the Doctor really is all he's interested in.

Someone turns on the radio, the Petrova parents dance, and Greta says she'll make the cocoa in just a few. Then there's a sudden, bright flash. A snap of electricity. A boom that shakes the house. And the music and the lights are gone.

Silence settles down with the dark. And then everyone starts talking. Can they change a fuse? Where are the candles? Who has a match? Eva backs up, finds the couch behind her and sits on it. A jolt of fear is coursing through her like the current they no longer have.

Thunder can sound like so many things.

Then there's a candle lit. And another, and the room is visible again. Thunder booms, not so close this time, but the blast of wind is violent. Everyone is laughing again, now that they can see. Jake, Eva thinks, is having a shower in the dark.

She should take a candle to him.

And then she realizes that Valentina is missing. Eva finds her huddling behind the couch. "Thank you," she whispers as Eva helps her to her feet. "I am not . . . like myself."

"I'm often not like myself," Eva replies.

Then Greta says what a perfect time it is to play hide-and-seek. And in such a big house, too. You can play in the dark, and everybody hides, but one person will be the murderer, and if you find someone playing dead, you yell murder and we all try to figure out who the murderer is.

Eva looks out the window, thinking of the gun in her purse. The dead Mr. Cruickshanks, his neck askew on the lawn.

"Eva, do you want to play murder?" Greta asks, her eyes bright with fun. The Petrova girls are bouncing.

"No, thank you." She doesn't want to tell Greta that this game is only fun when it isn't real to you. "I'll walk Valentina upstairs. She's not feeling well."

"Oh, sure. Thanks." Greta hesitates at the sight of Valentina's sweating face. But she doesn't want to ruin the good time for the girls.

The two Mr. Petrovas and Mr. Kushner go to bed while Greta passes out cards to decide who the murderer is, Mrs. Petrova and even Mrs. Kushner playing along. Eva takes one of the candles and picks up Valentina's hand as the players scatter to hide all over the dark house. Valentina obeys. Does exactly as she's told. A piece of machinery with the switch flipped on.

"Valentina," Eva whispers, shuffling her along in their circle of candlelight. The front hall is cavernous and black, flashing blue with the lightning. "Which room is yours?"

She doesn't respond, and they're alone now. Eva can hear a clock ticking beneath the roar of the wind. She wonders if Valentina shares a room with anyone. She isn't sure she should be left alone tonight.

They start up the stairs, and out of nowhere from the dark hall someone shouts, "Murder!" With all the theater of an actor on a stage. "Murder! Murder!"

And Valentina lets out a shriek that Brigit never thought of. Fear in the form of sound. She screams again, without reason or thought, echoing through the house, and then sits straight down on the steps.

Eva sets down the candle, taking Valentina by the shoulders. Her body is stiff, her brown eyes wide open. Unseeing. She falls over sideways. "Help!" Eva shouts, but footsteps are already coming.

"What's happened?" says Greta.

"I don't know . . ."

Valentina is like Brigit having a seizure, only there's no movement at all. She needs a doctor. Mr. Kushner, mustache illuminated by a candle, peers down over the rail.

There's another booming clap of thunder, the house shakes, and this time, glass breaks somewhere. Greta is looking up at her, open-mouthed. Everyone is looking at her. Eva stands.

"Take Valentina to her room," she says to Greta. "Carry her, and stay with her. Make sure she breathes. And everyone should go to their rooms." She looks at the tall windows of the hall. "The wind is dangerous. I will call a doctor. And see what has broken."

They move quickly to do as she says. A group effort of two of the Petrova sisters, Mrs. Petrova, and Greta to carry Valentina up the steps, Mr. Kushner holding a light. Eva takes her candle through to the dining room, where the wind is howling through a broken window, playing havoc with the curtains, and into the back hallway.

It's a moonless night in the hall, where there are no windows, the sound of the storm muffled. She hurries, looking for the office with the telephone in her small circle of candlelight, wondering why Jake didn't come when Valentina screamed. He couldn't still be in the dark shower.

She finds the room with the shelves, a desk with ledger books, and an old-fashioned telephone. The kind you can't dial. She sets the candle on the desk, picks up the earpiece, and jiggles the little cradle it sits in.

"Hello? Hello?" But there's not even a crackle. Either the line is down or she doesn't know how to use it. "Hello?"

"Hallo, mein Vögelchen."

Eva stands. Motionless. The voice had been behind her. In the office.

With her.

And something inside her shifts. But she does not feel ready. She doesn't feel much of anything at all. She sets the earpiece of the telephone gently back in its cradle. And turns. And smiles.

"Hello, Papa."

CHAPTER FIFTY

—— *September 1946* ——

THE DOCTOR STANDS in the doorway, his green cardigan beneath an unbuttoned coat dotted with rain. His whitening beard spreads as he smiles, and his smile is soft. Just for her. He takes a step forward, speaking gently in German.

"You have grown so much since I saw you last, my little bird. Such a young lady. Are you well?"

"Yes, Papa."

"Have you missed me?"

"Yes, Papa."

"You came to see me today, didn't you, little bird? I wish you had come inside. That would have been so nice."

It's such a shame, Eva thinks, that she didn't. A terrible shame. She can smell his tobacco.

"I'd like for you to make a telephone call for me. But the phone, it is not working?"

She shakes her head.

"Then we must go on a trip together, little bird. To find a telephone."

"Who would you like me to call, Papa?"

"I would like to speak to a Mr. Cruickshanks. Do you know the telephone number for a Mr. Cruickshanks?"

"Yes, Papa. It's on a little card. In my purse."

"Then let's go get that, shall we?"

She picks up the candle, smiling, and leads her father out of the office, down the hall and into the dining room, where the rain spatters the rug through the broken glass. They can hear the storm now, the thunder a constant rumble and roll. Like tanks across the sky. Eva walks slowly, so her father can keep up. Into the dark front hall, empty now, and to the living room, where the candles are dripping down onto the mantelpiece.

"This is a nice room," her father says. "Very comfortable. Have you been having a show?"

"Yes, Papa."

"How nice. And where are your friends?"

"Gone to bed," she says.

He looks at the water scouring the windows, lays his hat on a table, and takes off his coat. "Why don't we talk here for a few moments? The weather is terrible, and the car is parked at the end of the drive. And we must wait for Rolf."

"Is Rolf here?"

"Rolf is always here, little bird. He is bringing me my file."

She nods, picks up her purse, and sits with it on her lap, perched on the very edge of the sofa. "And do you have Anna here with you, too, Papa?"

Her father smiles. "Oh, yes, I think so."

He takes his tobacco pouch from his coat and settles in the arm chair. She watches him fill the pipe bowl, tamp it down, the glow as he pulls the flame through the tobacco with his breath. A puff of smoke, and the smell goes straight into her head. And the pieces of herself howl, clamor, rage and storm like the sky outside. But she's not listening to them. Not right now.

The Doctor crosses his legs, relaxing in the cushioned chair. His fingers are pink and soft, his shoes a little shabby. "Rolf says he saw you, just before we left Germany. He tells me you were not very nice to him."

"Oh, that wasn't me, Papa," she says.

"Even so. You must ask him to forgive you, yes?"

But she only says, "Why do you want me to call Mr. Cruickshanks, Papa?"

"So we can have a new life together, my little bird. A very prosperous, happy life. You will attend to Rolf. And you will take care of me, when I am not working."

"But what about Anna? Doesn't Mr. Cruickshanks want Anna, too?"

"Yes, you are right. How good you are, to remember. But Mr. Cruickshanks does not need Anna. Mr. Cruickshanks can't have her."

"Where did Anna come from?"

The Doctor leans back. "That is an interesting question. You have never asked me that question. Where do you think she comes from?"

"Poland."

"Does Anna remember anyone from Poland?"

"Only a little."

"She should not remember it. Those are the thoughts that will make her ill. Are they, making her ill?" His gaze is intent over the bowl of the pipe.

"Some."

"Then she does not have to think of them, does she? She will stay safe with Rolf and her Papa. You are lucky, little bird. To be so loved."

Her gaze drifts over the empty teacup sitting on the table. She looks up.

"Mama didn't love me."

"She didn't? Tell me why you think that. Come, tell Papa everything."

"Because she didn't shoot me like the others."

"Ah. Well. That was just a mistake, my little bird. A mistake." He blows another column of thick, rich smoke, making her blink. "Tell me something, Anna. Do you remember the bird?"

"Yes."

"And did you do as your Papa asked, and kill the bird, Anna?"

She looks through the smoke, right into her father's eyes. "Of course, I killed the bird, Papa."

The windows flash with lightning behind his head. And then he laughs. He laughs and laughs until his laughter has outlasted the thunder. He wipes his eyes, wagging a short, pink finger. "You," he says, "have been reading my papers. What have I told you about such things? That is what you get for being nosy, little bird. Fair is fair."

She opens her eyes wide. "What do you mean, Papa?"

"You may stop your little game now, Inge. Though you did have me hopeful for a just moment. A tiny moment. Very, very good. You always were the interesting one." He leans forward, pointing with the pipe, his eyes dancing. "This will be the first lesson of our new life together in America. Do not believe everything you read."

Eva sits still, purse perched on her knees.

You have been reading my papers.

Do not believe everything you read.

There were lies in Anna Ptaszynska's file. The Doctor has been writing down lies.

Anything real could be unreal, and anything unreal could be the truth.

And now he will have to explain which is which.

The Doctor is smiling. Watching her think.

Eva stands, walking briskly through the candlelight, and sets her purse on a table, blocking it from her father's view. She doesn't turn around when she says, "You know I am not coming with you."

He chuckles. "Of course you shall. My friend Dr. Schneider was approached by a Mr. Cruickshanks and was assured that you were part of the 'package.' But we have not been contacted again . . ."

She looks back. "That's because Mr. Cruickshanks is dead."

"Ah, well. I am sure you've realized by now that there is more than one Mr. Cruickshanks. But luckily, you were so kind as to put a notice in the paper, and even to come to the Schneider's today. Wasn't little Marta's party nice? And you had a young man with you, too. Rolf says he is the nephew of one of the surgeons, a Jewish surgeon, and that he has been asking uncomfortable questions at the hospital. Rolf was very hurt, to think you might prefer a Jew. We shall have to have some little talks together, I think. Once we are settled."

Eva turns, back against the table, keeping a hand on the purse behind her. "So Rolf doesn't mind, then? That I am Anna Ptaszynska?"

The Doctor puts his brows together, pipe in the corner of his mouth. "Tell me the truth. Does it make you ill, to ask me that?"

"No," she says. And it's almost not a lie.

"Oh, Inge. My little bird. I am going to enjoy having you back so very much. There is still much to learn from you, I think, and it will be fascinating to see how you have progressed. But let us have one thing clear between us. You are not Anna Ptaszynska." He sits forward in his chair. "Because Anna Ptaszynska does not exist."

Eva keeps her face serene. Because that can't be true. "I know who I am."

"Do you? You have no question in your mind?" He looks at her face carefully. Knowingly. "No questions for your papa?"

She looks back at him, smoking and musing in his chair, and for a moment, she's six years old with a nuthatch in her hands, squirming beneath the same shrewd gaze. She has to ask. She can't help it. "Who was Erich?"

"Oh, Inge." His face looks sad. "Do you not remember? Erich was your brother."

She shakes her head. "Mama couldn't have children, could she?"

"Think carefully. Adolf was born the night I took you to Berlin, to hear Wagner. You were so excited to find him, when we came home . . ."

She had been excited. And Adolf must have been six or seven months old.

"All right, then. Who is Annemarie?"

"Who?" the Doctor asks.

"Annemarie Toberentz."

"You can't have forgotten your neighbor. Wasn't she your friend? Yes, we will have to have many little talks . . ."

"She was with Anna. I remember."

"And are you very certain about your memories, Inge?"

"Stop calling me that. And yes, I am certain."

"So, tell me, if your memory serves you so well. What did you do with the bird?"

Eva grips the table behind her, the rain scouring the windows, reaching inside herself. Searching. She can see the box. Feel the soft, blue feathers, the grip of her tightening hand. But she can't remember what comes next.

The Doctor's eyes are dancing again. Eva narrows her gaze.

"If Anna Ptaszynska does not exist, then I wonder who Mr. Cruickshanks thinks he will be reading a file about."

"Ah, well," says the Doctor, sucking on his pipe. "I am sure he would like to have an Anna. Very much so. But he doesn't need her. He only thinks he does. The process of splitting the personality, of placing a hypnotic suggestion, bending a mind to a certain will, it's all so . . . messy. Overcomplicated, inefficient, and the outcomes are impossible to predict. When all you really need to make another person do what you wish is the application of the right leverage. That is simple science. And a more elegant solution. I proved this time and time again at the camp, in experiment after experiment . . ."

He smiles. "But this, it isn't what others want to hear, is it, little bird? You must show progress to keep the interest of those in power. You must pique their curiosity. And the idea of the ultimate control . . ." He pretends to shiver. "It is so tempting."

"Just not reality," she says.

"Reality is the condition we create for ourselves. If one side believes the other can do it, then the power is already gained and with much less fuss. It is the idea they need. And it is our ticket to a new life. New research. Isn't that wonderful? And imagine, Inge . . ."

He scoots forward in the chair. Eva presses her back into the table.

"Imagine the secrets to be discovered. We have lost so much this past year. A golden age of science. The Führer was a man cruelly let down by those around him, but he was a man of principle. A man of vision . . ."

Like Cruickshanks said. Apparently it was impossible to have "vision" and morals at the same time.

"And as such a man, the Führer removed all barriers to scientific discovery. Think of it, Inge. Take two parents of lesser blood. They have one child that is exactly as one might expect, while the other, through some far-off mixing of the bloodlines, shows all the signs of being racially valuable. What an opportunity! To see how the inferiority of one might be bettered, elevated, when compared to the other who is so naturally superior? And if such experiments could still be done, if we could learn from them, could we not create techniques to better all of the lower races? Create a new world? A better world, full of better people?"

And who gets to decide, Eva thinks, who is better? And who isn't?

She'd seen a glimpse of his "better world." It was a pile of dead bodies.

"And yet, who would allow such learning now?" the Doctor says. "The world is weak. Sentiment is allowed to rule science. But we are being given a second chance. Men of vision are willing to let me work on. To create the new world, no matter what they think I am actually doing. And I think that is worth a little fib or two in a file, don't you? To catch the interest of those in power? Anna Ptasyznska is my own invention. The key to the new beginning. And really . . ." He sits back in his chair. "I must say, I prefer it to a noose."

He smiles.

And Eva smiles back. Don't believe everything you read, he says. So she won't. She will believe what she remembers.

And she remembers being Anna. She remembers violets and gunshots and Annemarie and her mother's voice. But those smooth, blank spaces in her mind, where Anna the killer's memories were supposed to have been, they have disappeared. Dissolved. Sugar in the stormy rain. Because they never happened. The Anna Ptaszynska with the special word, who would shoot a man and finish her dinner, who would kill who she was told, when she was told, that Anna had never existed. Because the Doctor had made her up.

And there is something else she knows. Something the Doctor does not. She has read the file from his desk. The file with her German name on the outside and her Polish name on the inside. And that hadn't been written for anyone but himself.

She keeps her smile. "You did not invent what I remember. I know who I am."

"I am tired of this game. Let us have no more of it. You are Inge Louisa von Emmerich. My little girl. There is no Anna Ptaszynska."

She is Anna. And Inge. And Eva. One person, united. Wanting the same thing.

Justice.

She turns her back on the Doctor and unsnaps her purse.

"I was Anna," she says. "And I am not your little girl, and I do not belong to you. And I will not be making that call. Because you cannot make me do anything that I don't want. . . ."

She opens her purse wide in the candlelight. Lightning sparks the thunder outside, but now it is her fear that is electric, zapping through her veins.

The gun is gone.

"Oh, my dear little bird," the Doctor says, standing up from the chair. "You might be surprised to know what I can make someone do."

CHAPTER FIFTY-ONE

SHE IS SO tired this time. She doesn't want to wear the pink dress.

She doesn't want what comes after.

But there is the brown box, and she knows what is inside. She can hear it scrabbling.

She lifts the lid, and the bird is soft, sweet, heart beating in her hand.

She will call him Papa, she will call the woman Mama. She will say the German. She won't do the things that make her sick.

She holds tight to the bird and goes to Papa's desk. And she picks up the paperweight, blue and orange. Pretty like the bird.

And so heavy in her hand.

CHAPTER FIFTY-TWO

—— *September 1946* ——

THE GUN IS NOT THERE.

Eva breathes. And breathes. Looking down into her purse. The holster is empty.

How can there be no gun?

"I will not call Cruickshanks for you," she says. She keeps her back turned, sliding her hand deep into her purse. Where her fingers find the handle of the bread knife.

She hears the Doctor sigh.

"You do not listen, Inge. Did I not say that I am very good at making others do what is best? Rolf?"

Slowly, Eva brings out the bread knife, up and up, trying not to let her arms move.

"Rolf, where are you?"

The knife is out. And then she's sliding it back down again, into the waistband of her skirt.

"Stop skulking, Rolf! We have been waiting. . . ."

Hinges creak on the other end of the living room, but when Eva turns, one arm bent to hide the knife handle, it isn't Rolf she sees walking through the door. It's Jake. Hair wet and glistening in the dimming candles, hands held up and away from his body. Because Rolf is behind him. Rolf has a handful of his shirt collar.

Rolf has the barrel of her mother's gun pressed into the back of Jake's head.

Eva takes a step and stops. Rolf is panting, sweating, twitching with something like anticipation as he walks Jake around the furniture. He wants to shoot him. He's only just keeping himself from pulling the trigger. And Jake knows it. She can see it when their eyes meet.

He knows how close Rolf is to killing him.

Eva blinks once, slow. And turns to her father. She's Inge's inferno now. A blaze. A seething, silent tornado of fire.

"Do you see how easy control is, my little bird?" The Doctor knocks his pipe into the cold fireplace, gets his hat and coat. "We are all going together, and you will make a telephone call, exactly as I wish. See? Leverage. Simple science."

"He was in her room," Rolf says. "Dressing himself!"

"And you should be glad of it," says the Doctor. "If she didn't like him, she wouldn't be likely to do what we say, now would she? Now where is my file?"

"It was not there. He would not say where!" He jerks Jake by the collar. "And you would not let me . . . I can make him . . ."

"No, no, It doesn't matter. It will be tedious, but I can write it out again." He smiles once at Eva and taps his forehead. "It's all up here. I might make them better, even. Mr. Cruickshanks would like that. The telephone is not working, Rolf, and we can't wait longer. We are leaving, rain or no. Get your purse, please, Inge . . ."

Rolf watches her walk back to the table. "You degrade yourself," he hisses. But he's also looking at her legs. His trigger finger is twitching.

She turns to her father, obedient, ready to go, purse in one hand, the other at her waist. She meets Jake's eyes once more, and he sees. He can't understand what any of them are saying, but he knows what she had in her purse, and he can guess what is now hidden beneath her hand. She turns her body, so Rolf and her father won't.

The Doctor is still smiling at her. So pleased.

He thinks he's won.

He opens the latch to the terrace door, and suddenly the storm is with them, rain slapping down in wind-driven sheets.

They step into the gale, the Doctor first, then Eva, then Rolf walking Jake in front of him. She's soaked in seconds, water running down her forehead and neck until there's no point in trying to wipe it away, her white blouse sticking and clinging. Up and off the terrace and across the lawn, through slick, wet grass, toward the little rise and the driveway beyond it. The lightning is farther away now, the thunder a more distant rumble. Eva scans the tree line, but it's inky black, and when she looks back at the house, the candlelight is so dim the room is almost invisible through the rain.

She stays as close as she can to Jake and Rolf's itchy trigger finger, the knife handle beneath her hand. Jake is going to do something. She sees it in the set of his mouth. The first time Rolf loosens his grip, he's going to make a move.

Eva is not sure he can make that move fast enough.

They climb the rise, Eva sliding in her black heels, and when they get to the place where Mr. Cruickshanks died, she hears her father cursing in German. There's no car in the driveway.

"Where is Schneider?" he says. He looks around, a little waterfall running off the edge of his hat, and sees the edge of the dilapidated summerhouse. He goes to the steps and looks down, then looks back to Rolf. "Wait here," he says. "Out of sight. And if either of them tries to leave, shoot him somewhere that won't kill him right away, yes? I'm going to find Schneider."

Rolf nods, then jerks his chin at Eva to go down the steps first.

It's all shadows inside the summerhouse, old furniture hunching like dark figures in the lightning flash, the glass walls smeared with rain. The trees creak over their heads on two sides, smacking the glass, water dripping down through the roof into puddles. And just beside her foot, a cigarette butt is ground into a crack between the flagstones.

"Sit," Rolf says in English, positioning Jake on the low wall of a disused fountain in the center of the room, so he can hold the gun more comfortably against his head. He jerks Jake's shirt collar, still bunched in his other hand, and Eva hears him mutter, "Move, Jew, so I can shoot you."

Jake has not made a sound since she first saw him, and he doesn't make one now. But she can see his white shirt in the gloom, the tension in the fast rise and fall of his chest. She can see the hazel of his eyes. Watching her.

She's a fire wind.

She smiles a little at Rolf, arm crossed at the waist over her soaked blouse, the knife handle biting into her arm. Then she says, in German, "The Doctor always makes people give him what he wants, doesn't he?"

"Yes," Rolf replies, wary.

"So what do you do? Do you fight it at first, or do you just give it to him?"

Rolf scowls at the back of Jake's head. "It is not like that. Not that way. Otto needs me . . ." He straightens, lifts his chin. "Otto needs me to find his patients. No one else can. He trusts me. It is important to choose . . . the right ones. And I am good. . . . at finding . . ."

Good at finding weakness, Eva thinks, and she has a sudden memory of that woman in the apartment, with the Doctor there. Rolf likes weakness, when it isn't his own, and the Doctor always gives a reward. And so what is Rolf's? Is Rolf allowed to be cruel? Do what he wants?

Or is she the reward?

Rolf had said as much, right before she hit him with that chunk of concrete. But she hadn't understood things then. And wouldn't the Doctor be so intrigued to discover what happens when you cross the lesser blood of a Polish Communist with a good German pedigree? One long, interesting experiment.

She looks Rolf in the eyes. "Was my father difficult to please?"

"Sometimes." He adjusts his grip on the gun and Jake's collar. "But your father is an important man. He . . ."

Rolf pauses. Swallows. Eva is coming across the summerhouse, walking slowly toward the fountain.

"He knows things . . . that other people do not. You should . . . respect him . . ."

Eva stops just before the tips of Rolf's boots without looking at Jake. Wind and rain smack the glass, but she has Rolf's full attention.

"You're cold," she says. "Would you like a cigarette?"

"Yes, all right," he whispers.

"He keeps them in here." And she runs her hand slowly down to Jake's shirt pocket. Rolf watches, fascinated, as she pulls out the pack of cigarettes, touching all the ends to find a dry one. She takes one out and puts it between Rolf's lips, then tosses the pack in Jake's lap, reaching in his pocket again for the matches. Slowly. She can feel Jake's heart hammering. She can also feel his hand, reaching very carefully beneath the hem of her skirt, looking for the blade of the knife.

She strikes the match, keeping Rolf's eyes upward. The scar on his cheek jumps out jagged and pale. He looks at everything of her he can see in the match light. Then she lights the cigarette, waves out the match, and throws it in the fountain.

The cigarette glows orange in the rainy dark. But maybe not bright enough.

"What has my father told you about me?" Eva asks. She takes the cigarette from Rolf's mouth, so he can exhale.

"What should he have told me?" Rolf asks, and Eva feels her brows go up. That had been remarkably shrewd. For Rolf.

Jake's hand is halfway up now, feeling for the knife.

"Did he tell you I used to run off with the chauffeur?" Eva takes a drag on the cigarette, and Rolf's mouth opens. Just a little. She can see the gap in his teeth. He shakes his head.

"That I used to steal his files and read them?"

"No. He did not say that." She holds the cigarette while Rolf inhales, making an ember of the tip.

"He probably told you I would be a good wife, didn't he? Do you think he told you the truth?"

Rolf looks her over again, appraising, breathing out a cloud.

"Do you think I will be an obedient wife?"

"I suppose he might have lied about that."

And Jake has the knife blade. Working it down.

"Inge!"

The Doctor's voice comes sharp from the steps. Jake freezes, knife in hand.

"Come away from him. I went all the way down the road and I can't find Schneider . . ."

Eva leans close, keeping Rolf's eyes fixed on her face.

"Did he tell you that I am his daughter?" she whispers. "Because if he did, he lied about that, too."

Rolf's half-closed eyes open up. "What?"

The Doctor is shaking the water off his hat. "Can't think why Schneider would have gone . . ."

"You are not his blood?" Rolf whispers.

"No." Eva smokes the cigarette.

"How do you know?"

"Because I can remember my parents, and he was not one of them."

". . . we will wait for that boy to come back," the Doctor is saying, "and take their car instead. Inge! I said to come away. Rolf, what is she saying to you . . ."

Rolf doesn't break his gaze with Eva. "But he said . . ."

Eva smiles. "Do I really look German to you?"

And Rolf looks at her. Really looks. Her hair, her eyes. And the expression on his face is not shock or even disgust. It is hatred. Pure betrayal.

"What kind?" he says. He isn't wet from rain. He's sweating. The gun has moved a little to one side. "What kind of people were your parents?"

Eva shrugs. "Polish. Communists . . ."

Rolf makes a noise in his throat.

"Rolf!" says the Doctor. "What are you . . ."

"She's not German," Rolf says. And then he screams. "She's not even German!"

And Jake rolls suddenly to one side, stabbing backward with the knife. The gun explodes, blinding, deafening. Eva throws herself at Rolf, knocking him off-balance. Another shot goes off and they fall to the cracked, wet floor. But Jake is up and turned around, coming with the knife. Eva scrambles, planting her knee on Rolf's wrist. The gun comes loose, and then Jake has the knife blade across Rolf's throat.

Rolf exhales and goes still.

And then there is no sound but the rain running down the windows, dripping through the roof, and the ringing echo in Eva's ears.

She sits up, her knee still on Rolf's arm. Jake must have gotten Rolf somewhere with the knife because there are streaks on the blade, dark against Rolf's throat. They exchange a quick look. Jake's jaw is set, his breath coming hard. And he has a narrow gash along his cheekbone. Where a bullet passed.

So close.

Then Jake reaches out into the darkness with his free hand and brings back the gun. He lays it on her palm.

And she's an explosion. A blast of heat and light. Eva jumps to her feet and turns.

The Doctor is sitting on the floor beside the fountain. Sweating, gasping, blood running through his fingers where he's holding his thigh. He has a bullet in his leg.

Good, Eva thinks. That's for Mina.

And it is time. For justice. She raises the gun.

"Inge," the Doctor says.

She walks forward. And now Rolf is laughing behind her, spread-eagled on the floor, muttering something about German babies. The Doctor scoots backward through the puddles.

"Inge, what are you doing . . ."

"This is for Mina," she says, "and Rosa, Alfred, Piotr, David, Matya, Oskar . . ."

She walks forward, watching her father's face change from confusion to fear. He's clutching his leg.

Rolf giggles. "Gods among men . . ."

She says the names. All of them. And then she is standing at the Doctor's feet. There's one bullet left in her mother's gun. "This," Eva says, "is your justice."

"Justice?" The Doctor pulls himself up to the edge of the fountain, leaving a bloody place behind on the floor. "What do you mean by justice? Do you mean, what is fair? You were not the valuable one, but I saved you. You would have been killed, but I made you my daughter. Made you better. And now you will kill me? Is that fair? Is that your justice?"

"Shoot him!" Rolf screams.

"Eva," Jake says. "You can still choose . . ."

The Doctor shakes his head. "Inge, you are not going to shoot your papa."

"Why not?" she asks.

He smiles through gritted teeth. "Because I love you."

"But emotion must never enter into judgment, Papa. Isn't that what you taught me? You wouldn't want me to be weak, would you?"

"You were never like them," the Doctor says, voice soft. "You became something more, just like he . . ."—he waves a dripping hand toward Rolf—"became something less . . ."

"Shoot him," Rolf begs.

Jake keeps his voice low. "Eva. You can choose."

"Would I have done so much, made you my little girl, if I did not love you, Inge? If I did not want so much to be your papa? And don't you think, my little bird, that it is fair to give your love to me in return?"

The smile on her papa's face is gentle. Knowing. And in the flash of a second, she remembers.

She knows what she did with the bird.

And the Doctor, she thinks, does not know love. He's never seen it. But she has. And it isn't fair. And it doesn't make her weak. It makes her strong.

She breathes. And breathes.

She is stronger than him. She has always been stronger than him.

"Eva," Jake says.

She looks back over her shoulder and smiles.

And pulls the trigger.

CHAPTER FIFTY-THREE

SHE HOLDS THE bird with one hand, Papa's paperweight with the other. The bird wants to ruffle its pretty feathers. Spread its wings. But it is trapped.

The bird is afraid.

She is so tired.

"Are you ready to obey, my Inge?"

"Yes, Papa."

The paperweight is pretty, too. Heavy. It will smash things. She looks her Papa in the eyes.

And throws the paperweight through the window.

The glass shatters, a harsh, wrong sound.

And she runs to the broken window and thrusts the bird through. The glass is sharp and stinging. It makes her bleed. But the sky is close. She can feel the wind.

And she opens her hand.

CHAPTER FIFTY-FOUR

September 1946

THE WALL OF glass behind the Doctor explodes, shattering into a million shards and tinkling pieces, a cascade of breaking noise over the softening storm. Eva waits for the shivering sound to settle, for a puff of wind to find its way through the summerhouse. For the stillness to come back.

And then the Doctor laughs. He cackles and giggles and wipes his forehead with the back of a bloody hand.

"I knew you wouldn't do it," he says. He clutches his leg. But he's still laughing. "I knew you couldn't. You were always weak. Interesting, but weak . . ."

Eva lets the gun go clattering across the floor. "It would have taken less strength to shoot you," she says. "But I am not your judge."

"Weak," the Doctor says. And he laughs.

She walks around the fountain. It's easier to see the lawn now that the streaming water has nothing to run down. The rain still falls, but in a soft way, a moon up somewhere behind the thinning clouds. And she thinks she can see them coming, shadows making their way across the pale wet grass. One from the trees on the opposite side of the house, two from the direction of the road.

Eva takes a step through the empty wall into the lawn, where they can see her. She looks back at the Doctor. "Your consequences are here."

He stops laughing.

And then Jake is beside her, knife still in his hand, watching the dark figures come. The graze from the bullet has bled down his cheek. But he isn't dead. And the relief is like air. New air when the cupboard door is opened.

"Is it the Russians?" he asks.

Eva nods.

"What?" says the Doctor. "The Communists? They are not here . . ."

She can hear him scrabbling to get upright, hissing when the weight hits his leg.

"Inge . . . no. You cannot . . ."

She keeps her eyes on the coming men and asks, "Where is Rolf?"

"He's not going anywhere," Jake replies. "He's bleeding pretty bad from his thigh. I tied his belt around it . . ."

"Inge . . . Eva. Listen to me!" the Doctor says. "You do not understand. You have to tell them . . ."

She looks back. The Doctor is wobbling, his coat and cardigan dark with stains. He seems to have just understood the disappearance of Dr. Schneider.

"Where are my papers?" His voice rises. "Where is Anna's file?"

"I burned your file."

"Then you have to tell them. Tell them what I can do!"

She shakes her head.

"They're here," Jake whispers.

"You do not understand! I must have something to offer!"

And then the man with shiny shoes is stepping into the summer-house, feet crunching across the floor.

The Doctor moves, quicker than she would have thought on his bad leg, hands scrabbling in the glass. He finds the gun. And he fires. Nothing happens. He tries again. And again.

"Two for Erich," Eva tells him. "Remember?"

He drops the gun. The Russian nods once at Eva and puts the Doctor on his face on the floor.

And when Eva turns, there is another man stepping through the broken wall. A man with the same shine on his shoes. The two don't look exactly alike, but when seen apart, and dressed the same, it would be difficult to tell the difference.

She should have known there was more than one man with shiny shoes.

The third figure arrives at the summerhouse, a tall man, blond and ghost-pale in a long, gray coat. He does not step through the glass. He is neat. And mostly dry. Collar turned up to the dying wind. Jake stands just behind Eva, hand on her back, slipping the bread knife deep into his pants pocket.

The blond man observes the Doctor, who is having his hands tied behind his back, trying to explain what he can do for the Soviet Union. But the men with shiny shoes don't speak much German. The blond man, however, has good English.

"That is him, I suppose," he says. "Dr. Otto von Emmerich?"

"Yes," Eva says. "He needs a doctor, and so does . . ."

But there is an odd sound coming from the darkness where Rolf is. A strangling noise. Eva takes a step, and then the shadow of Rolf's body bucks up suddenly from the floor.

"Come this way, please," says the blond man, extending an arm.

Eva hesitates, but Jake presses his hand against her back, urging her away. The blond man gives a short order in Russian to the other two, and then he joins them.

"Cyanide is an ugly way to die," he says. "And it is not so quick. But the Nazis, it is always what they want. Come over here, please. To wait."

He steps gingerly across the wet lawn, and when Eva looks back, she can see the Doctor's coat and pockets being searched, making sure he doesn't have a cyanide pill, too. Then Rolf makes the horrible choking sound and Jake pushes her on a little faster, to where the blond man has stopped beneath a large branch at the tree line. The pine needles are fresh with rain, Sky Island a brooding shape without even the glow of a candle showing. And when she looks up, the blond Russian is studying her.

"You are Anna Ptasyznska?" he asks.

"No," says Jake, firm, but not unfriendly. "Her name is Eva Gerst."

The man gives Jake a long look in the half-light. The wound on his face, a glance at his pocket. He knows that knife is there. They can hear the trees drip.

Then the man says, "Von Emmerich's stories are not of interest to me. The Sachsenhausen prison has held Communists for many years. Thousands of Soviet prisoners of war have died there. We want everyone who was in charge. And many of von Emmerich's patients were Soviet . . ."

"I want him to go to trial," Eva says.

He examines her again. His eyes are the clearest blue. Bright even in the darkness. And they are cold. A pond in winter. For a Russian, he looks exactly the way a Nazi would wish to. "There will be a trial," he says.

"Not Nuremberg. A trial where the Americans cannot be involved."

"It will be Soviet."

"I want proof."

After a moment, he lifts a shoulder. "I will arrange your proof."

"And who are you, exactly?" Jake asks.

The cold eyes brush past him again. Over Eva. And then away. The shoulder lifts again. "It does not matter so much," he says. "We will clean up and we will go. When the Americans come, say nothing. You have not seen us. You have not seen the Doctor. In two days, von Emmerich will be out of the country."

Eva wants to ask where they are taking him. What her proof will look like. But the blond man has closed the door to questions without saying a word. His gaze is narrowed at the house. Or maybe at nothing at all. Then he reaches into his coat and hands Eva an envelope.

"Wait here," he says. "Until we are gone. You will not see me again."

And he just walks away, something rhythmic in his stride. Eva watches him dissolve into the dark, then looks at the envelope in her hand.

And discovers that she is shaking.

Then Jake has her, pulling her face into the dent in his chest. He's crushing her. She tries to crush him back.

"I thought you'd shot him," he says.

"I thought I was going to," she breathes. "But then I remembered. I remembered what I did with the bird."

"What did you remember?"

"That I let it go."

Jake sighs, his chin in her hair. "I thought you might have."

She can feel his blood beating strong against her cheek.

"Tell me what happened," he whispers.

Eva tells him. All of it. About Valentina, her father in the office and the things he said. The parts of her father's file that had been real—her training to forget, her punishments, the bird—and the parts that had been lies. For show. Like Anna the killer. She tells him everything he couldn't understand in the summerhouse.

There's a light in there now. She can just see it. A flashlight, maybe, dimmed with a cloth. Whatever they're doing, it's silent. She can't hear Rolf dying. Maybe he's dead. She can't hear her father. She closes her eyes. Jake is holding tight to her hair.

"I don't know if I did the right thing."

"You did the best thing you could," Jake says, "so that makes it the right thing."

She's not sure that's good enough. Jake rests his cheek on the top of her head.

"For what it's worth," he whispers, "I think you did the right thing."

But the guilt is there, anyway.

They both look up at the sound of a motor. Soft, far away, and fading down the hill. The summerhouse is dark. Still. They walk back across the lawn and peer into its shadows.

And it's like nothing happened. There are no Soviets. No Rolf. No Doctor. The floor is wet. She thinks the blood is gone. Even the cigarette butts are gone. There's just a mess of broken glass, and Eva's black purse, sitting on the edge of the fountain. She opens it and finds the gun inside. And then she discovers the envelope in her hand. She doesn't think there's writing on it, but it's too dark to see.

"What did he give you?" Jake asks.

"I'm not sure."

"I'd light a match, but you took all mine." He gives her a sideways glance. "I didn't know you smoked."

"I don't."

"The hell you don't, Bluebird." He almost laughs. But he doesn't.

She puts the envelope in her purse and snaps it shut, and Jake is still, hands in pockets, looking down at the clean stones. Where Rolf had been.

"I guess that's what it would have been like," he says. "In the war. Really knowing that the other guy wants you dead. Thinking you're about to die. And you don't want it to be you. You want it to be him. You'd do anything to make sure it's him. And then, when he does die, feeling sorry about it, all the same." He blows out a breath. "I guess I wouldn't have done so well."

"Why?" Eva says. "Because you shouldn't want to save your own life? Because you shouldn't be afraid when there is a gun against your head? Then you would just be . . . you would be *unvernünftig*."

That makes him look up. She comes around the fountain to stand beside him.

"It means stupid," she says. "That would make you stupid."

He lets out another deep breath. But his shoulders have lost some of their tension. And she's made him smile. And wince.

"Does your face hurt?" she asks.

"Like fire."

He takes her hand, looking at her red fingernails in the darkness, his brows together. And Eva knows guilt when she sees it. The guilt for being alive when someone else is dead. She sees it in the mirror every time she thinks of her brothers.

"Shut up," she says, even though he hasn't said anything, and she kisses him. Once. Gentle on his mouth, like she had in the abandoned office. She doesn't want to hurt his cheek. "I won't do it again," she whispers. But she doesn't step away.

"Shut up," he says, and then he's kissing her, hard, only this time, he's the one that doesn't stop. She doesn't want him to. He kisses her mouth and her chin and her cheeks and her neck and up to her mouth again, and then the wall of the summerhouse is behind her with the branches tapping, and he doesn't seem worried about hurting his face. He seems glad to be alive.

She wants to make sure he is glad to be alive.

And then she turns from Jake's lips, putting a finger on them, listening.

There's a motor coming, but it's not soft. It's the Studebaker, protesting its way up the hill. She can feel Jake's breath, coming fast on her fingertip. He smiles from the corner of his mouth, and shakes his head no.

"Valentina," she whispers.

He shakes his head no again. She kisses him once more, quick, feeling his sigh when he lets her go. She grabs her purse, leaving Jake with his hands on his head as she hurries up the summerhouse steps, and flags down the car as the lights pull around the drive. The brakes squeal to a stop, and then Jake is just behind her.

Mick is at the wheel, Tony peering out from the back seat. Patricia cranks down the window glass.

"What in the world happened to you two?" she says.

"The storm," Jake says, "it took down a wall of the summerhouse . . ."

"Man, did it take down your face?" Mick asks. "What were you doing in . . ."

"Valentina needs a doctor," Eva says. "The telephones are not working . . ."

"A big tree came down across the road," Tony says, "took the lines down, but the farmer's got it out of the way . . ."

"It's an . . ." Eva waves her hands. She can't think of the word.

"An emergency," Jake says.

"Oh," says Patricia. "Wow. Okay . . ."

"Jake, man, you're the one who needs the doctor. I think you need stitches."

"Look," says Patricia, "we were coming to tell you that Bets has been trying to call. She finally got somebody in the drugstore and . . . Anyway, Eva your friend is waking up. At the hospital."

Eva straightens. Like a mother who has just remembered her child. Jake leans down to the window. "Mick, how much gas is in this thing?"

"Well, you can't go this second," Patricia says. "You two look like you've been rolling up and down the lawn."

They arrange for Mick to go get the doctor in the Studebaker—which he says won't take more than half an hour, depending on how fast the guy can get out of bed—and then hurry back upstairs. Eva cleans up Jake's face while he cleans the knife in the sink, and he gets into a dry shirt borrowed from Tony while she puts on the blue dress, since her only other skirt has the hem ripped out. Her shoes are still wet.

They straighten up her room together, quick, before someone can come up and see there's been a fight inside it. Making the bed, righting the lamp, repacking the suitcases where Rolf had searched for the file, erasing the signs like the men with shiny shoes. Eva looks at the letter with the earrings and tucks it back into Brigit's suitcase.

If the surgery has made Brigit worse, she's going to need them. She may need them now, just to pay for it.

In twenty-five minutes, they are waiting with a lantern in the driveway, as the brakes of the Studebaker once again squeal to a stop. A man with a black bag steps out with his shirt half tucked in, and Eva tells him quickly about Valentina. How she's started moving again, but is seeing things that aren't there. The doctor hurries into the house with Mick and their lantern, Jake gets behind the wheel, and they are headed back down the mountain. Again.

It's after midnight.

Eva tries to pin up her wild hair, and then she stares out the window. At the blown leaves and twigs littering the road, at the passing farms, and the signs on the highway. Wondering if Brigit has opened her eyes already. If Dr. Schneider is never coming home. What you do with a dead body. If she'd done the right thing.

She looks up when Jake exits the highway too soon.

"We need to switch cars," he says. "We're nearly out of gas, and Uncle Paul's has a parking place at the hospital." He takes them to a spot about two blocks away from Auntie Joyce's, where an all-night diner is open, the neon glowing red and yellow. Jake turns the key and takes it out.

"Back in five minutes. I'd take you with me, but I'm going through the yards and I have to jump a fence." He pauses. She can see a bruise starting below the stubble on his jaw. Then he leans over and kisses her before he goes, and says, "Lock the doors."

He doesn't say he won't do it again.

She watches him trot away, over puddles in the pavement, shining with the reflections of the streetlights. She reaches across the seat and pushes down the door lock on his side, then the one beside her.

It's quiet in the car. A heavy sort of quiet. Her purse is on the floorboard at her feet. She picks it up and takes out the envelope. There isn't any writing after all, just the neon of the diner splashing color on the paper. She breaks the seal, and it's not a letter or a document about the Doctor, like she'd thought. It's a photograph. A portrait of a family.

Eva stares. She stares and stares at the photograph until her eyes are dry and her lungs burn. Four people. A man. A woman, and two little girls.

Imagine, the Doctor had said, two little girls. One racially valuable, while the other is not. What an opportunity, to see how the inferiority of the one might be bettered, elevated, when compared to the other, who is so naturally superior . . .

Two little girls in tones of gray. One is small, tiny, big-eyed with dark curls. A child-size version of herself. And the other could not be more different. With eyes a color that can be easily guessed, dimples, and beautiful fair hair that is long and straight. Eva turns over the photograph, and there is one word written on the back, in stark black ink.

Ptaszynski.

She looks up. Around. There's no one on the street. Eva fumbles with the car lock. She gets the door open, grabs her purse and the photograph, and goes running, heels clacking on the sidewalk, splashing through the puddles. Where is Jake? She has to find Jake. And she does. Coming around the corner in the big green convertible.

He leaves rubber on the road. Leaps out of the car in the middle of the street, leaving the door open and swinging.

"Jake!" she yells. One or two heads stick out the diner door.

"What's wrong?" he says, looking for who or what could be chasing her. "What's happening?"

Eva thrusts the photograph into his hands.

"Brigit is my sister!"

CHAPTER FIFTY-FIVE

—— *September 1946* ——

JAKE DROPS EVA off at the double glass doors of the hospital while he parks the car and goes to get his face seen to, telling her to find him in the waiting room afterward. She runs straight to the nurse at the desk, breathless, fidgeting while the roster is checked and a telephone call made, and as soon as she gets the room number, she is running again for the elevator.

Her sister. How could she not have known?

Or maybe she had. Hadn't she already decided that Brigit was her family? Hadn't she always taken care of Annemarie?

What if she's awake now? Confused. Needing her?

Out of the elevators onto the eighth floor, down a long hall, and Eva finds a private room, with glass for the upper half of the wall, so the nurses can see in as they pass. She stops and stands outside it, looking in at Brigit.

She isn't awake. Not yet. Her hair is gone, head wrapped in a white bandage, a green hospital gown around her front, and she's pale. Purple smudges of bruising beneath her eyes. But Eva can see the face in the photograph. She can see her small and dimpled. With violets in her hair. Even now, she's still lovely.

Her sister.

And Brigit must know it, too. She must remember somewhere inside her head. Like the Polish.

Or maybe she won't remember anything. Maybe she'll be worse off than she was before. And that will be Eva's fault, too.

Eva steps quietly into the blank room—white walls, white bed frame, white floor—and Bets is in a chair just below the window glass, head back, mouth a little open, in her suit with the AFSC badge. There's a vase of flowers on the table beside Brigit's bed.

A nurse comes and asks Eva's name, checks the watch pinned to her uniform, and says she will be back. Eva brings the other chair gently to the bedside without waking Bets. Brigit's eyes are moving beneath the lids, and every now and then, a finger twitches.

Eva takes Brigit's hand. Holding it against her cheek. Waiting, watching while people walk by. While the bag of fluids attached to Brigit's arm drips and drips. Then she reaches down with her other hand, into her purse, and pulls out the photograph, studying it in the hospital light.

Anna looks like her father. Her real father, and Eva doesn't remember him at all. But her mother, that face is like a song forgotten, a song she can still sing the words to. Her mother is smiling in the picture, chin tilted, a little mischievous, but Eva can see what she looks like when she frowns, too. When she plays the piano. And the hands, folded in her lap, have painted fingernails. Red, Eva thinks. That's what color they are. But even though the expression is different, the features are all Brigit. Same eyes. The same hair. The same upright back. And then Eva pauses. Sits up.

Her mother looks like the blond man. The Soviet agent. And not a little. She looks like him exactly.

She grips the photograph like she could shake it and make it speak. Ptaszynski would be her father's name, or the family name.

Ptaszynska for the women. Polish. But who had her mother been? The Doctor's notes said they were Communists. Had her mother been Russian? With someone, a younger brother, perhaps, now working for Stalin? A brother whose eyes are clear blue and cold. Who tells men which necks to break. Who'd studied her so carefully, and said she would never see him again. Who walks with the same rhythmic stride as Brigit.

A man with a personal vendetta to capture the Doctor, maybe, as well as a Soviet one.

What had her mother been doing, living in Germany, when Hitler came to power? She could have asked him. And now she'll never know.

She lays her head on the bed beside Brigit. What had Brigit's name been, her real name, so long ago? She can't remember. But she can hear a voice. Like music. She can see red fingernails on the piano keys. On a knife, cutting a cake, inviting the wrong man into their house. The man who brought the guns. . . .

"Inge?"

Eva's mind is a haze. Blurry. She doesn't know that name. And then she remembers the hospital. The dripping bag. She raises her head, and Brigit's eyes are open. Clear and lovely, like in the photograph. Eva smiles. Brigit's brows come together.

"Inge . . . my head hurts . . ."

Brigit's voice. Her real voice, not the childlike one. And she'd called her Inge. And said four words that made sense. In German. Eva calls the nurse, and Bets wakes up with a start. The nurse calls Dr. Forrester, and he says this is a very good sign.

And Eva can't stop smiling. She must have made the right decision. The surgery must have been right. Brigit is her sister and they have a future.

Brigit goes back to sleep again.

The second time Brigit opens her eyes Eva is already awake, and Jake is asleep where Bets had been, having charmed one nurse into giving him the room number, and another into letting him stay. He has four stitches beneath a little bandage on his face. He needs a shave. She'd like to find a blanket and tuck him in. And when her gaze wanders back to the bed, Brigit is looking at her with drowsy eyes.

"Have I . . . had an . . . accident?" she asks in German. Her words are slurred, but intelligible. They've given her a little something for pain, but not much.

Eva smiles and takes her hand. "You've hurt your head. You've had an operation."

She doesn't know if Brigit is ready yet, to be asked what she can remember. Eva doesn't know if she is ready to ask her.

"I could hear . . . people. Talking. And I . . . I can't understand . . ."

"They're speaking English," Eva says. "You've been sick for a long time now. We're in America. Can you remember? Coming to America?"

Brigit closes her eyes. Frowns. "I don't . . . understand. America is . . . the enemy . . ."

"No, darling. The war is over now. It's all right . . . if you don't remember . . ."

"It is not all right." Brigit tosses her head, wincing. "Where is . . . Mama? And Heinz and Magda . . ."

Brigit had had other brothers and sisters. When she was Annemarie. And Eva had seen them all lying dead in front of her burning house.

"I'll stay with you," Eva whispers. "I will always take care of you."

"I want . . . Mama," Brigit mumbles, and her eyes fall shut.

Eva holds her hand.

The third time, it is Eva who opens her eyes, to find Brigit staring at the wall. And this time she is much more alert, with thoughts happening inside her head. Eva can see them. She smiles, rubbing the sleep from her eyes.

"Hello," she whispers. She takes Brigit's hand, but Brigit pulls it away.

"Inge," she says. "Who is that?"

Jake is still asleep, head back, arms crossed over his chest. "That's Jacob. Do you remember meeting . . ."

"My hair is gone."

Eva sits up, adjusting the sheets. "You've had an operation, darling. They had to shave it, to fix . . ."

Brigit turns to look at her. She has tears in her eyes. "You left me," she says. "I remember. There were soldiers, and you left me. You drove past me in the car."

Eva whispers, "I came back for you . . ."

"You're always running off and doing whatever you want. You never did care about anybody else." Brigit turns on her side, wincing as she moves her head. "You are so selfish, Inge."

Eva swallows. But if this is what Brigit is focused on, she must not remember what came next. Not yet. Jake is awake now, watching.

"I've been taking care of you," Eva says. "For more than a year now . . ."

"I don't want you to take care of me. I want my mother."

Eva reaches out for her, but Brigit slaps away her hand.

"Where is my mother?" she shouts.

Then the nurse is there, soothing, telling Brigit to shush in words she can't understand. Brigit doesn't shush. She never did, when she was upset.

"Go away! I hate you!" she screams. "I want my mother!"

"Step out for a bit," the nurse says, not unkindly. "She needs to sleep yet, so she doesn't hurt herself, and he needs to go on as well . . ." She nods her head at Jake. "I have to change her sheets and things. And you're not doing her any good making her upset."

"But I . . ."

"Eva," Jake says, hand on her back. "Let's go for a walk."

Brigit is screaming and screaming.

"She doesn't understand English," Eva says. "Do you have a German nurse?"

"Ah. Yes. I'll see what I can do . . ."

Eva picks up her purse, tucking the photograph into the lining, where it won't wrinkle. Brigit is crying when she leaves the room.

Jake takes her hand and leads her along the hall and out of the hospital, across the street and down a few blocks, turning into a little park with trees, where wrought iron fencing and lampposts line a riverbank. A good place for walking dogs and reading newspapers. The sun is out, but it's a cooler sun, the sky brilliant blue. The year is turning.

Jake swings her hand. "She's still sick, you know."

"I know." It hadn't been that long since she'd thought Brigit would never speak again. It had only been hours since she'd thought Jake would die. And neither of those things had happened. She's not ungrateful.

"Anyone been hanging around?" Jake asks.

"I haven't been looking. Was Cruickshanks still there last night?"

"Asleep in his car. For all I know, he thinks you're still at Auntie Joyce's."

She smiles. "How's your face?"

"They told me I'm going to have a very handsome scar. Make me look like a gangster, don't you think?"

"I'm sorry."

"I'm not sure you should be."

Except he shouldn't have a scar because of her. And neither should Brigit.

But if Brigit is going to be better, so much better, her memories are going to be difficult. And not just the soldiers and her missing family. Brigit must have had the same kind of training as Anna. To forget who she'd been. And when the Cruickshanks realize there is no Doctor to find, and with Brigit in more of her right mind, what is to keep them from turning their full attention on Anna Ptaszynska? They always had assumed Anna was Brigit.

She wonders how long until they find out.

There's a stone tower ahead of them, tall and skinny, and then they turn onto a bridge, high, but only a few feet wide, for walking instead of cars. Stone arches stretch below, the open sky above, the city on either side of them. Jake stops near the center, elbows on the iron railing, watching the slow roll of the river. Eva watches it with him.

"I took the gun," Jake says. "From your purse. I forgot to tell you."

She'd forgotten to ask.

Jake shakes his head. "I thought nobody should be up there alone, and then I didn't lock the door. I'm sorry. I never thought . . ."

"You never thought I would need a gun in Sky Island's living room?" she finishes for him. "You probably didn't expect a Nazi in my bedroom, either. A Nazi that wasn't me," she adds.

Jake shrugs. "Call yourself a Nazi if you want, Bluebird, but . . . you're just so damn bad at it."

She opens her mouth and shuts it again.

"Not that I want to hurt your feelings or anything."

He has a grin in the corner of his mouth, and she knows what he's doing. That had been exactly like a cup of tea with lemon and no sugar.

Eva unsnaps her purse and takes out the gun in its holster, cradling it in both her hands. Jake straightens, giving a quick glance around them, but there's no one near. She leans over the railing and lets the gun go.

She'd dropped herself in brown water once. Trying to disappear. But she'd decided to swim back up again. Annemarie had done that for her. She watches the gun fall until the river swallows it whole.

Then she offers Jake her open purse. "Do you want to do this one?"

He takes out the knife, glances over it once, and gives it a good toss, end over end, way out into the current. "I couldn't have watched Peggy cut bread with that thing again, anyway," he says. "And how about this?"

He reaches into his pants pocket and brings out a much-creased and wrinkled photograph. Of her, with the eagle, in the awful pink dress. She recoils.

"Why do you have that?"

"It was supposed to remind me of all the reasons why I should never look at you again, only that didn't work so well. And then Rolf found it in my jacket, and . . . he didn't like it. And when he was on the floor in the summerhouse and you were holding the gun like some kind of avenging German angel, I took it back. I don't even know why." He shakes the photograph. "I mean, I don't even know this girl. I've never seen her."

"I'm not sure I ever knew her."

Eva takes the photograph and rips it into long strips, and then the strips become shreds. Tiny pieces of Inge. She opens her hands like she'd opened them for the bird, and they blow, scatter on the wind like confetti.

Gone.

When they walk back into the hospital, the nurse in the waiting room calls out, stopping them on the way to the elevators. Miss Heidelmann, she says, has requested no visitors.

"Oh," Eva says. "Did Dr. Forrester say she needs to sleep?"

"No . . ." The nurse hesitates.

Eva turns to Jake. "Maybe you should stay down . . ."

"Actually," says the nurse, "it's you she's asking to stay away, sweetie."

Eva steps back. Like the nurse had shoved her. Or hit her in the stomach. She sees Jake's brows come down. "I don't understand . . ."

"Look, I'm sorry, but what she says goes, and until she changes her mind, Miss Heidelmann does not want to see you."

CHAPTER FIFTY-SIX

THE BIGGER SISTER is crying, wiping her eyes, ruining her pretty crown of purple flowers. The bigger sister doesn't like the bangs, either.

She tugs the bigger sister's hand. She's smaller. But she is stronger.

"Under here," she whispers. "Follow me."

She leads the way, crawling across the rug, thick and squishing beneath her hands. Around the chair. Across the square of yellow sunshine. Under the bench. She likes that part.

And then they are underneath the piano, in the very back, where there is a triangle place to stand. Where no one can see behind the leg. The bigger sister only just fits.

"Shhh," she whispers to the bigger sister. "Don't make a noise, and no one can find you. When you hide here, no one can find you . . ."

Seven, eight, nine. The bangs are a bad sound.

She wishes bad sounds did not have to happen.

But no one can see her sister.

She always takes care of her sister.

CHAPTER FIFTY-SEVEN
— *September 1946* —

SHE FOLLOWS JAKE onto the subway, going where he leads. He'd been angry at the hospital. She'd seen it in the set of his jaw, in the way he walked, taking her by the hand again and straight out the double glass doors.

Eva thinks she might be angry. They don't really know how to take care of Brigit at the hospital. They have no idea what kind of memories could be in her head. And what if one of the Cruickshanks comes?

She thinks she might be guilty. Brigit is her fault. Always her fault.

She thinks she might be in pain. But mostly she is numb, floating, like a part of herself has splintered. She knows it hasn't. She's one person now. One person who chose to shoot the glass.

She's just saving her pain for later.

She is so tired.

They're getting off the subway at 96th Street before Eva looks up at Jake and says, "Where are we going?"

"You're coming home with me."

The streets in Jake's neighborhood are a little narrower, a little louder, with shops and awnings downstairs, apartments on top, the fire escapes zigzagging down their fronts. A group of boys run past shouting, kicking a can, and the barber washing his front window yells out, "Hey, Jake, what happened to your face?"

Jake waves. A man selling meat from a truck asks the same thing, and Jake waves at him, too, before swinging Eva around the corner. Here it's all houses, brownstone, three and four stories high, and about halfway down, she follows Jake through a gate to an arched door beneath a set of wide front steps. He puts a key to the lock.

"It's just us," he says over his shoulder. "Mom won't be home until five or six."

Eva realizes she has no idea what time of day it is. It might be afternoon.

Jake lets her in first, pointing her down a long hallway. The walls are light, the wood trim dark and polished, with shelves built in along one side, closed doors on the other, the floor made of old, patterned tiles. The air is cool. It smells like bread. And Jake's clothes.

At the end is a living room with windows across the back, stepping up into a little garden full of plants and vines, making the light filter green. There's a fireplace, a thick rug, magazines on the table, and one chair that obviously belongs to a cat.

"The building was my grandfather's," Jake says, tossing his keys. "Uncle Paul has it now. He lives upstairs. Usually he rents this place, but he's been letting us stay for a couple of years now. Be glad to see the back of us, probably."

"I like it," Eva says, looking out the windows. The room is a nook. A haven. She can't even hear the street. "What does your mother do?"

"Works in a dentist's office. Here . . ." He nips down the hall, coming right back with a bathrobe. "Bathroom is second door down. Do whatever you want and use whatever you find. I'll make us something to eat."

He smiles, disappearing through a door beyond the fireplace. She hears a dish clatter. Water running.

She makes her way down the hall. One of the doors is cracked open now, and behind it is Jake's room. Small, and full, with books stacked on cluttered shelves, a shirt tossed over an unmade bed. And one wall is almost completely covered with newspaper clippings. She turns on the lamp and looks at them. War stories, mostly, but sometimes articles about a place. Or people. Little things. There's a desk with a typewriter, and on a stack of papers beside it, a passport.

Eva picks it up, looking over her shoulder first, like a thief. His middle name is Benjamin. He'll be twenty in January. And the passport is new. Unmarked. He's never been out of the country. She puts it back exactly as she found it. There's a framed picture of a man on the desk, with the round glasses and high collars people wore thirty years ago. His father, probably. Eva hugs the bathrobe to her chest.

She remembers what it feels like, to live in your grandfather's house. Like you're connected. Part of something. Only, for her, it had all been a lie. The portraits on the wall had not been her grandparents. Grandmama's silver had nothing to do with her. Mama had probably wanted Annemarie for a daughter. In fact, Eva is sure she had. But the Doctor brought home the "interesting" one instead.

All she has of family now is a photograph. And a sister. A sister she would have done anything for—everything for—who doesn't want to see her face.

But there is one more thing she could do for her sister. One more thing that would keep Brigit safe.

She could call that number on Cruickshanks's card and tell him that she, not Brigit, is Anna Ptaszynska.

What is your name? She hears her father's voice in her head. *Tell me who you are!*

She knows her name now. Her real name. But she's not sure it's the answer to the question.

Eva takes a bath, a steamy one, in a tub with feet, and when she finds her way to the kitchen, hair still dripping, wearing Jake's enormous robe like an unruly blanket, there's toast and coffee and scrambled eggs.

Jake smiles. "It's what I know."

They sit together at a little yellow table at one end of the kitchen. Jake butters the toast, and Eva pours the coffee, stirring a spoonful of sugar into his. There's a radio playing swing, with occasional advertisements for dish soap and toothpaste, and Jake says swing is fun, like candy, but eventually you want something with salt. Eva tells him music should be more about the color of your mood. They don't talk about what has happened or what might happen next. They eat, a lot, and Eva finishes her coffee with her eyes half-closed.

Jake takes her back to the living room. Sits her on the couch, coming back from the hallway with the pillow she'd seen in his room. "I'd give you my bed," he says, "but Mom will be coming home and I wouldn't do that to you."

She curls up on her side on the pillow. Jake grabs a knitted afghan from a nearby chair and spreads it over her, sitting on the floor beside her head, elbow on the couch cushion. Eva smiles. Closes her eyes. She's like a chick in its shell.

"So now that I've softened you up with hospitality and my cooking skills," Jake says, "maybe it would be a good time to tell you that my mother thinks we eloped."

She opens her eyes again. "Your mother thinks we are married?"

"When I was getting the car keys last night, my rat fink cousin Andy jumped to a conclusion or two about your old boyfriend and the state of my face. I might have teased him a little. And he told

Auntie Joyce, who of course called my mother, who somehow got the impression that we'd managed to get our blood tests and already tied the knot."

He sighs. "I gave half the waiting room the laugh of their lives when I called home from the hospital this morning. So, no. Mom does not think we are married. Anymore. But she also does not know that you are on the couch, looking so pretty in my bathrobe. But you can handle my mother, can't you, Bluebird?"

Eva smiles. She'll handle her later. Jake's brows draw together, thinking, and she rubs out the crease between them with a finger, just touching the bandage on his cheek. He definitely has a bruise underneath the stubble, and smudges of shadow beneath his lovely eyes.

"Come up here with me," she says. For a second, she thinks he's going to say no. Then he kicks off his shoes, and they work out an arrangement that makes them both fit. Eva breathes, head tucked between Jake's arm and chest, her arm around his waist, his chin in her damp hair. She closes her eyes again.

"I think he must have loved me," she says. "At least a little bit."

"Who?"

"My father."

"Why do you say that?" She can hear the murmur in his chest. He's half-asleep.

"He didn't need me to call. He just needed the telephone number on the card. I think he loved me like . . . an interesting pet. Or a favorite shoe."

"Yeah, I'm not sure that's actual love, Eva."

She knows. This is what it feels like, she thinks, to be loved. Surrounded. She feels Jake's finger on her cheek, moving a piece of her wet hair.

"I didn't really forget, you know."

"Forget what?"

"To lock the door. I left it open. For you. I'd hoped it was you, coming in. I hoped you were coming upstairs . . . to me." He pauses. "Were you coming up? To me?"

Eva knows what he's asking. "Yes," she says, without opening her eyes. "I was coming. To you."

"Okay," he says. She feels him breathe. "Okay."

A minute goes by. "Eva," he says. "Why did the Russians take away my cigarettes?"

"Torture," she replies.

His laugh is sleepy. "You're torture."

She smiles again. And the silence is soft. Still.

And when Eva wakes up, the sun is dim through the windows, Jake's arm is heavy across her, and a fat, yellow cat is on the back of the couch, watching them sleep. The next time she wakes up, the cat is gone, and Jake is on the floor, stretched out on his stomach, head on a pillow. He's having a dream. A bad one. Tense and sweating in his sleep. She knows about bad dreams. She reaches down and strokes his back until he goes still. Relaxes. And the next time she wakes up, it's to a woman saying, "Oh, for God's sake."

Eva leaves Jake on the floor and has cake and milk in the kitchen with Mrs. Katz. Which doesn't go that badly, probably because Mrs. Katz is so relieved not to have a daughter-in-law. Not that she doesn't want one, she says. She just doesn't want one until Jake has money, because she doesn't want one moving in with her.

Eva helps do the dishes, since everything is still dirty from when Jake cooked, and she listens. She's good at listening to other people's stories. They talk about Jake's father, who'd had cancer, about how Mrs. Katz would maybe like to be on her own for a little while. About the cutest cottage she'd found in the suburbs—all the plumbing just redone—but she couldn't rent it because the neighborhood didn't allow Jews.

She tells her what a relief it was when the last girl Jake brought home went away. That one, she said, put three spoonfuls of sugar in her coffee, and who would drink something so sweet? Much too flighty and out for fun.

Mrs. Katz would be glad to have that girl back, Eva thinks, if she had any idea who Eva had been.

And how could she blame her.

In the morning, Jake has to leave for a job Eva didn't know he had. In the print room at the newspaper. It's a job Jake doesn't know if he has, because he's missed three days of work.

"You're all right?" he asks.

She's drinking coffee on the sofa with a cat, in his mother's nightgown and his robe, her hair sticking out in all directions. It's a strange place to find herself, after everything that's happened. She nods.

Jake has that little worry line between his brows again.

"Really. I'm fine."

But the line doesn't completely go away. "Let's talk tonight, then." He steals a kiss, then he steals another, and now he's smiling, going quick for the door before his mother comes out of the bathroom and tries to examine his face in the daylight. Eva thinks this hasn't worked, because there are voices in the hallway, but then she hears the front door close and Martha is standing in the living room, her round cheeks pushing up her glasses.

"Oh, hello," Eva says, setting down her cup. The cat leaps down in displeasure.

"Good morning," Martha says. "Could I sit and talk with thee a moment?"

Dr. Forrester called, Martha says, to have a talk with her. Brigit, it seems, has no memories of the time between her injury and the surgery, and the German-speaking nurse, who had been told some of Brigit's background, was sadly unaware of this fact. So the nurse mentioned certain things. Like that Brigit's family was dead.

Eva draws her knees up beneath the bathrobe. The anger, guilt, and pain she'd been saving has come. And with a vengeance. She should have been there. If they'd just asked her one question about how to take care of Brigit instead of pushing her out the door, this would not have happened. She should have been the one to tell her. She should have been taking care of her.

Why is she always failing her sister? The one person she has tried so hard not to fail.

"Also," Martha says gently, "she insists on being called Annemarie. Is this . . . understandable to thee?"

"Yes," Eva says. "They should call her Annemarie."

That Martha does not question this, Eva thinks, makes her a saint.

Martha pats her arm. "Grief," she says, "can be harsh. Dr. Forrester says we do not yet know . . . Annemarie's level of comprehension or her psychological state. He's having Dr. Holtz speak with her. She will be kept at the hospital for another week or so, and then go to a sanitarium for recovery. But for now, they will be honoring her wishes not to have you there."

Eva nods, staring up at the wild little garden through the window glass. She is a snipped thread, dangling.

Fair is fair. Her father's voice cuts through her thoughts. Because you left her.

Only, that last voice had been her own.

"Dear," says Martha. She waits for Eva to look around. "We have a saying. Right is right, even when all are against it, and wrong is wrong, even when all are for it. And that includes outcomes, which is my own little addition. Annemarie's recovery so far is remarkable. She will have a new life. Thee made the right decision, and the outcome is a wonderful thing. And thee could just . . . rest in that, perhaps. For a little while."

The right decision. She'd done the best she could, and Jake had said that made it right. But her best has not been good enough, and she does not think she can rest in it.

Brigit isn't safe. And she has no way of making any of them understand that.

"Martha!" says Mrs. Katz, coming though the living room with curlers in her hair. "Good morning! I'm getting you coffee." And she disappears into the kitchen.

"I cannot stay," Martha says, ineffectually.

Eva wipes her eyes. "I need to ask about the cost. For the operation."

"Yes. Some has been covered, and some has not. And the sanitarium will be expensive. But your question leads me to one of my own. I wonder what you would think, dear, about moving in with Dr. Holtz?"

"What?" says Mrs. Katz, coming in with the coffee.

Mrs. Holtz, Martha explains, is a lovely woman, who has unfortunately been hit by a bus. No! says Jake's mother. Mrs. Holtz has broken her leg badly, and is going to have a long recovery, which she would prefer to do at home. She will need help. Sure she will! says Mrs. Katz, sipping her coffee. And Dr. Holtz would much prefer someone who could live in their spare room and help with all the little things, rather than a nurse.

"And when he heard what excellent care thee took of Brigit—of Annemarie," Martha says, "which was difficult care, in very difficult circumstances, he was more than willing to give the situation a try. And there would be pay, of course."

Mrs. Katz sets down her coffee and looks at Eva. Eva looks at Martha.

Dr. Holtz "heard" about how she'd taken care of Annemarie because Martha had picked up the telephone and told him so. She probably came up with the whole idea. Eva goes to the other end of the sofa and hugs her, a long, hard squeeze around the neck.

"Well, then," Martha says, saving her glasses. "Aren't thee nice?"

Then she says that Bets is coming back with the car in fifteen minutes, and would Eva like them to drop her at Dr. Holtz's on the way? To talk things over?

Eva gets her purse and hurries down the hall while Martha and Mrs. Katz talk, and there, in its little nook in the wall, is the telephone. She could call the number. Tell Cruickshanks the truth. And she would know that Annemarie is safe. Then Mrs. Katz comes into the hall and Eva darts into the bathroom, putting the blue dress back on, hanging up the nightgown and the robe. She's struggling with three bobby pins and hair that looks like it dried in a windstorm, when Mrs. Katz passes by the open door.

"Oh, stop, dear. Stop!"

Eva stands, obedient, staring into the mirror while Mrs. Katz works magic with hairpins. "You weren't supposed to have hair like this, where I come from," Eva says.

"Oh, sweetie," Mrs. Katz replies, "that's because they were all schmucks."

Eva gets in the car with Bets and Martha, looking a little less like a waif.

Bets threads her way through the traffic, telling Eva that she's going up to Sky Island, to help close down the house and to check on Valentina, who is spending a few weeks somewhere having "a little rest." And should she pack up Eva's things and bring them back with her?

Eva has been watching the streets. For a pinstripe suit. A pair of shiny shoes. A face behind a steering wheel in a plain black car. But now, she's just watching Bets.

Because Bets is radiant. All her medium-ness sparkling. Her brown eyes. Her smile. She's practically bouncing in her seat at the red lights. And then, out of nowhere, Bets shouts, "I'm getting married!"

Martha chuckles.

Bets says her new husband-to-be is a history teacher, and they're buying a farm in Georgia. Eva doesn't know where Georgia is, but it's impossible not to be happy for Bets. Her joy is infectious. They drop her off at Dr. Holtz's apartment building with smiles and waves, and Eva waves back before she climbs the steps. Slowly.

She's not sure what she has to offer. Even some of her hairpins are borrowed. She could bring bad people to this house. She could disappear. She's a mess, inside and out. Dr. Holtz might change his mind. He would be right to change his mind. She stands a long time before she raises a hand and knocks.

"Come in," says Dr. Holtz, opening the door. "*Komm bitte rein.* Please." He's wearing soft, faded corduroys and house slippers.

A little dog comes yapping at her ankles. White with brown spots, and for a moment, Eva can hear another dog barking like this, a long, long time ago. Saying there's a stranger in the house. She lets it sniff her hand, and it runs away.

Dr. Holtz's apartment is comfortable but small, with plants on all the windowsills. And it's obvious his wife has not been home. The sink is full and so are the ashtrays. There are pots of tomato plants on the fire escape.

They sit on the sofa and have a long talk, about what Mrs. Holtz will need. About what Dr. Holtz can pay. Dr. Holtz is nervous. He seems to think he's offering her a job no right-thinking young girl would ever take. Eva thinks he is offering her riches. He shows her a tiny room, with a bed made up for a guest, where they have also been storing whatever they don't want to use at the moment. But there's a window with a deep sill and tree branches outside. And a door. A door that doesn't particularly need a lock.

"I love it," she tells him.

Dr. Holtz smiles, and she feels guilty. Like she's tricked him.

But by 3 p.m., she's moved in with Dr. Holtz.

And by 9 a.m. the next morning, there's a man with shiny shoes, smoking on the front stoop of Dr. Holtz's apartment building. He doesn't stay long. Just long enough to be seen. And that afternoon, when Dr. Holtz comes back from a funeral service for a colleague, a Dr. Schneider, who has been killed in a car accident, he brings in the mail and hands Eva a letter.

It has her name on it, in a plain, indistinct hand. No return address. She smiles, cheery, tells Dr. Holtz thank you, and shuts the door to her room before she slits open the envelope.

There's a photograph inside. An image of the Doctor. Dark, with the light on only one side of his face, and his expression is haunted. Animal-like. Like the faces she'd seen hanging in his bedroom. The metal rivets of a ship dot the wall behind his head.

Her proof.

And there is the sadness. And the guilt. A poisonous tentacle.

She finds another photograph behind the first, and this is a sight she's seen before. A young woman, a stranger, lying dead and open-eyed in a pile of rubble. This is Germany, she thinks. Maybe even Berlin, during the war. And this time, on the back is written a name.

Anna Ptaszynska.

So Dr. von Emmerich is crossing the ocean. And Anna Ptaszynska is dead.

Or that's what the Soviets want the Americans to believe.

Or maybe that's what the Soviets want her to believe that the Americans believe.

She wishes she could know if she's done the right thing.

CHAPTER FIFTY-EIGHT

—— *September 1946* ——

FOR TWO DAYS, Dr. Holtz goes to see patients while Eva tidies up the apartment, walks the dog, and organizes his notes and files, because she reads German. Then he comes back with groceries and cooks dinner, as they've agreed upon, because he usually does it anyway, and because he'd rather not suffer through her learning. Dr. Holtz is very patient when he teaches her how to slice a tomato. She tells him it's a shame he doesn't need a quonset hut, because she'd really been much better at that. They fall into a comfortable rhythm.

And then Mrs. Holtz comes home from the hospital, carried up the stairs in her wheelchair by the two brothers in the apartment below, fresh home from the war.

Mrs. Holtz is Hungarian. She wears a soft, gray bun with two curls beside each cheek. She's kind and in pain, and Eva is busy. Running, fetching, feeding, and distracting. Listening. All the things she'd been good at before. Mrs. Holtz lost two sisters and a father to the Nazis. Eva brings her pills and bathes her as gently as she can and feels like a fraud while she's doing it.

Jake is also working, picking up every hour they'll give him in the print room. But the telephone cord, Eva has discovered, stretches all the way onto the fire escape, where she can put on a coat and sit among the tomato plants while Mrs. Holtz is asleep. She explains, at his insistence, that yes, everyone had smoked in Düppel Center, but she really had decided it was too expensive. You could buy a meal, sometimes, with a cigarette. He tells her about Martha inviting the family of the teenage boy who'd smashed Augusta's art over to Powell House for a nice dinner.

And he tells her that he's been having dreams. Waking him up in a sweat. The sound of the gun firing behind his head, only he's paralyzed this time and can't move. Eva tells him about the dreams she'd had for months. That the planes are coming, and no matter how hard she pushes the gas, the car just goes slower. A soldier's hand reaching suddenly beneath the desk to grab her hair. That she is in a pile of bodies at Sachsenhausen, on the bottom of the stack.

She hasn't told him that her dreams have changed. That she's chasing Annemarie down a long white hall where she cannot hide her. That she's pointing the gun in the summerhouse and this time it fires, though she never pulled the trigger. That her father's voice comes to her. *Weak. Less. Do you love your Papa, little bird? Say your name!*

She knows Jake has had something more on his mind than dreams.

They'd been twice out to a jazz club, twice out dancing. One memorable night when a chuckling policeman threw them out of Central Park, and Eva lost a shoe and Jake had to go back for it. She'd come creeping in so late, it was early, softly, so she wouldn't wake anyone, only to find Dr. Holtz on the sofa, smoking a cigarette, because he couldn't sleep. He'd only said he wished he was young. That if he tried to dance the way they danced now, he'd be in a cast with Mrs. Holtz.

But even when they're out, even when Jake smiles, his smile has been quieter. He'd called her from New Jersey, where he'd gone with the family for the Jewish holidays, and she could hear his thoughts weighing heavy. She thinks maybe she's given him a scar. On the inside as well as the outside. Like she'd given Annemarie. She has a scar, too. More like a hole, torn right through the pieces of herself. A gap where her sister belongs.

And then Martha calls and says that Annemarie has asked if Eva would come and see her.

Eva goes to meet Jake at the bus station. She has a new hat, a fortunate discovery at the secondhand shop, in a deep, peacock blue. She holds it on her head, standing on her tiptoes, craning her neck. And then she finds him, leaning against the wall in his suit with the jacket unbuttoned, reading a newspaper. He was supposed to be working, but he'd made sure he could come with her for this. He looks up, smiles when he sees her coming.

"Hi, Bluebird," he says, and kisses her. But he always hesitates first. For a split second. Like maybe he shouldn't be doing that. He has a little pink line about an inch long on the highest part of his cheekbone. They get in line for the bus. "Did you see about Nuremberg?" he asks.

She had. The judges at the Nuremberg trial had given most of what was left of Hitler's government a death sentence. But it's the doctor's trial Eva is waiting for. Next year. To see if Dr. Kurt Blome will be acquitted, like Cruickshanks said.

"I have something to show you," she tells him, waiting until they find two empty seats. Then she takes out a package, untying the ribbon, opening the paper without wrinkling it. It's a framed photograph of the Ptaszynski family.

They'd talked a long time about what should and shouldn't be said to Annemarie. But they'd agreed she should know she has a sister. And so Eva asked Dr. Holtz for an advance—her first month of salary had gone to the AFSC, to start paying off Annemarie's medical bills—to use for a bus ticket to the sanitarium, and to have a negative and a print made. She'd found a nice frame to fit it in a secondhand shop—the same day she'd found the hat—and wrapped it all up in tissue and ribbon. And at the last second, she'd wrapped up the earrings, too, in a little box Mrs. Holtz had given her.

The earrings always had been for Annemarie.

"You look exactly the same," Jake says, smiling at the photograph. "Like trouble."

"Well, that's good, because you enjoy trouble, don't you? But that isn't what I really want to show you. Look what I found in my purse after I left the photography shop this morning."

She hands him a little white card. It's just like before, with Mr. Cruickshanks's name printed on it, a bluebird drawn in blue ink on the other side. But the phone number has been blacked out. And underneath is written one word: *Disconnected.*

"Did you see him?" Jake asks.

She shakes her head, drops the card in her purse, and starts tying the paper and ribbon back around the picture. "But I think it means they believe it," she says quietly. "What the Soviets showed them."

Which means they will leave Annemarie alone. She wonders if a man with shiny shoes checks on Annemarie, too. They must know who she is. She looks so much like the blond Russian.

Jake's brows are together again, thinking. He puts an arm around her, and doesn't say much else. Sometimes he picks up her fingers and looks at them. Her nails are red. She'd found the bottle of polish in her suitcase from Sky Island. From Greta. Sometimes, he puts one of her fingers to his lips, watching the city go by.

Jake has something on his mind.

The sanitarium is a nice place, a low, modern building with garden walks and a rolling, clipped lawn. They walk together to the front desk, and an attendant shows them past a sunroom where patients are in reclining chairs, with nurses and little tables for medicine bottles beside them, and then down a wide hall. To Annemarie's room.

Eva stands in front of the door. She's been longing for this moment. And dreading it. Jake tilts his head, telling her to go on. She knocks twice and opens the door.

And there is Annemarie. Sitting in the sun, straight-backed in a white wicker chair, a white satin robe—the emblem of the sanitarium to one side—flowing down to her slippered feet. Someone has given her a scarf to wrap around her head, a blue that matches her eyes, the ends trailing over her shoulders, blowing in the breeze from an open window. She looks like a painting. A Madonna.

She smiles until her dimples show, holding out both her hands. "Inge!" she cries.

Eva goes to her, takes her hands, surprised, but pleased. "I'm so glad . . ." She switches to German. "I'm so glad to see you looking so well."

Annemarie turns her gaze on Jake hanging back near the door with his hands in his pockets. "Hello," she says in English. "How are you, Jacob?"

Jake smiles. "Hello, Annemarie." He throws a little look at Eva.

Annemarie says in German, "Tell him I'm working on my English." She dimples again while Eva tells him.

"Do you remember Jacob?" Eva asks her, pulling a chair close to sit next to her.

"He was at the hospital," Annemarie says promptly. "When I woke up."

And she'd remembered his name.

"Jake gave you the harmonica. It was in the suitcase I sent you. You loved it when he . . ."

"Oh, is that what that was?" She waves an ivory hand. "I got rid of all those things. So shabby."

Eva bites the inside of her lip. The contents of that suitcase probably had been shabby. But they had also been hard won. Annemarie gives Jake another studying glance. He's seated a little closer to the door so they can talk, elbows on his knees, looking at his hands. There is definitely something on his mind.

"Are they taking good care of you here?" Eva asks her.

"Oh, it's not home, of course. But tell me what you have been doing since you came to America, Inge."

It's so startling, to hear Annemarie speaking like . . . Annemarie, that it takes her a moment to answer. "It's Eva now," she says. "I don't use that name anymore."

"That will be hard to get used to. It may take me a long time."

Eva takes Annemarie's hand again. "It's difficult to answer your question about what I've been doing, because you were with me for so much of it, and I don't know what you remember. The doctor said . . ."

"Hello!" says a voice at the door. A voice with the sun in it. "And there's my girl . . ."

Eva turns, and Happy Angel is there, waving. "Mrs. Angel," she says. She goes to the door to take her hands. "I've missed you!"

"Well, I missed you, too," Mrs. Angel says. She gives Eva and Jake a quick peck on the cheek. "I heard there was a visiting day, and talked Martha into bringing me. I just had to come see my girl . . ."

Martha is beaming, her cheeks as round as her glasses. Then Eva turns to Annemarie and her smile falters.

Annemarie has drawn back a little in her chair, staring at Mrs. Angel. Then she looks away. Like something just crawled across the carpet, something it would be embarrassing to call attention to. Eva steps quickly between them.

"Let's find everyone a chair," she says.

There's a little scramble for chairs, and Eva exchanges a quick glance with Jake. Mrs. Angel hadn't seen Annemarie's reaction, but he had.

"Annemarie is just beginning to learn English," she says quickly to Martha and Mrs. Angel. "So I'll interpret for you. Also, I don't think she remembers anything from Powell House, so . . ."

She turns quickly to Annemarie and says in German. "These are the people who helped you so much when you were sick . . ."

And when she turns back again, Mrs. Angel has taken Eva's seat. Next to Annemarie. Annemarie puts a smile on her face. A stiff one. Frozen.

"Tell her I've brought her a surprise," says Mrs. Angel, digging in her purse. And she brings out the kitten, mewing and blinking, like he's just woken up. Like he rides around in Mrs. Angel's purse all the time.

Annemarie recoils again, and Eva says quickly, "Isn't it sweet?" She jumps forward and takes the kitten, so it won't be obvious that Annemarie isn't going to.

Eva smiles, cuddling the squirming kitten, and says in quick German. "She took care of you and brought you this kitten when you were sick and you loved it and you loved her. Stop being rude."

Annemarie nods. But her lips are pressed together. And she has slid all the way to the other side of her chair.

"Hasn't he grown?" Eva says, scratching behind the kitten's ears.

"Please tell Annemarie how glad we are that she's doing so well . . ." Martha says.

But it's too late. Mrs. Angel has seen the way Annemarie is leaning. The way she averts her eyes. She reaches out a hand, to touch Annemarie's arm, and Annemarie moves it away, her eyes back on the carpet. Mrs. Angel's face is like a balloon deflating.

There's a tense little silence.

And Eva erupts inside. Boiling. Furious. Her cheeks are hot.

Jake gets up. "Mrs. Angel, could I buy you lunch?"

Martha stands. "What a nice idea, Jacob. Would you like to do that?" she asks Mrs. Angel.

"Well, yes," she replies. "I don't mind if I do." Mrs. Angel reaches all the way over to Annemarie's lap and gives her arm a good pat. A little hard. Annemarie turns her head the other way. Then Mrs. Angel stands, slowly, straightening her yellow dress. She takes Jake's arm.

"Thank you, Mr. Katz."

They walk to the door, Martha a little behind them. Eva follows them out into the hall. She still has the kitten.

"Wait," she says.

But she doesn't know what to say. That the girl in that room had been fed lies until she was full of them? That her dearest goal in life before she'd been hit on the head was to have a baby for Hitler? That to her, her behavior was reasonable. Normal?

There's actually nothing to say. So Eva says, "I'm sorry."

Mrs. Angel shakes her head. "I know how the world works, sweetie. Just didn't see that one coming, that's all." Then she says, "Bless her heart, I think I liked her better when she was sick."

"So did I." Eva holds out the kitten and Mrs. Angel takes it, along with a good look at Eva's face.

"Well, I wouldn't want to be that girl right now. You look like the wrath of God."

Martha smiles, sadly, and Eva sees Jake lift a brow, telling her to go do what she has to. The three of them walk away down the nice, new carpeted hall, and Eva steps back inside Annemarie's room. She shuts the door, and leans on it.

Annemarie is up from her chair, pouring water from a pitcher into a glass. She looks strong, steady on her feet. And the window behind her is shut now.

Annemarie likes the windows shut. That might explain some things.

Annemarie glances over her shoulder. "Oh, no," she says. "Inge has her mad face on." She comes back to her little throne, adjusting her white robe. "Was that your newest boyfriend?" she asks. "Katz, is it? Is he Jewish?"

The chair where Mrs. Angel had been sitting is pushed away, up against the wall. Eva crosses the carpet, pulls it back out again and sits in it, crossing her legs. "Does that disgust you?"

"I'm not the one it should disgust, Inge."

Eva stares at her. This, she realizes, is what Inge had been like. Maybe not to the same extreme. Annemarie had always been the good Nazi. But if she'd seen Annemarie like this, heard her say things like this in 1944, Inge wouldn't have blinked.

She would not have blinked.

And that is what disgusts her.

"I don't believe in the ideas we were taught," Eva says. "Not anymore. If you had seen what I saw, what was done because of . . ."

"Oh, is this where you tell me all the things I don't remember? All the terrible hardships you had that I don't even know? But you're not in a hospital, are you? You didn't have all your hair shaved off. You've been off doing whatever you want, like you always did."

Eva takes a breath. Slow. "I think if you count your days, Annemarie, you'll see that there were fifteen months in a war zone where I nearly starved to keep you fed, while you didn't remember how to go to a toilet."

"I remember the soldiers," Annemarie says.

"I got you out . . ."

"Not soon enough. And I remember why I was there. Because you left me. You drove away."

Annemarie takes a sip of her water while Eva sits, mute. She'd just driven away from the dead bodies of her murdered family. Been shot at by airplanes. But maybe that's something like what Annemarie had been running from, too.

Annemarie is so angry. At her. The blame is all on her.

"The problem with you, Inge," Annemarie says, setting down her glass, "is that you don't have any real backbone. No loyalty. You go to a new place and forget everything you've been taught. You degrade yourself . . ."

Rolf had said that.

". . . let yourself become just like . . . them."

And she can hear the words Annemarie isn't saying. Weak. Less.

Eva bends down and takes the tissue-wrapped frame from her purse. "I didn't come here today to fight with you . . ."

"Oh, why did you come, then, Inge? "

"Because you invited me. And to bring you a gift and . . . to tell you about our family."

"Don't talk to me about my family," Annemarie snaps.

Eva was going to do this delicately. Now she's not. "While you were ill, I came across information. Not about your family. About our family."

"What are you talking about?"

Eva hands her the package, and Annemarie pulls away the ribbon and the paper. Her lovely face never even changes expression.

"Our parents were Polish and probably Russian. Communist political prisoners. We were taken away when they were arrested and raised to be German. I came here to tell you that . . . you are my sister."

Annemarie's bottom lip sucks in just a little. And she remembers something. Eva can see it in her face. Then Annemarie looks up and holds out the photograph. "You're mistaken. That's not me."

Eva doesn't take it. Annemarie laughs.

"What an imagination you have. There might be a little resemblance. But that isn't . . ."

There's a knock on the door, and a young doctor steps through, stethoscope around his neck. "Miss Toberentz, I was, oh . . . I'm sorry. I didn't know you still had a visitor."

The doctor is tall, with light eyes and sandy hair, and would look well in a Wagner opera. And he's speaking German. And Annemarie has slipped the framed photograph under one side of her robe.

"Dr. Braun," she says, dimpling. "This is my old friend from Germany, come to see me. Isn't that wonderful?"

"Hello," the doctor says. "I'm so glad you came. She's been longing to have visitors."

When she hadn't been allowing them.

"The attendant said there was a Negro here . . ."

"Oh!" says Annemarie. "A mistake." She casts her blue eyes down, like it's embarrassing. The doctor smiles.

"There was a Jewish doctor involved with her case as well," Dr. Braun says to Eva, smiling. Like he's sharing a secret among friends. "But we got that changed, didn't we?"

Dr. Holtz. He's talking about Dr. Holtz. And when Eva looks around, Annemarie is looking up at Dr. Braun with a sweet little smile, one tear running demurely down her cheek.

"Are you in pain?" Dr. Braun asks, feeling gently around her skull.

She shakes her head, but her tear says something different.

Annemarie, Eva realizes, can cry when she wants to.

Eva thinks back, to their yellow clubroom with the swastika buntings, the charts for determining heredity and race on the walls.

Where she'd felt so much belonging. The belonging she didn't have at home. And now she can see that Annemarie had enjoyed standing up there with Frau Koch. Being their German ideal. The martyr, embarrassed to be so perfect, a tear running down her cheek. All the sympathy, the admiration, all the superiority, and with none of the ill will she might have gotten otherwise. All that with one little tear.

And she isn't even German. It's almost funny.

Annemarie had gone to sleep in that world. And woken up in this one.

Eva watches her simper, flatter Dr. Braun, gazing up into his eyes like an innocent. He leaves the room, looking smitten and stunned.

Annemarie smiles, her blue eyes bright and lovely. She takes the photograph out from beneath her robe and hands it back to Eva. Eva takes it.

"Have it your way," she says. "But you won't forget the truth, now that you've heard it. I don't think you've ever really forgotten. You were speaking Polish when you were ill. We all heard it." Eva walks across the room and places the frame carefully on the table beside Annemarie's bed. "And you may decide you want this. Someday."

She picks up her purse, the little package with the earrings still inside. "You can always find me through Dr. Holtz. When you are curious about the truth. Until then . . ." She puts a hand on the door knob. "Goodbye, Annemarie."

Annemarie says nothing, her smile still in place. Eva is partway down the hall when she hears the crash of glass, shattering against the wall of Annemarie's room.

She'd come there that day hoping Annemarie would no longer hate her.

She'd never considered that she could leave being the one to hate Annemarie.

CHAPTER FIFTY-NINE

SHE CRAWLS OUT fast from under the piano. The triangle place is empty, and there are purple flowers scattered on the rug.

The bigger sister has gone away.

She told her to hide. She told her to stay quiet. And the bigger sister didn't hide and she didn't stay quiet and now she's gone away.

Alone is not allowed. You always take your sister.

Sisters are not supposed to go away.

CHAPTER SIXTY

—— *October 1946* ——

JAKE FINDS HER on a bench in the sanitarium's garden, having seen Martha and Mrs. Angel off on a different bus. He doesn't say anything. Just takes her by the hand.

She knows she's wounded. That the hole inside her—the place where Annemarie had belonged—has been blasted wide open. She'd thought Annemarie needed time to grieve. To heal. She probably does. But the girl in that room is also who Annemarie really is. It's who she always was. Or who she became.

Annemarie hasn't changed. Eva is the one who changed.

"But she still can," Jake reminds her. "People are always changing. You know that, don't you?"

She does. But sometimes, they decide not to.

Eva is too angry to be sad. But the sadness is coming. The anger is Inge, but the sadness will always be Anna to her.

She wishes she could remember what Annemarie's name used to be. She'd like to think of her sister like that. With violets in her hair.

Eva's the snipped thread. Cut off at both ends.

The sun is lowering through the long sleek windows of the bus, lights beginning to shine in the windows of houses, electric stars passing them by in the twilight. Her shoulder jostles with Jake's as they bump and sway on the green and yellow seats. Jake is silent. And on his third cigarette. The air around them is a haze and she's in no mood for dithering.

"Is it time for you to tell me?" she asks him. "What's been bothering you?"

She sees his brows come together. She sees the end of the cigarette glow. He doesn't deny it. He doesn't look at her, either.

"Yes," he says, finally. "It is time. Only it's the worst time. I'd hoped . . . Yeah, things didn't go like I'd hoped."

She waits, but nothing happens. Jake stares into his own cloud. Then he shrugs.

"There's just no good way to say it."

"There's no good way to say what, Jake?"

"The truth of it is, I'm letting you go."

Eva stares and the bus engine hums a different note, changing its gears. "What does that mean?"

"It means that you need to fly free and I'm going to let you do it."

He means he's walking away. From her.

She turns to the window. Of course, he's walking away. He'd always known he shouldn't want to be with her, and she'd known it, too. They'd torn up that picture, but the memory was still there, wasn't it? And the idea is all you need, in the end. Her father had said that. Seeing Annemarie today had probably reminded him.

What an idiot she'd been, to have forgotten that she could never do anything—be anything—that would deserve Jacob Katz.

He still won't look at her.

"Stop it, Eva," he says. Angry. At her. "I knew you were going to pull this crap and that's why I didn't . . . I couldn't . . ." He stubs out the cigarette in the ashtray in the arm of the seat. "I'm leaving. Tomorrow. On a boat."

She stares at him again. "A boat to where?"

"Liverpool. London. France. And then to Oxford."

Eva closes her mouth. She sees that new, unstamped passport sitting in his room. "Tomorrow," she says. "You are leaving the country tomorrow and you just . . . forgot to say anything."

"I didn't say anything. And that's me being a coward and a bastard."

"How long will you be gone?"

"Just over eleven months."

A year. He's leaving for a year. And he's known all along.

The bus jerks to a stop. Eva looks around. They've pulled into a gas station with a little store and a diner and toilets. Their half hour pit stop, the driver says over the loudspeaker. The passengers are already up from their seats, milling in the aisle. She hooks her purse on her arm and stands.

"Excuse me," she says to Jake.

He doesn't move.

"I said, excuse me."

He doesn't move, so she puts her black strap pumps right on her seat and steps over him, nearly skewering his leg to get into the aisle. She hops down, adjusts her hat, ignoring a few snickers.

"Eva," Jake says.

But she has lived in New York long enough to know how to push her way off a bus. She steps out onto a sidewalk and looks around. It's nearly dark. She has no idea where they are. She has no idea where she's going. She walks down the pavement, swinging her purse. Past a feedstore and a beauty parlor, both closed for the night. And here come the footsteps behind her.

"Eva, listen," he says, voice echoing on the empty street. "It's the opportunity of a lifetime. I'm doing a semester at Oxford. I'll be traveling with a war correspondent, seeing what the Nazis did to

London. To Paris. I've been saving every penny for a year! I didn't know any of this . . . I didn't know you were going to happen!"

No, Eva thinks. That must have been inconvenient. Her heels stomp down the concrete.

"Why do you think I waited so long to tell you?" he yells. "Because it was easy? Because I didn't care?"

She picks up the pace. The streetlights come on, making circles of white light where the shadows had been.

"Look, I'm leaving. It's a fact. I should have told you sooner and I didn't. But you can't sit around for a year, waiting on me. . . . I don't want you to . . ."

She turns into a little park at the center of a town square.

"I don't want you to wait for me! And I don't want to take you around town and get kicked out of the park and sit up all night talking to you on the telephone. I don't want to have a fling with you. I'm way more serious than that. Listen! I am more serious than that. And you . . . you don't even know me."

Eva stops and turns around. "Yes, I do."

He puts his hands in his pockets. "Well, maybe that's so," he says. "But the trouble is, you don't know anybody else, either. Including yourself. How could you? You haven't had the chance."

Eva closes her eyes.

"Look, I don't want to be some lucky first strike. I want to be what you choose when you know all the options. And by all the options, I mean, you've got to know what you want your life to be like. And that might mean nobody. It might mean . . . somebody else. But you have to know, right? That's why I'm letting you fly. I have to."

Eva opens her eyes. Jake's gaze is on the pavement. He has one tear rolling down from the corner of his eye.

"I don't believe you," she says. And turns. And walks away.

Jake stays where he is the circle of the streetlight.

"Are you coming back to the bus?"

"No." She listens to the bright clip of her shoes.

"Come to the boat in the morning. At the ferry, where we picked you up. Six o'clock!"

She shakes her head.

"Come to the boat and say goodbye to me," he calls.

She keeps walking. Around the corner, and there's a bench in front of a closed candy shop. She sits on it.

She'd believed Annemarie's tear, once.

One month, she thinks. She gives him one month, and he will meet the girl. That sweet, uncomplicated girl who has never been anything that doesn't deserve him. She will have never splintered into pieces. Will not be shot through with holes. She will be nothing, in fact, like Eva Gerst.

Eva has a hole blown through her insides big enough to drive a truck through.

And when she looks up, it's dark, completely dark, the collar of her blouse is damp, and there really is a truck, idling beside her on the curb.

"Hey, miss?" A young man leans across the seat, shouting through the open window. "You okay, miss?"

The truck is a little battered, with a load of orange gourds in the back, and the young man has a white stripe of skin showing beneath his sleeve, where the sun hasn't found him. He's wearing a baseball cap pushed back on his head, and his eyebrows look friendly. And concerned.

"Only, this place pretty much puts itself to bed at night, and I didn't want . . ."

"The bus left without me," she says.

"Oh, say, that's too bad. Were you heading into the city? 'Cause I've got to take this load to a place in Jersey, you know, for the kids, for Halloween. But . . ."

Eva doesn't know what he's talking about. "Could you take me to a subway?"

"Well, sure, I guess I could run you across the bridge. I . . ."

Eva gets in the truck and slams the door. The young man says his name is Walter. He's dusty. And nice. "Say, where are you from, then?" he asks.

"Berlin." Or close enough.

Walter scratches his head. "That's a long way."

Yes, Walter, she thinks. It is. The truck rides worse than Patricia's jalopy. They cross the bridge and he drops her near a subway station, and she realizes she's close to the hospital. She knows exactly how to get home from here. She scoots across the seat and gives Walter a kiss on the cheek. Which makes him blush.

Take that, Jake, she thinks.

She rides the subway back to Dr. Holtz's apartment, and she knows she's being Inge right now. Angry. Defiant. Stupid. But she can't help it. She doesn't want the real sadness yet. And it is coming. Like a tidal wave. And the fear. Eva is fear. She's made of it. Because the future had always been something that stalked her like a predator, and now she is caught. It has her in its jaws, and it is a void. A black hole. A nothing.

She feels like nothing.

Something must be happening somewhere, because the train is full. Crammed with long coats and hats, arms and legs and shopping bags. There's a man directly across from her, reading the exact same newspaper as the man next to him. Swaying with the train. But when she looks again, there's something familiar about his fingernails. The way they look against the page.

Eva leans to one side, and then the other, annoying the people beside her, trying to see. And when the train pauses, and the navy skirt standing between them leaves, just before a trench coat takes its place, she has a clear view. The man looks up. Directly into her eyes.

It's Mr. Liebermann.

And he knows her.

Eva opens her mouth, but his eyes dive downward, the newspaper rising to cover his face. She's so glad to see Mr. Liebermann alive, well, in a hat on a train that she can only just keep from rushing over to hug him. His newspaper is shaking a little.

At the next stop, he makes a dash for the door, but Eva had been ready. She chases him through the crowd, knocking into people with her purse, making them swear. "Mr. Liebermann!"

He's running. She's running faster.

"Mr. Liebermann! Wait!"

And finally, he does. Just before the turnstiles to exit the station. He turns, and Eva stops. He looks sick at the sight of her.

Mr. Liebermann had seen people do horrific things. Because they'd been coerced, not controlled, but how could he know the why of his nightmare? Her father, she thought, had probably made sure he didn't. And now a piece of that nightmare has come to life out of nowhere on a subway in the middle of New York City. Eva digs in her purse.

"Here," she says, holding out the little ribbon-wrapped package of earrings that had been for Annemarie. She should have sold them on the road to Berlin. "Here. This is for you. Please."

He shuffles forward, forehead wrinkled, taking it from her hand with as much distance as he can manage. Mr. Liebermann is such a little man. She hadn't remembered that. Maybe that's why they had worked so well together, pulling that cart to Berlin.

"Sell them. And I want you to know there was justice. I made sure. I did everything to make sure."

He looks into her eyes. And there come her tears again. Out of nowhere. She doesn't know where they hide.

Mr. Liebermann nods, tips his hat, and Eva walks away down the platform. To catch the next train. To leave him in peace. When she looks back, he's looking at the package. When she looks back again. He's gone.

She comes quietly into the Holtz's apartment. They're side by side, Mrs. Holtz's wheelchair pulled up next to Mr. Holtz, holding hands while they listen to Orson Welles play The Shadow on the radio. The organ swells while someone's confesses to something, and Mrs. Holtz is wiping her eyes. They look lovely.

Eva gives them a wave and disappears into her little room. She throws off her clothes and sits in her dressing gown. She sits until the radio turns off, and the moon comes up, and the mantel clock strikes three, four, and then five.

She was wrong about the void.

The future is not nothing. It is there. It's going to happen. Like it just did with Mr. Liebermann. It's just still hidden behind the wall.

She'd thought the other side of the wall would mean taking care of Annemarie. Annemarie does not need her or want her.

She'd come to think, without realizing it, that the other side of the wall would mean Jake. Jake does not need her or want her. And if he thinks he does, he'll soon change his mind.

She used to think that when justice happened, the wall would crumble, fall down on its own. Like she'd thought was happening the first time Annemarie opened her eyes.

It's not going to. If she wants that wall down, she's going to have to take it down. Block by block. Brick by brick. She's going to have to scrabble until her fingers bleed.

And she will have to do it alone.

It's probably fair, but it doesn't feel that way. It's probably justice.

It feels like a horrible, rotten deal.

But it's her rotten deal. Not somebody else's.

The clock in the living room strikes six. Eva gets dressed. She doesn't go to the boat. She's waiting at the street door of Powell House when Olive unlocks it.

"Eva! Hello."

She follows Olive to the Refugee Office, sitting down in the chair on the other side of her desk.

"Olive," she says, "tell me what I have to do to get a degree in music composition."

"Oh!" Olive pops on her glasses, a manic gleam in her eye. "I'd be happy to help!"

CHAPTER SIXTY-ONE

SHE PUTS HER hand through the broken window, where the sun sparkles along the edges of cutting glass.

She is stinging, bleeding. She will have to face what stands behind her. But the sky is so close. She can feel the wind on the other side.

She opens her hand.

The bird leaps from her palm in a flutter of feathers. Blue wings flapping, swooping, rising, around the branches, through the sunlight, up and away and into the sky.

And the bird flies free.

CHAPTER SIXTY-TWO

—— *May 1947* ——

EVA HURRIES DOWN the street, hanging on to her blue hat, darting by the newsstand on the street corner. "You're gonna get wet!" Frank yells from the stand.

"So's your mother!" she yells back.

He laughs and she laughs. But she actually doesn't want to get wet. She doesn't have time for it.

She skids around Mrs. Carter and her dog, around the man in a red tie at the bus stop, up the steps of the apartment building, and into the little vestibule where the mailboxes are, just as the first fat drops begin to fall. She puts the shopping bag between her legs, strips off a glove with her teeth, digging in her purse for the mailbox key. And when she turns to shut the door, she sees a man smoking a cigarette on the opposite stoop. A man who looks like he's just had his shoes shined.

She doesn't know which one he is. She never does. Eva smiles, just a little. He gives the barest nod in acknowledgment. They only come every now and then. Sit and watch. And probably report back to her uncle. Or whoever he is. She shuts the door, wondering what he would do if she offered him an umbrella.

The key sticks in the mailbox, like it always does, and when she gets it open, she understands why the man with shiny shoes is here. There's a letter for her. Plain, square writing. No return address.

It's not the letter she was hoping for.

She doesn't get those letters anymore.

Eva leans back against the wall of the vestibule.

The first letter from Jake came two weeks after his boat sailed. The postmark was Liverpool, and she'd thrown it in the trash. Then she'd taken it out of the trash. And tossed it back in again. Then she'd turned on her lamp in the middle of the night and torn open the envelope.

And it wasn't what she'd thought it would be. No Nazis, no murder plots, no leaving him behind on a bus. No explanations. Just a letter telling her what he thought about the ocean. The sky. The boat and the people on it. And it was surprising. Funny. Unexpected and beautiful. A soul on six pages, front and back.

She'd understood then, why he wanted to write. She understood why he loved his music. The rhythms were the same. At the bottom of the page, he left an address.

And that was the night Dr. Holtz found her, tearful in the living room at three o'clock in the morning. He made them cocoa. He often couldn't sleep, he'd said. Bad dreams. From before. And they'd talked about her bad dreams, and she told him a little bit about herself. From before. Nothing about Soviets and Americans and justice. Just who she'd been. And somehow, he didn't despise her. It was like talking to her father, in a strange way. A doctor, but without the darkness.

Dr. Holtz said it was nicer, of course, to live without holes inside you. But that she could choose to live with them, and she could do it well. If she wanted to.

Did she know that Mother Martha was at Powell House because she had just lost her husband of over forty years? That Olive had grown up in orphan asylums, unwanted and unloved. That Mrs. Angel's first grandchild, a twin, had died two months ago. People could choose to live well with holes, Dr. Holtz said. Because he was doing it, too.

Her second letter from Jacob came the day of Elizabeth Whittlesby's going-away party at Powell House. It had been fun, considering so many people were sad, but that was mostly because Bets was so dazzlingly happy. And Patricia had come, and Olive had a gangly young man, and Mrs. Angel brought her daughter and her little granddaughter. Martha pulled Eva aside at the punch bowl to say that Annemarie's recovery was going well. So well, in fact, that she had gone to live with Dr. Braun and his mother and they planned a June wedding.

When her hair will have grown out, Eva thought. She wouldn't wait for an invitation.

Why did everyone have to be so in love?

It didn't seem fair. But what was ever fair? She couldn't have afforded to go to Annemarie's wedding, anyway. She still had eight months of payments for her hospital bill.

Annemarie—her family—was a hole she was having to learn to live with.

She let Larry take her for ice cream after the party, and then there was Jake's letter, on the hall table. She left it there. Mrs. Holtz's leg had been painful that night, and Eva got her bath and took care of her medicine, tidying her room and the kitchen while Mr. Holtz read her to sleep. Eva sat on the sofa, staring at the letter. Then she opened it, and let Jake tell her about the English countryside.

She'd thought he loved the city, noise and lights and music and pavement. But he liked grass, too. And stones. He wrote her a little diary, a day-by-day account of trying to coax a fox from its den, leaving her tense with the suspense, until finally, the fox came out and ate a biscuit. The cookie kind.

No past and no future. Just an address at the bottom of the page.

Dr. Holtz came into the living room, shook his head, and went to make the cocoa, while she got a sheet of paper and told Jake about her first time holding a baby. She'd never realized there was something to like about a baby. Or maybe Mrs. Angel's granddaughter would be the only one. She'd never known, she wrote, that when a baby knows you love it, it will love you right back. No questions asked. Then she told him she'd been listening to Liszt, and why did she dislike Liszt so very much?

She wrote it out neatly and carefully. She wrote it all in German. She held the letter for two days. Then she went to the post office, past the man with shiny shoes who was actually getting his shoes shined, and mailed it.

His reply had an express stamp. Listening to Liszt, Jake said, was just like sitting next to a woman drenched in perfume. Too sweet and too much.

That was all. In the whole letter. And that had made her smile.

His letters came every week after that. She answered them. In German.

And then Olive called Eva with a surprise. Could she come to Powell House to chat with a professor of piano at the New York College of Music? Professor Turner was married to a violinist who had found a job through Martha during the war.

Professor Turner listened to Eva play and asked what she wanted to do. Maybe compose, she'd said. And he'd said that was good, play something from her head. So she had, which felt exactly like taking off all her clothes. But Professor Turner told her it was interesting, which was good, and to sign in at the college and use the practice rooms whenever she wanted. Dr. Holtz said she should, and gave her three mornings off a week to do it. She went at night, too, sometimes. And sometimes out for coffee, or concerts, with the other students.

And also at the advice of Dr. Holtz, Eva went to Peggy's Tuesday Luncheon and discussed what it had been like to grow up in Hitler's Germany. To be steeped in an ideology, only to come face-to-face with the fact that what had been made to seem so normal and right was, in reality, the exact opposite. It was difficult, and embarrassing, and started a lively discussion about the citizens of America who were subjected to beliefs not so different from the Nazi ones. And Mrs. Katz came. She didn't mention Jake, but she did kiss Eva's cheek. She gave Eva a hug. She had tears in her eyes. And somehow, Eva was not despised. At least, not inside Powell House.

She wrote to Jake and told him what it felt like to find acceptance where you thought there would be rejection, love where you thought there would be hate. Beautiful. Unexpected. A surprise. Like music. And she sent him the titles of five songs. In German.

Express Mail: Lyrical. Illuminating. Boring. Piquant. Melancholy.

She was learning to live reasonably well while shot full of holes.

And then, Jake's letters had stopped. Abruptly. Nothing for the past two months.

Eva looks at the letter in her hands, the wrong letter, and the rain clouds open, a sudden splat against the door glass. The man with shiny shoes saunters off with a newspaper over his head, the man in the tie at the bus stop opening up an umbrella.

She knows exactly why Jake's letters have stopped coming. It took longer than she'd thought, but it has happened.

She has happened.

Mrs. Angel had told Martha about it while Eva was washing her hands in the little toilet above the Refugee Office. That Mrs. Katz had said she was so pleased with Jacob, because after such a string of bad apples, he seemed to have chosen someone with his head, for once, and that this one, at least, was steady and sensible.

So the girl of the future is the girl of now. The one who deserves him. The lovely girl with dark hair. Or that's how Eva has imagined her. She thinks Jake is partial to dark hair. And painted fingernails. But her eyes will be different. And she'll be taller. Curvier. With the right parents and the right religion and the right nationality. With nothing to wake her up at night. A girl who doesn't lie. Or ask him to do terrible things. Or drive his uncle's car too fast. And she'll take the perfect amount of sugar in her coffee.

Eva hates her. She always has.

And Jake, she has decided, is going to be so bored. And lately, she's begun to think, if Jacob Katz really wants to be that bored, then maybe he's the one who doesn't deserve her.

This hole is going to be difficult to live with.

Like the Doctor's voice. Telling her she's weak. Less. Like when the memories come, and she can feel the bird soft and wriggling in her hand. "But always remember," Dr. Holtz tells her over cocoa, "you let the bird go."

She remembers.

She says who she is. Just once. Because it is simple.

She is Eva and she belongs to herself.

Eva puts the rest of the mail under her arm and tears open the wrong letter while the rain comes down.

It's a photograph. The back view of an old man walking with a cane through an iron gate set inside white brick walls. And she knows those walls. She knows the gate. Even at a glimpse. It's Sachsenhausen. And that is the back of the Doctor. He's shrunken. Thin. But it's him. On the back of the photograph, in the same plain hand is written *Trial, September, 1947.*

Eva slumps back against the wall again. A trial in September. In Sachsenhausen. The scene of so many of the Doctor's crimes. And this is her proof.

Or that's what they want her to think.

She shivers once. With the sadness. With the sickness of her guilt.

And then she looks out the window. At the pouring rain. Who waits at a bus stop in the rain, when the bus doesn't come for another two hours? Someone who mixed up the schedule?

Or someone who doesn't want to look like they're watching her door?

Eva stands up straight, tucks away the photograph, and picks up her shopping. She doesn't choose suspicion today. Or guilt or sadness. She has other things to do.

She hurries up the stairs. "Hello!" she calls, coming through the door.

"In here," says Mrs. Holtz from the kitchen. She's at the table, her gray bun smooth with the two curls just so, her leg—cast free—propped up on the opposite chair. "What is happening? You look like the sun came out," she says, the rain scrubbing the window beside her.

Eva smiles. "Look what I bought at the secondhand shop." Out from the bag comes a sleeveless black dress, slinky with chiffon. "Where's Dr. Holtz?" she asks.

"In the bedroom . . ."

Eva starts unbuttoning and Mrs. Holtz yells, "Don't come in here, Leopold!"

"What?"

"Stay away!"

"Okay, okay . . ."

Eva drops her skirt and blouse to the floor and steps into the black dress. It's plain, but nicely cut and well fitted, with a low-cut back and a sweep of cloth that gathers behind her thighs, making her shapely. Which isn't as hard as it used to be, because of the way Dr. Holtz feeds her. And miracle of miracles, the length of the black chiffon hits just above her ankles.

"That, my darling," says Mrs. Holtz, "is a lovely dress. And the hair?"

"Red flower?" Eva asks.

Mrs. Holtz makes a kissy noise. Eva makes one back.

"Can I come in?" says Dr. Holtz. "I am wanting my tea—" And then he shakes his head. "Oh, no. Oh, dear. I do not like it. If you go out like that, you will leave us sooner than later."

Eva kisses his cheek and picks up her clothes, telling him to hurry up and get ready. They need to leave in an hour.

She slips into her little room, goes to her closet, and tucks the photograph into the lining of her old skirt—she's made a slit at the top now, just beneath the waist, so she doesn't have to keep sewing it back up again—letting it rest with the Doctor on the ship and the photograph of the dead girl that says *Anna Ptaszynska*.

She should burn those photographs. But you never know what a Cruickshanks might believe and what he might not.

Eva gets dressed and does up her hair. And when she goes to the living room, Dr. Holtz is calling a cab, because of the rain. So they won't be wet. And late. Because tonight they are going to Powell House for the very last time. Because Powell House is being sold.

Mrs. Powell, to the sadness of everyone except her bank manager, accepted an offer for the house she could not afford to refuse. And while the AFSC had considered buying it, the money, they'd decided, was better spent on their relief work in Japan, much needed since the drop of the atomic bomb. The program will continue, they say, but at the Quaker Meeting House at Gramercy, instead.

Everyone knows it won't be the same.

But tonight, they are celebrating, anyway. With a little concert given by newcomers to America. Informal. No program. Nothing to be concerned about. And sitting in the cab with Dr. and Mrs. Holtz, the rain coming down in sheets, in her new secondhand dress with a red flower in the back of her hair, Eva is fairly certain it's the stupidest thing she's ever agreed to.

There's already a good crowd when they get there. Eva says hello to Martha, and Olive, and Mrs. Powell. To Lucy and to Collette, who is just back from her honeymoon. The rooms look sad, bereft, with much of the borrowed furniture and paintings already gone, though someone has managed to bring in fifty or so folding chairs, for the concert, set in rows in the back parlor. Eva slips up the stairs to take one last look in the blue room. There's no bed, no chairs or rug. Only the wardrobe is left, and the mirror, standing on its own in the corner.

This time, the girl looking back is someone she thinks she can recognize.

And she is so nervous.

She hurries downstairs before they start.

There is a lovely girl, Ukrainian, playing the guitar and singing folk songs. A soprano performing a Negro spiritual. A recited poem that is frankly Socialist, but nobody really minds. The mood of the audience is chatty. Easy to please. But they are silent when Eva sits down at the keys. And as soon as she does, something inside her shifts into gear.

Ready.

She's never really afraid once the battle is on her.

She's playing Debussy, but not "Clair de Lune." She'd outgrown her teenage love for that one, opting instead for "The Sunken Cathedral." It's not showy. It's quiet. Deep. Unusual and ethereal, making pictures for the mind. And it feels easy, natural, because somewhere in her mind, she is four years old, lying underneath the piano on a blue rug with her eyes closed, listening to her mother play this song.

She gets a nice round of applause and goes to sit at the end of the row, smiling at Dr. Holtz, who is still clapping, at Martha, who is beaming. Waving back to Olive, who gives her a thumbs-up. And when she lifts her eyes to the back of the room, everything inside her stops. Motionless.

Because there is Jake.

CHAPTER SIXTY-THREE
—— *May 1947* ——

JACOB KATZ.

In New York. Not on the other side of the ocean. In Powell House. When he was supposed to be away for three more months.

He's thinner, and it makes him look older. But his suit is the same, jacket unbuttoned. And she can just make out the scar line, white and thin on his cheek. She can see it because his head is turned away from her, whispering to a girl.

And there she is. Right where she's supposed to be. Exactly how she's supposed to be. Dark-haired. Tall. Smiley and pretty. Happy. Curvey.

Scheisse.

Eva hates her.

She moves her eyes quick, before Jake knows she's seen him. Mrs. Katz is with them, and she looks happy, too. Of course, she is. They're all standing together, right beside the door.

She can't get out. Not without breaking a window.

Scheisse. Scheisse. Scheisse.

The right thing to do would be to say hello. Congratulate them.

But she's got a hole inside her as cold and deep as the Baltic Sea. And she's not sure she can live with it.

She'll have to live with it.

Eva claps for the other performers. She smiles and has eyes only for them. And as soon as the concert is over and people start milling for the coffee, she sees Jake sidestepping through the crowd. Making a beeline. For her.

And she can't. It's unlivable. After all those cups of cocoa.

Eva grabs her purse and makes a run for it. Darting along the edge of the chairs, smiling and shaking a hand or two as she passes, around to the back of the room. And she's got the advantage, because he'd gone the other way and is now trapped by the chairs. She bolts straight past Mrs. Katz and the beautiful girl she hates with every beat of her heart and out into the front parlor. There's some kind of crash behind her, but she's in the foyer and out the front door, hurrying down the steps.

It's still drizzling. Puddles all over the sidewalk, one big one soaking her heels. And she hears the front door of Powell House opening and Jake yelling, "Hey!"

She runs like she's late for a train, around the corner to Lexington, past the subway station. But he's seen. He doesn't think she went in. She gets the advantage again when he has to stop for a passing taxi, and then she is on Madison, where there are people, and shops open.

She glances back. He's still coming. She hikes up her skirt. Skims right across the intersection ahead of the traffic and pushes open the door to Shrafft's. She doesn't say anything to Fred. She doesn't even ask. Just runs right past him in her black dress, through the kitchen, where there is no woman cleaning the vats, out into the alley, and back toward the street. To run the other way.

And she stops. There is Jake at the end of the alley, leaning against the wall.

"Aww, Bluebird. You know you can't pull that on me. I'm the one who taught it to you."

He stands up and Eva stands still, panting, clutching her purse.

"Now, exactly what in the hell was that?" he says. "Do you realize I've just busted half Martha's chairs and probably my knee?"

She straightens her back. "Am I supposed to run to you every time you happen to be in a room?"

"Well, I can't say I thought you'd run the other way. After eight months, I thought a hello might be in order."

"You were supposed to be gone eleven."

"I got off for good behavior. What is wrong with you?"

"What is wrong with you? Do you think I want to just walk up and introduce myself to your wife?"

There's a man behind them emptying his garbage. Eva has an idea he's been emptying his garbage slowly.

Jake sighs. "What do you mean, my wife?"

Eva waves a hand. "Girlfriend, then!"

"This girlfriend you're talking about would not, by any chance, be my cousin Julie? Pretty little thing who doesn't have a brain in her head? She can't be more than sixteen years old, Eva!"

The man behind her tsks, loud and disapproving. Eva turns around.

"Oh, just shut it, why don't you!" she yells.

The man scoots back inside, and when she turns around, Jake is exactly as she left him, only with his brows up. And he doesn't have a wife. Or a girlfriend. Or at least, not with him tonight. He puts his hands in his pockets.

"I'm going to hazard a guess and say you didn't get my last letter."

"Your last letter was an express that said 'tart' and 'enchanting.'"

"Yeah, well. That wasn't it."

There's a little silence.

"How long have you been back?" she asks.

"Two days. Mom told me to go and see you. But I had an idea I was being rejected. More than an idea when you took off out the door at the first sight of my face. But Julie does look older than she is, to be fair." He looks at his feet. Takes a hand out of his pocket and holds it out. "Would you take a walk with me?"

Eva steps forward, but she doesn't take his hand. They turn out of the alley and walk down the street. Jake looks sideways at her, up and down.

"How do you run in that thing? You were a streak of light."

It's the shoes he should be impressed with. Her feet are screaming.

"The song was good," he says. Meaning the one she played. "It was deep water. You like it."

He doesn't have to ask. He knows.

"I auditioned for the New York College of Music last week," she tells him. "I got in. For composition."

"Oh, that's good, Eva," he says. "Hey, that's really good." She can tell he means it, by the way he's holding in his smile. Then the brows come down again. "You've probably been meeting lots of people, then. Making friends."

"Isn't that what you wanted me to do?"

"That's what I said, wasn't it? When do you start?"

"Mid-September."

He nods. He's thinking. Antsy, like he wants a cigarette, and now they're at the park. And she knows that look on his face. He's got something to say, and he's not saying it.

And it's her. The one his mother was talking about. The girl who deserves him. She's probably still overseas, waiting on a visa. On her way. And now, Eva doesn't get to read it in a letter. He has to tell it to her himself. To her face.

Maybe she should have kept running.

Jake veers onto a pathway. The branches are hanging heavy from the rain, the lampposts doing little to light the dark beyond themselves. There's a fog coming up. They walk in silence. A silence that is a string pulled too tight, ready to snap.

Eva stops. Let's a man pass by them on the path. Jake turns, waiting. And as soon as they're alone, Eva says, "Just say it."

The brows are all the way together now. "You want me to lay it on the table, do you?"

"Yes," she says.

It's always better to know. Even though every single piece of herself is screaming the opposite.

"Tell me why you stopped writing," she says. "Just say it."

She watches his jaw clench and unclench.

"All right. I'll say it. I got sick and tired of writing you letters. I mean, here I was, having this great trip. I wanted to know how things were, and I got it. London is a mess, and Paris is worse, and this guy I was traveling with, he'd seen it all. And I loved my term at Oxford. But there I am, in Paris, with a pen in my hand, ready to write to you about rubble or Mozart or something, and I thought, this is stupid. I hate writing this when I ought to be telling you . . ."

"You came home three months early because you needed to tell me about Mozart and rubble? Or because you suddenly hated writing?"

"And then I get this letter from Larry and he says he took you out . . ."

"You came back from Paris because Larry bought me an ice cream?"

"Will you shut up?"

Eva closes her mouth.

"And so I sat down and I wrote you a different kind of letter, and

I asked you if . . ." He rubs the back of his neck. "I asked you if you wanted to go to California with me."

"What?"

He sighs. "Look, if I asked nice, would you sit?" He goes to a bench beneath a lamppost, standing, waiting to see what she'll say. She walks to the bench and sits, Jake dropping down beside her, elbows on his knees. It's wet, but it doesn't matter.

"Look, the AFSC in London, they've got really good tracing services. They work with everybody, all the organizations, and I thought, just how many Ptaszynskas could there have been in Germany before the war, right? And so I asked them to look . . . and they found them."

Eva blinks. Breathes. And doesn't let it out.

"There wasn't a lot. Just that your father Marek was arrested in 1932, your mother, Klara, in 1933. For distributing Communist propaganda. She was a professor of music, at the University of Berlin, and there wasn't any mention of you or your sister. By 1937, they had both died. In prison. It wasn't really clear how."

Eva looks at her red fingernails in her lap, bright against the black chiffon. "Which prison?" she whispers.

"They'd been in different ones. But the last one was Sachsenhausen."

Where her uncle had said the political prisoners were sent. Where a doctor went after he became interested in two little girls, one valuable, and one not. By getting the Doctor to a trial there, maybe it was her own parents she'd given some justice to. And herself.

How could that be? That it was her justice, all along?

She looks up. Jake is sitting still, hands together, waiting. Little drops of fog dotting his dark hair.

"Why did you look for my parents?"

"That's a really stupid question, Eva. Why do you think I did it?"

She closes her eyes. For her. Not another girl. He did it for her. Because he loves her. And love isn't fair.

She doesn't have to deserve him.

"I didn't want to write you letters, Eva, like I didn't want to take you out on a date or talk to you on the telephone. I wanted to make you eggs and let you wear my bathrobe. And then your letters would come and you wouldn't believe what it took to get them translated, to find all that music. And you had me running to do it, because I was afraid if I wasn't quick enough, you wouldn't write to me again. And then you didn't and I caught a boat. I missed you. Like I was broken. And I realized exactly how big the world was, and what a lucky strike I got handed, to have you come across an ocean and climb into that car. And there I was. Sitting in Paris. Tossing it."

Lucky. She'd thought the luck was all on her side. How could she have gotten in a car with someone who should have despised her, and find the one person in the world who would do for her what he had done?

"I need you to believe me this time. I really thought I was doing the right thing. I wasn't playing around—I'm still not—and you needed to know your options. I wanted to be your first choice. But I don't care right now if I'm at the end of a line if you'll just choose me and there it is. All on the table. And you need to tell me, tell me if I've messed this up and waited too . . ."

"Shut up," she says. And kisses him. He lets her, his dark brows still down, like he's waiting to see if she means it. She kisses him again.

He decides she means it.

He takes her head in his hands. Puts his forehead on hers. And sighs. And they sit like that. In the fog, and she can feel his smile beneath her fingertips. And she is not less. She is just whole.

And then Jake whispers, "Eva, come to California with me."

"What is in California?"

"Your aunt Irina."

Eva leans back to look at him. Feels her mouth open. Her forehead wrinkle.

"I hadn't been the only one looking," Jake says. "Your father had a sister. She left a Sacramento address with the Red Cross." His smile is still there while he searches her face. "So let's go see her."

Eva breathes. And breathes again. An aunt. Family. She laughs. And then she cries. He puts his forehead on hers again, rubbing her jaw with his thumb. She's getting his hands wet. And then she laughs again.

"Come to California with me," he says, giving her a kiss. "Come tonight. Right now."

She smiles and gets another kiss. "I can't go tonight. Mrs. Holtz . . ."

"Does she need you?"

"No . . ."

He kisses her again. And again. "Then we swing by, you grab a suitcase, and we'll call them on the way. You'll be back in two months. Plenty of time for September. You can do that, Bluebird."

She laughs, and then she can't laugh, because Jake's mouth is on hers, and then she laughs again because his breath is warm on her neck.

"I sold a story to the *Daily* while I was gone," he says into her hair. "They offered me a job. A real one. I'm not going back to school. I start in October. And I bought Uncle Paul's car. Yesterday. He's getting married and sold it to me for a song. My suitcase is in the back." He kisses her jaw. "So come to California with me."

She makes him stop and look at her. "Wait. Why did you buy that car?"

"To take you to California in. And there's a lot of America to see between here and there."

The new world, she thinks.

"Come with me," he whispers. "Let's go. Right now."

It's daring. Reckless. It might be just what she came for. She looks at Jake and she nods.

"Yes?" he asks.

"Where's the car?"

He grins. And then he's up, dragging her by the hand, down the path, out of Central Park, back the way they came.

"What about your mother?" Eva says.

"She'll think we eloped."

"She doesn't think I'm sensible, does she?"

"What?"

"Never mind!"

They hurry around the corner, and there is the green convertible. They jump in. Jake starts the engine, adjusts the mirror, leans over to kiss her one more time, and whispers. "You know the guy who walked past us in the park? With the red tie? He's getting into a car half a block behind us."

Eva doesn't look around. She knows better than that. "That's interesting," she says. "Because the same man stood in the rain for a bus that wasn't coming in front of the apartment this afternoon."

"Are you sure it was him?"

"I saw his eyebrows."

"Do you think he wants to come to California?"

She gives Jake a smile, a kiss. And climbs right over him in her black dress and heels.

"Move," she says. "I'm driving."

EPILOGUE

— August 1947 —

EVA ROLLS OVER on the beach blanket, chin on her hands, feet in the air, lulled by the swish and fizz, bluster and boom of the rolling Pacific. The sun is warm, hot on her skin, but the air is cool, and high and dark above her head, a bird rides the breezes from the hills.

Then Jake drops down on the blanket beside her, dripping with the ocean. Jake has tanned to the most beautiful bronze. She got three freckles and burned. He runs a finger down the dented trail of her spine, letting the cold water trickle on her sun-warmed skin so she'll squeal.

This is not unexpected.

When she's squealed enough, he rolls over with an arm behind his head, his eyes closed behind the sunglasses. And then Eva drops a hermit crab onto his stomach, saved for the occasion.

This is very unexpected. And makes him swear.

"You should be nice to that boy," says Aunt Irina, settling back in her beach chair. She's left a book open over her face, and the words are muffled. But her voice had been smiling.

Aunt Irina likes Jake. This is not unexpected, either. But that Aunt Irina could fill a hole shaped for a mother, sister, and grandmother all at once, this Eva had not expected at all.

– 436 –

"Yeah, Eva. Be nice," Jake agrees, releasing the crab back to the beach. He grins, kissing her with the thumb he runs over the corner of her mouth. "Anyone?" he asks, low. He always asks.

"No one," she says, and kisses his thumb back. She hasn't seen anyone following since they lost the man with the red tie in Pennsylvania. Or maybe he'd just gotten bored.

Aunt Irina falls asleep, and Eva grabs the newspaper from the bag before Jake can. So he won't get it wet. She opens it, holding it tight against the wind, looking for something he'll find interesting. She's gotten good at spotting what Jake will find interesting. She's read him a newspaper every day, bare feet propped up on the convertible's dash, all the way across America.

America, it turns out, is enormous.

And then she sits up on the blanket. Jake sits up, too. He knows her mood has changed. She hands him the newspaper and lets him get it wet, pointing to a little article in the corner. A few lines tucked beside an advertisement for ladies' shoes.

Dr. Kurt Blome has been acquitted of all crimes at Nuremberg.

Just like Mr. Cruickshanks had said. A doctor. A war criminal. Like her father. Free to continue his crimes. Working for the United States.

"So it was for nothing, then," Eva says.

Jake tosses down the paper. "No. I think it means they would've gotten the Doctor off, too, if you'd done anything else. You can't make the whole world better, Bluebird. Just your corner of it. I think it means you did the right thing."

Eva closes her eyes.

And for the first time, she is certain. Really certain. She chooses to be certain.

She did the right thing.

What a beautiful and unexpected feeling. Like music. Like family. Like love.

It feels a little bit like flying.

"Hey," Jake says, kissing the back of her hand. "Somebody had to do it, didn't they, Bluebird?"

They did.

Even if somewhere, the experiment goes on.

AUTHOR'S NOTE

Bluebird is one author's imagining of what could have been, based on the history that was. Below are some notes on the research and historical context that helped this author create *Bluebird*.

Project Bluebird

Project Bluebird was a top secret program begun by the United States Central Intelligence Agency after Germany's surrender in 1945. It was the very beginning of the Cold War, and the race with the Soviet Union to acquire German technology was not just about information. It was a struggle for any advantage that might tip the balance of power in a postwar world.

Unlike the more infamous and well-documented Operation Paperclip, also run by the CIA, Project Bluebird is murky. Operation Paperclip brought an estimated sixteen hundred Nazi experts from all areas of the sciences to the United States and put them to work, cleansing their backgrounds of atrocities and war crimes. But Bluebird was more specifically targeted: to continue the human medical experimentation begun in Dachau and other concentration camps for the purpose of mind control.

Project Bluebird sought to answer questions like:

"Can we create, by post-H (post-hypnotic) control, an action contrary to an individual's basic moral principles?"

"Could we seize a subject and in the space of an hour or two by post-H control, have him crash an airplane, wreck a train, etc?"

"Can we 'alter' a personality? How long will it hold?"

"Can we guarantee total amnesia under any and all conditions?"*

Based on experiments by doctors such as Kurt Blome and Kurt Plötner, whose notes and papers were found at Dachau, the aim of Project Bluebird was to split the human personality, to create a sliver of the mind that could be controlled, either with drugs or without. It was the stuff of science fiction, like *The Manchurian Candidate.* Assassins and saboteurs who would follow orders without hesitation, without remembering what they had done. Agents impervious to interrogation because they would have no idea they were agents. And not only did the CIA want this ability, they were afraid the Soviet Union had already beat them to it.

Despite overwhelming evidence and a previous confession, Dr. Kurt Blome was acquitted at Nuremberg in 1947, widely accepted to have happened through the interference of the CIA. Dr. Blome dropped out of sight until he was officially hired by the United States in 1951, just after the dissolution of Bluebird, to work on a top secret project that has never been declassified. Dr. Kurt Plötner disappeared from an Allied prison in Germany, and when the French government tried to prosecute him in 1946, the US simply said he could not be located. He appeared again in West Germany, under his own name, in 1952. Neither Blome nor Plötner was ever brought to justice for the grisly and inhumane experiments they conducted in the concentration camps, experiments believed to have been continued on American citizens under the guidance and funding of the CIA.

In 1951, Project Bluebird was renamed Project Artichoke, which was renamed Project MK-Ultra in 1953. MK-Ultra became infamous for giving LSD to unwitting American citizens as a supposed form of mind control, and like the Nazis had done, the CIA chose their victims carefully. Rather than Jews, Roma, and political or social dissidents, MK-Ultra used prostitutes, gang members, prisoners, and mental patients. Elements of society that "could not fight back." Ultimately, MK-Ultra ran out of control, and the project's administrators were accused of using their own agents as test subjects, leading to at least one death. In 1973, CIA Director Richard Helms ordered all documents pertaining to Bluebird, Artichoke, and MK-Ultra destroyed. Twenty-thousand documents, however, had been stored incorrectly and were found in 1977, prompting an investigation by Congress. These documents are available today through the Freedom of Information Act.

The Central Intelligence Agency insisted in 1977 that the program had been long abandoned. Others say it still goes on today. While much is known and documented—particularly the horrific shock experiments used to erase memory and personality by Dr. Ewen Cameron, who is no relation to this author, thankfully—the extent of experimentation done on unwitting American citizens in the name of keeping ahead of the Soviets remains a dark and shameful secret in our nation's history. But one Bluebird document does contain a clue: a description of a psychiatrist recruited for human experimentation in mind control in 1950:

> *Through internal agency channels, Bluebird was given the name of_____, an individual of _____ extraction. . . .*

_____ *was reported to have done considerable work in SI [special interrogation] and H [hypnosis] and to have an unusual and interesting background.* _____ *is considered reliable, trustworthy, and a known anti-Communist.*
_____ *only apparent weaknesses were his foreign background and non-United States citizenship.**

All personal information, including two pages of background, has been redacted. But in 1950, a noncitizen psychiatrist who is a known anti-Communist, having done "considerable" work in special interrogations research, sounds very much like a Nazi. It's also very likely that no one will ever really know.

Sachsenhausen

The Sachsenhausen Concentration Camp is located in Oranienburg, north of Berlin. The camp opened in 1936 and was intended to be a model for all the others. Because of its early opening date, many of the prisoners were political dissidents, then POWs. The drug testing, boot factory, the running in boots while drugged, and the punishments of the prisoners depicted in this novel are all based on real accounts, and while I do not have records of psychological experimentation, there certainly was medical experimentation, particularly with stimulant drugs. The commandant, officers, and camp doctor were all arrested when the camp was liberated in April of 1945, and as the camp remained in the Soviet Zone, a Soviet trial took place in September 1947. All were found guilty and sentenced to hard labor, as the Soviet Union had just made the death penalty illegal. The hatred between Soviets and Nazis was so intense, however, this might have been a worse sentence for the convicted men. Sachsenhausen was operated as a Soviet prison camp until 1950 and approximately 12,000 prisoners died there during that time. Though we may never know the reality of that number, either.

Lebensborn and Children Stolen from Poland

An estimated 26,000 children were stolen from Poland during World War II by Nazi soldiers, based on the premise that children who looked Aryan must have a racially valuable bloodline and should therefore be "harvested" and replanted in Germany. These children were removed from their parents—sometimes brazenly kidnapped out of classrooms or their front yards—and put into group homes, where they were conditioned to be German. Food deprivation, beatings, and sensory deprivation were all employed to make the children "forget" their previous parents and upbringing, to learn to speak German and never Polish, and to ensure that all became good German citizens who would live up to Nazis ideals.

The younger the child, the more successful this program was. Children who would not conform were sent to concentration camps or murdered outright. Children who did conform were given new names, new birth certificates, and were adopted by unsuspecting German families. Some of these children never forgot their Polish upbringing, even in their new German homes. They just kept it secret. For survival. Others completely forgot their own background. For them, being removed from their new German parents and siblings, then returned to Polish parents they no longer recognized and whose language they could no longer speak, was a horrific trauma, and the memoirs written by some of these children, the families, and the representatives tasked with removing them, are heartbreaking. It was a postwar dilemma that still has no correct answers.

The program to steal children was part of Lebensborn, which means "well of life," a program created to grow Germany's population and fill their new territories with valuable bloodlines, essential to creating the "master race." Group homes were established, where racially valuable young women could meet with SS officers and "give Hitler" a good German baby. This was not only encouraged among the League of German Girls, it was a requirement for SS officers, and in occupied countries considered particularly racially valuable, like Norway, the program was forced on the female population. I don't have any documentation of children taken from Communist dissidents. But Communists were being arrested and imprisoned in Germany from the beginning of Hitler's rise to power, and all the ideas for Lebensborn and preserving racial purity were certainly already in place at that time.

Powell House and the American Friends Service Committee

The American Friends Service Committee, or the AFSC, won the Nobel Peace Prize in 1947, in conjunction with the British Friends Service Committee, for their global relief work during and after both world wars.

Gunnar Jahn, the chairman of the Nobel Peace Prize Committee, said:

> *It is through silent assistance from the nameless to the nameless that they have worked to promote the fraternity between nations cited in the will of Alfred Nobel . . . The Quakers have shown us that it is possible to carry into action something which is deeply rooted in the minds of many: sympathy with others; the desire to help others . . . without regard to nationality or race; feelings which, when carried into deeds, must provide the foundations of*

a lasting peace. For this reason, they are today worthy of receiving Nobel's Peace Prize.

By the end of the war in 1945, the AFSC alone was distributing hundreds of tons of food, clothing, and medicine to Austria, Finland, France, Holland, Switzerland, Spain, Italy, Portugal, French North Africa, China, India, and Mexico. By 1946, this included Japan, after the devastation of the atomic bombs. There was also domestic work underway, in Appalachia, in setting up hostels for disinterred Japanese-Americans, institutes and conferences focused on race and international relations, and of course, services for refugees coming into America.

In Germany, the AFSC was the only charitable organization allowed to remain in operation during the Third Reich, because they were apolitical and, speculatively, because of the fond associations with the AFSC milk trucks that were set up to feed children after World War I, and were still in operation. But as the danger level rose in Germany, the AFSC quietly turned its attention to facilitating visas and travel arrangements for those under threat from the regime, particularly in getting children out of Vichy France. This work continued up until the bombing of Berlin, which meant the AFSC was on the ground postwar, immediately ready to begin relief work. The Berlin offices were damaged, but not destroyed, and are still housed in the same building today. And since the AFSC considered no one "the enemy," they were one of the few organizations willing to work immediately with non-Jewish German immigrants.

Powell House was one small program in a vast organization, and yet it stands as a shining example of how small things can make the biggest difference to individual lives. A new suit, help with a résumé or finding an apartment, even learning some American slang helped ease many an immigrant's transition into a new country. But I believe the most important offering that came out of Powell House was friendship, and in this, the program was incredibly ahead of its time. Powell House acted as a liaison between Jewish organizations, Christian organizations—both Protestant and Catholic—and the African American churches of Harlem, where the Powell House staff ate dinner once a week. This spirit of cooperation was also fostered by assigning new immigrants a "friend," irrespective of race or religion.

All the programs and classes mentioned in the novel are real. The *Exhibition of White and Negro Artists* was also a true event, revolutionary for its time, a veritable who's who of the Harlem Renaissance. And there was much, much more that could not be fit into a novel: financial services, family tracing services, translations, concerts, dances, symposiums on race, on Nazi philosophy, American history, field trips to Harlem, to musicals, museums, and farms, all done through a score of hardworking volunteers, donations, and a shoestring budget.

The house itself still stands as a private family home on the Upper East Side of New York City. As a program, Powell House operated from 1943 to 1950, though in reality the house was sold by Mrs. Powell at the end of 1945. I gave the house eighteen months longer as the hub for the program, so apologies to any Powell House scholars for this creative license. After the sale of the house, the program itself was still called Powell House and was moved to the Quaker Meeting House at Gramercy Park, which had been a stop on the Underground Railroad. That building is now the Brotherhood Synagogue.

In the novel, the volunteers of Powell House and the refugees who came through the program are all homages to real people who were there, without being completely accurate as to names and personalities, particularly if I have not spoken to the family. Happy Angel was a real person. She was part of a Harlem religious organization run through a man known as Father Divine, who instructed all his followers to choose new names. Finding Happy Angel was one of the most enjoyable romps through the 1940 census I've ever had. There was also a Powell House volunteer, a Quaker who was a conscientious objector, given malaria by the US Army as part of nonconsenting human medical experimentation during the war. And he did marry his "assigned friend," a young Jewish woman who had escaped the Nazis in France.

The character of Peggy is based on Margaret Loring Thomas, a Powell House volunteer and children's book author. One of my favorite pieces of discovered ephemera from Margaret is a birthday card she sent to an Italian anarchist on death row. She also wrote a draft of a manuscript about the beginnings of Powell House and Sky Island, 130 pages of humor and wit, including the story of Mrs. Turgonov's bloomers. Her Tuesday Luncheon Club ran for years and years. I was also lucky enough to have access to a short memoir written by Olive, which was such a lovely insight into her personality, though for the purposes of the book, I changed her background slightly and made her much younger. Martha, recently widowed, had just come from running an AFSC hostel for wartime refugees in Iowa called Scattergood. Scattergood is worthy of a novel all by itself.

To Lucy, one of the immigrants turned volunteer, I owe a particular debt of gratitude. She was a sociology student at Hunter College, and wrote case studies of many of the immigrants who came through Powell House, all of which are preserved in the AFSC archives. Patricia was studying to be a social worker, and also wrote case studies of the visitors to Sky Island. I was able to meet Patricia in 2019. She was ninety-nine years old, delightful, sharp as a tack, and may never get over her regret of the "murder" game. "We were young, and so enthusiastic, and had no concept of the kind of trauma we were dealing with," she said. Patricia devoted her life to service in the AFSC all over the world.

Also in 2019, I stayed for five days with the daughter of Elizabeth "Bets" Whittlesby, who so generously shared not only her home but her mother's life, letters, and papers. This was invaluable for understanding the beliefs of Quakers and the goals of peace and friendship that were the ultimate aim of the Powell House program. Bets married her history teacher and raised three children on that farm in Georgia. She was a lovely, special person who perfectly embodied the spirit of Powell House, and she has passed that spirit on to her children, grandchildren, and great-grandchildren.

The records kept in the American Friends Service Committee archives were unbelievable in their detail. From personal accounts of war-torn Berlin to Happy Angel's salary to the color of the walls of Powell House, it was all there. Approximately 22,000 files of immigrants who came through the AFSC's programs during the 1940s are currently housed at the United States Holocaust Memorial Museum. There is an archivist there, working to reunite these files with their families, who spent an hour and half on the phone with me, explaining the Powell House program and how closely they worked with Jewish organizations. Having access to such a wealth of information and reality is an author's dream. But in all that research, what impressed me most was that the ideals being espoused by the people of Powell House were not just ideals. They were lives lived. And well lived. And those ideals are still being lived out among the AFSC today.

Postwar Germany

As so often happens, research on one subject will lead to another, and when researching my last book, I took some time—"some time" meaning hundreds of hours—to listen not only to oral histories of Jewish survivors of the Holocaust, but to the memories of Germans who had lived through that time as well. The stories were fascinating, and they were heartbreaking. Particularly the stories of girls who were fifteen, sixteen, and seventeen years of age at the end of the war. Girls who had been raised in the League of German Girls, steeped in Nazi ideology, who had no real memory of a life before Hitler. Who had been given no reason to question what to them had seemed the very fabric of the world.

What they knew and did not know near the end of the war varied. Some girls were running the signals for enemy aircraft and learning to shoot bazookas. Others had little idea that the Nazis were losing until foreign tanks rolled into their villages. Some knew about concentration camps, torture, and harvesting the gold from teeth. Others had no idea the camps existed. The difference seemed mostly one of location, city versus rural, though there had to be many cases of willful ignorance as well. Who wants to admit they knew about such atrocities and did nothing? But one element of experience seemed to be shared by all of them: a single, horrific moment when the realization of what Nazi belief had done to the world really hit home. Truth became a lie, and life completely and utterly upended, not only externally, as the Third Reich collapsed, but internally.

And the price paid was terrible. Seven of the eleven girls interviewed for a single documentary had been raped, some multiple times, all by Soviet soldiers. Almost all of them had either seen or knew someone who had committed suicide. Most of them knew many. Suicide after the death of Hitler and at the approach of the Soviet army was rampant, encouraged by fear and the Nazi government. Such as in the village of Demmin, where 1,000 people committed suicide or were murdered by their own friends and family members in a seventy-two-hour period. But it was the guilt—guilt for surviving, guilt for not knowing, guilt for participating, for cheering on a value system that led to the deaths of millions—this is what haunted them. Guilt, individual and collective, is something that still haunts Germany today.

But for the children of the perpetrators—those high in Hitler's government, running and organizing the concentration camps—the realization was even more terrible. How do you reconcile not only that your truth has been a lie, but that your own parent has done something monstrous? That your parent is the monster? Some coped by turning completely against their parents, others by denying their parent had ever done anything wrong. Others lived a life trying to compensate. And where is the line of responsibility? When is a child or a teenager responsible for their own beliefs, and when are they themselves the victim of abuse?

What gives a person the strength to upend their own beliefs and start again with something new?

"I had never known love. Not from anyone," said Martin Bormann Jr., son of Hitler's private secretary and godson of Hitler. "We weren't taught it. I didn't know what it was."

And what would happen, I thought, if someone raised in Nazism, steeped in the trauma and guilt of a terrible past, stepped straight into a belief system that was diametrically opposed to everything they had known before? Where love is undeserved, unearned, and unconditional?

The answer, I hope, is that they would transform.

And that, ultimately, is why I came to write *Bluebird*.

Because we can transform.

*Quoted material excerpted from "Special Research, Bluebird" published in 1952, available via the Freedom of Information Act Electronic Reading Room of the Library of the Central Intelligence Agency: https://www.cia.gov/library /readingroom/document/0000140401.

ACKNOWLEDGMENTS

Once again, I attempt an impossible task: thanking everyone who deserves to be thanked for helping make a novel come to life. *Bluebird* was one of the most challenging research projects I've done and I had incredible help. Here are some of the people who so willingly gave me their time, patience, and knowledge.

First, to my critique group, Ruta Sepetys, Angelika Stegmann, Amy Eytchison, and Howard Shirley. *Bluebird* was written during our fifteenth year of writing books together. You have been there from the very beginning and taught me all I know. Thank you for reading lots of pages at the last minute! And a special thanks to Angelika, for her memories of life in Germany.

Lisa and Martin Ogletree. Thank you for opening up your hearts and home, and of course, for allowing me such an intimate peek into the life of Quakers and Elizabeth Whittlesby Hendricks. The meals, car rides, bus schedules, train schedules, videos, and lovely bed made my research easy as well as illuminating. Your friendship made it fun. The looms in the basement are fascinating. I would love to learn.

Patricia Dunham Hunt. Thank you for your interview, dinner, and your memories. They changed me, just like your service to the AFSC has changed so many lives.

Donald Davis, Archivist at the American Friends Service

Committee Headquarters in Philadelphia. What an enormous help you were to me. Thank you so much for the guidance and patience. Thank you so much for taking care of such a precious archive of lost history. I will never get over putting that file in the wrong box. I hope you've managed to forgive me.

Swarthmore College. Thank you for your carefully curated archive of all things Quaker. And the serendipitous historic map lecture was wonderful.

John T. Reddick, Harlem architect and cultural historian. Thank you for your fast and scrupulous read, and for keeping my facts straight.

Ronald Coleman of the United States Holocaust Memorial Museum Archives. Thank you for your emails and phone calls, your careful explanations, and your dedication to reuniting the refugee files of the AFSC with their families. My appreciation for the work you do, and the work of the museum archives, knows no bounds.

Marla Abraham, Director, Western Region of the United States Holocaust Memorial Museum. Your support of my books and research is so appreciated. Thank you for taking the time to connect me to all the right people.

Lisa Sandell, my one and only editor, my dearest of friends. Thank you for having so much confidence in me when I really had no confidence in me. You are beautiful inside and out.

Kelly Sonnack, my one and only agent and dearest of friends. I rest so easy knowing you have it all in hand. Your strength and wisdom passes right on to me.

Every time I write acknowledgments to my editor and agent, I think four words: *fortunate, favored, lucky, blessed.*

And speaking of lucky, my people at Scholastic: the incredible David Levithan, Elizabeth Parisi, Ellie Berger, Olivia Valcarce, Lori

Benton, Leslie Garych, John Pels, Stephanie Peitz, Janell Harris, Brittany Schachner, Dave Ascher, JoAnne Mojica, Anne Henderson, and Jenn Epstein. My awesome team in Marketing and Publicity: Sydney Tillman, Rachel Feld, Shannon Pender, Zakiya Jamal, Lizette Serrano, Emily Heddleson, Danielle Yadao, Matt Poulter, Lauren Donovan, Alex Kelleher-Nagorski, and Erin Berger. The intrepid champions in Sales: Alan Smagler, Elizabeth Whiting, Jacquelyn Rubin, Jarad Waxman, Savannah D'Amico, Roz Hilden, Daniel Moser, Nikki Mutch, Sue Flynn, Tracy Bozentka, Chris Satterlund, Terribeth Smith, Betsy Politi, Jody Stigliano, Barbara Holloway, Caroline Noll, and so many others, and of course, Duryan Bhagat-Clark and Randy Kessler, in memoriam. The powerhouse Foreign Rights team: Jennifer Powell, Hannah Babcock, Rachel Weinert, and Jazan Higgins. And Jana Haussman and Robin Hoffman of Book Fairs.

It's a lot of names, and I'm perfectly aware that it can't be all the names, and that I'll probably never know all the things those names really do to support my work. Thank you, all of you, for being my fans and my publishing family.

And finally, to the most important people in my life: Elizabeth, Stephen, Christopher, and Siobhan. Thank you for being my precious family, and for being patient through all the distracted moments and missed phone calls. And Philip, the best husband and partner that anyone could ever ask for. You probably didn't sign up for a wife who looks up from her computer only long enough to say things like "Quick. New York subways, 1946. Tokens or nickels?" Or "All the things about a chronic subdural hematoma, STAT." And yet, you find it all. In detail. And stick around and make me cups of tea. And do the laundry. I love you.

ABOUT THE AUTHOR

Sharon Cameron's debut novel, *The Dark Unwinding*, was awarded the Society of Children's Book Writers and Illustrators' Sue Alexander Award for Most Promising New Work and the SCBWI Crystal Kite Award and was also named a YALSA Best Fiction for Young Adults selection. Sharon is also the author of its sequel, *A Spark Unseen*; *Rook*, which was selected as an IndieBound Indie Next List Top Ten Pick, a YALSA Best Fiction for Young Adults selection, and a *Parents' Choice* gold medalist; *The Forgetting*, a #1 *New York Times* bestseller and an Indie Next List selection; its companion, *The Knowing*; and the widely acclaimed historical World War II novel *The Light in Hidden Places*, which was a Reese's Book Club YA Pick.

She lives with her family in Nashville, Tennessee, and you can visit her online at sharoncameronbooks.com or follow her on Facebook, Twitter, and Instagram at @CameronSharonE.